PRAISE FOR

The Winter of the Witch

"Visceral descriptions of battle, an atmospheric sense of place, and some truly heartbreaking moments of loss make this a gut-wrenching read, but there's ample hope and satisfaction to be found as Vasya chooses her own unique path to triumph." —*Booklist*

"Luxuriously detailed yet briskly suspenseful . . . a striking literary fantasy informed by Arden's deep knowledge."
—*Kirkus Reviews* (starred review)

PRAISE FOR

The Girl in the Tower

"A compelling, fast-moving story that grounds fantasy elements in a fascinating period of Russian history." —*Kirkus Reviews*

"Arden once again delivers an engaging fantasy that mixes Russian folklore and history with delightful worldbuilding and lively characters." —*Library Journal*

PRAISE FOR

The Bear and the Nightingale

"Arden's debut novel has the cadence of a beautiful fairy tale but is darker and more lyrical." —*The Washington Post*

BY

KATHERINE ARDEN

The Bear and the Nightingale

The Girl in the Tower

The Winter of the Witch

FOR CHILDREN

Small Spaces

Dead Voices

THE
WINTER OF
THE WITCH

The
Winter
OF THE
Witch

BOOK THREE OF
*The Winternight
Trilogy*

A NOVEL

Katherine
Arden

DEL REY · NEW YORK

2019 Del Rey Trade Paperback Edition

Published in the United States by Del Rey,
an imprint of Random House,
a division of Penguin Random House LLC, New York.

DEL REY and the HOUSE colophon are registered
trademarks of Penguin Random House LLC.

RANDOM HOUSE READER'S CIRCLE & Design is a
registered trademark of Penguin Random House LLC.

Originally published in hardcover in the United States
by Del Rey, an imprint of Random House,
a division of Penguin Random House LLC, in 2019.

LIBRARY OF CONGRESS CATALOGING-IN-PUBLICATION DATA
NAMES: Arden, Katherine, author.
TITLE: The winter of the witch: a novel / Katherine Arden.
DESCRIPTION: New York: Del Rey, 2019. | Series: Winternight trilogy; 3
IDENTIFIERS: LCCN 2018038385 | ISBN 9781101886014
(trade paperback) | ISBN 9781101886007 (Ebook)
SUBJECTS: | BISAC: FICTION / Literary. | GSAFD: Fantasy fiction.
CLASSIFICATION: LCC PS3601.R42 W56 2019 | DDC 813/.6—dc23
LC record available at https://lccn.loc.gov/2018038385

Printed in the United States of America on acid-free paper

randomhousebooks.com

6 8 9 7

Book design by Barbara M. Bachman

To my brothers
By birth and by adoption
Sterling, RJ, Garrett
I love you

The sea is fair in the storm-shadow
The sky wondrous without its blue
But trust me; on the rock, the girl
Excels the wave, the sky, and the storm

—A. S. PUSHKIN

Part One

Marya Morevna

Dusk at the end of winter, and two men crossed the dooryard of a palace scarred by fire. The dooryard was a snowless waste of water and trampled earth; the men sank to their ankles in the muck. But they were speaking intently, heads close together, and did not heed the wet. Behind them lay a palace full of broken furniture, smoke-stained; the screen-work smashed on the staircases. Before them lay a charred ruin that had been a stable.

"Chelubey disappeared in the confusion," said the first man bitterly. "We were busy saving our own skins." A smear of soot blackened his cheek, blood crusted in his beard. Weary hollows, like blue thumbprints, marred the flesh beneath his gray eyes. He was barrel-chested, young, with the fey energy of a man who has driven himself past exhaustion to a surreal and persistent wakefulness. Every eye in the dooryard followed him. He was the Grand Prince of Moscow.

"Our skins, and a little more," said the other man—a monk—with a touch of grim humor. For, against all hope, the city was mostly intact, and still theirs. The night before, the Grand Prince had come close to being deposed and murdered, though few people knew that. His city had nearly burned to ash; only a miraculous snowstorm had saved them. Everyone knew that. A swath of black gashed the heart of the city, as though the hand of God had fallen in the night, dripping fire from its nails.

"It was not enough," said the Grand Prince. "We may have saved ourselves, but we made no answer for the treachery." All that bitter day, the prince had reassuring words for every man who caught his eye, had calm orders for the men wrangling his surviving horses and hauling away the charred beams of the stable. But the monk, who knew him well, could see the exhaustion and the rage just beneath the surface. "I am going out myself, tomorrow, with all that can be spared," the prince said. "We will find the Tatars and we will kill them."

"Leave Moscow now, Dmitrii Ivanovich?" asked the monk, with a touch of disquiet.

A night and a day without sleep had done nothing for Dmitrii's temper. "Are you going to tell me otherwise, Brother Aleksandr?" he asked, in a voice that made his attendants flinch.

"The city cannot do without you," said the monk. "There are dead to mourn; there are granaries lost, and animals and warehouses. Children cannot eat vengeance, Dmitrii Ivanovich." The monk had no more slept than the Grand Prince; he could not quite mask the edge in his own voice. His left arm was wrapped in linen where an arrow had gone into the muscle below the shoulder, and been dragged through and out again.

"The Tatars attacked me in my own palace, *after* I had made them welcome in good faith," retorted Dmitrii, not troubling to keep the rage from his reply. "They conspired with a usurper, they *fired my city*. Is all that to go unavenged, Brother?"

The Tatars had not, in fact, fired the city. But Brother Aleksandr did not say so. Let that—mistake—be forgotten; it could not be mended now.

Coldly, the Grand Prince added, "Did not your own sister give birth to a dead child in the chaos? A royal infant dead, a swath of the city in ashes—the people will cry out if there is not justice."

"No amount of spilled blood will bring back my sister's child," said Sasha, sharper than he meant. Clear in his mind was his sister's tearless mourning, worse than any weeping.

Dmitrii's hand was on the hilt of his sword. "Will you lecture me now, priest?"

Sasha heard the breach between them, scabbed over but unhealed, in the prince's voice. "I will not," said Sasha.

Dmitrii, with effort, let go the twining serpents of his sword-hilt.

"How do you mean to find Chelubey's Tatars?" Sasha asked, trying for reason. "We have pursued them once already, and rode a fortnight without a glimpse, though that was in deepest winter, when the snow took good tracks."

"But we found them, then," said Dmitrii, and his gray eyes narrowed. "Did your younger sister survive the night?"

"Yes," said Sasha warily. "Burns on her face, and a broken rib, Olga says. But she is alive."

Now Dmitrii looked troubled. Behind him, one of the men clearing away the wreckage dropped the end of a broken roof-beam, swearing. "I would not have come to you in time, if it weren't for her," Sasha said to his cousin's grim profile. "Her blood saved your throne."

"The blood of many men saved my throne," snapped Dmitrii without looking round. "She is a liar, and she made a liar of you, the most upright of men."

Sasha said nothing.

"Ask her," said Dmitrii, turning. "Ask her how she did it—found the Tatars. It can't be only sharp eyes; I have dozens of sharp-eyed men. Ask her how she did it, and I will have her rewarded. I do not think any man in Moscow would marry her, but a country boyar might be persuaded. Or enough gold would bribe a convent to take her." Dmitrii was talking faster and faster, his face uneasy, the words spilling out. "Or she may be sent home in safety—or stay in the terem with her sister. I will see she has enough gold to keep her comfortable. Ask her how she did it, and I will make all straight for her."

Sasha stared, full of words he could not say. *Yesterday she saved your life, slew a wicked magician, set fire to Moscow and then saved it all in a single night. Do you think she will consent to disappear, for the price of a dowry—for any price? Do you know my sister?*

But of course, Dmitrii did not. He only knew Vasilii Petrovich, the boy she had pretended to be. *They are one and the same.* Beneath his bluster Dmitrii must realize that; his unease betrayed him.

A cry from the men around the stable spared Sasha from answering. Dmitrii turned with relief. "Here," he said, striding over. Sasha trailed, grim-faced, in his wake. A crowd was gathering where two burned roof-beams crossed. "Stand aside—Mother of God, are you sheep at the spring grass? What is it?" The crowd shrank away from the steel in his voice. "Well?" said Dmitrii.

One of the men found his tongue. "There, Gosudar," he said. He pointed at a gap between two fallen posts, and someone thrust down a torch. An echoing gleam came from below where a shining thing gave back the torchlight. The Grand Prince and his cousin stared, dazzled, doubting.

"Gold?" said Dmitrii. "There?"

"Surely not," said Sasha. "It would have melted."

Three men were already hauling aside the timbers that pinned the thing to the earth. A fourth plucked it out and handed it to the Grand Prince.

Gold it was: fine gold, and not melted. It had been forged into heavy links and stiff bars, oddly jointed. The metal had an oily sheen; it threw a shimmer of white and scarlet onto the ring of peering faces and made Sasha uneasy.

Dmitrii held it this way and that, then said, "Ah," and switched his grip so that he held it by the crownpiece, reins over his wrist. The thing was a bridle. "I have seen this before," said Dmitrii, eyes alight. An armful of gold was very welcome to a prince whose coffers had been shrunk by bandits and by fire.

"Kasyan Lutovich had it on his mare yesterday," said Sasha, disliking the reminder of the day before. His eye dwelled with disfavor on the spiked bit. "I would not have blamed her for throwing him."

"Well, this thing is a forfeit of war," said Dmitrii. "If only that fine mare herself had not vanished—damn those Tatars for horse-thieves. A hot meal and wine for all you men; well done." The men cheered raggedly. Dmitrii handed off the bridle to his steward. "Clean it," the Grand Prince said. "Show it to my wife. It might cheer her. Then see it safely locked away."

"Is it not strange," Sasha said warily when the reverent steward had departed, the golden thing in his arms, "that this bridle should have lain in the stable as it burned and yet show no hurt?"

"No," said Dmitrii, giving his cousin a hard look. "Not odd. Miraculous, coming on the heels of that other miracle: the snowstorm that delivered us. You are to tell anyone who asks exactly that. God spared this golden thing, because he knew our need was great." The difference between uncanny happenings of the benevolent and the wicked sort was no thicker than rumor, and Dmitrii knew it. "Gold is gold. Now, Brother—" But he fell silent. Sasha had stilled, his head lifted.

"What is that noise?"

A confused murmuring was rising from the city outside: a roar and snap, like water on a rocky shore. Dmitrii frowned. "It sounds like—"

A shout from the gate-guard cut him off.

A LITTLE WAY DOWN the hill of the kremlin, the dusk came earlier, and the shadows fell cold and thick over another palace, smaller and quieter. The fire had not touched it, except for singeing from falling sparks.

All Moscow roiled with rumors, with sobs, curses, arguments, questions, and yet here a fragile order reigned. The lamps were lit; servants gathered what could be spared for the comfort of the impoverished. The horses drowsed in their stable; tidy columns of smoke rose from the chimneys of bakehouse and cookhouse, brewhouse, and the palace itself.

The author of this order was a single woman. She sat in her workroom, upright, impeccable, starkly pale. Sweeping lines of strain framed her mouth, though she was not yet thirty. The dark streaks beneath her eyes rivaled Dmitrii's. She had gone into the bathhouse the night before and delivered her third child, dead. In that same hour, her firstborn had been stolen, and nearly lost in the horrors of the night.

But despite all that, Olga Vladimirova would not rest. There was too much to be done. A steady stream of people came to her, where she sat by the workroom oven: steward and cook, carpenter, baker, and washerwoman. Each one was dispatched with an assignment and some words of thanks.

A pause came between petitioners, and Olga slumped back in her chair, arms wrapped around her belly, where her unborn child had been. She had dismissed her other women hours ago; they were higher in the terem, sleeping off the shocks of the night. But one person would not go.

"You ought to go to bed, Olya. The household can manage without you until morning." The speaker was a girl, sitting stiff and watchful on a bench beside the oven. She and the proud Princess of Serpukhov both had long black hair, the plaits wrist-thick, and an elusive similarity of feature. But the princess was delicate, where the girl was tall and long-fingered, her wide eyes arresting in the rough-hewn angles of her face.

"You should indeed," said another woman, backing into the room bearing bread and cabbage stew. It was Lent; they could not eat fat meat. This woman looked as weary as the other two. Her plait was yellow, just touched with silver, and her eyes were wide and light and clever. "The house is safe for the night. Eat this, both of you." She began briskly ladling out soup. "And then go to bed."

Olga said, slow with exhaustion, "This house is safe. But what of the city? Do you think Dmitrii Ivanovich or his poor fool of a wife are sending servants out with bread to feed the children that this night has orphaned?"

The girl sitting on the oven-bench paled, and her teeth sank into her lower lip. She said, "I am sure Dmitrii Ivanovich is making clever plans to take vengeance on the Tatars, and the impoverished will just have to wait. But that does not mean—"

A shriek from above cut her off, and then the sound of hurrying footsteps. All three women glared at the door with identical expressions. *What now?*

The nurse burst into the room, quivering. Two waiting-women panted in her wake. "Masha," the nurse gasped. "Masha—she is missing."

Olga was instantly on her feet. Masha—Marya—was her only daughter, the one who had been stolen from her bed just the night before. "Call in the men," Olga snapped.

But the younger girl tilted her head, as though she were listening.

"No," said the girl. Every head in the room whipped round. The waiting-women and the nurse exchanged dark glances. "She's gone outside."

"Then that—" Olga began, but the other interrupted, "I know where she is. Let me go and get her."

Olga gave the younger girl a long look, which she returned steadily. The day before, Olga would have said that she'd never trust her mad sister with one of her children.

"Where?" Olga asked.

"The stable."

"Very well," said Olga. "But, Vasya, bring Masha back before the lamps are lit. And if she is not there, tell me *at once*."

The girl nodded, looking rueful, and got to her feet. Only when she moved could one see that she was favoring one side. She had a broken rib.

VASILISA PETROVNA FOUND MARYA where she'd expected, curled up asleep in the straw of a bay stallion's stall. The stall door was open, though the stallion was not tied. Vasya entered, but did not wake the child. Instead she leaned against the great horse's shoulder, pressing her cheek to the silky skin.

The bay stallion put his head around and nosed irrepressibly at her pockets. She smiled, her first real smile of that long day, drew a crust of bread from her sleeve and fed it to him.

"Olga will not rest," she said. "She puts us all to shame."

You have not rested either, returned the horse, blowing warm air onto her face.

Vasya, flinching, pushed him away; his hot breath pained the burns on her scalp and cheek. "I do not deserve to rest," she said. "I caused the fire; I must make what amends I can."

No, said Solovey, and stamped. *The Zhar Ptitsa caused the fire, although you should have listened to me before setting her loose. She was maddened with imprisonment.*

"Where did she come from?" Vasya asked. "How did *Kasyan*, of all people, put a bridle on a creature like that?"

Solovey looked troubled. His ears tilted forward and back, and his tail lashed his flanks. *I do not know how. I remember someone shouting, and someone weeping. I remember wings, and blood in blue water.* He stamped again, shaking his mane. *Nothing more.*

He looked so distressed that Vasya scratched the stallion's withers and said, "Never mind. Kasyan is dead and his horse is gone." She changed the subject. "The domovoi said Masha was here."

Of course she's here, returned the horse, looking superior. *Even if she doesn't know how to speak to me yet, she knows I will kick anyone who tries to hurt her.*

This was not an idle threat coming from seventeen hands of stallion.

"I cannot blame her for coming to you," Vasya said. She scratched the horse's withers again, and the stallion's ears flopped with delight. "When I was small, I always ran to the stable at the first sign of trouble. But this is not Lesnaya Zemlya. Olya was frightened when they found her gone. I must take her back."

The little girl in the straw stirred and whimpered. Vasya dropped gingerly to her knees, trying not to jar her sore side, just as Marya came awake, thrashing. The child's head butted into Vasya's ribs, and she narrowly avoided a scream; her vision went black around the edges.

"Hush, Masha," Vasya said, when she could speak again. "Hush. It's me. It's all right. You're all right. You're safe."

The child subsided, rigid in the older girl's arms. The big horse put down his head and nosed her hair. She looked up. He lipped her nose very gently, and Marya squeaked out a tiny giggle. Then she buried her face in the older girl's shoulder and wept.

"Vasochka, Vasochka, I don't remember anything," she whispered between sobs. "I just remember being scared—"

Vasya remembered being scared, too. At the child's words, images from the night before crossed her mind like flung darts. A horse of fire, rearing up. The sorcerer withering, crumpling to the floor. Marya ensorcelled, blank-faced, obedient.

And the winter-king's voice. *As I could, I loved you.*

Vasya shook her head, as though motion could dispel memory.

"You don't have to remember; not yet," she said gently to the girl. "You are safe now; it is over."

"It doesn't feel like it is over," whispered the child. "I can't remember! How do I know if it's over or not?"

Vasya said, "Trust me, or if you will not, trust your mother or your uncle. No more harm will come to you. Now, come, we must get back to the house. Your mother is worried."

Marya immediately wrenched away from Vasya, who had little strength to stop her, and wrapped all four limbs around Solovey's foreleg. "No!" Marya shouted, face pressed to the horse's coat. "You can't make me!"

An ordinary horse would have reared at such antics, or shied, or at the very least hit Marya in the face with his knee. Solovey only stood there, looking dubious. Gingerly, he put his head down to Marya. *You can stay here if you like,* he said, although the child did not understand him. She was crying again: the thin exhausted wail of a child at the end of endurance.

Vasya, sick with pity and anger on the girl's behalf, understood why Marya did not want to go back to the house. She had been taken from that house, subjected to half-remembered horrors. Solovey's large and self-confident presence was nothing if not reassuring.

"I have been dreaming," the little girl mumbled into the stallion's foreleg. "I can't remember anything—except for the dreaming. There was a skeleton that laughed at me, and I kept eating cakes—more and more—even though they made me sick. I don't want to dream anymore. And I'm not going back to the house. I am going to live here in the stable with Solovey." She renewed her grip on the stallion.

Vasya could see that unless she chose to pry Marya off and drag her away—a procedure that her broken rib wouldn't bear and Solovey would heartily disapprove of—the girl wasn't going anywhere.

Well, let someone else explain to an irascible stallion why Marya could not stay where she was. In the meantime— "Very well," Vasya said, and made her voice cheerful, "no need to go back to the house unless you wish it. Shall I tell you a story?"

Marya's death-grip on Solovey loosened. "What kind of story?"

"Any story you like. Ivanushka and Alenushka?" Then Vasya's

heart misgave her. *Sister, dear sister Alenushka, said the little goat. Swim out, swim out to me. They are lighting the fires, boiling the pots, sharpening the knives. And I am going to die.*

But his sister couldn't help him. For she'd already been drowned herself.

"No, perhaps not that one," said Vasya hastily and thought. "Ivan the Fool perhaps?"

The child pondered, as though the choice of tales were a momentous one that could change the history of that bitter day. For her sake, Vasya wished it were so.

"I think," said Marya, "that I would like to hear the story of Marya Morevna."

Vasya hesitated. As a child, she had loved the story of Vasilisa the Beautiful, her own fairy-tale namesake. But the tale of Marya Morevna would cut deep—perhaps too deep—after the night before. Marya wasn't finished though. "Tell about Ivan," she said. "That part of the story. About the *horses.*"

And then Vasya understood. She smiled, and didn't even care that smiling tugged at the burnt skin on her face.

"Very well. I will tell that part, if you will let go of Solovey's foreleg. He is not a post."

Marya let go of Solovey reluctantly, and the stallion lay down in the straw, so that both girls could curl against his warm side. Vasya wrapped Marya and herself in her cloak and began, stroking Marya's hair:

"Prince Ivan tried three times to rescue his wife, Marya Morevna, from the clutches of the evil sorcerer Kaschei," she said. "But each time he failed, for Kaschei rode the fastest horse in all the world, and moreover one who understood the speech of men. His horse could outrun Ivan's, no matter how great his start."

Solovey snorted out a complacent, hay-scented breath. *That horse couldn't outrun me,* he said.

"At last, Ivan bid his wife Marya to ask Kaschei how he had come to ride such a matchless horse.

"'There is a house on chicken legs,' replied Kaschei. 'Which stands upon the shore of the sea. A witch lives there: a Baba Yaga, who breeds the finest horses in all the world. You must cross a river of fire to get to her, but I have a magic kerchief that parts the flames. Once you have come to the house, you must ask to serve the Baba Yaga for three days. If you serve her well, she will give you a horse. But if you fail, she will eat you.'"

Solovey slanted a thoughtful ear.

"And so Marya, that brave girl"—here Vasya tugged her niece's black plait, and Marya giggled—"stole Kaschei's magic handkerchief and gave it to Ivan in secret. And he went away to the Baba Yaga, to win the finest horse in all the world for his own.

"The river of fire was great and terrible. But Ivan crossed it by waving Kaschei's handkerchief and galloping through the flames. Beyond the fire, he found a little house by the shore of the sea. There lived the Baba Yaga and the finest horses in all the world—"

Here Marya interrupted. "Could they talk? Like you can talk to Solovey? Can you really talk to Solovey? Does he talk to people? Like the Baba Yaga's horses?"

"He can talk," said Vasya, putting a hand up to stem the flow of questions. "If you know how to listen. Now hush, let me finish."

But Marya was already asking her next question. "How did you learn how to listen?"

"I—the man in the stable taught me," said Vasya. "The vazila. When I was a child."

"Could I learn?" said Marya. "The man in the stable never talks to me."

"Yours is not strong," said Vasya. "They are not strong in Moscow. But—I think you could learn. Your grandmother—my mother—knew a little magic, they say. I have heard a tale that your great-grandmother rode into Moscow on a magnificent horse, gray as the morning. Perhaps she saw chyerti just as you and I do. Perhaps there are other horses, somewhere, just like Solovey. Perhaps we all—"

She was interrupted by a decisive step in the aisle between the stalls. "Perhaps we all," said Varvara's dry voice, "are in need of supper. Your sister trusted you to go and get her daughter, and here I find you two rolling in the straw like a couple of peasant boys."

Marya scrambled to her feet; Vasya followed painfully, trying not to favor her injured side. Solovey stood up with a heave, his ears pricked toward Varvara. The woman gave him a strange look. For an instant, there was a kind of remote longing in her face, as a woman looks upon something she coveted long ago. Then, ignoring the stallion, she said, "Come on, Masha. Vasya can finish your story later. The soup will be cold."

THE STABLE HAD FILLED UP with shadows in the time Vasya and Marya had been talking. Solovey stood still, ears pricked. "What is it?" Vasya asked the horse.

Can you hear that?

"What?" said Varvara, and Vasya looked at her strangely. Surely she hadn't . . .

Marya looked suddenly frightened. "Does Solovey hear someone coming? Someone bad?"

Vasya took the girl's hand. "I said you are safe and I meant it. If there is any danger, Solovey will take us all galloping far away."

"All right," said Marya in a small voice. But she held tight to Vasya's hand.

They walked out into the blued evening. Solovey went with them, huffing uneasily, his nose at Vasya's shoulder. The blood-colored sunset had diminished to a faint smear in the west, and the air was still and strange. Outside the thick walls of the stable, Vasya could hear what Solovey had heard: the rush and tramp of many feet and a muted rumble of voices.

"You are right; something is wrong," said Vasya to the horse, low. "And, curse it, Sasha is not here." Aloud, she added, "Do not worry, Masha, we are safe here behind the gates."

"Come on," said Varvara, and made for the outer door, the anteroom and the stair that would lead them back up to the terem.

2

Reckoning

THE DOORYARD WAS STRANGELY QUIET; THE DAY'S BUSTLE HAD
given way to a heavy calm. Varvara slipped through the outer door of
the terem, holding Marya tight by the hand. Vasya turned back at the
foot of the stairs, pressed her forehead to Solovey's silky neck. She
wondered why it was so still in the dooryard. Many of Olga's guards
had died or been wounded in the fighting in the Grand Prince's dvor,
but where were her sister's grooms, her bondsmen? From beyond the
gates, the shouting rose. "Wait for me," she told the horse. "I am going
up to my sister, but I'll come back soon."

Hurry, Vasya, said the stallion, unease in every line of his body.

Up the stairs to Olga's workroom. Vasya's broken rib ran a claw of
fire down her side as she climbed. The big, low-ceilinged workroom
had a stove for heat, a narrow window for air. It was crowded now;
Olga's attendants had been awakened by the noise. The nurse sat near
the stove, clutching Olga's son, Daniil. The child was eating bread; he
was a placid boy, if a bit bewildered. The women were whispering as
though they feared to be heard. An air of disquiet had invaded the palace of Serpukhov. Vasya found her blistered palms sweating.

Olga was standing at the narrow window, looking out beyond the
dooryard. Marya ran straight to her mother. The princess put an arm
around her daughter's shoulders.

The hanging lamps threw sinister shadows, quivering with the breeze of Vasya's entrance. Heads turned, but Vasya only had eyes for her sister, who stood unmoving beside the window.

"Olya?" Vasya asked. The voices in the room sank to hear her. "What is it?"

"Men. With torches," Olga said, still not turning around.

Vasya saw the women exchanging frightened glances. But still she did not understand. "What are they doing?"

"See for yourself." Olga's voice was calm. But she wore layers of chains draped over her breast, hanging from her headdress. The lamplight shimmered on the gold, blindingly, showing the speed of her breathing.

"I would send for the guards," added Olga. "But we lost so many last night, in the fire, or fighting the Tatars. The rest are at the city-gates; the bondsmen are in the city on errands of mercy. All the men we could spare, and they have not returned. Perhaps some were prevented from coming back, perhaps others heard something we did not."

Daniil's nurse clutched the child until he squawked. Marya was watching Vasya with hope and blind trust: the aunt who had a magic horse. Trying not to limp, Vasya crossed to the window. As she passed, a few of the women averted their eyes and crossed themselves.

The street before the gates of Serpukhov was thronged with people. Many bore torches; all of them were shouting. Near the open window, their rising voices came clear at last to Vasya's straining ears.

"Witch!" they shouted. "Give us the witch! Fire! She set the fire!"

Varvara said flatly to Vasya, "They are here for you," and Marya said, "Vasochka—Vasochka—do they mean *you*?" Olga's arm was stiff, holding her daughter close.

"Yes, Masha," said Vasya, dry-mouthed. "They do." The crowd before the gate spread like a river against a rock.

"We must bar the door to the palace," Olga said. "They might break the gate. Varvara—"

"Have you sent for Sasha?" Vasya interrupted. "For men from the Grand Prince?"

"Whom exactly is she supposed to send?" said Varvara. "All the men were in the city when this started. Curse it. I would have had some warning myself, were I not in the terem all the day, and so weary."

"I can go," said Vasya.

"Don't be a fool," snapped Varvara. "Do you think you'll not be recognized? Do you mean to ride that great bay stallion too, that every man, woman, and child in this city will know on sight? *I* will go, if anyone."

"No one is going," said Olga coolly. "Look, we are surrounded."

Vasya and Varvara turned toward the window again. It was true. The pool of torches had spread.

The women's whispers were shrill now with fright.

The crowd swelled; people were still streaming in from side-streets. They began pounding on the gate. Vasya could not make out individual faces in the crowd; the torches dazzled her eyes. The dooryard beneath them lay cold and silent.

"Be easy, Vasya," said Olga. Her face was rigidly calm. "Don't be frightened, Masha; go and sit by the fire with your brother." To Varvara— "Take women to help you; put whatever you can find against the door. It will buy time, if they break the gate. The tower was built to withstand Tatars. We will be all right. Sasha and the Grand Prince will get word of the disturbance; men will arrive in time."

The shimmer of Olga's golden chains still betrayed her unease.

"If it is me they want—" Vasya began.

Olga cut her off. "Give yourself over? Do you think *that* can be reasoned with?" A sharp gesture took in the seething mob. Varvara was already chivying women off their benches. The wood was sturdy. It would buy them time. But how much time?

Just then a new voice spoke. *"Death, "* it whispered.

Vasya turned her head. The voice belonged to Olga's domovoi, speaking from the oven-mouth. His voice was the whisper of settling ashes after the fire has died.

Every hair on Vasya's body rose. It is given to the domovoi to know what will happen to his family. In two limping strides, Vasya crossed to the stove. The women stared. Marya's eyes met Vasya's in horror; she too had heard the domovoi.

"Oh, what will happen?" Marya cried. She seized Daniil's bread, making the child wail, and dropped to her knees on the hearth beside Vasya.

"Now Masha—" the nurse began, but Vasya said, *"Leave her,"* in such a tone that the whole room drew back in fright. Even Olga's breath whistled out audibly between her teeth.

Marya thrust her bread at the faded domovoi. "Don't say that," she said. "Don't say death. You are frightening my brother."

Her brother could neither hear nor see the domovoi, but Marya in her pride would not admit that she was frightened. "Can you not protect this house?" Vasya asked the domovoi.

"No." The domovoi was little more than a faint voice, and a shape cast by the ember-light. "The sorcerer is dead; the old woman wanders in darkness. Men have turned their eyes to other gods. There is nothing left to sustain me. To sustain any of us."

"We are here," said Vasya, fierce with fear. "We see you. Help us."

"We see you," Marya echoed, whispering. Vasya took the child's hand, held it tight. She had already reopened one of her innumerable cuts from the night before. She smeared a bloody hand on the hot brick in the oven-mouth.

The domovoi shivered and suddenly looked more like a living creature and less like a speaking shadow. "I can buy time," he breathed. "A little time, but that is all."

A little time? Vasya was still holding her niece's hand. The women were massed at their backs, wearing various expressions of fright and condemnation.

"Black magic," said one. "Olga Vladimirova, surely you see—"

"There is death in our fortunes tonight," Vasya said to her sister, ignoring the others.

Olga's face drew into grim lines. "Not if I can help it. Vasya, take the end of the bench; help Varvara bar the door—"

In Vasya's head beat a swift litany: *It is me they want.*

Out in the dooryard, Solovey squealed. The gates shook. Varvara stood nearest the door, silent. Her eyes seemed to convey something. Vasya thought she knew what it was.

She knelt, stiffly, to look her niece in the face. "You must always take care of the domovoi," she said to Marya. "Here—or wherever you are—you must do your best to make him strong, and he will protect the house."

Marya nodded solemnly, and said, "But Vasochka, what about you? I don't know enough—"

Vasya kissed her and stood. "You will learn," she said. "I love you, Masha." She turned to Olga. "Olya, she—soon, you must send her to Alyosha, at Lesnaya Zemlya. He will understand; he knew me, growing up. Masha cannot stay in this tower, not forever."

"Vasya—" Olga began. Marya, puzzled, clutched at Vasya's hand.

"For all of this," said Vasya, "forgive me." She let go of Marya's hand and slipped out the door, which Varvara opened for her. For an instant, their eyes locked in a look of grim understanding.

SOLOVEY WAS WAITING FOR Vasya by the palace door, seemingly calm, save that a white rim showed about his eye. The dooryard was dark. The shouting had grown louder. A splintering crash came from the gate. The light of torches gleamed between the cracking timbers. Her mind was racing. What to do? Solovey, unmistakable, was in danger. They all were: herself, her horse, her family.

Could she and Solovey hide in the stable, the door barred? No—the maddened crowd would make straight for that vulnerable terem-door, for the children inside.

Give herself up? Walk up to them and surrender? Perhaps they would be satisfied, perhaps they would not break in at all.

But Solovey—what would they do to him? Her horse, standing stalwart at her side, would never leave her willingly.

"Come on," she said. "We are going to hide in the stable."

Better to run, said the horse. *Better to open a gate and run.*

"I am not opening any gate to that mob," Vasya snapped. She made her voice coaxing. "We must buy all the time we can, so that my brother will come, with men from the Grand Prince. The gate will hold long enough. Come, we must hide."

The horse, uneasy, followed her, while the shouting rose up all around them.

The great double door of the stable was made of heavy wood. Vasya opened it. The horse followed her, huffing uneasily into the dimness.

"Solovey," Vasya said, drawing the door nearly to. "I love you."

He nuzzled her hair, careful now of her burns, and said, *Don't be frightened. If they break the gate and come in here, we will just run away. No one will find us.*

"Take care of Masha," said Vasya. "Perhaps one day she will learn to speak to you."

Vasya, said Solovey, throwing his head up in sudden alarm. But she had already pushed his head away from her, slipped out the narrow opening of the door and shut the stallion securely in the stable.

Behind her she heard the stallion's furious squeal, heard also the splintering, barely audible over the shouting, of his hooves on the sturdy wood. But even Solovey could not break through the massive door.

She started making her awkward way to the gate, cold and terrified.

The cracks in the gates widened. A single voice soared up into the night, urging the crowd on. In answer, the shouting rose to a greater pitch.

A second time the same voice called, silken, half-singing, cutting through the noise with its purity of tone. The slow, stabbing ache in Vasya's side worsened. The lamps had been put out in the terem above.

Behind her, Solovey squealed again.

"Witch!" called the powerful voice a third time. It was a summons; it was a threat. The gate was splintering faster by the instant.

This time she recognized the voice. Her breath seemed to leave her body. But when she answered, her voice didn't shake. "I am here. What do you want?"

At that moment, two things happened. The gate gave way in a shower of splinters. And behind her, Solovey burst the stable door and came galloping through it.

3

Nightingale

THEY WERE NEARER HER THAN SOLOVEY, BUT NOTHING WAS FASTER than the bay stallion. He was coming for her at full gallop. Vasya saw a final chance. Goad the mob into pursuit; lead it away from her sister's door. And so, as Solovey flew past her, she timed his stride, running alongside him, and then leaped to his back.

Pain, weakness disappeared in the urgency of the moment. Solovey was charging straight toward the smashed gate. Vasya shouted as they went, drawing the mob's eyes from the tower. Solovey lashed out with all of a war-stallion's viciousness, tearing through the crowd. People clawed at them, only to be flung back and away.

Near the gate now. Her whole being was bent on escape. On open ground, nothing could outrace the bay stallion. She could draw them off, buy time, come back with Sasha, with Dmitrii's guards.

Nothing could outrun Solovey.

Nothing.

She never saw what hit them. It might have been only a log meant for someone's fireplace. All she heard was the hiss as it swung, and then she felt the shock, vibrating through the stallion's flesh, as the blow landed. Solovey's leg went sideways. He fell, a stride before the ruined gate.

The crowd shrieked. Vasya felt the *crack* like a wound herself. Instinct rolled her clear, then she was kneeling at the horse's head.

"Solovey," she whispered. "Solovey, get up."

People pressed nearer; a hand seized her hair. She whipped round and bit it; the owner swore and fell back. The stallion struggled, kicking, but his hind leg lay at a terrible angle.

"Solovey," Vasya whispered. "Solovey, please."

The stallion breathed a soft, hay-scented breath into her face. He seemed to shudder, and the mane pouring over her hands felt spiky as feathers. As though his other, stranger nature, the bird she'd never seen, was going to fight free at last and take wing.

Then a blade came down.

It bit into the horse just where his head met his body. A howl went up.

Vasya felt the blade go through the stallion just as though it had cut her own throat, and she did not know she was screaming as she whirled like a wolf protecting her cub.

"Kill her!" cried someone in the crowd. "There she is—the unnatural bitch. Kill her."

Vasya launched herself at them, heedless of anything, careless of her own life. Then a man's fist fell on her, and another, until she could not feel them at all.

SHE WAS KNEELING IN a starlit forest. The world was black and white and quite still. A brown bird fluttered in the snow just out of reach. A figure, black-haired and bone-pale, knelt beside it, extending a cupped hand toward the creature.

She knew that hand; knew this place. She thought she could even see feeling behind the ancient indifference in the death-god's eyes. But he was looking at the bird, not at her, and she could not be sure. He was stranger and farther away than he had ever been, his whole attention fixed on the nightingale in the snow.

"Take us together," she whispered.

He did not turn.

"Let me come with you," she tried again. "Let me not lose my horse." Far away, she could feel the blows on her body.

The nightingale hopped into the death-god's hand. He closed his fingers delicately about the creature, picked it up. With his other hand, he scooped up a handful of snow. The snow melted to water in his hand; it dripped upon the bird, who at once went still and stiff.

Then, at last, he raised his eyes to hers. "Vasya," he said, in a voice she knew. "Vasya, listen to me—"

But she could not reply.

For in the true world, the crowd drew back at a word from a man's thunderous voice, and she was wrenched back to nighttime Moscow, bleeding in the trampled snow, but alive.

Perhaps she only imagined it. But when she opened her blood-smeared eyes, the death-god's dark figure was still beside her, fainter than a noontime shadow, eyes urgent and quite helpless. He held the stiff body of a nightingale most tenderly in one hand.

Then he was gone. He might never have been there at all. She was lying across the body of her horse, sticky with his blood. Above her stood a man with golden hair, his eyes blue as midsummer. He wore the cassock of a priest and was looking at her with an expression of cold and steady triumph.

THROUGH ALL THE LONG ROADS and the griefs of his life, Konstantin Nikonovich had one gift that had never failed him. When he spoke, crowds grew pliant at the sound of his voice.

All that night, while the midnight snowstorm raged, he'd said extreme unction for the dying and comforted the wounded.

Then, in the black hour before dawn, he spoke to the people of Moscow.

"I cannot be silent," he said.

At first his voice was low and gentle, addressing now this person, now that. As they began to pool about him, like water in the hollow of his hand, he raised his voice. "A great wrong has been done you."

"Done us?" asked the soot-smeared, frightened people. "What wrong has been done us?"

"This fire was God's punishment," said Konstantin. "But the crime was not yours."

"Crime?" they asked, uneasy, clutching their children.

"Why do you think the city burned?" Konstantin demanded. Real sorrow thickened his voice. Children, smothered with smoke, had died in their mothers' arms. He could grieve for that. He was not so far gone. His words were hoarse with feeling. "The fire was God's punishment for the harboring of a witch."

"A witch?" they asked. "Have we harbored a witch?"

Konstantin's voice rose. "Surely you remember? The one you thought was called Vasilii Petrovich? The boy—who was in truth a girl? Remember Aleksandr Peresvet, whom all men thought so holy, tempted into sin by his own sister? Remember how she deceived the Grand Prince? *That very night the city caught fire.*"

As he spoke, Konstantin felt their mood shift. Their rage and grief and fright were turning outward. He encouraged them in this, deliberately, deftly, like a blacksmith putting an edge on a sword-blade.

When they were ready, he had only to take up the weapon.

"Justice must be done," said Konstantin. "But I know not how. Perhaps God will know."

NOW SHE LAY IN her sister's dooryard with the blood of her horse drying on her hands. Her own blood stained lip and cheek and her eyes were full of tears. She breathed in wrenching gasps. But she was alive. She crawled gracelessly to her feet.

"Batyushka," she said. The word cracked her lip anew and set the blood seeping down. "Call them back." Her breaths came quick and painful between words. "Pull them back. You have killed my horse. Not—my sister. Not the children."

The crowd spilled around and past them, their bloodlust unslaked. They were beating at the door of the palace of Serpukhov. The door was holding, just. Konstantin hesitated.

Low she added, "Twice I saved your life." She could barely stand.

Konstantin knew himself powerful, riding the crowd's fury, like a rider on a half-tamed horse. Abruptly he put his hand to the reins.

"Back!" he cried to his followers. "Get back! The witch is here. We have taken her. Justice must be done; God will not wait."

She shut her eyes in relief. Or perhaps it was weakness. She did not fall at his feet; she did not thank him for his mercy. Venomously, he said, "*You* will come with me and answer to God's justice."

She opened her eyes again, stared at him, but did not seem to see. Her lips moved in a single word. Not his name, not a plea for mercy, but, "Solovey . . ." Her body bent suddenly, with grief more than pain, bowed as though she'd been arrow-shot.

"The horse is dead," he said, and saw her take the words like fists. "Perhaps now you will turn your mind to things proper for a woman. In the time that is left to you."

She said nothing, her eyes lost.

"Your fate is decided," Konstantin added, bending nearer, as though he could force the words through her mind. "The people have been wronged; they want justice."

"What fate is that?" she whispered through bruised lips. Her face was the color of the snow.

"I advise you," he whispered, gently, "to pray."

She threw herself at him, like a creature wounded. He almost laughed with unlooked-for joy, when a blow from another man's fist flung her down, crumpled at his feet.

4

The Fate of
All Witches

"WHAT IS THAT NOISE?" DMITRII DEMANDED. FEW OF HIS GATE-GUARDS had survived the night unwounded; the few that had all seemed to be shouting. Outside the walls of his palace came a tumult of voices and the sound of many feet in the snow. The only light in his dooryard was torchlight. The noise in the city rose steadily; there came a shattering crash. "Mother of God," said Dmitrii. "Have we not had trouble enough already?" He turned his head to snap swift orders.

Next moment, the postern opened amid a flurry of shouting. A servant with yellow hair strode without diffidence up to the Grand Prince, trailing Dmitrii's bewildered retainers in her wake.

"What is this?" Dmitrii demanded, staring.

"That is my sister's body-servant," said Sasha. "Varvara, what do—"

Varvara had a bruised cheek, and her expression chilled him to the marrow.

"Those people you hear," Varvara snapped, "have broken the gates of the palace of Serpukhov. They killed the bay stallion that Vasilisa loved"—here Sasha began to feel the blood draining from his face—"and they have dragged off the girl herself."

"Where?" said Sasha, his voice remote and terrible.

Beside him, Dmitrii was already calling for horses, for men-at-arms: "—Yes, even if they are wounded, get them on horses, it cannot wait."

"Down," said Varvara, panting. "Down toward the river. I fear they mean to kill her."

━━◈━━

VASYA WAS NEARLY SENSELESS with the mob's fists, her clothes torn and bloodied. She was borne along, half-dragged, half-carried, and the world was full of noise: shouting, a cold, beautiful voice controlling the crowd, and the word, endlessly murmured—*Father. Batyushka.*

Down, they were going downhill; she stumbled in the hardened slush of the street. Hands—many hands—scoured her body; her cloak and letnik had been ripped away, leaving her in her long-sleeved shift, her kerchief gone, her hair falling about her face.

She was barely aware of it. She was locked in a single memory: the impact of a club, a blade, the shock that ran through her own body. *Solovey. Mother of God, Solovey.* As the mob raged, all she could see was the horse, lying in the snow, all the love and the grace and the strength broken and muddied and stilled.

More people were tearing at her clothes; she knocked one groping hand aside, and a fish-smelling fist struck her across the face, bringing her teeth together. Pain like stars exploded on her mouth; the neck of her shift tore. Konstantin's even voice remonstrated, too late, with the crowd. They drew back, a little chastened.

Still they dragged her downhill. All around was torchlight, throwing sparks across her sight. "Finally frightened?" Konstantin murmured to her under his breath, his eyes bright, as though he had bested her at some sport.

She hurled herself at him a second time, in a rush of rage that swallowed up her pain.

Perhaps she was trying to get them to kill her. They nearly did. Konstantin let the crowd punish her. A gray fog slipped slyly over her sight, but *still* she did not die, and when she came back to herself, she realized that they had borne her past the gates of the kremlin. Now they were in the posad, the part of Moscow that lay outside the walls. Still hurrying; they were going down to the river. A little chapel loomed up. They paused there for a swift debate. Konstantin spoke, though she caught only a word here and there.

Witch.

Holy father.

Bring wood.

She wasn't really listening. Her senses were numb. They had not harmed her sister, they had not harmed Marya. Her horse was dead. She cared not what they did with her. She did not care for anything.

She felt the change in the air, when she was thrust from the beating, insistent torchlight into the darkness of a candlelit chapel. She tumbled to the floor not far from the iconostasis, jarring her torn mouth.

There she lay, breathing the smell of dusty wood, passive with shock. Then she thought that she might try to rise at least, stand with a little courage. A little pride. Solovey would have. Solovey . . .

She dragged herself to her feet.

And found herself alone, and face-to-face, with Konstantin Niko-novich. The priest had his back to the door, half the length of the nave between them. He was watching her.

"You killed my horse," she whispered, and he smiled, just a little.

SHE HAD A CUT ACROSS her nose; one eye was swelling shut. In the half-light of the chapel, her bruised face looked more unearthly than ever, and more vulnerable. The old desire flared, and the accompanying self-hatred.

But—why should he be ashamed? God cared not for men and women. All that mattered was his own will, and she was in his power. The thought heated his blood, as much as the worship of the crowd outside. His eyes swept her body again.

"You have been condemned to die," he told her. "For your sins. You have been granted these few moments to pray."

Her face did not change. Perhaps she had not heard. He spoke louder. "It is the law of God, and the will of the people, whom you have wronged!"

Her face was salt-white, so that each faint freckle stood out on her nose like spots of blood. "Kill me then," she said. "Have the courage to do it yourself, not leave it to a mob and call it justice."

"Do you deny then that the fire was of your making?" Lightly, he stepped toward her. Free, he told himself. Free at last of her power over him.

Her expression didn't change. She didn't speak. She didn't move even when he curled his fingers behind the bone of her jaw and lifted her face to his. "You cannot deny it," he said. "Because it is true."

She didn't flinch when he pressed his thumb into the bruises blossoming flowerlike along her mouth. She barely seemed to see him.

She really was ugly. Big eyes, wide mouth, the jutting bones. But he could not look away. He wouldn't ever be able to look away, not until those eyes closed in death. Perhaps even beyond she would haunt him.

"You took all that mattered from me," he said. "You cursed me with demons. You deserve death."

She made no reply. Tears ran unheeded down her face.

In sudden rage, he caught her shoulders, drove her against the iconostasis, so that all the saints shook, and pinned her there. The breath left her body, any vestige of color left her face. His hand closed on her throat, pale and vulnerable, and he found himself breathing fast. *"Look at me, damn you."*

Slowly, her eyes focused on his face.

"Beg for your life," he said. "Beg, and perhaps I will grant it you."

She shook her head slowly, her eyes dazed and wandering.

He felt a surge of hatred; he bent his lips to her ear and whispered in a voice even he hardly recognized, "You will die in the fire, Vasilisa Petrovna. And you will scream for me, before the end." He kissed her once, hard as a blow, holding her jaw in a vise-grip and tasting the blood on her split lip.

She bit him, bloodying his mouth in turn. He recoiled, and then they were staring at each other, with the hatred of each mirrored in the other's eyes.

"God go with you," she whispered, in bitter mockery.

"Go to the devil," he said, and left her.

SILENCE FELL IN THE DUSTY CHAPEL, after Konstantin left. Perhaps they were building a pyre, perhaps they were readying something worse. Perhaps her brother would come at last, and this nightmare would be over. Vasya didn't care. What had she to fear, in dying? Perhaps, beyond life, she would find her father again, her mother, her beloved nurse Dunya.

Solovey.

But then she thought of fire, of whips and knives and fists. She was not dead yet; she was terrified. Perhaps she could just—step away— walk into the gray forest beyond life and be gone. Death was someone she knew.

"Morozko," Vasya whispered, and then his older name, the name of the death-god, "Karachun."

No answer. Winter was over; he had faded away from the world of men. Shivering, she sank to the floor, leaned against the iconostasis. Outside people shouted, laughed, swore. But in that chapel, there was only the silence of the saints in the icon-screen, staring steadily down. Vasya could not bring herself to pray. Instead she tipped her aching head back and shut her eyes, measuring out her life in heartbeats.

She could not have slept, not there. Yet somehow the world faded away and she found herself walking once more in the black forest beneath a starry sky. She knew a dim, shocked relief. It was over. God had heard her plea; this was what she longed for. She stumbled forward, calling.

"Father," she cried. "Mother. Dunya. Solovey. *Solovey!*" Surely he would be here. Surely he had waited for her. If he could.

Morozko would know. But Morozko wasn't there; only silence met her cry. She struggled on, scrabbling, but her limbs were so heavy, and her ribs hurt worse and worse with every breath.

"Vasya." He called her name twice before she heard. *"Vasya."*

She tripped and fell before she could turn, found herself kneeling in the snow without the strength to rise. The sky was a river of stars, but she didn't look up. The death-god was the only thing she could see. He was little more than a confluence of light and dark, wispy as cloud across the moon. But she knew his eyes. He was waiting for her, in the gray forest. She was not alone.

Between gasps she managed, "Where is Solovey?"

"Gone," he said. There was no comfort in the death-god, not here; there was only the knowledge of her loss, echoed in his pale eyes.

She did not know such a sound of agony could come from her throat. Mastering it, she whispered, "Please. Take me with you. They are going to kill me tonight and I do not—"

"No," he said. The faintest of pine-tinged breezes seemed to touch her bruised face. He wore his indifference like armor, but it was wavering. "Vasya, I—"

"*Please,*" she said. "They killed my horse. There is only the fire now."

He reached out to her, just as she reached back, through whatever memory or illusion or walls divided them, but it was like touching a wisp of mist.

"Listen to me," he said, mastering himself. *"Listen."*

She lifted her head with effort. Why, listen? Why couldn't she just go? But the bonds of her body called her; she could not win free. The faces of the icons seemed to be trying to break in upon her sight and come between them. "I wasn't strong enough," he said. "I have done what I could; I hope—it may be enough. You won't see me again. But you will live. You must live."

"What?" she whispered. "How? *Why?* I am about to—"

But icons were thrusting themselves before her eyes, more real than the faint death-god. "Live," he said to her again. And then he was gone a second time. She was awake, alone, lying on the cold, dusty floor of a church, still, horribly, alive.

Alone, save for Konstantin Nikonovich. He was saying, over her head, "Get up. You have missed your chance to pray."

HER HANDS WERE ROUGHLY bound behind her back; a few men came up at Konstantin's beck and made a square around her. They weren't anything like soldiers; they were peasants or tradesmen, ruddy and determined. One held an ax, another a scythe.

Konstantin's face was white and set; their eyes met once, in a look of pure violence, before he looked away, serene, his lips set in the austere lines of a man doing his duty to his faith.

The crowd was thick about the chapel, lining the road that wound down to the river. They had torches in their hands. They smelled like cooking and char and old wounds and sweat. The nighttime wind scoured her skin. They took away her shoes—for penitence, they said. Her feet scraped and throbbed on the snow. Triumph in their faces; naked worship of the priest, naked hatred of her. They spat on her.

Witch, she heard again and again. *She set fire to the city. Witch.*

Vasya had never been so frightened. Where was her brother? Perhaps he could not get through the mob; perhaps he feared the people's madness. Perhaps Dmitrii thought her life a small price to quiet his raging city.

She was prodded forward, stumbling. Konstantin walked beside her, head piously bent. The red light of the torches leaped before her eyes and blinded them.

"Batyushka," she said.

Konstantin broke off. "Beg me now?" he breathed, below the roar of the crowd.

She did not speak; she had all she could do to fight the panic that was threatening to madden her. Then she said, "Not like this. Not—in fire."

He shook his head, and gave her a half-smile; quick, almost confiding. "Why? Did you not condemn Moscow to burn?"

She said nothing.

"The devils whispered," said the priest. "At least I can get some good of your curse; the devils spoke true. They whispered of a maiden with a witch's gifts, and a monster all of fire. I didn't even have to lie, when I told the people of your crime. You should have thought of that before you cursed me with the ears to hear them."

With visible effort, he turned away from her and resumed his praying. His face was the color of linen, but his steps were steady. He seemed transfixed by the crowd's rage, consumed by what he himself had summoned.

Vasya's vision took on a black-and-white clarity, grim and shocking. The air was cold on her face; her feet burned as they began to freeze in the snow. Moscow's smoke-tinged air ran quicksilver through her veins, drawn in with each panicked breath.

Before her, on the ice of the Moskva, massed a sea of upturned faces, snarling or weeping, or merely watching. Down on the river stood a stack of logs, illuminated on all sides with torches. A pyre, hastily constructed. And atop it, stark against the sky, the cage of the condemned, lashed down with many ropes. The crowd made a low, continuous sound now, like the growl of an animal rising.

"Forget the cage," Vasya said to Konstantin. "These people will tear me to pieces before I get there."

The look he gave her was almost pitying, and she suddenly understood why he walked beside her, why also he prayed with that calculated grace. This was Lesnaya Zemlya writ large; he had gathered them up in their grief and terror, gathered them into his hand with his golden voice and his golden hair, so that they became a weapon in his grip, a tool of vengeance, and a sop to his pride. They would not attack while he was with her, and he wanted to see her burn. He had been cheated of it, after all, the night before. Always, always she had underestimated the priest.

"Monster," she said, and he almost smiled.

Then they were down on the ice itself. A shriek went up like a dozen dying rabbits. The people were pressing close about her now, spitting and striking. Her guards could barely keep them back. A stone came whistling through and cut her cheek, gashed it deep. She put a hand to her face and blood spilled through her fingers.

Dazed now, she twisted her head one more time to look at Moscow. No sign of her brother. But she saw the devils, despite the dark. They were silhouetted atop roofs and walls: domoviye and dvoroviye and banniki, the faint house-spirits of Moscow. They were there, but what could they do but watch? Chyerti are formed of the currents of human life; they ride them, but they do not interfere.

Except two. But one was her enemy, the other was far away, made nearly powerless by spring and by her own hand. The most she could hope for from him was a death without agony. She held that hope in a desperate grip as they prodded and shouted and chivied her toward the pyre. Across the ice, through a narrow corridor in the throng. Tears poured down her face now, from her own helplessness, and an involuntary reaction against their hatred.

Perhaps there was some justice in it. Again and again, she saw folk limping, burned, with bandages on their arms or faces. *But I did not mean to free the firebird,* she thought. *I did not know what would happen. I did not know.*

The ice was still hard, as thick as a man was tall, shining in spots where wind or sledges had swept away the snow. It would be a long time still until the river released its bonds. *Will I live to see it?* Vasya wondered. *Will I feel sun on my skin again? I think not, I think—*

The crowd ebbed and surged around the pyre. Konstantin's golden hair turned gray-silver in the torchlight, his face a maelstrom of triumph, anguish, lust. His voice and his presence were undiminished, but now his power was divorced from the restraining impulses of religion. Vasya wished suddenly that she could warn her brother, warn Dmitrii. *Sasha, you know what he did to Marya. Do not trust him, do not—*

Then she thought: *Sasha, where are you?*

But her brother was not there, and Konstantin Nikonovich was bending his eyes down to hers for the last time. He had won.

"What will you say to the God you despise," Vasya whispered, breathing short and thin with fear, "when you go into the darkness? All men must die."

Konstantin only smiled at her again, lifted his hand to make the sign of the cross, raised his deep voice to intone a prayer. The crowd fell silent to hear him. Then he bent forward to whisper in her ear. "There is no God."

Then they were dragging her up, and she was struggling like a wild thing in a trap: pure instinct, but the man was stronger than she was, and her arms were bound, the blood ran down her fingertips where the ropes bit into her thrashing wrists. They forced her up, and Vasya thought, *Mother of God it is happening.*

Dying, she thought, *ought to bring some sense of completion, of a journey ended.* But this was just being caught out of life, as she was, with all her sweat and tears and terrors, her wishes and regrets.

The cage was small enough that she would have to crouch inside it. A blade at her back prodded her forward. The barred wooden door slammed, was tied securely shut.

Vasya's sight fractured with fear. The world became a series of disjointed impressions: the black, fire-lit mass of the crowd; a last glimpse of sky; and memories, of her childhood in the forest, of her family, of Solovey.

The men were tossing torches onto the wood. Smoke billowed, and then the first log caught, crackling. For an instant, her eyes found the stark-white face of Konstantin Nikonovich. He lifted his hand. The hunger, the grief, the joy in his gaze was for her alone. Then a curl of smoke blotted him out.

She wrapped both hands around the bars. Splinters stabbed into her fingers. The smoke stung her face and set her coughing. Somewhere dim and far away, she thought she heard hoofbeats, new voices calling, but they were in another world; her world was made of fire.

Many say, better to die, until the time comes to actually do it, Morozko had told her once. He was right. The heat was already unbearable. But he was nowhere to be seen; there was no refuge for her yet in the forest beyond life.

She couldn't breathe.

My grandmother came to Moscow and never left. Now it is my turn. I am never going to leave this cage. I will be ash on the wind, and I will never see my family again . . .

Rage filled her suddenly; it opened her eyes, sent her back, crouching, to her feet. Never? All those hours, those memories stolen by one mad priest, who had seen his chance for vengeance and taken it? Would they say of her one day, *She never left; her tale ended there on the ice?* And what of Marya? Brave, doomed Marya? Perhaps Konstantin would turn on her next, the witch-child who knew his crime.

There was no way out. She was crouched on the floor of a locked cage, flames rising all around, burning her already-blistered face. There was no way out, save by dying. The cage would not break. It was impossible.

Impossible.

Morozko had said that when she dragged him against hope into the inferno that was Moscow.

Magic is forgetting the world was ever other than as you willed it.

On a surge of blind will, Vasilisa Petrovna set her hands onto the thick, burning-hot bars of her cage, and *pulled*.

The heavy wood broke apart.

Vasya clung, disbelieving, to the new-made gap. Her vision was graying. The cage smoldered; beyond hung a curtain of fire. What matter if she'd broken the bars? The fire would take her. If by some miracle it did not, then she'd be torn apart by the crowd.

But still she crawled out of the cage, put her hands, then her face, into the fire, got to her feet. An instant she stood there, wavering, beyond fear, untouched by the flames. She'd forgotten they could burn her.

And then she leaped down.

Down through the flames of her own funeral pyre; she struck the snow and rolled, sweating, sooty, bloody. A soundless cry went up from all the watching chyerti. She was blistered, but not on fire.

Alive.

Vasya scrambled up, looking wildly about her, but no one cried out; Konstantin—*everyone*—was still watching the fire, as though she had not come hurtling down at all. It was like being a ghost. Was she dead? Had she fallen into another world, like a devil that could not touch the earth, but only live above or beneath it? Dimly, she thought she heard the sound of hoofbeats getting louder, thought she heard a familiar voice shouting her name.

But she didn't heed. For a different voice spoke, low and amused, seemingly in her ear. "Well," it said, "I thought I was beyond surprising."

And then it laughed.

VASYA WHIPPED HER HEAD AROUND, fell sprawling into the melted slush. The haze of smoke choked her; the air rippled like cloth in the heat, made formless shadows of the ring of people. Still they didn't see her. Perhaps she had died, or fallen in truth into a world of devils. She couldn't feel her wounds, only her weakness. Nothing seemed real. Certainly not the man standing over her.

Not a man. A chyert.

"*You,*" she whispered.

He stood too close to the fire and should have been scorched, but wasn't. His single eye glittered in a face seamed with blue scars.

The last time she'd seen him, he had killed her father.

"Vasilisa Petrovna," said the chyert called Medved.

Vasya lurched to her feet, caught between the devil and the fire. "No. You're not here, you cannot be here."

He did not answer in words, but caught her chin in his hand, tilted her face up to his. The lid of his missing eye was sewn shut. His thick fingers smelled of carrion and hot metal and were quite real. He grinned down at her. "No?"

She wrenched back, wild-eyed. There was blood from her split lip on his fingers; he licked it off and added, confidingly, "Tell me: how long do you think your newfound power will avail you?" He cast an appraising eye upon the mob. "They are going to tear you to pieces."

"You—were bound," Vasya whispered, in the voice of a girl in a nightmare. It could have been a nightmare. The Bear had haunted her dreams since her father died, and now they stood face-to-face in a storm of smoke and red light. "*You cannot be here.*"

"Bound?" said the Bear. In the single gray eye flashed a memory of fury; his snarling shadow was not the shadow of a man. "Oh, yes," he added, with irony. "You and your father bound me, with the help of my skulking twin." He bared his teeth. "Aren't you fortunate that I am free? I am going to save your life."

She stared. Reality wavered like the air around the fire.

"Perhaps I am not the savior you want," added the Bear, sly now, "but my noble brother could not come himself. You shattered his power when you shattered his blue jewel; and then spring came. He is less than a ghost. So he freed me and sent me. Went to a lot of trouble, really." The single eye slid over her skin, and he pursed his lips. "No accounting for taste."

"No," was all she could manage. "He would not." She was going to be sick, from terror and shock, from the animal-stink of the half-seen crowd, concealed by smoke.

The chyert reached into his ragged sleeve. With a look of distaste, he thrust a palm-sized wooden bird into her hand. "He gave me this to give you. A token. He traded his freedom for your life. Now we must go."

The words seemed to run together in her mind; she couldn't make sense of them. The wooden bird was carved, agonizingly, to look like a nightingale. She had seen the winter-king, the Bear's brother, carving a bird once, beneath a spruce tree in the snow. Her hand closed about the carving even as she said, "You're lying. You didn't save my life." She wished for a drink of water. She wished she could wake up.

"Not yet," the Bear said and glanced up at the burning cage. The mockery vanished from his face. "But you will not escape the city, unless you come with me." He caught her hand suddenly, grip sure. "The bargain was for your life. I have sworn it, Vasilisa Petrovna. Come. Now."

Not a dream. Not a dream. *He killed my father.* She licked her lips, forced her voice to work. "If you are free, what will you do after you save my life?"

His scarred mouth quirked. "Stay with me and find out."

"Never."

"Very well. Then I will see you safe, as I promised, and the rest doesn't concern you."

He was a monster. But she didn't think he was lying. Why would the winter-king do such a thing? Was she now to owe this monster her life? What would that make him? What would that make her?

With death all around her, Vasya hesitated. Shrieks rose suddenly from the crowd and she flinched, but they were not screaming at her. A mass of horsemen was beating a way through the mob. Eyes turned from the fire to the riders; even Medved glanced up.

Vasya jerked herself away and ran. She didn't look back, for if she did, she would stop, would yield in her despair to her enemy's promises or to the death still beating at her back. As she ran, she tried to be like a ghost, like a chyert herself. *Magic is forgetting the world was ever other than as you willed it.* And perhaps it worked. No one called out; no one so much as glanced in her direction.

"Fool," said the Bear. His voice was in her ear, though a whole mass of people stood between them. His weary amusement was worse than rage. "I am telling you the truth. That is what frightens you." Still she darted through the crowd, a fire-smelling ghost, trying not to hear that dry, metallic voice. "I will let them kill you," said the Bear. "You can leave here with me, or you will not leave at all."

That she believed. Still she ran, sinking herself deeper in the crowd, sick with terror, sick at the stink, expecting every instant to be seen, to be seized. The carved nightingale felt cold and solid in her sweaty fist: a promise she didn't understand.

And then the Bear's voice was raised up again, not directed at her. "Look! Look—what is that? A ghost—no—it is she the witch; she has escaped the fire! Magic! Black sorcery! She is there! She is there!"

Vasya realized with horror that the crowd could hear him. A head turned. Then another. They could see her. A woman screamed, just as a hand closed on Vasya's arm. She pulled away, thrashing, but the hand only tightened its grip. Then a cloak was flung over her shoulders, concealing her blackened shift. A familiar voice spoke in her ear, even as the hand dragged her deeper into the crowd. "This way," it said.

Vasya's savior yanked the hood over the girl's charred hair, hiding everything except her feet. The crush of people hid them; most people were trying not to be trampled. It was too dark to see her red footprints. Behind her the Bear's voice rose, savage now: "There! There!"

But even he could not guide a crowd in such confusion. Sasha and Dmitrii and the Grand Prince's riders had finally arrived, had won their way through to the pyre, shouting. They tore the burning logs away, swearing as they scorched their hands; one man caught fire and shrieked. All around Vasya, people were surging, fleeing, crying out that they had seen the witch's ghost, that they had seen the witch herself, escaped from the fire. No one remarked a skinny girl, stumbling in a cloak.

Her brother's voice soared over the din; she thought she heard the strident tones of Dmitrii Ivanovich. The crowd surged backward from the riders. *I must go to my brother,* Vasya thought. But she could not bring herself to turn; her every sense was bent on escape, and somewhere at her back was the Bear . . .

The hand on her arm continued to drag her along. "Come," said that familiar voice. "Hurry."

Vasya lifted her head, stared uncomprehending into Varvara's grim, bruised face.

"How did you know?" she whispered.

"A message," said Varvara jerkily, still dragging her.

She didn't understand. "Marya," Vasya managed. "Are Olga and Marya—"

"Alive," said Varvara, and Vasya sagged in gratitude. "Unhurt. Come." She pulled Vasya on, half-carrying her through the retreating crowd. "You have to leave the city."

"Leave?" Vasya whispered. "How? I have—I have not . . ."

Solovey. She could not form the word; grief would take the last of her strength.

"You do not need the horse," said Varvara, voice hard. "Come."

Vasya said nothing more; she was fighting a desperate battle to stay conscious. The ends of her ribs ground together. Her bare feet didn't hurt anymore, numbed on the ice. But they didn't work very well either, and so she stumbled and stumbled again, until Varvara's arm was the only thing keeping her from falling.

The crowd churned behind them, scattering under the whips of Dmitrii's men-at-arms. A voice called to Varvara, asking if the girl was sick, and Vasya felt a new bolt of terror.

Varvara returned a cool explanation, of a niece who'd fainted with the bloodletting, and all the while her hand made more bruises on Vasya's arm as she dragged her up from the riverbank and into the darkness of the sapling woods that grew beside the posad. Vasya tried to understand what was happening.

Varvara halted abruptly near an oak-sapling, bare with the end of winter. "Polunochnitsa," she said to the dark.

Vasya knew a person—a devil—called Polunochnitsa, Lady Midnight. But what could her sister's body-servant know of—

The Bear loomed out of the shadows, firelight striping his face. Vasya wrenched back. Varvara followed her gaze, her eyes darting into the dark like a blind woman's. "Do you think I'd lose *you* in this?" the Bear demanded, half-angry, half-amused. "You reek of terror. I could follow that anywhere."

Varvara could not see him, but her hand tightened convulsively on Vasya's arm. Vasya realized that she had heard him. "Eater," Varvara breathed. "Here? *Midnight*." The voices of the dispersing mob filtered up from the river below.

The Bear shot Varvara a speculative look. "You're the other one, aren't you? I forgot the old woman had twins. How did you contrive to live so long?"

Vasya thought the words should make some kind of sense, but understanding slipped away before she could seize it. To Vasya, the Bear added, "She means to send you through Midnight. I wouldn't, if I were you. You will die there, just as surely as in the fire."

The voices of the crowd came closer as the people cut through the woods back to the posad. In moments, someone would see them, and then . . . Torches threw flickers of light through the scraggly trees. A man caught sight of the two women. "What are you doing, skulking there?"

"Girls!" said another voice. "Look at them, all alone. I could have a girl, after watching that . . ."

"You can die at their hands or you can come with me now," the Bear said to Vasya. "It is all one to me; I will not ask again."

One of Vasya's eyes was swollen shut, the other blurred; perhaps that had made her slow to pick out a fourth person, watching from the shadows. This person had skin that was violet-black, and her hair was pale, blowing white across eyes like two stars. She was looking from the women to the Bear and said not a word.

This was the demon called Midnight.

"I do not understand," Vasya whispered. She stood frozen between

Varvara, who had kept secrets, and the Bear, who offered poisonous safety.

Beyond them, silent, stood Lady Midnight. At the demon's back, the woods seemed to have changed. They grew thicker, wilder, darker.

Varvara said, low and fierce in Vasya's ear, "What do you see?"

"The Bear," Vasya breathed. "And the demon called Midnight. And—a darkness. There is darkness behind her, such darkness." She was shaking from head to foot.

"Run into the dark," Varvara whispered to Vasya. "That was the message I had, and the promise. Touch the oak-sapling and run into the dark. That is the road, from here to the oak-tree by the lake. The road through Midnight opens every night to those with eyes to see. There will be refuge for you by the lake. Hold it in your mind; a stretch of water, shining, with a great oak that grows at the bow-curve of its shore. Run into the dark, and be brave."

Whom to trust? The voices of men were growing louder. Their crunching footsteps broke into a run. Her only choices were fire or darkness or the devil in between.

"Go—*go!*" shouted Varvara. She placed Vasya's bloody palm on the bark and shoved. Vasya found herself stumbling forward. The darkness loomed up, and then the Bear's hand closed about her arm, an instant before the night swallowed her. She was spun to face him, her numb feet clumsy and scraping on the snow. "Go into the darkness," he breathed. "And you will die."

She had no words, no courage, no defiance left. She made no answer at all. The only thing that drove her to gather all her strength and wrench away from him, fling herself into the night, was the desire to get away, from him, from the noise, from the smell of fire.

She broke his grip and hurled herself into the dark. Instantly, the lights and the noise of Moscow were swallowed up. She was in a forest all alone, beneath an unsullied sky. She took one step forward, and then another. And then she tripped, fell to her knees, and could not muster the strength to rise. The last thing she heard was a half-familiar voice. "Dead just like that? Well, perhaps the old woman was wrong."

Behind her, somewhere, it seemed the Bear was laughing again.

And then Vasya lay still, unconscious.

In the true world, the Bear's breath hissed between his teeth, still with that edge of angry laughter. He said to Varvara, "Well, you have killed her. I didn't even need to break my word to my brother. I thank you for that."

Varvara said nothing. *The Eater's greatest power is his knowledge of the desires and weaknesses of men.* Varvara's mother had taught her much of the ways of chyerti. Varvara had tried to forget what she knew. What did it matter? She had not the eyes to see them, as her sister liked to remind her.

But now the Eater was free, and her mother and her sister were gone.

Two young men came stumbling up, drunk. In their eyes was a hungry light. "Well, you're old and you're ugly," said one. "But you'll serve."

Without a word, Varvara kicked the first man between the legs, put a hard shoulder into the second. They fell yelping to the snow. She heard the Bear's sigh of satisfaction. *Above all,* her mother had said, *he is a lover of armies, of battles, and of violence.*

Holding her skirts, Varvara ran, back to the lights, the chaos of the posad and thence up the hill of the kremlin. As she ran, she heard the Bear's voice in her ears, though he had made no move to follow her. "I must thank you again, No-Eyes, that the little witch is dead, and my promise is unbroken."

"Don't thank me yet," Varvara whispered between clenched teeth. "Not yet."

Part Two

5

Temptation

THE CAGE COLLAPSED IN A SHOWER OF SPARKS, JUST AS SASHA AND Dmitrii battered through the ring of people and began to break the fire apart with their smoldering spear-hafts. The chaos rose to a fever pitch.

In the confusion, Konstantin Nikonovich slipped away, hood drawn up over the deep gold of his hair. The air was hazed with smoke; the maddened crowd jostled him, not knowing who he was. By the time the men had scattered the logs of the fire, Konstantin had passed through the posad unremarked, was making his soft-footed way back to the monastery.

She didn't even deny her guilt, he thought, hurrying through the half-frozen slush. She had set fire to Moscow. It was the people's righteous wrath that had swept her up. What blame could attach to him, a holy man?

She was dead. He'd taken the full measure of his vengeance.

She had been seventeen years old.

He barely made it to his cell and shut the door before he broke into a fit of sobbing laughter. He laughed at all those nodding, adoring, snarling faces out in Moscow, taking every word of his as gospel, laughed at the memory of her face, the fear in her eyes. He even laughed at the icons on the wall, their rigidity and their silence. Then he found his laughter turning to tears. Sounds of anguish tore from his throat, quite against his will, until he had to thrust a fist into his mouth to muffle the noise. She was dead. It had been easy, in the end. Perhaps the demon, the witch, the goddess had only existed in his mind.

He tried to master himself. The people had been as clay in his hands, softened as they were in the heat of Moscow's fire. It would not always be so easy. If Dmitrii Ivanovich discovered that Konstantin had raised the mob, he would see him as a threat to his authority at least, if not the murderer of his cousin. Konstantin did not know if his new-made influence would be enough to counter the Grand Prince's wrath.

He was so busy weeping, pacing, thinking and trying not to think, that he failed to notice the shadow on the wall, until it spoke.

"Crying like a maiden?" murmured a voice. "On tonight, of all nights? What are you doing, Konstantin Nikonovich?"

Konstantin leaped back with a sound not far from a scream. "It is you," he said, breathing like a child afraid of the dark. And then, *"No."* And finally, *"Where are you?"*

"Here," said the voice.

Konstantin twisted round, but saw only his own shadow, cast by the lamp.

"No, here." This time the voice seemed to come from his icon of the Mother of God. The woman beneath the gold icon-cover leered at him. She was not the Virgin at all, but Vasya with her red-black hair shaken loose, her face one-eyed and scarred with fire. Konstantin bit back another scream.

Then the voice said a third time, from his own cot, laughing, "No, here, poor fool."

Konstantin looked and saw . . . a man.

Man? The creature on his bed *looked* like a man; such a man as had never before been seen in a monastery. He lounged smiling upon the bed, hair tumbled, feet incongruously bare. But his shadow—his shadow had claws.

"Who are you?" asked Konstantin, breathing fast.

"Did you never see my face before?" asked the creature. "Ah, no, at Midwinter you saw the beast and the shadow, but not the man." He got slowly to his feet. He and Konstantin were nearly of a height. "Never mind. You know my voice." He cast down his eyes like a girl. "Do I please you, man of God?" The unscarred side of his mouth twisted in a half-smile.

Konstantin was pressed hard against the door, his fist against his mouth. "I remember. You are the devil."

The man—the chyert—looked up at that, single eye alight. "I? Men call me the Bear, Medved, when they call me anything at all. Have you never thought that heaven and hell are both nearer you than you like to believe?"

"Heaven? Nearer?" said Konstantin. He could feel every ridge of the wooden wall pressed against his back. "God abandoned me. He gave me over to devils. There *is* no heaven. There is only this world of clay."

"Exactly," said the demon. He spread his arms wide. "To mold to your liking. What do you desire of this world, little father?"

Konstantin was shaking in every limb. "Why are you asking?"

"Because I need you. I am in need of a man."

"For what?"

Medved shrugged. "Men do the work of devils, do they not? It has always been so."

"I am not your servant." His voice shook.

"Nay—who wants a servant?" said the Bear. He stepped closer and closer still, voice dropping. "Enemy, lover, passionate slave you may choose, but servant—no." His red tongue just touched his upper lip. "See, I am generous in my bargains."

Konstantin swallowed, his mouth dry. His breath came short, with eagerness and despair; it felt as though the walls of his cell were closing in. "What would I get in return for my—allegiance?"

"What do you want?" returned the chyert, so near that he could murmur the question into Konstantin's ear.

In the priest's soul was a desperate mourning. *I prayed—all the years of my life, I prayed. But you were silent, Lord. If I am making bargains with devils it is only because you abandoned me.* This devil looked as though he were following his thought with an easy and a secret delight.

"I want to forget myself in men's devotion." It was the first time he had ever spoken the thought aloud.

"Done."

"I want the comforts that princes have," Konstantin went on. He was going to drown in that single eye. "Good meats and soft beds." He breathed out the last word. "Women."

The Bear laughed. "That too."

"I want earthly authority," Konstantin said.

"As much as your two hands, your heart, and your voice can compass," the Bear said. "The world at your feet."

"But what do you want?" breathed Konstantin Nikonovich.

The devil's hand curled into a clawed fist. "All I wanted was to be free. My bastard brother penned me up in a clearing on the edge of winter for life after life of men. But at long last he wanted something more than he wanted me confined and I am freed at last. I have seen the stars and smelled the smoke, and tasted men's fear."

Softer, the devil added, "I have found the chyerti faded to shadows. Now men order their lives to the sound of damned bells. So I am going to throw the bells down, throw down the Grand Prince while I am about it; set fire to this whole little world of Rus' and see what grows out of the ashes."

Konstantin stared, fascinated and afraid.

"You will like that, won't you?" asked the Bear. "*That* will teach your God to ignore you." He paused and then added more prosaically, "In the short term, I want you to go tonight where I bid you and do what I tell you."

"Tonight? The city is unsettled; midnight has come and gone and I—"

"Are you afraid that you might be seen out past midnight, consorting with the wicked? Well, leave that to me."

"Why?" said Konstantin.

"Why not?" returned the other.

Konstantin made no answer.

The devil breathed against his ear, "Would you rather stay and think of her dying? Sit here in the dark, and lust after her, dead?"

Konstantin tasted blood where his teeth had come together on the inside of his cheek. "She was a witch. She deserved it."

"That does not mean you didn't enjoy it," murmured the devil. "Why do you think I came to you first?"

"She was ugly," said Konstantin.

"She was as wild as the sea," he rejoined. "And full, like the sea, of mysteries."

"Dead," said Konstantin flatly, as though speaking could cut off memory.

The devil smiled a secret smile. "Dead."

Konstantin felt the air thick in his lungs, as though he were trying to breathe smoke.

"We cannot dally," said the Bear. "The first blow—the first blow must be struck tonight."

Konstantin said, "You tricked me before."

"And I might again," returned the other. "Are you afraid?"

"No," said Konstantin. "I believe in nothing and I fear nothing."

The Bear laughed. "As it should be. Because that is the only way you can play for everything, when you do not fear to lose."

6

No Bones, No Flesh

Dmitrii and his men tore apart the fire on the river. Sasha worked alongside the others in the most hopeless and terrible desperation. In the end, a field of smoldering logs lay glowing across a stretch of pitted and steaming ice. The cage looked just like the rest of the charred wood; they could barely tell which pieces had formed it. The crowd had fled; it was the coldest and blackest part of the night. They stood in a field of dying fire, caught between the cold earth and the spring stars.

The terrible strength that had animated Sasha's limbs suddenly vanished. He leaned against his mare's smoke-smelling shoulder. Nothing. There was nothing left of her. He could not stop shivering.

Dmitrii pushed the loose hair from his brow, made the sign of the cross. Low he said, "God rest her spirit." He laid a hand on his cousin's shoulder. "It is for no man to undertake justice in my city without my leave. You will have vengeance."

Sasha said nothing. But the Grand Prince was surprised at the look on his cousin's face. Grief, of course, anger. But also—puzzlement?

"Brother?" said Dmitrii.

"Look," Sasha whispered. He kicked one log apart, and then another, pointed to the remains of the cage.

"What?" said Dmitrii warily.

"No bones," said Sasha, and swallowed. "No flesh."

"Burned away," said Dmitrii. "The fire was hot."

Sasha shook his head once. "It didn't burn long enough."

"Come," said Dmitrii, looking worried now. "Cousin, I know you wish her alive, but she did go in. She could not have come out again."

"No," said Sasha, drawing a deep breath. "No, that would be impossible." But still he glanced again at the red and black hellscape of the river, and then abruptly went to his horse. "I am going to my sister."

Startled silence. Then Dmitrii understood. "Very well," he said. "Tell the Princess of Serpukhov that I—that I am sorry for her grief, and yours. She—was a brave girl. God be with you."

Words, only words. Sasha knew that Dmitrii could not wholly regret Vasya's death; she had been a problem he didn't know how to solve. Yet—the fire had contained no bones. And Vasya—you could not always predict Vasya. Sasha wheeled his mare and kicked her to full gallop up the hill of the posad and through the gates of Moscow.

Dmitrii turned, scowling, to snap orders and marshal his guards. He was very weary, and now there had been two fires in Moscow, the second, in its own way, as destructive as the first.

SASHA FOUND OLGA'S GATES SMASHED, the dooryard trampled. But Dmitrii had sent all of his own men-at-arms that could be spared. They had established some kind of order, kept the outbuildings from looting. The dooryard was quiet.

Sasha passed Dmitrii's men with a soft word. A few of the grooms had straggled back after the crowd went down to the river. Sasha roused one in the stable and thrust him the reins of his mare, barely pausing.

The snow of the dooryard was daubed and spattered with blood, and there were the marks of boots and blades on the door to the terem. A fearful serving-woman opened at last to his knocking; he had to persuade her to let him in.

Olga was sitting by the hot brick of the stove in her bedchamber, still awake and still dressed. Her face was drawn and gray in the candlelight; exhausted shadows smeared her milky beauty. Marya was weeping hysterically into her mother's lap, black hair flung about like water. The two were alone. Sasha paused in the doorway. Olga took in his filthy, blistered, soot-streaked appearance and blanched.

"If you have news, it can wait," she said, with a look at the child.

Sasha hardly knew what to say; his faint, terrible hope seemed foolish in the face of the blood-spattered dvor, in the face of Marya's wild grief. "Is Masha all right?" he said, crossing the room and kneeling beside his sister.

"No," said Olga.

Marya lifted her head, wet-eyed, with marks like bruising about the lids. "They killed him!" she sobbed. "They killed him and he would never hurt anyone but the wicked, and he loved porridge and *they shouldn't have killed him*!" Her eyes were savage. "I am going to wait for Vasya to get back, and we are going to go and kill all the people that hurt him." She glared about the room and then her eyes welled once more. The rage drained out of her, fast as it had come. She fell to her knees, hunched up small, weeping into her mother's lap.

Olga stroked her daughter's hair. Up close, Sasha could see Olga's hand tremble.

"There was a mob," said Sasha, low-voiced. "Vasya—"

Olga put her finger to her lips, with a glance at her sobbing child. But she shut her black eyes the briefest instant. "God be with her," she said.

Marya lifted her head once more. "Uncle Sasha, did Vasya come back with you? She needs us; she will be sad."

"Masha," said Olga gently. "We must pray for Vasya. I fear she has not come back."

"But she—"

"Masha," said Olga. "Hush. We do not know all that happened; we must wait to find out. Mornings are wiser than evenings. Come, will you sleep?"

Marya would not. She was on her feet. "She has to come back!" she cried. "Where would she go if she didn't come back?"

"Perhaps she has gone to God," said Olga, steadily. She did not lie to her children. "If so, let her soul find rest."

The child stared between her mother and her uncle, lips parted with horror. And then she turned her head, as though someone else in the room were speaking. Sasha followed her gaze to the corner by the stove. There was no one there. A chill ran down his spine.

"No, she hasn't!" cried Marya, scrambling free of her mother's arms. She scrubbed at her wet eyes. "She's not with God. You're wrong! She's—where?" Marya demanded of the empty place near the floor. "Midnight is not a place."

Sasha and Olga looked at each other. "Masha—" Olga began.

There was an abrupt movement in the doorway. They all jumped; Sasha spun, one dirty hand on the hilt of his sword.

"It is I," said Varvara. Her fair plait straggled; there was soot and blood on her clothes.

Olga stared. "Where have you been?"

Without ceremony, Varvara said, "Vasya is alive. Or was when I left her. They were going to burn her. But she broke the bars of the cage and leaped down unseen. I got her out of the city."

Sasha had hoped. But he hadn't really thought how . . . "Unseen?" Then he thought of more important things. "Where? Was she wounded? Where is she? I must—"

"Yes, she is wounded; she was beaten by a mob," said Varvara acidly. "She was also near mad with magic; it came on her suddenly, in desperation. But she is alive and her wounds aren't mortal. She escaped."

"Where is she now?" asked Olga sharply.

"She took the road through Midnight," said Varvara. There was the strangest combination of wonder and resentment in her face. "Perhaps she will even reach the lake. I did all I could."

"I must go to her," said Sasha. "Where is this road through Midnight?"

"Nowhere," said Varvara. "And everywhere. But only at midnight. It is no longer midnight now. In any case, you have not the sight: the power to take the Midnight-road alone. She has gone beyond your reach."

Olga looked, frowning between Marya and Varvara.

Incredulously, Sasha said, "You expect me to take your word for it? To *abandon my sister*?"

"There is no question of abandonment; her fate is out of your hands." Varvara sank onto a stool as though she weren't a servant at all. Something had changed, subtly, in her bearing. Her eyes were intent and troubled. "The Eater is loose," she said. "The creature that men call Medved. The Bear."

Even after Vasya had told them the truth, in the hours after Moscow had caught fire and been saved by snow, Sasha had hardly believed his sister's tale of devils. He was about to demand again that Varvara tell him properly where Vasya was, when Olga broke in: "What does that mean, that the Bear is *loose*? Who is the Bear? Loose to do what?"

"I do not know," said Varvara. "The Bear is among the greatest of chyerti, a master of the unclean forces of the earth." She spoke slowly, as though remembering a lesson long forgotten. "His chief skill is knowing the minds of men and women, and bending them to his will. Above all he loves destruction and chaos, and will seek to sow it as he can." She shook her head, and suddenly she was the body-servant Varvara again, clever and practical. "It must wait until morning; we are all mortally weary. Come, the wild girl is alive and beyond reach of friend or foe. Will you all sleep?"

There was a silence. Then, grimly, Sasha said, "No—if I can't go to her, then at least I am going to pray. For my sister, for this mad city."

"The city isn't mad," Marya protested. She had been following their conversation, her black eyes ferocious, and then had turned her head to listen to that unseen voice near the floor. "It was a man with golden hair—he made them do it. He spoke to them, he made them angry." She had begun to shake. "He was the one who came last night, who made me come with him. People listen when he talks. His voice is very beautiful. And he hates Aunt Vasya."

Olga gathered her daughter into her arms. Marya had begun weeping again, slow exhausted sobs. "Hush, sweet," she said to her daughter. Sasha felt his face settling into bleakness. "The priest with golden hair," he said. "Konstantin Nikonovich."

"Our father sheltered him. You brought him to Moscow. I succored him here," said Olga. Her habitual composure could not hide the look in her eyes.

"I am going to pray now," said Sasha. "If a devil has come to this city, all I can do against it is pray. But tomorrow I will go to Dmitrii Ivanovich. I will see this priest tried and justice done."

"You must kill him with your sword, Uncle Sasha," said Marya. "For I think he is very wicked."

Sasha kissed them both and departed in silence.

"Thank you for saving our sister's life," Olga said to Varvara, when Sasha had gone.

Varvara said nothing, but the two women clasped hands. They had known each other a long time.

"Now tell me more of this demon that has come to Moscow," Olga added. "If it concerns the safety of my family, it cannot wait until morning."

7

Monster

In ANOTHER PART OF MOSCOW, IN THE BLACK AND FRIGID HOUR BEFORE dawn, a peasant man and his wife lay awake atop his brother's oven. They had lost their izba, their possessions, and their firstborn in the fires of the night before, and neither of them had slept since.

A light, insistent tapping came from the window.

Tap. Tap.

Below them, on the floor, the brother's family stirred. The knocking went on, steady, monotonous, first at the window, then at the door. "Who could that be?" muttered the husband.

"Someone in need perhaps," said his wife, voice hoarse from the tears she had shed that day. "Answer it."

Her husband reluctantly slid down from the oven. He stumbled to the door, over the complaining bodies of his brother's family. He opened the inner door, unbarred the outer door.

His wife heard him give a single, sobbing gasp, and then nothing. She hurried up behind him.

A small figure stood in the doorway. Its skin was blackened and flaking away; you could see hints of white bone through rents in his clothing. "Mother?" it whispered.

The dead child's mother screamed, a scream to wake the dead—but the dead were already awake—a scream to awaken their neighbors, sleeping uneasily with the memory of fire. People opened their shutters, opened their doors.

This child did not go into the house. Instead he turned away and began walking up the street. He walked drunkenly, lurching from side to side. His eyes, in the moonlight, were bewildered and afraid and intent all at once. "Mother?" he said again.

Above, on either side, the awakened neighbors stared and pointed. "Mother of God."

"Who is that?"

"What is that?"

"A child?"

"Which child?"

"Nay—God defend us—that is little Andryusha—but he is dead . . ."

The voice of the child's mother rose up. "No!" she cried. "No, I am sorry; I am here. Little one, don't leave me."

She ran after the dead boy, tripping on the half-frozen earth. Her husband ran stumbling out after her. There was a priest among the awed crowd on the street; the husband seized him and dragged him along. "Batyushka, do something!" he cried. "Make it go! Pray—"

"Upyr!"

The word—the dread word of legend and nightmare and fairy tale—was taken up from house to house, as understanding dawned. The word hissed its way down the street, up and back down, growing and growing until it became a moan, a scream.

"The dead boy. He is walking. The dead are walking. We are cursed. *Cursed!*"

Every instant the turmoil grew. Clay lamps were lit; torches made gold points of light under the sickly moon. Cries flew. People fainted, or wept, or called down God's aid. Some opened their doors and ran out to see what the trouble was. Others barred their doors tight and set their families to praying.

Still the dead child walked on unsteady legs, up the hill of the kremlin.

"Son!" panted his mother, running at the thing's side. She still did not dare touch him; the way he moved, ill-jointed, was not the way the living moved. But in his eyes—she was sure of it—lay something of her son. "My child, what horror is this? Has God sent you back to us? Have you come to give a warning?"

The dead child turned and said "Mother?" again, in a soft, high voice.

"I am here," whispered the woman, putting out a hand. The skin of his face peeled away at her touch. Her husband shoved the priest forward. "Do something, for God's sake."

The priest, his lips quivering, stumbled forward, and raised a trembling hand. "Apparition I charge thee . . ."

The child looked up, his eyes dull. The crowd drew back, crossing themselves, watching . . . The child's eyes wandered around the assembled faces.

"Mother?" the child whispered one last time. And lunged.

Not fast; injury and death had weakened the thing, made it clumsy on its half-grown limbs. But the woman put up no resistance. The vampire buried its face in her wrinkled throat.

She gave a gurgling cry of pain and of love, and clutched the thing to her, gasping in agony and crooning to the thing in the same breath. "I'm here," she whispered again.

And then the little dead creature was painting itself with her blood, jerking its head back and forth in a mockery of infancy.

People were running, screaming.

Then a voice rang out from the street above, and Father Konstantin came down, walking fast, fierce, dignified, his gold hair silver in the moonlight.

"People of God," he said. "I am here; fear no darkness." His voice was like church-bells at dawn. His long robe snapped and flared behind him. He thrust his way past the husband, who had fallen to his knees, one hand helplessly outstretched.

Crisp as a man drawing a sword, he made the sign of the cross.

The child upyr hissed. Its face was black with blood.

There was a one-eyed shadow behind Konstantin, watching the tawdry, bloody encounter with delight, but no one saw it. Not even

Konstantin, who was not looking. Perhaps he had forgotten in that moment that it was not his voice alone that bid the dead rest.

"Back, devil," Konstantin said. "Get back to where you came. Do not trouble the living again."

The little vampire hissed. The wavering crowd had paused in its flight; the nearest watched with frozen fascination. For a long moment, the upyr and the priest seemed to lock eyes in a terrible battle of wills. The only sound was the gurgling breath of the dying woman.

An observant person might have noticed that the dead thing was not looking *at* the priest, but beyond him. Behind Konstantin, the one-eyed shadow jerked its thumb in a peremptory gesture, the way a man dismisses a dog.

The vampire snarled again, but softly, as the power that had given it life and breath and movement faded. It crumpled onto its mother's breast. No one could tell if the final sound from the pair was her last breath or his.

The husband stared at the corpses of his family: empty, shocked and still. But the crowd was not looking at him. *"Go back,"* hissed the Bear into Konstantin's ear. "They think you a saint; it is not the time to stand about. So much as sneeze and you ruin the effect."

Konstantin Nikonovich, surrounded by faces slack with awe, knew that perfectly well. He made the sign of the cross over them all again: a benediction. Then he swept back up the narrow street, striding through the darkness, hoping he wouldn't trip on a frozen rut in the road. People drew back before him, weeping.

Konstantin's blood was singing with the memory of power. Years of praying, of earnest searching, had left him an outcast of God, but this demon could make him great among men. He knew it. If part of him whispered, *he will have your soul,* Konstantin did not heed. What good had his soul ever done him? But he muttered, as though despite himself, "That woman died for your show."

The devil shrugged. The scarred side of his face was lost in darkness; he looked ordinary, except for his soundless bare feet. Now and again he glanced up at the stars. "Not *exactly* dead; the dead do not lie quiet when I'm about." Konstantin shuddered. "She will walk the streets at night, calling for her son. But that is all to the good. More fuel for their fear." He looked at the priest sidelong. "Regrets? Too late for scruples, man of God."

Konstantin said nothing.

The devil murmured, "There is nothing but power in this world. People are divided into those who have it and those who have it not. Which will you be, Konstantin Nikonovich?"

"At least I am a man," Konstantin snapped, shrill. "*You* are only a monster."

Medved's teeth were white as a beast's; they gleamed briefly when he smiled. "There are no monsters."

Konstantin snorted.

"There are not," said the Bear. "There are no monsters in the world, and no saints. Only infinite shades woven into the same tapestry, light and dark. One man's monster is another man's beloved. The wise know that."

They were nearly at the monastery-gate. "Are you *my* monster then, devil?" Konstantin asked.

The shadow at the corner of Medved's mouth deepened. "I am," he said. "And your beloved too. You are not one to distinguish." The devil caught Konstantin's golden head between his hands, drew him down and kissed him, full on the mouth.

Then he disappeared into the darkness, laughing.

8.

Between the City
and Evil

Brother Aleksandr left his sister's palace in the gray-blue hour before the sun rises. All around him, Moscow was stirring, sullenly. The city's rage and wildness had shifted to a deeper unease. Dmitrii had every man he could spare in the streets—soldiers at the kremlin-gate, at the gate of his own palace, guarding the boyars' houses—but their presence only seemed to feed the sense of dread.

A few people recognized Sasha, despite the hour, despite his hood. Once they would have asked him for his blessing; now they gave him black looks, and drew their children aside.

The witch's brother.

Sasha strode on, lips set thin. Perhaps a better monk would have fixed his gaze on heavenly things, forgiven and forgotten, not mourned his sister's torment, or his own lost reputation. But—if he had been a better monk he would have stayed in the Lavra.

The sun had made a copper rim on the horizon and water was running beneath the softening snow when Sasha passed the Grand Prince's gate, and found Dmitrii in low-voiced conversation with three of his boyars. "God be with you," said Sasha to them all. The boyars made the sign of the cross, identical troubled expressions half-hidden in their beards. Sasha could hardly blame them.

"The great families do not like it," said Dmitrii when the boyars had bowed and left, and his attendants gone out of earshot. "Any of it. That a traitor came so close to killing me, that I lost control of the city last night. And—" Dmitrii paused. His hand toyed with his sword-hilt. "There are rumors that a demon was seen in Moscow."

Sasha thought of Varvara's warning. Perhaps Dmitrii expected him to scoff, but instead he asked, warily, "What nature of—demon?"

Dmitrii shot him a glance. "I know not. But that is why those three came to me so early and so uneasy; they heard the rumors too and fear that the city must be under some curse. They say that people talk of nothing now but devils, and of spoiling. They say that the only reason the city did not fall to evil last night was because a priest named Father Konstantin banished the demon. They are saying he is a saint, that he is the only one standing between this city and evil."

"Lies," said Sasha. "It was that same Father Konstantin yesterday who drove the city to riot and put my sister in the fire."

Dmitrii's eyes narrowed.

"His mob smashed the gates of my sister's palace," Sasha went on. "And he—" Sasha broke off. *He stole my niece from her bed and gave her to the traitor,* was what he wanted to say, but . . . *No,* Olga had said. *Don't you dare say aloud that my daughter left the terem that night. Get justice for Vasya if you can, but what do you think folk will say of Marya?*

"Have you proof of this?" asked Dmitrii.

Once Sasha would have replied, *Is my word not enough?* Dmitrii would have answered, *Yes it is, brother,* and that would have been the end of argument. But a lie had come between them and so instead Sasha said, "There are witnesses that will place Father Konstantin among the mob at the palace of Serpukhov, and at the burning."

Dmitrii didn't answer directly. He said, "After I heard the rumors this morning, I sent men to the Monastery of the Archangel, with orders to escort the priest here. But he wasn't at the monastery. He was in the Cathedral of the Assumption, with half the city attending him, praying and weeping. He chants like an angel, they say, and Moscow is full of tales of his beauty and his piety and how he freed the city from devils. All these rumors alone would make him dangerous, even if he is not the villain you make him out to be."

"Since he is dangerous, why have you not arrested him?"

"Weren't you listening?" demanded Dmitrii. "I can't have a holy man dragged out of a cathedral before half of Moscow. No, he will come today by quiet invitation, and I will decide what to do."

"He set the mob to break Serpukhov's gates," said Sasha. "There is only one thing to do with him."

"Justice will be done, cousin," returned Dmitrii. In his eyes was a warning. "However, it is for me to administer it, not you."

Sasha said nothing. The dooryard was full of the sound of hammers, of men calling, of horses. Beyond was the murmur of the waking city. "I have ordered divine service sung," Dmitrii added. Now he sounded tired. "I have set all the bishops to praying. I do not know what else we can do. Curse it, I am not a holy man, to answer questions of curses and devils. The people are unsettled enough without wicked rumors. There is the city to rebuild and Tatar bandits to find."

ALL MOSCOW, IT SEEMED to Konstantin, followed him from the cathedral to the Grand Prince's palace. Their voices pulled at him; their stink surrounded him. "I will return," he told the people, before passing the gates. They waited outside, icons in their hands, praying aloud, better than a hundred guards.

Nonetheless, Konstantin's sweat was cold as he crossed the dooryard. Dmitrii had guards of his own, heavily armed and watchful. The devil had not left Konstantin's side since that morning; now he walked beside him, insouciant, invisible to all but the priest and looking about him with interest. The Bear was, Konstantin realized with a sinking feeling, enjoying himself.

All about the dooryard stood the wisps of small demons, hearth-creatures. Konstantin's skin crawled, seeing them. "What do they want?"

The Bear smirked at the assembled devils. "They are afraid. The bells are blotting them out, year by year, but the destruction of their hearths will kill them quickly. They know what I am going to do." The Bear bowed to them, ironic. "They are doomed," he added cheerfully, as though to make sure they could hear, and strode on.

"Good riddance," Konstantin muttered, and followed. The stares of the hearth-chyerti seemed to bore into his back.

There were two men waiting for him in the audience-chamber: Brother Aleksandr and Dmitrii Ivanovich, with Dmitrii's attendants standing woodenly behind him. The place still smelled of smoke. One wall was scarred with sword-cuts, the paint hacked away.

Dmitrii sat in his carved chair. Brother Aleksandr stood, watchful, beside him.

"That one will kill you if he can," remarked the Bear, with a jerk of his chin at Sasha. Sasha's eyes narrowed; was it Konstantin's imagination or did the monk's gaze flicker from him to the devil beside him? He knew an instant of panic.

"Be easy," added the Bear, eyes still on Sasha. "He has the same blood as the witch-girl. He senses what he cannot see, but that is all." He paused. "Try not to get yourself killed, man of God."

"Konstantin Nikonovich," said Dmitrii coldly. Konstantin swallowed. "A girl, my kinswoman, was killed by fire yesterday, without trial. They are saying you set the mob of Moscow to do this. What have you to say?"

"I did not," said Konstantin, making his voice calm. "I tried to restrain the people from worse violence, from breaking into the terem of Serpukhov and killing the women there. That much I did, but I could not save the girl." He did not have to feign the sorrow in his voice, just let it float up from the tangle of other emotions. "I prayed for her soul. I could not stay the people's wrath. By her own confession she set the fire that slew so many."

He struck the perfect note of regretful admission. The Bear snorted beside him. Konstantin narrowly missed whipping round to glare.

Sasha, beside his cousin on the dais, stood perfectly still.

The Bear said suddenly, "The monk knows how the fire began. Press him; he will not lie to the Grand Prince."

"That is a lie," Dmitrii was saying to Konstantin. "The Tatars set the fire."

"Ask Brother Aleksandr," returned Konstantin, letting his voice fill the room. "Ask the holy monk there, if the girl set the fire or no. In the name of God, I charge him to speak truly."

Dmitrii rounded on Sasha. The monk's eyes were starry with rage, but Konstantin saw with astonishment that it was true. He wouldn't lie. "An accident," Sasha bit off. He and Dmitrii looked at each other as if they were the only two people in the room. "Dmitrii Ivanovich—"

Dmitrii's face shuttered; he turned without a word back to Konstantin. The priest felt swift pleasure; he saw the Bear grin. They exchanged a look of perfect understanding, and Konstantin thought, *Perhaps I was always cursed, that I can know this monster's mind.*

"She saved the city too," murmured the Bear. "Although her brother can't say so without accusing his own sister of witchcraft. Mad girl; she was nearly as bad as a chaos-spirit." He sounded almost approving.

Konstantin pressed his lips together.

Dmitrii said, recovering smoothly, "I hear also that you fought a demon last night and banished it."

"Demon or poor lost soul, I do not know," said Konstantin. "But it had come in anger to torment the living. I prayed"—he had better control of his voice now—"and God saw fit to intercede. That is all."

"Is it?" said Brother Aleksandr in a low measured voice. "And what if we do not believe you?"

"I could bring a dozen witnesses from the city to prove it," returned Konstantin, with more confidence. The monk's hands were tied now.

Dmitrii leaned forward. "So it is true?" he said. "There was a demon in Moscow?"

Konstantin crossed himself. Head bowed, he said, "It is true. A dead thing. I saw it with my own eyes."

"Why do you think there was a dead thing in Moscow, Batyushka?"

Konstantin noted the use of the honorific. He breathed again. "It was God's punishment for the harboring of witches. But the witch is dead now, and perhaps God will relent."

"Not likely," said the Bear, but only Konstantin could hear him.

⌒

CURSE THE SILVER-TONGUED PRIEST, Sasha thought. *And curse Vasya too, wherever she is.* For he could defend her good intentions and her good heart, but he could not in conscience say that his sister was blameless. He couldn't in truth say she was not a witch. He could not speak aloud of Marya's kidnapping.

So now he must stand before this murderer, listening to his half-truths, and he had no good answers and unbelievably Dmitrii was listening to the priest. Sasha was white with rage.

"Will the dead thing come again?" Dmitrii asked.

"Who knows but God?" Konstantin replied. His glance shifted a fraction to the left, though there was nothing there. The hairs on the back of Sasha's neck prickled.

"In that case—" Dmitrii began, but he got no further. A clamor on the stairs got their attention, and then the doors to the audience-chamber opened.

They all turned. Dmitrii's steward came stumbling into the room, followed by a man in fine clothes, travel-stained.

Dmitrii stood. All the attendants bowed. The newcomer was taller than the Grand Prince, with the same gray eyes. Everyone recognized him on sight. He was the greatest man in Muscovy, after the Grand Prince, the only one who was prince in his own right, of his own lands, without vassalage. Vladimir Andreevich, Prince of Serpukhov.

"Well met, cousin," said Dmitrii, with delight; they had been boys together.

"Scorch marks on the city," returned Vladimir. "I am glad she is still standing." But his eyes were grave; he was worn thin with winter travel. "What happened?"

"There was a fire, as you saw," said Dmitrii. "And a riot. I will tell you everything. But why have you come in this haste?"

"The temnik Mamai has provisioned his army."

A silence fell in the room; Vladimir hadn't tried to soften the blow. "I had word in Serpukhov," he continued. "Mamai has a rival farther south who is growing more powerful by the day. To stave off the threat he must have Muscovy's allegiance and our silver. He is coming north himself to get it. There is no doubt. He will be in Moscow by autumn, if you don't pay him, Dmitrii Ivanovich. You will have to muster your silver or muster an army, and there is no more time to delay."

On Dmitrii's face was a strange mix of anger and eagerness. "Tell me everything you know," he said. "Come, let us drink and—" Sasha saw, with fury, that his cousin was relieved, for the moment, to set aside all questions of devils and the dead, and of culpability in the riot and the burning. Matters of war and politics were more pressing and less fraught.

Through a cold sinking tangle of anger and dismay, Sasha could have sworn that there was someone in the room laughing.

"SEND THE PRIEST AWAY UNPUNISHED?" Sasha demanded later. He could barely speak. There had been scarce a moment to catch his cousin alone, after Vladimir Andreevich came. Sasha finally caught Dmitrii in the dooryard, just as he was about to mount his horse to go look over the burned parts of Moscow. "Do you think Vladimir Andreevich will accept that? Vasya was his sister-in-law."

"I have had the chief men of the riot arrested," said Dmitrii. He took the reins from a groom, a hand on his horse's withers. "They will be put to death for damaging the Prince of Serpukhov's property, for laying hands on his kin. But I am not going to touch that priest—no, listen to me. Charlatan the priest may be, but a very good one. Didn't you see the crowd outside?"

"I saw," said Sasha, unwillingly.

"They will riot if I kill him," Dmitrii went on, "and I can afford no more riots. He can control the mob, and I can control *him;* that is the kind of man who wants gold and glory, despite all his pretension of piety. The news from the south changes everything; you know it does. I can either squeeze all my boyars, all my princes, and the wretched city fathers of Novgorod for silver, or I can undertake the far more difficult route of calling all the princes of Rus'—the ones that will come—and equipping an army. I will try the former, for my people's sake, but I cannot afford to be at odds with my city over it. That man may be useful. I have decided, Sasha. Besides, his story is plausible. Perhaps he is telling the truth."

"Do you think *I* am lying then? What about my sister?"

"She caused the fire," said Dmitrii. His voice grew suddenly cold. "Maybe her death by fire was justice. You certainly didn't tell me of it.

It seems we are back where we started. Telling lies, and omitting truths."

"It was an accident."

"And yet," said Dmitrii.

They looked at each other. Sasha knew that the fragile, regained trust had eroded once more. There was a silence.

Then— "There is something I want you to do," said the Grand Prince. He let go the reins of his horse and drew Sasha aside. "Are we still kin, Brother?"

"I COULD NOT PERSUADE DMITRII," said Sasha wearily to Olga. "The priest goes free. Dmitrii is going to raise silver, to placate the Tatars."

His sister was darning stockings, plain needles and swift hands incongruous in the magnificence of her embroidered lap. Only the jerky movements of her fingers revealed her feelings. "No justice then, for my sister, for my daughter, for my smashed gates?" she asked.

Sasha shook his head slowly. "Not now. Not yet. But your husband has returned. You are safe now, at least."

"Yes," Olga replied, in a voice dry as summer dust. "Vladimir has returned. He will come to me—today or tomorrow—after he has delivered all his news and made his plans and bathed and eaten and caroused with the Grand Prince. Then I may tell him that his hoped-for second son was a daughter, and she is dead. In the meantime, there is a demon loose and— Do you think there will be war?"

Sasha hesitated, but Olga's set face dared him to pity her, and in the end, he accepted the change of subject. "Not if Dmitrii pays. Mamai cannot really want a war; he has a rival south of Sarai. He only wants money."

"A great deal of money, I imagine," Olga said, "if he is going to the trouble of mustering an army to extort it. There were bandits in Muscovy all winter, and Moscow in flames not long ago. Will Dmitrii be able to get his money?"

"I don't know," Sasha admitted, then paused. "Olya, he has sent me away."

That broke through her composure. "Sent you—where?"

"To the Lavra. To Father Sergei. The troubles of men and armies, Dmitrii understands. But with all the talk of wickedness, spoiling, and demons, he wants Father Sergei's advice, and sent me to get him." Sasha rose to pace, restless. "The city is against me now, because of Vasya." The admission cost him. "He says it would be unwise for me to stay. For your sake and my own."

Olga's narrowed eyes followed him as he swept back and forth. "Sasha, you cannot leave. Not when there is such wickedness loose. Marya has the same gifts as Vasya, and this priest who tried to kill our sister knows it."

Sasha paused in his pacing. "You will have men. I have spoken to Dmitrii and Vladimir about it. Vladimir is calling up men from Serpukhov. Marya will be safe in the terem."

"As safe as Vasya was?"

"She left."

Olga sat very still, said nothing.

Sasha went to kneel at her side. "Olya, I *must*. Father Sergei is the holiest man in Rus'. If there is a demon loose, then Sergei will know what to do. I do not."

Still his sister said nothing.

Lower, Sasha said, "Dmitrii has asked it of me. As the price of his trust."

His sister's hands closed on her needles, crumpling the stockings. "We are your family, vows or no, and we need you here."

Sasha bit his lip. "All of Rus' is at stake, Olya."

"So you care more for children unknown than for mine?" The strains of the past days were catching both of them.

"That is why I became a monk," he retorted. "That I might care for all the world together and not be tied to a little corner of it. What has it all been for, if I cannot protect all of Rus' instead of just a patchwork of fiefdoms, a few people among the many?"

"You are as bad as Vasya was," Olga said. "Thinking that you can just shake off your family like a horse slipping its traces. Look where it got her. You are not responsible for Rus'. But you can help keep your niece and nephew safe. Do not go."

"It is your husband's task—" began Sasha.

"He will be here a day or a week, then gone again, on the prince's work. Just as always," said Olga furiously, with a catch in her voice. "I cannot tell him about Marya; what do you think he would do with a daughter so afflicted? Arrange at once, with generosity and foresight, to have her sent to a nunnery. Brother, please."

Olga ran her household with a steady grip, but the last days had shown her limits; when the world moved outside her walls, there was very little she could do. Now she was reduced to pleading: a princess without power enough to keep her family safe.

"Olya," Sasha said. "Your husband will see that there are men at your gate; you will be safe. I cannot—I cannot refuse the Grand Prince. I'll come back as soon as I can, with Father Sergei. He will know what to do. About the demon—and Konstantin Nikonovich."

While he spoke, she controlled her rage; she was the immaculate Princess of Serpukhov once more. "Go then," she said with disgust. "I do not need you."

He went to the door, hesitated at the threshold. "God be with you," he said.

She made no reply, though as he went out into the dripping gray of early spring, he heard her breath catch once, as if she fought to control her weeping.

IT WAS NIGHT AGAIN in Moscow, and nothing moved but beggars, trying to keep warm in the spring damp, and the faint house-spirits, walking, stirring, whispering. For there was change in the air, in the water beneath the ice, in the damp wind. Chyerti murmured rumors to one another, much as folk did in the city all around.

The Bear walked softly through the streets, a cold rain on his face, and the lesser chyerti shrank away. He did not heed them. He reveled in the sounds and the scents, the moving air, the fruit of his cleverness taking shape. The news of the Tatar army had been a lucky stroke, and he meant to use it to full advantage.

He must succeed. He must. Better to unmake the world—better to be unmade himself—than go back to the grim clearing at the edge of winter, dreaming the years away. But it would not come to that. His brother was far away, and so deeply imprisoned that he would never come out again.

The Bear smiled at the indifferent stars. *Come spring, come summer, and let me make an end to this place, let me silence the bells.* Each time they rang the monastic hours of worship, he flinched a little. But men were men, whatever gods they followed—hadn't he tempted a servant of the newer God into his service?

Hoofbeats sounded in the darkness ahead, and a woman on a black horse rode out of the shadows.

The Bear greeted her with a lifted head, looking unsurprised. "News, Polunochnitsa?" he said, a hint of arid humor in his voice.

"She did not die in my realm," said the midnight-demon, her voice quite expressionless.

The Bear's eye sharpened. "Did you help her?"

"No."

"Yet you watched her. Why?"

The midnight-demon shrugged. "We are all watching. All the chyerti. She has refused both of you, Morozko and Medved, and so made herself a power in her own right in your great war. The chyerti are choosing sides once more."

The Bear laughed, but the gray eye was intent. "Choose her over me? She is a child."

"She defeated you before."

"With my brother's help and her father's sacrifice."

"She has passed three fires, and she is not a child anymore."

"Why tell me?"

Midnight shrugged again. "Because I have not chosen a side either, Medved."

The Bear, smiling, said, "You will regret your indecision, before the end."

Midnight's black horse shied, and gave the Bear a wild-eyed look. Midnight smoothed a hand through his mane. "Perhaps" was all she said. "But you see, now I have helped you too. You will have the whole spring to do as you please. If you cannot secure your position, then perhaps the chyerti will be right to look instead to the powers of a half-grown girl."

"Where will I find her?"

"Summer, of course. Beside the water." Midnight looked down on him, from her horse's back. "We will be watching."

"I have time then," said the Bear, and looked again up at the wild stars.

Part Three

9

To Travel by Midnight

Vasya woke to a darkness so deep, she thought she had been struck blind. She lifted her head. Nothing. Her body had chilled and stiffened; moving sent a cascade of pain through neck and back. She wondered vaguely why she was not dead, wondered also why she was lying on bracken instead of snow. It was quiet, except for the faint creaking of branches overhead. Gingerly, she put a trembling hand to her eyes. One was swollen shut. The other seemed all right, except the lashes were gummed together. Gingerly, she pried it open.

It was still dark, but now she could see. A faint sickle moon cast wavering light over a strange forest. Snow lay only in patches; mist veiled the trees, luminous in the moonlight. Vasya smelled cold, wet earth. She stumbled to her feet, turning in a circle. Darkness all around. She tried to remember the last hours, but there was only a vague memory of terror and flight. What had she done? Where was she?

"Well," said a voice, "you are not dead after all."

The voice had come from above. Vasya wrenched instinctively back, even as she searched for the speaker, her good eye watering. Finally, on a limb overhead, she caught sight of star-pale hair and bright eyes. As her own eyes adjusted, Vasya began vaguely to make out the shape of the midnight-demon, perched on the branch of an oak-tree and leaning against the trunk.

A deeper patch of black stirred in the shadows below the tree. Vasya, squinting, could just make out a marvelous black horse, grazing by moonlight. He lifted his head to look at her. Vasya's heart thumped once, loud in her ears, and memory came rushing back: blood sticky on her hands, Father Konstantin's face, fire . . .

She stood perfectly still. If she moved, if she made a sound, she would flee, scream, go mad with memory, or the impossibility of this darkness, with Moscow nowhere in sight. What was real? This? Her horse dead, her life saved by magic? She shuddered, fell to her knees, pressing her hands into the icy, wet earth. Trying to understand was like grasping at rain. For a long time, all she could do was breathe, and feel her hands on the ground.

Then, with a terrible effort, she raised her head. The words came slowly. "Where am I?"

The demon let out a little sigh. "And in your right mind, too." She sounded faintly surprised. "This is my realm. The country called Midnight." The curve of her mouth was cold. "I bid you welcome."

Vasya tried to slow her breathing. "Where is Moscow?"

"Who knows?" said Polunochnitsa. She slid from the limb of her tree, fell lightly to earth. "Not nearby. My realm is not made up of days or seasons, but of midnights. You can cross the world in an instant, so long as it is midnight where you are going. Or, more likely, you can die trying, or go mad."

"I was told," Vasya said thickly, remembering, "that I must find a lake. With an oak-tree growing on the shore."

Polunochnitsa lifted a pale brow. "Which lake? My realm contains enough lakes to keep you searching for a thousand lives of men."

Search? Vasya could barely stand. "Will you help me?"

The black horse flicked his ears.

"Help you?" answered Midnight. "I did help you. I have made you free of my realm. I even *kept* you here just now while you lay insensible. Must I do more?" Polunochnitsa's hair fell like cold rain over the darkness of her skin. "You were discourteous at our last meeting."

"Please," said Vasya.

Midnight half-smiled and came closer still, whispered her answer as though it were a secret. "No," she said. "Find it yourself. Or die here, die now. I will tell the old woman. She might even mourn, though I doubt it."

"Old woman?" said Vasya. The darkness seemed to press around her, horribly. "Please," she said again.

"I do not forget insults, Vasilisa Petrovna," said Lady Midnight, and turned away, laid a hand on the withers of the black horse. Then she was astride, wheeling, gone into the trees without a backward glance.

Vasya was alone in the darkness.

SHE COULD LIE DOWN in the leaf-litter and wait for dawn. But how could there be dawn in a country made of midnights? She could walk, though her legs shook when she stood. But where was she to go? She wore only Varvara's cloak and the bloody, reeking remains of her shift. Her feet were bare and torn. It hurt to draw breath, and she was shivering. This night was a little warmer than the night near Moscow, but not much.

Had she come through fire, defied the Bear, escaped Moscow by magic only to die in the darkness? *Go to the lake,* Varvara had said. *You will be safe there. The lake with an oak-tree growing at its shore.*

Well, if Varvara had thought she could find it, then perhaps she had a chance. Probably Varvara had thought Midnight would help her, as Vasya had no idea of direction. But at least she would die on her feet, in search of sanctuary. Gathering the last of her strength, Vasya walked into the darkness.

SHE DID NOT KNOW how long she walked. Beyond the uttermost end of her strength, yet still she stumbled on. The light never changed; the sun never rose. Vasya began to be desperate for light. Her feet left bloody footprints.

Polunochnitsa had spoken true. This was a country made of midnights. Vasya could not discern a pattern among them. One moment, she was walking on cold dead grass, with a half-moon overhead. Then she passed into tree-shadow and found with a cold shock that the moon had disappeared and muddy earth squelched under her feet. It was always early spring, more or less, but the place changed every few steps: a mad, patchwork country.

I am still here, Vasya told herself, over and over. *I am still myself. I am still alive.* Gripping hard to that thought, she walked on. Wolves cried in the distance, and she lifted her head to hear them; then the wind struck like icy water on her face. She saw new lights—firelights—on a hill in the distance, hurried toward them, only to have them vanish. Then she was walking under pale birch trees, white as dead fingers, beneath a scarlet moon.

It was like walking through a nightmare; she could not orient herself, did not know north from south. On she stumbled, gritting her teeth, but now the earth was sucking at her feet and she found that she had fallen into a bog. Mud everywhere; she could not muster the strength to break its grip. Tears of purest exhaustion leaked from her eyes.

Let go, she thought. *Enough; let go. At least here there will be no mob laughing when I go to God.*

The black, sucking mud of the bog seemed to agree, gurgling. There were wicked eyes, like green lamps, watching her from beneath the water. They belonged to a bolotnik, swamp-dweller, breathing out stinking plumes of marsh-gas. He could kill her quickly, if she let him. He could pull her down into the frigid dark and she wouldn't have to walk again on her torn feet, or breathe against her broken ribs, or remember the last two days.

But Marya, Vasya thought dimly. *Marya is in Moscow, and my brother and sister, defenseless against the Bear.*

And so? What could she do? Sasha and the Grand Prince could . . .

Could they? They could not see. They did not understand.

My brother has traded his freedom for your life, the Bear had said. The carved nightingale was in the sleeve of her shift. Her filthy, groping hand closed tight around the wooden creature and it seemed a little warmth crept into her chilled limbs.

Winter-king, why would you do such a terrible thing?

He had a reason. Morozko was no fool. Shouldn't she find out *why*, rather than allow his bargain to go for nothing? But she was so tired.

Solovey would have said she was being foolish; he would have made her get on his back and carried her along steadily to wherever they were going, ears flicking cheerfully back and forth.

Hot tears spilled from her eyes. On a surge of rage she yanked herself from the mud, scrambled up the bank. In desperation she put a hand into the water, and spoke in her choked, smoke-damaged voice. "Grandfather," she said to the lurking swamp-demon, "I am looking for a lake, with an oak-tree growing on the shore. Can you tell me where it is?"

The bolotnik's eyes had just breached the water; she could make out his scaly limbs churning below the surface. He looked almost surprised. "Alive still?" he whispered. His voice was the sucking sound of the swamp, his breath the smell of decay.

"Please," said Vasya. With her fingers, she split one of the clotted cuts on her arm, and let her blood fall on the water.

The bolotnik's tongue flicked, tasting, and his eyes glowed suddenly bright. "Well, you are a courteous maiden," he said, licking his chops. "Look then."

She followed the turn of his marsh-light eyes. A reddish flicker showed between the black trees. Not daylight. Perhaps fire? A rush of fear sent her to her feet, cloak heavy with mud.

But it was not fire. It was a living creature.

A tall mare, limned with light, stood hock-deep in the marsh. Sparks like fireflies tumbled from her mane and tail, molten white against the silver-gold of her coat. Head up, she watched Vasya, motionless except for her tail, which lashed her sides with arcs of light.

Vasya took an involuntary, stumbling step toward the mare, caught between wonder and rage. "I remember you," she said to the horse. "In Moscow, I set you free."

The mare said nothing, only flicked her great, golden ears.

"You could have just flown away," Vasya said. Her voice cracked; her throat was raw. "But instead you dripped sparks over a city of wood and they—and they—" She could not say the words.

The golden mare pawed defiantly, splashing, and spoke, *I would have killed them all, if I could,* she returned. *Killed all the men in the world. They dared trick me, bind me.* Scars of saddle and spur marked the mare's golden perfection, and her face was striped with white where the golden bridle had been. *I would have killed the whole city.*

Vasya said nothing. Grief was a frozen ball in her mouth; she could only stare with mute hatred at the mare.

The mare spun and galloped away.

"Follow her, fool," hissed the swamp-demon. "Or if you prefer, stay here, and I will eat you."

Vasya hated the mare. But she did not want to die. She began to make her way through the trees, stumbling on bloody feet. On and on she went, following the dot of golden light, until she was quite sure that she could not walk a step more.

But then she did not have to.

The trees ended; she found herself in a sloping meadow leading down to a vast, frozen lake. It was earliest spring. Stars cast a faint silver sheen on the long grass of an open field. All around she could discern the shapes of great trees, black against the silver sky. Snow lay on this field only in hollows and patches. Faintly she could hear the sound of water under the lake's ice.

There were more horses grazing in the meadow. Three—six— a dozen. The night faded them all to gray except for the golden mare. Standing among them, she glittered like a fallen star, head up in challenge.

Vasya halted, full of agonized wonder. Part of her was half-convinced that her own horse must be here, among his kin, that in a moment he would gallop toward her, flinging snow from under his feet, and she wouldn't be alone anymore. "Solovey," she whispered. "Solovey."

A dark head rose, then a paler one. All of a sudden, the horses were wheeling, fleeing. On four legs they fled from the sound of her voice, straight down toward the lake, but just before their hooves struck water, their hooves became wings. As birds they took to the air, and soared over the starlit water.

Vasya watched them go, tears of pure wonder in her eyes. They winged across the lake, no two alike. Owl and eagle and duck and smaller birds: purely, miraculously, strange. Last of all to leave the earth was the golden mare. Her wings swept wide, trailing smoke, and her plumed tail was every color of flame: gold and blue-violet and white. She flew after her kin, calling. In moments, they were all swallowed by the darkness.

Vasya stared at the place the horses had been. It was as though she'd dreamed them. Her vision swam with weariness. Her feet and her face were numb, and she had gone beyond shivering, cocooned icily in shock. *Solovey,* she wondered dimly. *Why didn't you fly away too?*

Just at the edge of the lake stood a single vast oak-tree. Its branches stood out like blackened bones against the moon-white ice. To her right, nestled among the trees, was a squat, dark shape.

It was a house.

Or rather, a ruin. The house's roof, sloped steeply to keep off the snow, had fallen in; no firelight showed behind window or door. There was only silence, the faint creaking of trees, the crack of thinning lake-ice. And yet this place, this clearing by the water, did not feel empty. It felt watchful.

The house had been built on a sturdy platform between two trees. The trees gave it a look of standing alertly on strong legs; the windows like black eyes, staring down. For an instant, the house didn't seem dead at all. It seemed to be watching her.

Then the illusion of menace faded. It was only a ruin. The steps were rotten, crumbling. There would be dead leaves within, and mice and unrelieved dark.

But there might be a working stove, even a handful of grain from the house's last occupant. At the very least, she could get out of the wind.

Only half-aware of what she was doing, Vasya crossed the meadow, stumbling on rocks, skidding on snow. Gritting her teeth, she crawled up the steps. The only sounds were the groaning of branches and her own hoarse breathing.

At the top of the stairs stood two posts, carved with figures starlit and fantastic: bears, suns, moons, small strange faces that might have been chyerti. Over the door was a lintel carved in the shape of two rearing horses.

The door hung askew on its hinges in a litter of slick, rotten leaves. Vasya paused to listen.

Silence. Of course, silence. Perhaps there were beasts denning here, but she was beyond caring. The half-fallen door gave with a squeal from rusted hinges. Vasya stumbled inside.

She found dust, old leaves, the smell of decay, and chill weary damp. It was no warmer than outside, though at least there was not the cold wind off the lake. Most of the house was taken up by a crumbling brick oven, its mouth a maw in the blackness. Across the room, where the icon-corner should be, there were no icons, only a big dark thing shoved against the wall.

Vasya groped her way cautiously to that corner and found a wooden chest: bronze-bound and securely locked.

She turned shivering back toward the oven. Mostly she just wanted to sink down on the floor in the dark and let unconsciousness take her; never mind the cold.

Gritting her teeth, she heaved herself atop the oven-bench and gingerly touched the rough brick, where a person might have breathed her last. But there was nothing; no blanket, certainly no bones. What tragedy had left this strange ruin deserted? The night outside cradled the house with a silent menace.

Her groping fingers found a few dusty sticks beside the oven. Enough for a fire, though she didn't want fire. Her memory was full of flames, the choking smell of smoke. The heat would hurt her blistered face.

But it was certainly cold enough for a wounded girl wearing only a cloak and shift to freeze to death. She meant to live.

So, moved only by the cold embers of will, Vasya set about making a fire. Her lips and fingertips were quite numb. She bruised her shins on things she could not see, scrabbling for the sticks and pine-needles for kindling.

After a half-blind effort that left her trembling, she had made a heap of sticks that she could barely see in the mouth of the oven. She felt over the entire house for flint and steel and charred cloth, but there were none.

She could make a fire with a flat piece of wood and patience, and strength in the forearms. But both her strength and patience were at an end.

Well, do it, or freeze. She took the stick between her hands. When she was a child, in the autumn woods, it had been a game. The stick, the board, the swift strong movement. Deftly handled, the smoke would turn into fire, and Vasya still remembered her brother Alyosha's grin of delight, the first time she did it unaided.

But this time, though she labored and sweated, not a single curl of smoke rose from the board between her knees; no ember glowed in the groove. At last Vasya let the stick fall, shivering, defeated. Useless. She was going to die after all, with only the dust of someone else's life for company.

She did not know how long she sat in the sour-smelling silence, not crying, not feeling anything, just hovering on the edge of unconsciousness.

She never knew what spurred her to raise her head once more, teeth sunk in her lower lip. She must have fire. She must. In her head, in her heart, was the terrible presence of fire, memory as strong as anything in her life, as though her soul were full of flames. Ridiculous that fire burned so bright in hated memory but there was no scrap of light here, where it could do some good.

Why should it be only in her mind? She shut her eyes, and for an instant, memory was so strong that she forgot it wasn't.

Vasya smelled smoke first, and her eyes opened, just as her sticks burst into flame.

Shocked, almost frightened of her success, Vasya hurried to add wood. The room filled with light; the shadows retreated.

The hut looked even worse by firelight: ankle-deep in leaves, crumbling, mildewed, thick with dust. But there was a little woodpile she hadn't seen: a few dry logs. And it was warmer now. The fire drove back the night and the chill. She was going to live. Vasya stretched out trembling hands to the fire.

A hand shot out of the oven and grasped her wrist.

10

The Devil in the Oven

VASYA DREW A SINGLE, STARTLED BREATH, BUT SHE DID NOT PULL away. The hand was as small as a child's, long-fingered, traced in red and gold from the firelight. It did not let her go. Instead, Vasya found herself pulling a tiny person into the room.

She was a woman no taller than Vasya's knee, with eyes the color of earth. She was licking embers hungrily off the end of a stick, but she paused to look up at Vasilisa and say, "Well, I have overslept and no mistake. Who are you?" Then the chyert caught sight of the decay all around them and her voice rose in sudden alarm. "Where is my mistress? What are you doing here?"

Vasya sank down onto the crumbling oven-bench in exhausted surprise. Domoviye did not live in ruins; they did not live on in houses at all when their families had gone. "There is no one here," Vasya said. "Only me. This place—it is dead. What are *you* doing here?"

The domovoi—no, a female—a domovaya—stared. "I do not understand. The house cannot be dead. I *am* the house, and I am alive. You must be lying. What have you done to them? What have you done to this place? Stand and answer me!" Her voice was shrill with fright.

"I cannot stand," Vasya whispered. That was true. The fire had taken the last of her strength. "I am only a traveler. I thought only to make a fire and stay here for the night."

"But you—" The domovoi—domovaya—peered again about the house, took in the extent of the rot. Her eyes widened in horror. "Over-slept indeed! Just look at this filth. I cannot just let vagabonds stay without my mistress's leave. You will have to go. I must set things to rights, against her return."

"I do not think your mistress is coming back," said Vasya. "This house is abandoned. I do not know how you managed to survive, in that cold oven." Her voice broke. "Please. Please let me stay. I cannot bear any more."

A small silence. Vasya could feel the domovaya's narrow regard. "Very well then," she said. "You will stay here tonight. Poor child. My mistress would want it."

"Thank you," Vasya whispered.

The domovaya, still muttering to herself, went at once to the chest shoved against the wall. She had a key hanging at her throat; she un-locked the iron hasp of the chest. It gave with a rusty click.

Before Vasya's astonished eyes, the domovaya produced linen and a clay bowl, laid them on the hearth. Then she took a bucket and went outside for snow, which she set at once to heating, and a branch of young pine-needles, which she scattered in the water.

Vasya watched the steam rise through the hole in the roof, only half-aware of the domovaya's deft movements as she peeled away the shift that had so nearly been Vasya's shroud, briskly sponged off the worst of the fear-sweat, the soot, and the blood, washed away the scum about Vasya's injured eye. The latter hurt, but when the crust was wiped away, Vasya could see through a slit. She was not blinded. She was too tired to care even for that.

From the chest in the corner, the domovaya produced a wool shirt. Vasya barely felt the domovaya put it on her, found herself lying atop the oven under rabbit-skin blankets with no idea how she'd gotten there. The brick was warm. The last thing she heard before oblivion claimed her was the small voice of the domovaya, saying, "A little rest will put you aright, but you are going to have a scar on your face."

VASILISA PETROVNA NEVER KNEW how long she slept. She had dim memories of nightmares, of screaming for Solovey to run. She dreamed the midnight-demon's voice—*It must be done,* Polunochnitsa said, *send her forth, for all our sakes*—and the domovaya's voice raised in distress. But before Vasya could speak, darkness pulled her under once more.

Uncounted hours later, she opened her eyes to dawn: the light almost shocking after the long dark. It was as though she'd only dreamed the tangled roads of Midnight. Perhaps she had. Lying in the blurred gray light of early morning, she could have been anywhere, atop any oven. "Dunya?" she called, her childhood strong in her mind. It had always been her nurse who comforted her after nightmares.

Memory crashed in. She made an inarticulate sound of distress. A small head appeared at once beside her pallet, but Vasya barely saw the domovaya. Memory had her by the throat. She was shivering.

The domovaya watched, frowning.

"Forgive me," Vasya managed at length. She pushed her ragged hair back from her face. Her teeth chattered. The oven was warm, but there was still a hole in the roof, and memory was colder than the air. "I—I am called Vasilisa Petrovna. Thank you for your hospitality."

The domovaya looked almost sad. "It is not hospitality," she said. "I was asleep in the fire. You awoke me. You are my mistress now."

"But this is not my house."

The domovaya made no reply. Vasya sat up, wincing. The domovaya had done her best while Vasya slept. The dust and dead mice, the rotten leaves, were gone. "It is much more like home now," Vasya said, cautiously. Now that it was daylight, she saw that most of the wood on the rooftree and table was carved like the lintel outside, worn to smoothness from use and care. The house had a dignity to match its hearth-spirit: an old, subtle beauty that time could not quite conceal.

The domovaya looked pleased. "You mustn't lie abed. The water is hot. Your wounds must be cleaned again and bound afresh." She disappeared; Vasya heard her adding wood to the fire.

Getting down to the floor left Vasya panting, as though she were new-recovered from fever. To add insult to injury, she was also hungry. "Is there—" croaked Vasya, swallowed, tried again. "Is there anything to eat?"

Lips pursed, the domovaya shook her head.

Why would there be? It was too much to suppose that the house's long-vanished mistress would have conveniently left a loaf and cheese.

"Did you burn my shift?" Vasya asked.

"I did," said the domovaya, shuddering. "It stank of fear."

Well it might. Then Vasya stiffened. "There was a token—a carving—I was carrying in it. Did you—?"

"No," said the domovaya. "It is here."

Vasya seized the little carved nightingale as if it were a talisman. Perhaps it was. It was dirty but undamaged. She wiped it clean, thrust it again into her sleeve.

A bowl of snowmelt steamed on the hearth. The domovaya said briskly, "Take off that shirt; I am going to wash your wounds again."

Vasya did not want to think about her wounds; she did not want to have flesh at all. Just below the surface of her mind lurked the most howling grief; the memory of death, of violation. She did not want to see those memories scribed on her skin.

The domovaya was not sympathetic. "Where is your courage? You do not want to die of a poisoned wound."

That at least was true; a slow and horrible death. Before she could lose her nerve, Vasya, wordless, peeled the shirt over her head, stood up shivering in the light from the crumbling roof and looked down at her body.

Bruises of every color: red and black, purple and blue. Cuts latticed her torso; she was glad she could not see her own face. Two teeth were loose; her lips were split and sore. One eye was still half swollen shut. When she raised her hand to her face, she was met with a clotted gash on her cheek.

The domovaya had produced dusty-smelling herbs, honey for bandaging, lengths of clean linen from the chest in the corner. Vasya, staring, said, "Who leaves such things in a locked box in a ruin?"

"I hardly know," said the domovaya shortly. "They were here, that's all."

"Surely you remember something."

"I don't!" The domovaya looked suddenly angry. "Why are you asking? Isn't it enough that it was here, that it saved your life? Sit down. No, there."

Vasya sat. "I am sorry," she said. "I was only curious."

"The more one knows, the sooner one grows old," snapped the domovaya. "Hold still."

Vasya tried. But it hurt. A few cuts had closed in their own blood; the domovaya left them alone. But many had been pulled open under the stresses of the night, and she had not got all of the soot and splinters, working by firelight.

But all were bound up and salved at last. "Thank you," Vasya said, hearing her voice shake. Hurriedly she put on her shirt to shut away the sight of herself, and then rubbed a bit of her charred hair between two fingers. Foul. Tangled, fire-smelling; it would never be clean again.

"Will you cut my hair off? As short as you can," said Vasya. "I have had enough of Vasilisa Petrovna."

The domovaya had only a knife to cut with, but she took it up without a word. Hanks of black hair tumbled down, soundless as snow, to be swept out and flung away for the nesting birds. When it was done, the air seemed to whistle strangely past Vasya's ears and down her neck. Not long ago, Vasya would have wept to lose her black hair. Now she was glad to have it gone. Her long, glossy plait belonged to another girl, in another life.

The domovaya, a little subdued, returned to the iron-bound chest. This time, boy's clothes appeared: loose trousers and sash, kaftan, even boots—good leather sapogi. They were badly creased, yellowed with time, but unworn. Vasya frowned. Bits of herbs were one thing, but this? Sturdy garments, sewn with a competent hand, out of close-woven linen and thick wool?

They even fit.

"Did—" Vasya could scarce credit it. She peered down at herself. She was warm, clean, rested, alive, clothed. "Did someone know I was coming?" The question was ridiculous; the clothes were older than she was. And yet . . .

The domovaya shrugged.

"Who was your mistress?" Vasya asked. "Who had this house before?"

The domovaya only looked at her blankly. "Are you sure it's not you? I almost remember you."

"I've never been here before," said Vasya. "Can't you remember?"

"I remember existing," returned the domovaya, a little affronted. "I remember these walls, my key. I remember names and shadows in the fire. Nothing more." She looked distressed; Vasya, in courtesy, let the subject drop. With gritted teeth, she concentrated on getting woolen stockings and sapogi onto her torn and burned feet. Gingerly, she put her feet to the floor, then stood and winced. "Now if only I *could* float along like the devil that cannot touch the earth," she said, trying a few limping steps.

The domovaya thrust an old reed basket into Vasya's hands. "If you want supper, you will have to find it," she said. There was a strange note in her voice. She pointed at the woods.

Vasya could hardly bear the thought of going gathering in her current state. But she knew it would only be worse the next day, as her bruises stiffened.

"Very well," she said.

The domovaya looked suddenly anxious. "Beware the forest," she added, following Vasya to the door. "It does not take kindly to strangers. Safer to come back by nightfall."

"What happens at nightfall?" asked Vasya.

"The—the season will turn," said the domovaya, twisting her hands together.

"What does that mean?"

"You cannot get back, if the season turns. Or you can, but by then it will be someplace different."

"How—different?"

"Different!" cried the domovaya, and stamped her foot. "Now go!"

"Very well," said Vasya, placating. "I will be back by nightfall."

11

Of Mushrooms

FOOD IN THE FOREST IS AT ITS SCARCEST AT THE END OF WINTER, and Vasya could barely touch anything with her blistered hands. But she must try or starve, and so she let herself be urged out the door.

The cool morning, pale as pearl, threw tendrils of mist over the blue-gray ice. Ancient trees ringed the frozen water; their dark limbs seemed to hold up the sky. Frost silvered the earth, and all around was the whisper of water, breaking loose winter's bonds. A thrush called from within the wood. There was no sign of the horses.

Vasya might have stood on the rotten steps until she froze, forgetting sorrow in the pure and untouched beauty. But her stomach reminded her. She must live. And to live, she must eat. Determinedly, she went into the forest.

In another life, Vasya had wandered the woods of Lesnaya Zemlya in all its seasons. In spring, she would walk in the wild places, sun in her hair, and sometimes call greetings to her friend the rusalka, coming awake from her long sleep. But Vasya was not soft-footed now. She limped. Every step seemed to uncover a new pain. Her father would have mourned, for his light-footed, lighthearted child was gone and would not return.

There were no people and, out of sight of the house, no sign that there ever had been. Walking in solitary silence loosened the chokehold of rage and terror and grief on Vasya's soul. She began to consider the shape of the land and wonder where food might be had.

A breath of wind, incongruously warm, riffled her hair. She was well out of sight of the house now. A patch of dandelion was flowering in a sunlit gap between the trees. Startled, Vasya bent and plucked the leaves. So early? She ate one of the flowers as she walked, chewing gingerly with her sore jaw.

Another patch of dandelions. Wild onion. The sun was over the treetops now. There—young dock, leaves curling. And—wild strawberries? Vasya halted. "It is too early," she murmured.

It was. And there—mushrooms? Beliye? The tops of their pale heads just showed above a heap of dead leaves. Her mouth watered. She went to cut them, then looked again. One had spots that seemed to glisten strangely in the sun.

Not spots. Eyes. The largest of the mushrooms peered up at her, eyes a livid scarlet. Not a mushroom at all, but a chyert, scarcely the length of her forearm. A mushroom-spirit, glaring, shook himself free of the leaf-litter. "Who are you?" His voice was shrill. "Why have you come into my woods?"

His woods? "Trespasser!" he squeaked, and Vasya realized he was frightened.

"I didn't know they were your woods." She showed the chyert empty hands, knelt stiffly so he could see her better. The cold moss soaked through the knees of her leggings. "I mean no harm. I am only looking for food."

The mushroom-spirit blinked, said, "Not *exactly* my woods—" and then added, hastily, "But it doesn't matter; you can't be here."

"Not even if I make an offering?" asked Vasya. She put a perfect dandelion down before the creature.

The chyert touched the flower with a grayish finger. His outline solidified; now he resembled a small person more than a mushroom. He looked down at himself, and back at her, in puzzlement.

Then he flung away the flower. "I don't believe you!" he cried. "Do you think to make me do your bidding? You will not! I don't care how many offerings you give me. The Bear is free. *He* says we are striking a blow for ourselves now. If we join him we will make men believe in us again. We will be worshipped again, and have no need to make bargains with witches."

Vasya, rather than answer, got hurriedly to her feet. "How exactly are you striking a blow for yourselves?" Wary, she looked about her but nothing stirred. There were only birds, flitting, and strong, steady sunlight.

A pause. "We will do great and terrible deeds," said the mushroom-spirit.

Vasya tried not to sound impatient. "What does that mean?"

The mushroom-spirit threw his head back proudly, but he didn't actually answer. Perhaps he didn't know.

Great and terrible deeds? Vasya kept an eye on the silent forest. In the midst of loss and injury and terror, she had not stopped to consider the implications of her last night in Moscow. What had Morozko set in motion by freeing the Bear? What did it mean, for herself, for her family, and for Rus'?

Why had he done it?

Some part of her whispered—*He loves you and so gave his freedom.* But that could not be the only reason. She was not so vain as to think the winter-king would risk all he had long defended for a mortal maiden.

More important than why, what was she going to do about it?

I must find the winter-king, she thought. *The Bear must be bound once more.* But she didn't know how to do either of those things; she was wounded still, and hungry.

"What makes you think I want you to do my bidding?" Vasya inquired of the mushroom-spirit. He had subsided under a log while she thought; she could just see the gleam of his eyes peeping out. "Who told you that?"

The mushroom-spirit poked his head out, scowled. "No one. I am no fool. What else would a witch want? Why else would you have taken the road through Midnight?"

"Because I fled for my life," said Vasya. "I only came into the forest because I am hungry." To illustrate, she took a handful of spruce-tips from her basket and began determinedly chewing.

The mushroom-spirit, still suspicious, said, "I can show you where better food is growing. *If,* as you say, you are hungry." He was watching her closely.

"I am," said Vasya at once, getting to her feet. "I would be glad of a guide."

"Well," said the chyert, "follow me then." He darted off at once into the undergrowth.

Vasya, after a moment's thought, followed, but she kept the lake always in sight. She did not trust the forest's hostile silence and she did not trust the little mushroom-spirit.

VASYA'S MISTRUST SOON MINGLED with amazement, for she found herself in a land of wonders. The spruce-tips were green and tender; dandelions nodded in the breeze off the lake. She ate and gathered and ate, and then she realized suddenly that there was a sprawl of blueberries at her feet, more strawberries hidden beneath the damp grass. Not spring anymore, but summer.

"What is this place?" Vasya asked the mushroom-spirit. In her mind, she had begun calling him Ded Grib: Grandfather Mushroom.

He gave her an odd look. "The land between noon and midnight. Between winter and spring. The lake lies at the center. All lands touch, here at the water, and you can step from one to the other."

A country of magic, such as she had once dreamed of.

After an instant of awed silence, Vasya asked, "If I go far enough will I reach the country of winter?"

"Yes," said the chyert, though he looked dubious. "It is far to walk."

"Is the winter-king there?"

Ded Grib gave her another odd look. "How would I know? I cannot grow in the snow."

Thinking, frowning, Vasya returned her attention to filling her basket and her belly. She found cresses and cowslips, blueberries and gooseberries and strawberries.

Deeper she went into the summertime forest. *How happy Solovey would have been,* she thought, while her feet bruised the tender grass.

Perhaps together we could have gone to find his kin. Sorrow drained away her pleasure in the sun on her back, in the sun-ripened strawberry between her lips. But she kept gathering. The warm, green world quieted her wounded spirit. Ded Grib was sometimes visible, sometimes not; he liked to hide under logs. But always she could sense him watching: curious, untrusting.

When the sun was high overhead, she remembered caution, and her promise to the domovaya. She had not yet regained her strength, and that she would need, whatever came next. "I have all I need," she said. "I must get back."

Ded Grib popped out from behind a stump. "You haven't come to the best part," he protested, pointing to a distant flash of trees clad in scarlet and gold. As though autumn, like summer, was a place you could walk into. "A little farther."

Vasya was intensely curious. She also thought hungrily of chestnuts and pine-nuts. But caution won. "I have learned the cost of being reckless," she told Ded Grib. "I have enough, for one day."

He looked disgruntled, but said nothing else. Reluctantly, Vasya turned back the way she had come. It was hot in this summer country. She was dressed for early spring, in wool shirt and stockings. Her laden basket swung from her arm. Her feet throbbed now; her ribs ached.

To her left, the forest whispered, and watched. To her right lay the lake, summer-blue. Between the trees, she glimpsed a little sandy cove. Thirsty, Vasya strayed nearer the water, knelt, drank. The water was clear as air, so cold it made her teeth ache. Her bandages itched. The sponge-bath that morning had done nothing to ease her bone-deep sense of filth.

Abruptly, Vasya stood and began to strip. The domovaya would be cross with her for undoing all the careful wrapping, but Vasya couldn't bring herself to care. Her hands were trembling with eagerness. As though the clean water could scour both the dirt from her skin and memory from her mind.

"What are you doing?" asked Ded Grib. He was staying well away from the sand and the rocks, hiding in the shade.

"I am going to swim," said Vasya.

Ded Grib opened his mouth, closed it again.

Vasya paused. "Is there a reason why I shouldn't?"

The mushroom-spirit shook his head, slowly, but he gave the water a nervous look. Perhaps he didn't like water.

"Well," said Vasya. She hesitated, but Mother of God, she wanted to peel off her own skin and become someone else; a plunge in the lake might at least quiet her mind. "I won't go far. Perhaps you will look after my basket?"

SHE WADED IN. AT FIRST, she walked on rocks, wincing. Then the bottom became slick mud. She dove and came up yelling. The freezing lake closed her lungs and set her senses ablaze. She put her back to the shore and swam. The water delighted her, beneath the heat of the unaccustomed sun. But it was very cold. At last she halted, ready to turn back, scrub herself in the shallows, lie drying in the sun . . .

But when she turned, all she saw was water.

Vasya spun in a circle. Nothing. It was as though the whole world had sunk suddenly into the lake. For a few moments she treaded water, shocked, beginning to be afraid.

Perhaps she was not alone.

"I mean no harm," said Vasya aloud, trying to ignore her chattering teeth.

Nothing happened. Vasya paddled in a circle again. Still nothing. Panic in this cold water and she was as good as dead. She must simply take her best guess and pray.

With a splash like a shout, a creature shot out of the water in front of her. Two slitted nostrils lay between its bulbous eyes; its teeth were the color of rock, hooked over a narrow jaw. When it exhaled, its breath steamed and oily liquid ran down its face.

"I am going to drown you," it whispered, and lunged.

Vasya made no answer; instead her cupped hand came down on the water like a thunderclap. The chyert jerked back and Vasya snapped, "An immortal sorcerer could not kill me and neither could a priest with all Moscow at his beck—what makes you think *you* can?"

"You came into my lake," returned the chyert, baring black teeth.

"To swim, not to die!"

"That is for me to decide."

Vasya tried to ignore the goad of her aching ribs and to speak calmly. "For trespassing, I am guilty before you, but I do not owe you my life."

The chyert breathed scalding steam onto Vasya's face. "I am the bagiennik," he growled. "And *I* tell you your life is forfeit."

"Try and take it then," snapped Vasya. "But I am not afraid of you."

The chyert lowered his head, churning the blue water to froth. "Are you not? What did you mean that the immortal sorcerer could not kill you?"

Vasya's legs were on the edge of cramping. "I killed Kaschei Bezsmertnii in Moscow on the last night of Maslenitsa."

"Liar!" snapped the bagiennik, and lunged again, nearly swamping her.

Vasya didn't flinch. Much of her concentration was taken with staying above water. "Liar I have been," she said, "and I have paid for it. But about this I am telling the truth: I killed him."

The bagiennik shut his mouth abruptly.

Vasya turned away, looking for the shore.

"I know you now," murmured the bagiennik. "You have the look of your family. You took the road through Midnight."

Vasya had no time for the bagiennik's revelations. "I did," she managed. "But my family is far away. As I said, I mean no harm. Where is the shore?"

"Far away? Near at hand too. You understand neither yourself nor the nature of this place."

She was beginning to sink lower in the water. "Grandfather, the shore."

The bagiennik's black teeth shone with water. He slid nearer, moving like a water-snake. "Come, it will be quick. Drown, and I will live a thousand years on the memory of your blood."

"No."

"What use are you otherwise?" demanded the bagiennik, gliding nearer and nearer still. *"Drown."*

Vasya was using the last of her strength just to keep her numb limbs churning. "What *use* am I? None. I have made more mistakes than I can count, and the world has no place for me. And yet, as I said before, I am still not going to die to please you."

The bagiennik snapped his teeth right in her face, and Vasya, heedless of her wounds, caught him round the neck. He thrashed and almost threw her loose. But he didn't. In her hands was the strength that had broken the bars of her cage in Moscow. "You will not threaten me," Vasya added, into the chyert's ear, and sucked in a breath, just as they plunged. When they surfaced, the girl still clung. Gasping, she said, "I may die tomorrow. Or live to sour old age. But you are only a wraith in a lake, and *you will not command me.*"

The bagiennik stilled and Vasya let go, coughing out water, feeling the strain in muscles along her broken side. Her nose and mouth were full of water. A few of her reopened cuts streamed blood. The bagiennik nosed at her bleeding skin. She didn't move.

With surprising mildness, the bagiennik said, "Perhaps you are not useless after all. I have not felt such strength since—" He broke off. "I will bring you to shore." He looked suddenly eager.

Vasya found herself clinging to a sinuous body, scorching hot. She shivered as life came back into her limbs. Warily, she said, "What did you mean, that I have the look of my family?"

Undulating through the water, the bagiennik said, "Don't you know?" There was a strange undercurrent of eagerness in his voice. "Once the old woman and her twins lived in the house by the oak-tree and tended the horses that graze on the lake-shore."

"What old woman? I have been to the house by the oak-tree and it is a ruin."

"Because the sorcerer came," said the bagiennik. "A man, young and fair. He said he wished to tame a horse, but it was Tamara, her mother's heir, whom he won over. They swam together in the lake at Midsummer; he whispered his promises in the autumn twilight. In the end, for his sake, Tamara put a golden bridle on the golden mare: the Zhar Ptitsa."

Now Vasya was listening closely. This was her own history, laid out casually by a lake-spirit in a country far away. Her grandmother's name had been Tamara. Her grandmother had come from a distant land, riding a marvelous horse.

"The sorcerer took the golden mare and left the lands by the lake," continued the bagiennik. "Tamara rode after him, weeping, swearing to recover the mare, swearing that she loved him in the same breath. But she never came back, and neither did the sorcerer. *He* made himself master of a great swath of the lands of men. No one ever knew what happened to Tamara. The old woman, in grief, shut and guarded every road to this place except the road through Midnight."

There were a hundred questions darting through her head. Her tongue snatched up the first. "What happened to the other horses?" Vasya asked. "I saw a few of them last night and they were wild."

The water-spirit swam in silence awhile; she did not think he would answer. Then the bagiennik said, his voice deep and savage, "The ones you saw are all that remain now. The sorcerer slew all that strayed away from the lake. Occasionally he caught a foal, but they never lasted long—they died or they escaped."

"Mother of God," Vasya whispered. "How? *Why?*"

"They are the most marvelous things in all the world, the horses of this land. The sorcerer couldn't ride them. He couldn't tame them or use them. So he killed them." Almost too low to hear, the bagiennik added, "The ones that were left—the old woman kept them here, safe. But she is gone now, and there are fewer every year. The world has lost its wonder."

Vasya didn't speak. Her memory was a welter of flame, and Solovey's lifeblood.

"Where did they come from?" she whispered. "The horses."

"Who knows? The earth brought them forth; their very natures are magic. Of course men and chyerti want to tame them. Some of the horses take riders willingly," added the bagiennik. "The swan, the dove, the owl, and the raven. And the nightingale—"

"I know what happened to the nightingale." Vasya could barely say it. "He was my friend and he is dead."

"The horses do not choose unwisely," said the bagiennik.

Vasya said nothing at all.

After a long silence, lifting her head, she asked, "Can you tell me where the Bear has imprisoned the winter-king?"

"Beyond recall; long ago and far away and deep in the dark that does not change," said the water-spirit. "Do you think the Bear would risk his twin winning free now?"

"No," said Vasya. "No, I suppose he wouldn't." Suddenly she felt unutterably tired; the world was huge and strange and maddening; nothing seemed real. She neither knew what to do nor how to do it. She laid her head on the chyert's warm back and did not speak again.

SHE DIDN'T NOTICE THE LIGHT change until she heard the murmur of water on pebbled cove.

In the time they'd been swimming, the sun had tilted west, cold and yellow-green. She was in summer twilight on the cusp of night. The golden day was gone, as though the lake itself had swallowed it. Vasya rolled with a splash into the shallows and stumbled onto the shore. The shadows of the trees stretched long and gray toward the water; her clothes were a cold heap in the shade.

The bagiennik was only a smudge of darkness, half-submerged in the lake. Vasya rounded on him in sudden fear. "What happened to the day?" She saw the bagiennik's eyes beneath the water, shining rows of teeth. "Did you bring me into twilight on purpose? Why?"

"Because you killed the sorcerer. Because you did not let me kill you. Because word has gone out among the chyerti and we are all curious." The bagiennik's answer floated, disembodied, out of the shadows. "I advise you to make a fire. We will be watching."

"*Why?*" Vasya demanded again, but the bagiennik had already sunk beneath the water and disappeared.

The girl stood still, furious, trying to ignore her fear. The day was rushing down around her as though the forest itself was determined to catch her at nightfall. Used to her own unthinking endurance, she now had to contend with the weakness of her battered flesh. She was half a day's walking from the house by the oak-tree.

The season will turn, the domovaya had said. What did that mean? Could she risk it? Should she? She looked up at the gathering dark, and knew she couldn't make it back before nightfall.

Stay then, she decided. And she would take the bagiennik's poisonous advice, and use the last of the light to gather firewood. Whatever dangers haunted this place, better to meet them with a good fire, and a full belly.

She set about gathering firewood, angry at her own credulity. The forest of Lesnaya Zemlya had been kind to her, and that trust was still there, though this place had no cause for kindness. A brilliant sunset reddened the water; the wind whistled through the pines. The lake was perfectly still, golden with sunset.

Ded Grib reappeared as she was chopping up a deadfall. "Don't you know you mustn't pass the night beside the lake in a new season?" he asked. "Or you will never get the old season back. If you go back to the house by the oak-tree tomorrow, it will be summer and no spring at all for you."

"The bagiennik kept me in the lake," Vasya said grimly. The girl was recalling white, sparkling days in Morozko's house in the fir-grove. *You will return on the same night you left,* he had told her. She had, even though she spent days—weeks—in his house. She had. And now— would the moon wax and wane in the wider world, while she passed a single night in this summer country? If you could spend a day in the lake in minutes, then what else was possible? The thought frightened her, as even the bagiennik's threats had not. The patterns of day and dark, summer and winter, were as much a part of her as her own breath. Was there no pattern here at all?

"*I* didn't think you'd come out of the lake at all," the chyert confided. "I knew the great ones were planning something for you. Besides, the bagiennik hates people."

Vasya had an armful of firewood; she flung it down in fury. "You might have told me!"

"Why?" asked Ded Grib. "*I* can't interfere with the great ones' plans. Besides, you let one of the horses die, didn't you? Maybe it would have been justice, if the bagiennik had killed you, for he loves them."

"Justice?" she demanded. All the rage and guilt and trapped helplessness of the last few days seemed to spill out. "Have I not had enough *justice* these last days? I only came here for food; I have done nothing to you, nothing to your forest. And *still* you—all of you—"

Words failed her. In bitter anger, she seized a stick and flung it down on the head of the little mushroom.

She wasn't prepared for his reaction. The cloudy flesh of his head and shoulder sheared away. The chyert crumpled with a shriek of pain, and Vasya was left standing, appalled, while Ded Grib went bloodlessly from white to gray to brown. Like a mushroom kicked over by a careless child.

"No," said Vasya in horror. "No, I didn't mean it." Without thinking she knelt, put her hand on his head. "I am sorry," she said. "I didn't mean to hurt you. I am sorry."

He stopped turning gray. She realized she was crying. She hadn't realized how deep the last days' violence had gone inside her, hadn't realized that it was still inside her, coiled up, ready to lash out in terror and rage. "Forgive me," she said.

The chyert blinked his red eyes. He breathed. He was not dying. He looked more real than he had a moment ago. His broken body had knitted itself.

"Why did you do that?" asked the mushroom.

"I didn't mean to hurt you," said Vasya. She pressed the heels of her hands to her eyes. "I never meant to hurt anyone." She was shaking in every limb. "But you're right. I did—I did . . ."

"You—" The mushroom was examining his cloudy-gray arm with puzzlement. "You gave me your tears."

Vasya shook her head, struggling to speak. "For my horse," she managed. "For my sister. Even for Morozko." She scrubbed at her eyes, tried to smile. "A little for you."

Ded Grib stared at her solemnly. In silence, Vasya struggled to her feet and set about preparing for the night.

SHE WAS ARRANGING FIREWOOD on a bare patch of ground, when the mushroom-spirit spoke again, half-hidden in a leaf-pile. "*For Morozko,* you said. Are you looking for the winter-king?"

"Yes," said Vasya at once. "I am. If you don't know where he is, do you know who might?" The Bear's words—*his freedom for your life*—beat at the back of her skull. Why had he done it? *Why?* And a deeper memory still, Morozko's voice saying, *As I could, I—*

Her firewood was stacked in a neat open square, with kindling laid between the bigger branches. As she spoke, she was arranging pine-needles for tinder.

"Midnight knows," said Ded Grib. "Her realm touches every midnight that ever was. But I doubt she'll tell you. As to who else might know——" Ded Grib paused, obviously thinking hard.

"Are you helping me?" Vasya asked in surprise. She sat back on her heels.

Ded Grib said, "You gave me tears and a flower. I will follow *you*, and not the Bear. I am first." He puffed out his chest.

"First to what?"

"To take your side."

"My side in what?" asked Vasya.

"What do you think?" replied Ded Grib. "You denied both the winter-king and his brother, didn't you? You made yourself a third power in their war." He frowned. "Or are you going to find the winter-king to join *his* side?"

"I am not sure what difference it makes," said Vasya. "All these questions of sides. I want to find the winter-king because I need his help." That was not the entire reason, but she was not about to explain the rest of it to the mushroom-spirit.

Ded Grib waved this away. "Well, even if he does join your side, I will always have been first."

Vasya frowned at her unlit fire. "If you don't know how to find the winter-king, then how do you mean to help me?" she asked cautiously.

Ded Grib reflected. "I know all about mushrooms. I can make them grow, too."

This pleased Vasya inordinately. "I love mushrooms," she said. "Can you find me any lisichki?"

If Ded Grib answered, it went unheard, for the next moment she drew a sharp breath, and let her soul fill with the searing memory of fire. Her pile of sticks burst into flame. She added twigs with satisfaction.

Ded Grib's mouth fell open. All around, a whispering rose, as if the trees were speaking to one another. "You should be careful," said Ded Grib, when he could speak.

"Why?" said Vasya, still pleased with herself.

"Magic makes people mad," said the mushroom. "You change reality so much you forget what is real. But perhaps a few more chyerti will follow you after all."

As though to punctuate his words, two fish flopped out of the lake and lay gasping, red-silver in the light of Vasya's campfire.

"Follow me where?" Vasya demanded in some exasperation, but she did go and take the fish. "Thank you," she added grudgingly in the direction of the water. If the bagiennik heard, he didn't answer, but she didn't think he'd gone away. He was waiting.

For what, she didn't know.

12

Bargaining

Vasya gutted the fish and wrapped them in clay to roast in the coals of her fire. Ded Grib, true to his word, scampered off and brought her handfuls of mushrooms. Unfortunately, not only did he not know which were lisichki, he didn't know which were edible. Vasya had to pick through alarming handfuls of toadstools. But the good ones she stuffed into her fish, along with herbs and wild onion, and when they were done, she burned her fingers eating them.

A full stomach was pleasant, but the night itself was not. The wind blew sharp off the lake, and Vasya could not shake the sense of being watched, of being measured by eyes she could not see. She felt like a girl hurled unwary into a tale she didn't understand, with folk all around waiting for her to take up a part she didn't know. Solovey's absence was a gnawing misery that did not ease.

Eventually Vasya fell into a chilly doze, but even sleep was no respite. She dreamed of fists and enraged faces, of shouting for her horse to run. But instead he turned into a nightingale, and a man with a bow and arrow shot him out of the sky. Vasya jerked awake with her horse's name on her lips, and heard somewhere in the darkness the thud of uneven hoofbeats.

SHE HAULED HERSELF UPRIGHT, stood barefoot in the cool summer bracken, painfully stiff. Her fire was down to a few red-edged coals. The moon hung low on the horizon. A light was coming through the trees. She thought of men with torches, and her first instinct was to flee.

But it wasn't torches, she realized, squinting. It was the golden mare, alone. Her glow from the night before had dimmed; she was stumbling on a bad foreleg, her breast spattered with foam. Vasya thought she heard whispers in the wood beyond the horse. A foul smell gusted on the wind.

Swiftly, Vasya threw wood onto her little campfire. "Here," she called.

The mare tried to run, tripped over nothing, turned her steps to Vasya. Her head hung low. In the newborn firelight, a gash in her fore-leg was clearly visible.

Vasya picked up her ax and a flaming log. She couldn't see what pursued the mare, though the smell of it thickened all around them, rotten-ripe, like carrion in the heat. Holding her pitiful weapons, she backed toward the water. Vasya had no love for the living spark that ignited Moscow. But—she had failed her own horse. She would not fail this one. "This way," she said.

The mare had no words in reply, nothing but terror, communicated with her whole body. Still she came toward Vasya.

"Ded Grib," Vasya called.

A patch of mushrooms, glowing sickly green in the darkness, quivered. "You had better survive this. What good will my being first be, otherwise? *Everyone* is watching."

"What—?"

But if he answered she did not hear, for the Bear stepped softly out of the trees, into the moonlight beside the water.

IN MOSCOW, HE HAD looked like a man. He still did, but it was a man with sharp teeth, and wildness in his single eye; she could see the beast in him stretching out like a shadow at his back. He seemed stranger, older: at home in this impossible forest.

"I suppose this is why the bagiennik wanted me to spend the night in the forest," she said, standing tense. Hoarse, snarling breaths sounded from the undergrowth. "He did want me dead, after all."

The unscarred corner of the Bear's mouth curled. "Perhaps. Or perhaps not. Stop puffing up like a cat. I didn't come to kill you."

The burning log had begun to scorch her hand. She flung it onto the ground in between them. "Hunting the firebird then?"

"Not even that. But my creatures will have their sport." He hissed at the mare, grinning, and she shied back, her hind feet in the water.

"Leave her be!" Vasya snapped.

"Very well," said the Bear, unexpectedly. He seated himself on a log beside her fire. "Won't you sit with me?"

She didn't move. His dog-teeth gleamed sharp and white in the gloom when he smiled. "Truly, I do not desire your life, Vasilisa Petrovna." He opened his empty hands. "I wish to make you an offer."

That surprised her. "You have already offered me my life. I didn't take it; I saved myself. Why would I take anything less from you?"

The Bear did not answer directly. Instead, he looked up at the tree-fringed starlight, breathed deep of the summer night. She could see the stars reflected in his eye, as though he were drinking the sky after long darkness. She did not want to understand that joy. "I passed uncounted lives of men bound to a clearing at the edge of my brother's lands," said the Bear. "Do you think he was a good steward of the world while I slept?"

"At least Morozko did not leave destruction in his wake," said Vasya. Beside her the mare was bleeding into the water. "What have you been doing in Moscow?"

"Amusing myself," said the Bear matter-of-factly. "My brother did the same once, although he likes to play the saint now. Once we were more alike. We are twins, after all."

"If you are trying to make me trust you, it isn't working."

"But—" the Bear went on. "My brother thinks that men and chyerti can share this world. These same men that are spreading like sickness, rattling their church-bells, forgetting us. My brother is a fool. If men are unchecked, one day there will be no chyerti, no road through Midnight, no wonder in the world at all."

Vasya did not wish to understand why the Bear raised his eyes in wonder to the night sky, and she did not want to agree with him now. But it was true. All over Rus', chyerti were faint as smoke. They guarded their waters and woods and households with hands that did not grasp, with minds that barely remembered. She said nothing.

"Men fear what they do not understand," murmured the Bear. "They hurt you. They beat you, spat on you, put you in the fire. Men will suck all the wildness out of the world, until there is no place for a witch-girl to hide. They will burn you and all your kind." It was her deepest and most wretched fear. He must know that. "But it doesn't have to be so," the Bear continued. "We can save the chyerti, save the land between noon and midnight."

"Can *we?*" asked Vasya. Her voice was not quite steady. "How?"

"Come with me to Moscow." He was on his feet again, the unscarred half of his face ruddy in the firelight. "Help me throw down the belltowers, break the grip of the princes. Be my ally and you will have vengeance on your enemies. No one will dare scorn you again."

Medved was a spirit: no more made of flesh than Ded Grib, and yet in that clearing he seemed to pulse with raw life. "You killed my father," Vasya said.

He spread his hands. "Your father threw himself upon my claws. My brother got your allegiance with lies, didn't he? With whispers and half-truths in the dark and his two blue eyes, so tempting to maidens?"

She fought to keep all feeling from her face. The corner of his mouth curled before he continued. "But here I am, asking for your allegiance with nothing but the truth."

"If you are here with the truth, then tell me what you want," said Vasya. "With less art and more honesty."

"I want an ally. Join me and take your vengeance. We, the old ones, will rule this land once more. That is what the chyerti want. That is why the bagiennik brought you here. *That* is why they are all watching. For you to hear me, and agree."

Was he lying?

She found herself, horribly, wondering how it would be, to agree, to let the rage inside her loose in a spasm of violence. She could feel the impulse echoed in the scarred figure before her. He understood her guilt, her sorrow, the fury that had come down on Ded Grib's head.

"Yes," he whispered. "We understand each other. We cannot make a new world without first breaking the old."

"Breaking?" said Vasya. She hardly recognized her own voice. "What will you break in the making of this new world?"

"Nothing that cannot be repaired. Think of it. Think of the girl-children that will not face the fire."

She wanted to go to Moscow in power and throw the city down. His wildness called to her, and the sorrow of his long imprisonment. The golden mare stood very still.

"I would have my vengeance?" she murmured.

"Yes," he said. "In full measure."

"Would Konstantin Nikonovich die screaming?"

She thought he hesitated before answering. "He would die."

"And who else would die, Medved?"

"Men and women die every day."

"They die according to God's will; they do not die for me," said Vasya. The nails of her free hand tore into her palm. "Not one life lost is worth the price of my grief. Do you think that I'm a fool, that you can drip words like sweet poison in my ear? I am not your ally, monster, nor will I ever be."

She thought that a murmur rose from the forest all around, but she couldn't tell if it was a sound of delight or disappointment.

"Ah," said the Bear. The regret in his voice seemed real. "So wise in some ways, little Vasilisa Petrovna, and yet so foolish in others. For of course if you do not join me, you cannot remain alive."

"My life was the price of your freedom," Vasya said. The lake was a cold presence at her back, the golden mare still stood warm and trembling beside her. "You cannot kill me."

"I offered you your life," said the Bear. "It is not my fault you are a stubborn fool and did not take it. My debt is paid. Besides, I am not going to kill you. You can join me alive. Or you can be my servant." His mouth quirked irrepressibly. "Less alive."

VASYA HEARD A SOFT, shuffling footstep. Another. Vasya's pulse sounded loud in her ears; in her mind echoed an old warning. *The Bear is loose. Beware the dead.*

"I am going to enjoy this," said Medved. "Tell me what you decide." He stepped back. "Either way, I will give my brother your regrets."

To her left, a dead man with red eyes and a filthy visage slunk into the light. To her right, a woman grinned, blood on her lips, a few locks of rotten hair still clinging to her bone-white skull. The dead things' eyes were pits of hell: scarlet and black. When their mouths opened, the points of their teeth dazzled, sharp, in the last of the firelight. Vasya and the mare were surrounded by a shrinking half-circle.

The golden mare reared. For an instant, it seemed as though vast wings of flame flared from her back. But she came to earth, a horse still, and wounded. She couldn't fly.

Vasya dropped her useless ax. Her soul was still full of remembered fire. She clenched her fists and forgot that the dead things were not burning.

It worked better than she could have hoped. Two went up like torches. The upyry screamed as they burned and blundered about, howling. She had to snatch up a branch and fend them off, her bare feet in the water. The golden mare backed up, striking out with frantic fore-hooves.

"Oh ho," said the Bear, in a new voice. "Moscow put the fire in your soul, did it? Truly, you are half chaos-spirit; you would like being my ally. Won't you reconsider?"

"Are you never silent?" Vasya demanded. Her body was streaming cold sweat. Another upyr burst into flames and reality began to waver. Now she understood. *Magic makes men mad. They forget what is real because too much is possible.*

But there were still four more; she had no choice. The dead things were advancing once more.

The Bear's eye locked on hers, as though he could see the seed of insanity there. "Yes," he breathed. "Lose your mind, wild girl. And you'll be mine."

She drew a deep breath and—

"Enough," said a new voice.

The sound seemed to shake Vasya out of a dark dream. An old woman, big-handed and broad-shouldered, strode between the trees, took in the lurid scene, and said irritably, as though it were the most natural thing in the world, "Medved, you shouldn't have tried it at midnight."

At the same moment, a wave from the lake nearly swamped Vasya, and the bagiennik appeared, floating in the shallows, teeth bared. "Eater, you didn't say anything about hurting the horses."

The old woman might have been tall once, but she was crabbed with age, her clothes rough, her hands long-nailed, her legs bowed. There was a basket on her back.

Vasya, standing with her feet in the lake, reality gone pliant as mist, could see the Bear startled, wary. "You are dead," he said to the old woman.

The old woman chortled. "At midnight? On my own lands? You should know better."

Vasya, as though in a dream, thought she caught the gleam of the midnight-demon's hair, her starry eyes, half-hidden in the trees, watching.

The Bear said, placating, "I should have known better. But why interfere? What care you for your traitorous family?"

"I care at least for the mare, you great hungry thing," retorted the old woman. She stamped her foot. "Go back to terrorizing Muscovy."

One of the upyry was creeping up behind the old woman. She didn't look, didn't even twitch, but the dead thing burst into white fire, and collapsed with a shriek.

"I suppose," said the Bear, "I'd have to wait a long time for you to go mad." There was respect in his voice. Vasya listened in astonishment.

"I have been mad for years," said the old woman. When she laughed, every hair on Vasya's body rose. "But at midnight, this is still my realm."

"The girl won't stay with you," said the Bear, with a jerk of his chin at Vasya. "She won't stay, however you try to persuade her. She'll leave you just like the others. When she does, I'll be waiting." To Vasya, he added, "Your choice still stands. You are going to be my ally one way or the other. The chyerti will not have it otherwise."

"*Go away,*" snapped the woman.

And, unbelievably, the Bear bowed to them both, and slunk away through the dark. His servants, shambling, the hell-light gone from their eyes, followed him.

13

Baba Yaga

THE SOUNDS OF THE NIGHT RESUMED. VASYA'S FEET WERE NUMB IN the water. The golden mare's head hung low. The old woman pursed her lips, inspecting girl and horse.

"Babushka," said Vasya cautiously. "Thank you for our lives."

"If you want to stand in the lake until you grow fins, that is your affair," the old woman replied. "Otherwise come to the fire."

She stumped away, added sticks to the blaze. Vasya waded out of the lake. But the mare did not move. "You are bleeding," Vasya said to her, trying to get a look at the gash on her foreleg.

The mare's ears were still pinned to her head. Finally, she said, *I ran, while the others flew, to lead the upyry away. But they were too fast, and then my leg was torn and I could not fly.*

"I can help you," Vasya volunteered.

The mare made no answer. But suddenly Vasya understood her stillness, the golden head sunk low. "Do you fear being bound again? Because you are wounded? Do not be afraid. I killed the sorcerer. Tamara is dead too." She could feel the old woman at her back, listening. "I have no rope here, let alone a golden bridle. I will not touch you without your leave; come to the fire."

Vasya suited action to word, making her own way to the fire. The mare stood still, the set of her ears uncertain. The old woman was

standing on the other side of the flames, waiting for Vasya. Her hair
was white. But her face was a distorted mirror of the girl's own.

Vasya stared, with shock, hunger, recognition.

The forest still seemed thick with eyes, watching. There was an instant of perfect silence. Then the woman said, "What is your name?"

"Vasilisa Petrovna," said Vasya.

"What was your mother's name?"

"Marina Ivanovna," said Vasya. "Her mother was called Tamara,
the girl who put a bridle on the firebird."

The woman's eyes roved over Vasya's torn and bruised face, her
cropped hair, her clothes, and perhaps more than anything the expression in the girl's eyes. "I'm surprised you didn't frighten the Bear
off," said the old woman, drily. "With your face so frightful. Or perhaps he liked it. Hard to know, with that one." Her hands were trembling.

Vasya said nothing.

"Tamara and her sister were my daughters. Long ago, it would seem
to you."

Vasya knew that. "How are you alive?" she whispered.

"I'm not," said the old woman. "I died before you were born. But
this is Midnight."

The golden mare broke their silence with splashing as she stepped
out of the lake. As one, they turned to the horse. The firelight gleamed
cruelly on the scars of whip and spur. "A pitiful pair you make," said
the old woman.

Vasya said, "Babushka, we are both in need of help."

"Pozhar first," said the old woman. "She is bleeding still."

"Is that her name?"

A shrug. "What name would compass a creature like her? It is only
what I call her."

BUT HELPING THE MARE was not so easy. Pozhar laid back her ears if
either of them tried to touch her. When she switched her tail, showers

of sparks tumbled to the summer earth. One began to smolder; Vasya put it out with a booted foot. "Wounded or no, you are a menace."

The old woman snorted. The mare glared. But Pozhar was exhausted, too. At last, when Vasya ran a hand from her shoulder to her knee, she only shuddered. "This is going to hurt," said Vasya grimly. "You are *not* to kick."

I am not promising anything, said the mare, ears pinned.

Between them, they convinced the mare to stand still long enough for the girl to sew up her leg, although Vasya had a few new bruises by the time it was done. After, when a shaken Pozhar had escaped, limping, to graze at a safe distance, Vasya sank to the earth beside the fire, pushing sweaty hair off her face. Her clothes had dried in the heat of the mare's body. It was still blackest night, although it seemed hours since the Bear had come.

The woman had a pot in her basket, salt, some onions. When she thrust her hand in the lake, she withdrew fish, as naturally as a woman pulls bread from her own oven. She set about making soup, as though it were not midnight.

Vasya watched her. "Is it your house?" she asked. "The house by the oak-tree?"

The old woman was gutting the fish and didn't look up. "It was, once."

"The chest—did you leave it there? For me to find?"

"Yes," said the woman, still not looking up.

"You knew that I—you are the witch of the wood then," said Vasya. "Who tends the horses." She thought of Marya and the old, dread name, the fairy-tale name, came to her lips unbidden. With a shiver, she said, "Baba Yaga. You are my great-grandmother."

The old woman brayed a short laugh. The fish guts shone darkly between her fingers when she flung them back into the lake. "Near enough, I suppose. This witch and that were woven into a single fairy tale. Perhaps I am one of the witches."

"How did you know I was here?"

"Polunochnitsa told me, of course," returned the old woman. She was rummaging in the contents of Vasya's basket now, adding greens to the pot. Her eyes gleamed in the dark, big and wild and reddened by the fire. "Although she almost waited until it was too late; she wanted you and the Bear to meet."

"Why?"

"To see what you'd do."

"*Why?*" Vasya asked again. She felt perilously close to breaking into a child's whining complaint. Her feet ached, and her ribs, and the cut on her face. More than ever she felt as if she'd been thrust into a tale she hardly understood.

The old woman didn't answer at once. She studied Vasya again. Finally she said, "Most of the chyerti do not want to strike a blow at the world of men. But they don't want to fade either. They are torn."

Vasya frowned. "Are they? What has that to do with me?"

"Why do you think Morozko went to such lengths to save your life? Yes, Polunochnitsa told me that, too."

"I don't know why," said Vasya, and this time her voice rose a note despite her best efforts. "Do you think I wanted him to? It was utter madness."

A quick, malicious gleam from beneath the old woman's lids. "Was it? I suppose you'll never know."

"I would if you'd tell me."

"That—no. It is something you must come to understand yourself, or not." The old woman grinned, still with that edge of malice. She tossed salt in the soup. "Is it an easy road you're after, child?"

"If it were, I'd not have left home," retorted Vasya, holding hard to courtesy. "But I am tired of stumbling blind in the dark."

The old woman was stirring the pot now; the firelight caught a strange expression on her face. "It is always dark here," she said.

Vasya, still bursting with questions, found herself silenced, ashamed of herself. In a different voice, she said, "You are the one who sent Midnight to me, on the road to Moscow."

"I am," said the old woman. "I was curious, when I heard a girl-child of my blood had gone wandering, with a horse from the lake."

Vasya flinched at the reminder of Solovey. The soup was ready; the witch ladled up a large bowl for herself, a meager one for Vasya. Vasya didn't mind; she'd stuffed herself on fish earlier. But the broth was good; she drank it slowly.

"Babushka," she asked, "did you ever see your daughters, after they left this place?"

Baba Yaga's old face grew still as carven stone. "No. They abandoned me."

Vasya thought of Tamara's withered ghost, wondered if this woman could have prevented that horror.

"My girl plotted with the sorcerer to take the firebird by force!" snapped the old woman, as though she could read Vasya's thought. "I could not catch them. The mare is the fastest thing that runs. But at least my daughter was punished."

Vasya said, "She was your child. Do you know what the sorcerer did to Tamara?"

"She did it to herself."

"Shall I *tell* you what happened to her?" Vasya asked, growing angry. "About her courage and her despair? Of how she was trapped in the terem of Moscow until she died? And even after! You shut your lands and didn't even try to help her?"

"*She* betrayed *me*," retorted the witch. "She chose a man over her own kin; gave the golden mare into Kaschei's keeping. My Varvara left me too. She tried first to take Tamara's place, but she could not. Of course she could not; she had not the sight. So, she left, the coward."

Vasya stilled, struck with sudden understanding.

"I didn't need either of them," the old woman went on. "I shut the way in. I shut every road but the Midnight-road and that road is mine, for Lady Midnight is my servant. I have kept my lands inviolate until a new heir should come."

"Kept your lands inviolate?" Vasya demanded incredulously. "While your children were trapped in the world of men, while your daughter was abandoned by her lover?"

"Yes," said the witch. "She deserved it."

Vasya said nothing.

"But," the old woman went on, her voice softening, "I have a new heir now. I knew you'd come, one day. You can speak to horses; you awakened the domovaya with fire, you survived the bagiennik. You will not betray me. You will live in the house by the oak-tree and I will come every midnight to teach you all I know. How to master chyerti. How to keep your own people safe. Don't you want to know those things, poor little girl, with your burned face?"

"Yes," said Vasya. "I do want to know those things."

The woman sat back, looking satisfied.

"When there is time to learn," Vasya continued. "But not yet. The Bear is free in Rus'."

The old woman bristled. "What is Rus' to you? They tried to burn you, didn't they? They killed your horse."

"Rus' is my family. My brothers and sister. My niece, who sees as I do. *Your* grandchildren. Your great-grandchildren."

The woman's eyes began, disconcertingly, to gleam. "Another with the sight? And a girl-child? We will walk through Midnight and get her."

"Steal her away, you mean? Take her from her mother, who loves her?" Vasya dragged in air. "You should think of what happened to your own children first."

"No," said the woman. "I didn't need them, little serpents." Her eyes were savage, and Vasya wondered if it were solitude or magic that had planted this deep seed of madness inside her, that she would reject her children so. "You will have my powers and my chyerti, great-granddaughter."

Vasya got up and went and knelt at the old woman's side. "You honor me," she said, forcing her voice to calm. "At dusk I was a vagabond, and now I am someone's great-grandchild."

The old woman sat stiff, puzzled, watching Vasya with reluctant hope.

"But," she finished, "it was for my sake that the Bear was freed; I must see him bound anew."

"The Bear's amusements do not concern you. He was long a prisoner; don't you think he deserves a little sunlight?"

"He just tried to kill me," said Vasya acidly. "That is one amusement that concerns me."

"You cannot stand against him. You are too young, and you have seen the dangers of too much magic. He is the cleverest of the chyerti.

If I had not come, you would have died." One withered hand reached out and caught Vasya's. "Stay here and learn, child."

"I will," said Vasya. "I will. If the Bear is bound then I will come back and be your heir and learn. But I must see my family safe. Can you help me?"

The old woman withdrew her hand. Hostility was winning out over the hope in her face. "I will not help you. I am steward of this lake, these woods; I care not for the world beyond."

"Can you at least tell me where the winter-king is imprisoned?" asked Vasya.

The woman laughed. Really laughed, throwing her head back with a cackle. "Do you think his brother will have just left him lying, like a kitten he forgot to drown?" Her eyes narrowed. "Or are you just like Tamara? Choosing a man over your own kin?"

"No," said Vasya. "But I need his help to bind the Bear again. Do you know where he is?" Despite her efforts at calm, a hard edge was creeping back into her own voice.

"Not on any of my lands."

Lady Midnight was still standing in the shadows, listening intently. *Baba Yaga has three servants, riders all: Day, Dusk, and Night,* that was how the story went. "Nevertheless," said Vasya, "I am going to find him."

"You don't know where to start."

"I am going to start in Midnight," said Vasya shortly, with another glance at the midnight-demon. "Surely if it includes *every midnight* that ever was, one of them contains Morozko in his prison."

"It is a land so vast your mind cannot understand it."

"Will you help me then?" Vasya asked again, looking into the face that was the mirror of her own. "Please. Babushka, I am sure there is a way."

The woman's mouth worked. She seemed to hesitate. Vasya's heart leaped with sudden hope.

But then the witch turned stiffly away, jaw set. "You are as bad as Tamara, as bad as Varvara, as bad as either of those wicked girls. I will not help you, fool. You will only get yourself killed, and for nothing,

after your precious *winter-king* went to such lengths to see you safe."
She was on her feet. Vasya was too.

"Wait," she said. "Please." Midnight stood motionless in the darkness.

Furiously the old woman said, "If you think better of your foolishness, come back and perhaps I will reconsider. If not—well, I let my own daughters go. A great-granddaughter should be even easier."

Then she stepped into the darkness and was gone.

14

Vodianoy

Vasya wished she could cry. Part of her soul yearned after her great-grandmother, as it yearned after the mother she'd never known, after her dead nurse, and the elder sister who'd gone away so young. But how could she live quietly in a land of magic while the Bear was loose, her family in danger, the winter-king left to rot?

"You are too alike," said a familiar voice. Vasya raised her head. Midnight slipped out of the shadows. "Rash. Heedless." The moonlight kindled the chyert's pale hair to white fire. "So, you mean to seek the winter-king?"

"Why are you asking?"

"Curiosity," said Midnight, lightly.

Vasya didn't believe her. "Are you going to tell the Bear?" she asked.

"Why should I? He will only laugh. You cannot get Morozko out. You will only die trying."

"Well," said Vasya, "*you* would rather I died, it seems, judging by our last meeting. Why not tell me where he is, and I'll be dead the sooner?"

Polunochnitsa looked amused. "It wouldn't do any good if I did. Getting somewhere in Midnight is not so simple as knowing where you mean to go."

"How do you travel by midnight then?"

Polunochnitsa said softly, "There is no north in Midnight, no south.

No east or west; no here or there. You must only hold your destination in your mind and walk, and not falter in the darkness, for there is no telling how long it will take to get where you wish to go."

"Is that all? Why did Varvara make me touch an oak-sapling then?"

Polunochnitsa snorted. "A little that one knows, but she does not understand. Affinity makes it easier to travel. Like calls to like. Blood calls to blood. It is easiest to go to your own kin. You couldn't reach the tree by the lake alone because you used a weak affinity—oak-tree to oak-tree." Her expression went sly. "Perhaps it won't be hard for you to find the winter-king, little maiden. There is an affinity there, surely. After all, he loved you enough to yield up his freedom. Perhaps he is longing for you even now."

Vasya had never heard anything more ridiculous. But all she said was, "How do I get *into* Midnight?"

"Every night, when the hour comes, my realm is there, for those with eyes to see."

"Very well. How do I get *out* of Midnight again?"

"The easiest way? Go to sleep." Midnight was watching her intently now. "And your sleeping mind will seek the dawn."

Ded Grib popped out from under a log.

"Where were *you* in all this excitement?" Vasya asked him.

"Hiding," said the mushroom-spirit succinctly. "I am glad you are not dead." He gave Midnight a nervous glance. "Better not go looking for the winter-king, though. You'll get killed, and after I have gone through so much trouble to be your ally."

"I must," said Vasya. "He sacrificed himself for me."

She saw Midnight's eyes narrow. She was deadly serious, but she'd not spoken in the tones of a lovelorn maiden.

"That was his choice, not yours," said Ded Grib, looking more uneasy than ever.

Vasya, without another word, went to Pozhar, stopped a healthy distance away from where the mare was grazing. Pozhar liked to bite. "Lady, are you all kin? You and the other horses that are birds?"

Pozhar flicked her ears in annoyance. *Of course we are,* she said. Her leg already looked much better.

Vasya took a deep breath. "Then will you do me a kindness?"

Pozhar at once shied. *You are not getting on my back,* she said.

Vasya thought she heard Polunochnitsa laugh. "No," Vasya said. "I would not ask it of you. I meant to ask—will you come through Midnight with me? Take me to Morozko's white mare? Blood calls to blood, I learn."

This last was for Polunochnitsa's benefit. She could almost feel Polunochnitsa's arrested stare.

Pozhar was still for a moment. Her great, golden ears flicked once, back and forth, uncertainly. *I suppose I will try,* said Pozhar irritably, and stamped. *If that is all. But you are still* not *getting on my back.*

"Just as well," Vasya said. "I have a broken rib."

Ded Grib was frowning. "Didn't you just say—?"

"Will no one credit me with common sense?" Vasya demanded, stalking back to the fire. "Affinity guides one through the land of Midnight. Well and good, but I am not fool enough to trust the tie between Morozko and me, that was made up of lies and longing and half-truths. Especially since I suspect that the Bear might be expecting me to, and get myself killed in the process."

Judging by Polunochnitsa's face, that was the exact thing he was expecting. "Even if you do find him," she said, recovering, "you won't be able to get the winter-king out."

"One task at a time," said Vasya. She took a handful of strawberries from her basket, held them out. "Will you tell me something else, Lady Midnight?"

"Oh, is it bribery now?" But Polunochnitsa took the fruit, bent her head to the sweetness. "Tell you what?"

"Will the Bear or his servants follow me, if I go into Midnight after Morozko?"

Midnight hesitated. "No," she said. "He has enough to do in Moscow. If you want to throw your life away on a prison that cannot be breached, then that is your affair." She smelled the strawberries again. "But I will give you a last warning. The midnights nearest you only cross distance. You can go into and out of them as you will. But the farther midnights—those cross years. If you fall asleep there, and lose the Midnight-road, then you will vanish like the dew, or your flesh fall at once to dust."

Vasya shuddered. "How will I know which is near and which is far?"

"It doesn't matter. If you wish to find the winter-king, you must not sleep until you do."

She took a deep breath. "Then I will not fall asleep."

VASYA WENT TO THE LAKE to take a long drink, and found the bagiennik writhing, furious, in the shallows. "The firebird has come back!" snarled the bagiennik. "Against all hope, to live again by the water. And perhaps there will be a great herd again, to fly over the lake at dawn. Now you are taking her away on your own foolish errand."

"I am not forcing her to come with me," said Vasya gently.

The bagiennik beat his tail against the water, wordlessly miserable.

Vasya said, "When Pozhar wishes to come back, she may. And—if I survive this, then I will come and live by the lake and learn, seek out all the scattered horses and tend them. In memory of my own, whom I loved very much. Will that content you?"

The bagiennik said nothing.

She turned away.

From behind the bagiennik said in a new voice, "I will hold you to your word."

VASYA COLLECTED HER BASKET, the remains of her fish. From the grass, Ded Grib piped, "Are you leaving me behind?" He was sitting on a stump now, glowing an unpleasant green in the darkness.

Vasya said, dubiously, "I may go far from the lake."

Ded Grib looked small and determined. "I am going with you anyway," he said. "I am on your side, remember? Besides, *I* can't fall to dust."

"How comforting for you," said Vasya coolly. "Why be on my side?"

"The Bear can make chyerti angry, stronger with wrath. But you can make us more *real*. I understand now. So does the bagiennik." Ded Grib looked proud. "I am on your side and I am going with you. You would be lost without me."

"Perhaps I would," Vasya said, smiling. Then a note of doubt crept into her voice. "Are you going to walk?" He was very small.

"Yes," said Ded Grib and marched off.

Pozhar shook her mane. *Hurry up*, she said to Vasya.

THE GOLDEN MARE WALKED into the night, taking mouthfuls of grass as she went. Sometimes if she found a good patch, she would put her head down to graze in earnest. Vasya did not hurry her, not wanting to irritate the gash in Pozhar's foreleg, but she was anxiously wondering when she would start to get sleepy, wondering how many hours it would take . . .

No point in thinking of it. She had decided. Either she would succeed or she wouldn't.

"I have never left the lake," Ded Grib confided to Vasya as they walked. "Not since there were villages of men there and the children dreamed me alive, when they went mushrooming in autumn."

"Villages?" asked Vasya. "By the lake?" By then they were walking in a strange glade, with rough grass and mud under her feet. The stars were low and warm in the generous sky: summertime stars.

"Yes," said Ded Grib. "There used to be villages of men on the borders of the magic country. Sometimes if they were brave, men and women would go in, seeking adventure."

"Perhaps men and women might be persuaded to do so again," said Vasya, fired with the idea. "And they could live in peace with chyerti, safe from the evils of this world."

Ded Grib looked doubtful, and Vasya sighed.

On they went, walk and halt and walk again. Now the night was cooler, now warmer. Now they were walking on rock, with wind whistling past Pozhar's ears, now they were skirting a pond, with a full moon lying like a pearl in the center. All was still, all was silent. Vasya was weary, but nerves and her long sleep in the house by the lake kept her moving.

She was barefoot, her boots tied to her basket. Though her feet were sore, the ground felt good on her skin. Pozhar was a silver-gold glimmer between the trees, a little short on her wounded foreleg. Ded Grib was a fainter presence still, creeping from stump to rock to tree.

Vasya hoped that Midnight had been right about the Bear not following her. But she looked often over her shoulder and once or twice had to stop herself from telling the mare to hurry.

Walking through a wooded hollow, with tall pines on all sides, she found herself thinking for the first time how pleasant it would be to make a bed of boughs and sleep until first light.

Hurriedly seeking a distraction, Vasya realized that it had been a while since she'd seen the mushroom-spirit's green glow. She peered into the darkness, searching. "Ded Grib!" She scarcely dared to speak above a whisper, not knowing what dangers stalked this place. "Ded Grib!"

The mushroom-spirit popped out of the loam at her feet, sending Pozhar skittering backward. Even Vasya jumped. "Where have you been?" she asked him, sharp with fright.

"Helping!" said Ded Grib. He thrust something into her hands. Vasya realized that it was a sack of food. Not wild food, like her strawberries and dandelions, but flat camp-bread, smoked fish, a skin of mead. "Oh!" said Vasya. She tore off a piece of flatbread, gave it to him, gave another to the offended Pozhar, and tore off a third for herself. "Where did you get this?" she asked him, gnawing.

"There are men over there," said Ded Grib. Vasya looked up and saw the faint glow of fires between the trees. Pozhar backed, nostrils flared uneasily. "But you shouldn't go any nearer," the mushroom-spirit added.

"Why not?" asked Vasya, puzzled.

"They are encamped near a river," said Ded Grib matter-of-factly. "And the vodianoy there means to kill them."

"*Kill* them?" said Vasya. "How? Why?"

"With water and fear I suppose," said Ded Grib. "How else would he kill anyone? As to why, well, the Bear probably told him to. Most water-creatures are his, and he is putting forth his power all through Rus' now. Let's get away."

Vasya hesitated. It was not pity for men drowned asleep that decided her; it was wondering why the Bear would want to kill *these* men in particular. *You travel by midnight through affinity.* What affinity would have drawn *her* here? Now? She peered again through the trees. Many fires; the camp was not a small one.

Then Vasya heard a faint, familiar rumbling, as though horses were coming near at a gallop over stones. But it was not horses.

The sound decided her. She thrust her basket at Ded Grib. "Stay here, both of you," she said to the mare and to the mushroom-spirit. Barefoot, she dashed toward the glow of the low-burning fires, raising her voice to shout through the dark, "You! The camp! Wake up! *Wake up!* The river is rising!"

She half-ran, half-slid down the steep sides of the gully where they had made camp. The horses were picketed and jerking at their lines; *they* knew what was happening. Vasya cut their pickets and the beasts bolted for higher ground.

A heavy hand fell on Vasya's shoulder. "Horse-thieving, boy?" asked a man, his hand pinching, smelling of garlic and rotten teeth.

Vasya wrenched away. She might otherwise have been afraid of him, for the touch and the reek brought back raw memories. But now she had more pressing concerns. "Do I look like I am hiding a horse in my hat? I have saved your horses for you. Listen. The river is rising."

The man turned his head to look, just as a wall of black water exploded from downstream, came racing past them. The hollow where the band had made camp was instantly awash. Men, half-asleep, were running everywhere in the darkness, shouting. The water was rising unnaturally fast, throwing men off their feet and frightening them by its very strangeness.

One man began calling orders. "First the silver!" he shouted. "Then the horses!"

But the water was rising faster and faster. A man was pulled down by the flood, then another. Many of the men made it to higher ground. But the one who'd been calling orders was still floundering in the wash.

As Vasya watched, the vodianoy, the river-king, shot out of the water directly in front of him.

The man couldn't see the chyert. But he jerked back anyway, on some instinct older than sight, and nearly went under.

"Prince?" said the vodianoy. His laugh was the grinding of rocks in the flood. "I was king here when princes groveled in the mud of my river and threw in their daughters to ensure my favor. Now—drown."

The black water surged and knocked the man off his feet.

Vasya had taken refuge in a tree, while the current raged below. Now she dove from a limb straight into the torrent. The water snatched at her with astonishing force, and she could feel the vodianoy's rage in it.

In her veins was the same strength that had broken the bars of her cage in Moscow. She wasn't sleepy now.

The leader of the camp came up for air, gasping. Men were shouting to him from above, cursing each other. Vasya swam three strokes, cutting across the current. The leader was a big man, but fortunately he could swim a little. She seized him under the arms, and on a last burst of strength, heaved him to shore. A stab of pain ran down her half-knitted ribs.

The man just lay in the mud, gaping at her. She could hear men converging on all sides, but she didn't speak, just whirled and dove back into the water, leaving the man clinging to the shore and staring after her.

SHE LET HERSELF BE SWEPT downstream until she caught a rock in the middle and clung there, gasping.

"River-king!" she shouted. "I want to talk to you."

The water rushed along, with broken trees borne on its flood. She had to clamber higher on her rock to avoid a huge limb spinning toward her in the current.

The vodianoy popped out of the water scarce an arm's length away. His grinning mouth was filled with needle-sharp teeth, his skin thick with slime and river muck. Water ran like diamonds down his warty skin and foamed and boiled around him. He opened his spine-toothed mouth and roared at her.

This is when I'm supposed to scream, Vasya thought. *Then he laughs— and I cry out in despair, believing in my own death, and that is when he sinks his teeth into me and drags me down.*

That was how chyerti killed people, by making them believe they were doomed.

Vasya spoke as composedly as one could, clinging to a rock in a current. "Forgive my intrusion."

It is not easy to startle the river-king. His gaping mouth closed abruptly. "Who are you?"

"It doesn't matter," said Vasya. "Why were you trying to kill these men?" The water surged, struck her in the face. She spat it out, wiped water from her eyes, hitched herself a little higher.

She only knew where the river-king was by his black bulk against the sky, the shine of his eyes. "I wasn't," he said.

Her arms had begun to shake. She cursed her lingering weakness. "No?" she demanded, breathless.

"The silver," he said. "I was to drown the silver."

"*Silver?* Why?"

"The Bear desired it of me."

"What do chyerti care for men's silver?" she panted.

"I know not. I only know the Bear bid me to do it."

"Very well," said Vasya. "It is done now. Will you quiet the water, river-king?"

The vodianoy rumbled with displeasure. "Why? Those men with their dust and their horses and their filth fouled my river. They left no offering, no acknowledgment. Better they drown with their silver."

"No," she said. "Men and chyerti can share this world."

"We cannot!" snapped the vodianoy. "They will not stop—the bells will not stop, the cutting of trees and the fouling of water, and the forgetting will not stop until there are none of us left."

"We *can,*" she insisted. "I see you. You will not fade."

"You are not enough." The black lips had pulled back again, revealing the needles of his teeth. "And the Bear is stronger than you."

"The Bear is not here," said Vasya. "I am here and *you will not kill these men*. Quiet the water!"

The vodianoy only hissed, mouth opening wide. Vasya did not recoil, but reached out a scraped hand and touched his warty face. She said, "Listen to me and be at peace, river-king." The vodianoy felt like living water, cold and silken and alive under her hand. She committed the texture of his skin to memory.

He shrank away. His mouth closed. "Must it be so?" he asked her, in a different voice. He sounded suddenly afraid. But beneath it was a thread of agonized hope. Vasya thought of what her great-grandmother had said, that the chyerti didn't really wish to fight, at all.

Vasya took a deep breath. "Yes," she said. "It must."

"Then I will remember," said the vodianoy. The raging force of the current slacked. Vasya drew a relieved breath. "You must also remember—sea-maiden." The vodianoy sank gurgling beneath the water and vanished before she could ask him why he called her that.

The level of the river began to drop. By the time Vasya dragged herself ashore, it was only muddy creek again.

The man that she had rescued was standing on the bank when she came wading out. She was bedraggled, panting and shivering, but at least she wasn't sleepy. She jerked to a halt when she saw him waiting, quelled a startled impulse to flee.

He raised his hands. "Do not be afraid, boy. You saved my life."

Vasya didn't speak. She didn't trust him. But the water was at her back, the night, the forest, the Midnight-road. All promised refuge. She was afraid of the man with an instinctive fear, but it wasn't like Moscow, where walls hemmed her in. So she stood fast and said, "If you are grateful, Gospodin, then tell me your name and your purpose here."

He stared. Vasya realized belatedly that he had thought she was a peasant boy but that she didn't sound like one.

"I suppose it is of no matter now," he said after a grim silence. "I am called Vladimir Andreevich, the Prince of Serpukhov. I, with my men, was to take a tribute of silver to Sarai, to the puppet-khan and his temnik Mamai. For Mamai has mustered an army and will not disperse it until he has his tax. But now the silver is gone."

Her brother-in-law, sent by Dmitrii on an errand meant to avert a war, now thwarted. Vasya understood why affinity had brought her here; knew also why the Bear had wanted to drown the silver. Why bring down Dmitrii himself when he could get Tatars to do it?

Perhaps the silver could be found. But not in darkness. Could she force the vodianoy to retrieve it? She hesitated between the forest and the water.

Vladimir was considering her, narrow-eyed. "Who are you?"

"You wouldn't believe me if I told you," she assured him with perfect honesty.

His sharp gray eyes took in the fading cuts and bruises on her face. "I mean you no harm," he said. "Wherever you ran away from— I won't send you back. Would you like something to eat?"

The unexpected kindness almost drove tears from her; she realized how bewildered and frightened she had been, and still was. But she had no time for tears.

"No," she said. "I thank you." She had decided. To end the Bear's mischief once and for all, she needed the winter-king.

So she fled, a wraith in the darkness.

15

Farther, Stranger Countries

THE MOON WAS HANGING NEAR THE HORIZON AND IT WAS STILL endless, sapping night. Vasya was barefoot, and now she was cold.

Ded Grib popped out from behind a stump, clutching Vasya's basket. He looked outraged. "You are *wet*," he said. "*And* you are lucky I kept you in sight. What if you and I and the horse had all gone into different midnights? You would have been lost."

Vasya's teeth were chattering. "I didn't think of it," she said to her little ally. "You are so wise."

Ded Grib looked a little mollified.

"I am going to have to find somewhere to dry my clothes," Vasya managed. "Where is Pozhar?"

"There," said Ded Grib, pointing to a glimmer in the darkness. "I kept you *both* in sight."

Vasya, in gratitude, bowed deeply and sincerely before him, and then she said, "Can you find a place where no one will see if I build a fire?"

Grumbling, he did. She laid a fire and then hesitated, looking at the wood, feeling the rage and terror—and flame—in her soul just waiting to be let out.

The sticks went up in a shower of sparks, almost before she thought of it, and reality at once yawed at her feet. The infinite darkness of this place already weighed on her; now it felt a hundred times worse.

Her shaking hand crept to the lump in her clothes, where the domovaya had sewn the wooden nightingale. Her hand closed around it. It felt like an anchor.

A light gleamed through the thick trees. Pozhar came out of the dark, mincing in the bracken. She shook her mane. *Stop making magic, foolish girl. You will be as mad as the old woman. It is easier than you'd think, to lose yourself in Midnight.* Her ears flicked. *If you go mad, I am leaving you here.*

"Please don't. I will try not to go mad," Vasya said hoarsely, and the mare snorted. Then she went to graze. Vasya stripped and began the tedious process of drying her clothes.

How she wanted to sleep now, and wake up in light. But she couldn't. So, she stood and paced naked, pinching her arms, going away from the fire so that the chill drove her to alertness.

She was standing, wondering if her clothes were dry enough to keep her from freezing, when she heard a squeal from Pozhar. She turned to see Midnight's black horse, almost indistinguishable from the night, step into the firelight.

"Have you brought your rider here to offer *more* advice?" Vasya asked the horse, not very kindly.

Don't be silly, said Pozhar to Vasya. *I called him. Voron.* She gave the black horse a wicked look, and the stallion licked his lips submissively. *The Swan is farther off than I thought, and Voron knows better than I how to get to her—he is more used to the ways of this place. I am getting tired of wandering about, especially when you make it hard for me to keep you in sight. At this speed, we aren't going to make it before you have to sleep.* She fixed Vasya with both ears. *Twice you have saved me: in Moscow and by the water. Now I will have saved you twice too, and there will be no more debt between us.*

"None," said Vasya with a surge of gratitude, and bowed.

The midnight-demon stalked into the firelight behind her horse, looking sour. Vasya knew that look. She had worn it herself, when Solovey badgered her into something. She almost laughed.

"Pozhar," said Midnight. "I have business far from here, and I cannot be—"

"Delayed because your horse is ignoring you?" interrupted Vasya.

Midnight gave her a venomous look.

"Well, then help me now," said Vasya. "And you can go about your business the sooner." The black horse twitched his heavy ears. Pozhar looked impatient. *Come on,* she said. *It was amusing at first, but I am tired of this darkness.*

A little reluctant humor came into Midnight's face. "What do you hope to do, Vasilisa Petrovna? He is trapped beyond recall, trapped in memory, in place, and in time: all three."

Vasya was frankly incredulous. "Am I so vain as to think that the winter-king would let himself be imprisoned for eternity for my sake? He is not a half-witted fairy-tale prince, and heaven knows I am not Yelena the Beautiful. So he must have had a reason, known there was a way out. Which means I *can* free him."

Midnight put her head to one side. "I thought you besotted, and that was why you were risking the depths of my realm for his sake. But it's not that, is it?"

"No," said Vasya.

Now the midnight-demon looked resigned. "Better put your boots on." She eyed Vasya's half-dry clothes critically. "You are going to be cold."

IT DID GROW COLD. The first Vasya felt of it was frost-crystals break-ing under her boots, as she stepped between midnights. The green smell of summer took on a wilder, earthy note; the stars grew sharp as sword-points, where they were not caught fast in racing clouds. The soft rustling of summer leaves became a dry rattle, and then nothing: only bare trees against the sky. And then between one midnight and another, Vasya's feet broke through a crust of wet snow. Ded Grib halted abruptly. "I cannot go on; I will wither." He eyed the white stuff with terror.

Vasya knelt before the little mushroom-spirit. "Can you go back to the lake alone? I have to go on."

He looked miserable. His sickly green glow wavered. "I can always go back to the lake. But I promised."

"You kept your promise. You found me food, you found me after the flood." She touched his head, gave him another piece of bread from her basket. She said, on sudden inspiration, "Perhaps you could talk to the other chyerti for me. Tell them that I—that I—"

Ded Grib brightened. "I know what I will tell them," he said.

That was somewhat worrying. She opened her mouth, thought better of it. "All right," she said. "But—"

"Are you sure *you* won't go back to the lake?" asked Ded Grib. He gave the snow a look of loathing. "It is dark and cold and the ground is hard."

"I cannot. Not yet," said Vasya. "But one day. When this is over. Perhaps you can show me where the lisichki grow."

"Very well," said Ded Grib sadly. "Mind you tell anyone who asks that I was first." He disappeared, not without a few backward glances.

Vasya straightened, and peered ahead. Winter midnights spread out before them: cold copses, ice-choked streams, and perhaps dangers she couldn't see, hidden in the darkness. A chill wind raced down over them, so that Pozhar, in her summer coat, switched her tail and flattened her ears.

"Are we deep in your country now?" Vasya asked Polunochnitsa.

"Yes," she said. "These are the winter midnights, and we started in summer."

"The domovaya said I couldn't get back," said Vasya. "If the season turned."

"In the lands by the lake," returned Polunochnitsa. "But this is Midnight. You can go anywhere you wish, in Midnight. Any place, any season. Except that, so far from where you began, you must not fall asleep."

"Let's go on then," said Vasya, with a glance at the frozen sky.

They walked on in silence. Occasionally there would be a chink, as Pozhar's hoof struck a rock beneath the snow. But that was all. They passed like ghosts over the silent earth.

One instant, they would be walking through cloud-torn darkness, but the next moment, the moon would beam down, almost too bright for Vasya's night-adjusted eyes. Then a great gust of wind would tear at her hair. It was getting even colder as they walked, the land wilder. Snow stung her face.

Once Polunochnitsa said, abruptly, "If you had tried to use your own bond to the winter-king you would have died quickly, lost. You were right; it is too capricious, mortal to immortal, and there are too many half-truths between you. But I never—the Bear never—thought of the horses."

Vasya said, "There is no bond at all now, between me and the winter-king. The necklace was destroyed."

"None at all?" Midnight looked amused.

"Misplaced longing was all there ever was," Vasya insisted. "I do not love him."

To that Midnight made no answer.

Vasya wished they could linger, for she began to get glimpses of things far off; of cities in festival, on high hilltops, where the shrieks of revelers by torchlight came clearly to her ears.

"There are farther, stranger countries," said Midnight. "Places you would have to journey long in the dark to get to. Places that you might never be able to get to, for your soul could not comprehend them. Places that are not a part of your lifetime of midnights; they are from when your earliest ancestor was born, or when your furthest grandchildren will die. Even I cannot get to all of them. By that I know that one day I will cease to exist, and not every midnight in the life of the world will know my hand."

Vasya felt a little thrill, deep inside her. "I would like to see the far reaches of your country," she said. "To feast in strange cities, break midnight bread in a bathhouse before a wedding, or see the moon on the sea."

Midnight glanced sideways at her. "You are a strange girl, to want that danger. And you have much to do before you can think of journeying, in Midnight or anywhere."

"And yet, I will think of the future," Vasya retorted. "To remind me that the present is not forever. One day I may see my brother Alyosha again, and my sister Irina. I might have a home of my own, a place and a purpose, a victory. What is the present without the future?"

"I do not know," said Midnight. "Immortals have no future: only now. It is our blessing and great curse."

It was growing steadily colder. Vasya began to shiver. Big, frosty stars showed overhead; the sky was clear through the leafless trees. Now her feet broke through deep snow with every step. Vasya began to stumble, dazed with tiredness. Only fear kept her awake.

Finally, Voron and Pozhar stopped. A slim creek, blue with ice, lay before them. Beyond that stood a small, palisaded village. It was a perfectly clear winter night. The stars lay overhead thickly as water slopped from a careless bucket.

The houses had holes for the smoke, not chimneys. The places under the eaves were carved but not painted, and the palisade was low and simple; designed to keep cows and children in, not marauders out. Strangest of all: there was no church. Vasya, in all her life, had never seen a community without a church; it was like seeing a person with no head. "Where are we?" she asked.

"The place you sought."

16

The chains of the Winter-King

"MOROZKO IS HERE?" VASYA ASKED. "*THIS* IS A PRISON FOR A frost-demon?"

"Yes," said Midnight.

Vasya eyed the village. What *here* could keep the winter-king imprisoned? "The white mare—the swan—is she close?" she asked Pozhar.

The mare lifted her golden head. *Yes,* she said. *But she is afraid. She has been waiting for him a long time in the dark. I am going to find her. She needs me.*

"Very well," said Vasya. She laid a hand on Pozhar's neck. The mare didn't even bite. "Thank you. When you see the white mare, tell her I am going to try and save him."

Pozhar stamped. *I will tell her.* She wheeled and galloped away, skimming the snow and melting it, the cut on her leg almost mended already.

"Thank you," said Vasya to Polunochnitsa.

"You are going to your death, Vasilisa Petrovna," said Midnight. But there was doubt now in her voice. Her black stallion arched his neck and blew softly; she scratched his withers, frowning.

"Even then," said Vasya. "Thank you." She began to make her painstaking way toward the village. She could feel Midnight watching her go. Just before she was out of earshot, Midnight called, as though she could not help it, "Go to the great house. But tell no one who you are."

Vasya glanced back, nodded, and walked on.

She would have expected Morozko's prison to look something like the Bear's clearing. Or perhaps a locked and guarded tower and he confined, like a princess, at the top of it. At least, she would have expected it to be a summer place: one where he was faint, powerless. But this was just a village. In winter. Gardens slept under snow; beasts drowsed in their warm stables. A single house in the very center streamed noise and light. Smoke poured from a hole in the roof. She could smell meat roasting.

How could Morozko be here?

Vasya climbed the palisade and crept toward the great house.

She was quite near when the fresh-fallen snow of its dooryard quivered and a chyert emerged. Vasya halted abruptly. It was the dvorovoi, the dooryard-guardian, and he was not tiny, like all the other dvoroviye she had ever known. He was as tall as she, his eyes fierce.

Vasya bowed, with wary respect.

"Stranger, what are you doing here?" he growled.

Her mouth and throat were dry, but she managed, "Grandfather, I am here for the feasting." Not quite a lie. She was hungry; Ded Grib's camp-rations seemed an age ago.

Silence. Then the dvorovoi said, "You have come a long way, only for the feasting."

"I am also here for the winter-king," she admitted, low. It was difficult to deceive a house-spirit, and unwise to try.

The dvorovoi's eyes measured her. She held her breath. "Go through the door then," he said simply, and vanished once more into the snow.

Could it be so simple? Impossible. But Vasya walked toward the door. Once she had loved feasts. Now all she heard was too much noise, all she smelled was fire. With an odd detachment, she looked down at her hand, realized that it was shaking.

Gathering her courage, she went up the stairs, between bars of lamplight. A dog began to bark. Then another, a third, a whole chorus. Next moment, the door opened, creaking in the cold.

But it was not a man who came out, or, what Vasya had feared, several men, with blades. It was a woman, alone. She was accompanied by a torrent of warm, smoky air, rich with the smell of cooking.

Vasya stood still, her whole being bent on not fleeing into the shadows.

The woman's hair was the color of good bronze. Her eyes were like amber beads; she was almost as tall as Vasya. The grivna on her throat was gold; gold there was too on her wrists and ears, set on her belt, plaited in her hair.

Vasya knew how she must look to this woman: wild-eyed after the long darkness, lips trembling with cold and terror, clothes crackling with frost. She tried to sound eminently sane when she said, "God be with you," but her voice was hoarse and faint.

"The domovoi said we had a visitor," the woman said. "Who are you, stranger?"

The domovoi? Can she hear——? "I am a traveler," Vasya said. "I came to ask supper and a place for the night."

"What is a maiden doing, traveling alone at Midwinter? And dressed so?"

So much for her boy's clothes. Vasya said carefully, "The world is not kind to a maiden alone. Safer to dress as a boy."

The frown between the woman's eyes deepened. "You have no sling, no pack, no beast. You are not dressed to spend even one night out of doors. Where have you come from, girl?"

"From the forest," Vasya improvised. "I fell into the river and lost all I had."

It was almost the truth. The woman's brows drew together. "Then why——" She paused. "Can you *see?*" she asked in a different voice. She looked suddenly half-afraid, half-eager.

Vasya knew what she meant. *Tell no one who you are.* "No," she said at once.

The eager light faded from the woman's eyes. She sighed. "Well, it was too much to hope for. Come, there are lords visiting from all about, and their servants; you will not be noticed. You may eat in the hall, and have a warm place to sleep."

"Thank you," said Vasya.

The tawny woman opened the door. "I am Yelena Tomislavna," she said. "The lord is my brother. Come."

Vasya, heart beating very fast, followed her in. She could feel the dvorovoi at her back. Watching.

YELENA CAUGHT THE SHOULDER of a servant. A few words passed between them. All Vasya heard was "get back to our guest" from Yelena. A strange expression of sympathy crossed the face of the old servant.

Then the servant bustled Vasya into a cellar full of chests, bundles, and barrels. Muttering to herself, she began to rummage. "No harm will come to you here, poor maiden," she said. "Take off those clothes; I will find you something proper."

Vasya debated arguing, realized that it might get her thrown out. "As you say, babushka," she said and began to strip. "But I would like to keep my old clothes."

"Well, of course," said the old servant kindly. "Never fling away wantonly." Eyeing Vasya's bruises, she clucked and said, "Husband or father's handiwork, I care not. Bold girl, to dress as a boy and run away." She turned Vasya's cut face to the light, frowned dubiously. "Perhaps, if you stay here and work hard, the lord will give you a little dowry, and you may find a new husband."

Vasya wasn't sure whether to laugh or be vexed. The servant thrust a coarse linen shift over Vasya's head. Over that went a length of cloth, hanging loose front and back, then belted. Bast shoes for her feet. The servant patted Vasya's cropped black head and produced a kerchief. "What were you thinking, child, to cut your hair?"

"I was traveling as a boy," Vasya reminded her. "Safer." She slipped the wooden nightingale into the sleeve of her shift. The clothes smelled of onion and their previous owner, but they were warm.

"Come into the hall," the servant said, after a pitying silence. "I will find you some supper."

THE SMELL OF THE FEAST hit her first: of sweat and honey-wine and fat meat roasted in a great pit of coals at the center of a long hall. The room was packed with people, richly dressed; their ornaments gleamed copper and gold in the smoke-haze. The heat went up, making the air dance, to a hole in the center of the roof. A single star gleamed in the blackness, swallowed by the rising smoke. Servants bore in baskets of fresh bread, dusted with snow. Vasya, trying to peer in every direction at once, nearly tripped over a bitch-hound that had retired, growling, to a corner with her litter and a bone.

The serving-woman pushed Vasya down onto a bench. "Stay here," she said, intercepting a loaf and a cup. "Sup at your leisure, and see what you can of the great folk. There will be feasting until dawn." She seemed to mark the girl's nerves, and added kindly, "No harm will come to you. You'll be put to work soon enough." With that she was gone. Vasya was left alone with her meal and a head full of questions.

"It is the lord's sister herself he wants," said one man to another, hurrying past, stepping on one of the bitch-hound's nursing puppies.

"Nonsense," said his fellow, with a heavy, measured sort of voice. "She is to marry; *he* will not give her up even to the winter-king."

"He will not have a choice," said the first voice, significantly.

Vasya thought, *Morozko is here then*. Frowning, she tucked the bread into her sleeve and got to her feet. The food made a small, comforting weight in her stomach. Wine heated her limbs and loosened them.

No one marked her rising; no one even glanced her way. Why should they?

Just then, the crowd parted, and gave her a look at the folk around the fire-pit.

Morozko was there.

Her breath stilled in her throat.

She thought, *That is no prisoner.*

He sat in the best place, near the fire. The flames gilded his face, cast dazzles of gold on the curling darkness of his hair. He was dressed like a prince: jacket and shirt both stiff with embroidery; fur about cuffs and collar.

Their eyes met.

But his face did not change; he showed no sign of recognition. He turned his head away to speak to someone sitting beside him. Then the gap in the crowd closed quick as it had opened. Vasya was left shaken, craning her head in vain.

What keeps him here, if not force?

Had he truly not known her?

The bitch on the floor growled. Vasya, whom the crowd was pushing nearer and nearer the wall, found herself trying not to step on the creature. "Could you not nurse in a quieter spot?" she asked the dog, and then a man stumbled into her, drunk.

Vasya lurched into the wall, sending the bitch up snapping. The man pinned her against the smoke-darkened wood. Clumsy with drink, he ran a hand down Vasya's body. "Well, you've eyes like green pools at twilight," he said, slurring. "But doesn't your mistress feed you at all?"

He poked a clumsy forefinger against the side of her breast, as though bent on finding out for himself. His open mouth descended on hers.

Vasya felt her heartbeat quick and furious against the man's chest. Without a word, she threw all her weight at him, heedless of the strain on her still-sore ribs, and slipped out from between man and wall.

He nearly went over. She tried to disappear into the crowd, but the man recovered, seized her arm and wrenched her back around. A look of injured pride had replaced his smile. All about them, heads turned. "Treat me like that?" he said. "On Midwinter night, too! What man would want you, frog-mouthed little weasel?" He looked crafty. "Get you gone. They will be wanting mead there at the high table."

Vasya didn't speak but reached for the memory of fire. The flames in the fire-pit blazed up, crackling. Those nearest drew back from the heat; the whole crowd heaved. Thrown off balance, the man's grip loosened. Vasya pulled away from him, melted into the crowd. The heat and the reek of tight-packed people sickened her; blindly she made for the door and stumbled out into the night.

For long moments, she stood in the snow, heaving for breath. The night was pure and cold; eventually she calmed.

She didn't want to go back in.

But Morozko was there, somehow imprisoned. She must get closer; she must discover the nature of his chain.

Then she thought, perhaps the man was right. What better way to go near the winter-king unremarked than as a servant bearing wine?

She took one last breath of the icy night. The scent of winter seemed to linger about her, like a promise.

She plunged back into the maelstrom inside. She was dressed as a servant; it was not difficult to acquire a wineskin. Carrying it carefully, feeling the strain of the weight in her battered body, Vasya slipped through the masses of people in the hall and came to the central fire-pit.

The winter-king sat nearest the flames.

The breath stilled in Vasya's throat.

Morozko's head was bare; the fire gilded the blackness of his hair. His eyes were a depthless and beautiful blue. But when their eyes met, there was still no recognition in his.

His eyes were—young?

Young?

Vasya had last seen him, frail as a snowflake, his gaze impossibly old, in the inferno of burning Moscow. *Call the snow,* she had begged him. *Call the snow.* He had, and then faded away with the dawn.

His last words, a reluctant confession. *As I could, I loved you.* She would never forget how he'd looked then. His expression, the impress of his hands, were seared into her memory.

But not in his memory. The years had disappeared from his gaze. She did not know how great the weight of them had been, until she could see them gone.

His idle glance found Vasya's, strayed away, lit on the woman beside him. Yelena wore an expression caught between fear and—something else. She was beautiful. The gold on her wrists and throat gleamed dully in the firelight. As Vasya watched, Morozko bent his wild, dark head to murmur into Yelena's ear, and she leaned nearer to hear him.

What could imprison a frost-demon? Vasya thought, suddenly angry. Love? Lust? Is that why he was here, when all Rus' was in peril? A woman with golden hair? He was so obviously here because he wished to be.

And yet, Rus' was in peril because Morozko had yielded up his freedom to save her from the fire. *Why did he do that? Why? And how can he have forgotten?*

Then she thought, *If I wanted to imprison someone until the end of days, would it not be best to use a prison that he has no desire to escape? Here in this place, this midnight, humankind can see him; they fear him and they love him in equal measure. What more can he want? What more has he ever wanted in all the years of his life?*

All these thoughts passed swiftly through her brain, and then Vasya collected herself and approached the place where the winter-king sat beside the lord's sister. She held the wineskin before her like a shield.

The frost-demon bent again to the woman, breathing more words into her ear.

A sudden movement drew Vasya's eye. Another man was watching the pair from the other side of the fire-pit. His embroidery and his ornaments indicated rank; his eyes were great and dark with pain. The sudden movement had been the involuntary dart of his hand to his sword-hilt. As Vasya watched, he let it go again, finger by finger.

Vasya did not know what to make of it.

Her feet carried her nearer the winter-king and the tawny woman beside him. She supposed that she was meant to drop her eyes, fill the cups, and scurry away. But instead she walked forward without affectation, her eyes on the eyes of the frost-demon.

He glanced up, and then, looking amused, watched her come forward.

At the last second, Vasya lowered her gaze and tipped her skin to fill the cups.

A thin, cold, familiar hand closed on her wrist. Vasya jerked back, splashing mead over them all.

Yelena managed to turn, keeping the wine from her gown. Then she recognized Vasya. "Go back," she said to Vasya. "It is not your task to serve us, girl." It seemed to Vasya that she was conveying a warning behind the words: Morozko, proud, young, death in his long hands, was dangerous.

He had not tried to retain her wrist when she jerked away from him. She was sure now that he did not know her. Whatever bond they'd shared—hunger, reluctant passion—that was gone.

"Forgive me," Vasya said to the woman. "I only wished to repay your hospitality."

Her eyes did not leave the eyes of the frost-demon. His glance, without hurry and without admiration, traced her cropped hair, her thin face, her body. She felt her color rise.

"I do not know you," Morozko said.

"I know that you don't," said Vasya. Yelena stiffened, either at Vasya's words or the tone of them. Morozko glanced at Vasya's arm. She looked too, saw the skin marked white where he'd touched her. "Have you come to ask a favor of me?" he asked.

"Do you mean to grant me one?" asked Vasya.

Yelena said sharply, "Little fool, go away."

Still no flicker of recognition in the frost-demon's eyes, but he put out a single finger and touched the inner part of her wrist. Vasya felt her heartbeat quicken under his fingers, though only a little. The tread of her heart had looked upon life and death and things in between without yet faltering.

Morozko's glance was quite cold. "Ask," he said.

"Come away with me," said Vasya. "My people have need of you."

Horror, shock, on Yelena's face.

He only laughed. "My people are here."

"Yes," she said. "And elsewhere too. You have forgotten."

The cold fingers released her abruptly. "I forget nothing."

Vasya said, "If I am lying, winter-king, then why would I risk my life to come before you in this hall at Midwinter?"

"Why are you not afraid of me?" He did not try to touch her again, but an icy wind stirred the hall, blueing the firelight and dampening the talk.

Yelena wrapped her arms about herself; a hush rippled through the raucous crowd. Vasya almost laughed. Was *that* supposed to make her afraid? Blue fire? After everything else?

"I am not afraid to die," she said. She wasn't. She had walked down that road. There was nothing in its cold stillness, the great sweep of stars, that could frighten her. Suffering was for the living. "Why should I fear you?"

His eyes narrowed. Vasya realized what a stillness had gathered about the fire, like the birds when a hawk comes soaring. "Why indeed?" Morozko said, holding her gaze. "Fools are often brave, for they do not understand. Leave us, girl, as your mistress bids. I will honor your courage, and forget your foolishness." He turned away.

Yelena sagged; she looked caught between disappointment and relief.

Not knowing what to do, Vasya slipped back into the crowd, her hand sticky with mead, her wrist tingling where his hand had lingered. How could she make him remember?

"Did she displease you, lord?" Vasya heard Yelena ask, with curiosity and censure mingled.

"No," said the frost-demon. She could feel him watching her go. "But I have never met anyone who was not afraid."

The people drew away from Vasya when she came among them, as though she were stricken with some sickness. The old serving-woman hustled up behind her, seized her elbow, relieved her of the wineskin and growled in her ear, "Mad thing, what possessed you to approach the winter-king so? It is the lady who gives him mead. She takes his gaze upon herself; that is her task. Do you not know what happens to girls that catch his eye?"

Vasya, feeling suddenly cold, asked, "What happens?"

"He might have chosen you, you know," muttered the woman just as Yelena rose to her feet. She was pale, but composed.

A deadly hush fell.

The blood began to beat in Vasya's ears. In the fairy tale, a father took his daughters into the forest and left them there, first one, then the other: brides of the king of winter. The winter-king sent one home with her dowry.

He killed the other.

Once they strangled maidens in the snow, Morozko had said. *To court my blessing.*

Once? Or now? Which midnight is this? Vasya had heard the fairy tale, but she had never imagined it: a woman separated from her people, the frost-demon vanished into the forest.

Vanished, but not alone.

Once he'd been nourished on sacrifices.

Morozko and Medved were alike once, she thought, her lips cold. In the winter-king's face was a clear and unthinking joy, the hawk's hunger when he tears the rabbit to pieces. He got to his feet, took the woman's hand.

All around, a new tension began to build.

Into the silence came a single sound; the ringing chime of a drawn sword. Heads turned; it was the man with dark eyes, who had not been able to keep his hand from his sword-hilt. His face was naked with agony.

"No," he said, "take another; you shall not have her." Many hands tried to hold him back, but he broke their grip, hurled himself forward, and swung his sword at the winter-king in a single, blind stroke.

Morozko held no weapon. But it didn't matter. With his bare hand, he caught the blade as it fell. A wrench and a twist and the sword clattered to the floor, sheathed with frost. The tawny woman cried out; the dark-eyed man blanched.

Morozko's hand streamed water like blood, but only for a moment. Frost crept over the cut place and sealed it.

The winter-king said softly, "You *dare.*"

Yelena fell to her knees. "Please," she begged. "Do not hurt him."

"Do not take her," pleaded the man, facing the winter-king with empty hands. "We need her. I need her."

Deathly silence.

Morozko, a line between his brows, might have hesitated.

In that moment, Vasya strode out into the open space herself. Her kerchief had fallen from her hair. All heads swiveled toward her.

She said, "Let them go, winter-king."

She was remembering Moscow, walking through the slush toward her own death. It was bitter memory that put the rage in her voice when she said, "Is this your power? Taking women from their fathers' halls at Midwinter? Killing their lovers too, when they try to prevent you?"

Her voice rang through the hall. Cries of anger rose. But none dared break into the ritual space nearest the fire-pit.

Yelena's hand crept out and took hold of the man's. Their knuckles were bone-white. "My lord," she breathed. "That is only a foolish girl, a mad girl, who came a beggar out of the snow on Midwinter night. Never mind her; I am the sacrifice for my people." But she did not let go of the man's hand.

Morozko was watching Vasya. "This girl doesn't think so," he said.

"No, I do not," snapped Vasya. "Choose me. Then take your sacrifice, if you can."

Everyone in the hall recoiled. But Morozko laughed; free and wild and so like the Bear that she flinched despite herself. In his eyes was a blaze of heedless joy. "Come here then," he said.

She did not move.

His eyes locked on hers. "Do you mean to *fight*, little maiden?"

"Yes," said Vasya. "If you want my blood, take it."

"Why should I, when there is another, fairer than you, waiting for me?"

Vasya smiled. Something of his unthinking joy—in challenge, in battle—echoed in her soul. "What pleasure in that, winter-king?"

"Very well," he said, drew a knife and lunged. When he moved, the knife caught the light with a wavering spark, as though the blade were made of ice.

Vasya backed up, her eyes on the weapon. Morozko had given Vasya her first knife and taught her how to use it. The way he moved was imprinted on her consciousness, but that patient teaching was a far cry from—

She seized a knife from the belt of one of the watchers. The man gaped at her, wordless. The knife was short-hafted: plain mortal iron against the winter-king's shimmering ice.

Vasya ducked Morozko's strike, and came up on the opposite side of the fire, cursing her rough shoes. She kicked them off, the floor icy on her feet.

The crowd fell silent, watching.

"Why come to me?" he asked her. "Are you so eager to die?"

"Judge for yourself," Vasya whispered.

"No—" he said. "Then why?"

"Because I thought I knew you."

His face hardened. He moved again, faster. She parried, but badly; his blade broke her guard and scoured her shoulder. Her sleeve tore, and blood ran down her arm. She could not match him. But she didn't need to. She only needed to make him remember. Somehow.

All about her, the crowd stood silent, watching like the wolf-ring when the hart is brought to bay.

The hot smell of her blood drove home to Vasya that this playacting was real to them. It had felt like a fairy tale to her, a game in a far-off country. Perhaps he would never remember her. Perhaps he would kill her. Midnight had known this would happen. *Well*, Vasya thought grimly, *I am the sacrifice after all*.

Not yet. Fury filled her; she drove suddenly beneath his guard, and dragged her knife in turn across his ribs. Cold water poured from the wound; a sound of hushed wonder came from the crowd.

He fell back. "Who are you?"

"I am a witch," said Vasya. Blood was running down her hand now, spoiling her grip. "I have plucked snowdrops at Midwinter, died at my own choosing, and wept for a nightingale. Now I am beyond prophecy." She caught his knife on the crosspiece of hers, hilt to hilt. "I have crossed three times nine realms to find you, my lord. And I find you at play, forgetful."

She felt him hesitate. Something deeper than memory ran through his eyes. It might have been fear.

"Remember me," said Vasya. "Once you bid me remember you."

"I am the winter-king," he said, and savagely, "What need have *I* for a girl's remembrance?" He moved again, not playing now. He forced her blade down, broke her guard; his knife cut through the tendons of her wrist. "I do not know you." He was immovable as winter, long before the thaw. In his words, she heard the echo of her failure.

And yet, his eyes were on her face. The blood ran off her fingertips. She forgot that the fire was not blue, and in an instant, it burst into brilliant gold. All the people cried out.

"You could remember me," she said. "If you tried." She touched him with her bloody hand.

He hesitated. She could have sworn he hesitated. But that was all. Her hand fell away. The Bear had won.

Tendrils of black mist crept around the edges of her vision. Her wrist was cut deeply, her hand useless, blood sliding down to bless the boards of this house.

"I came to find you," she said. "But if you do not remember me, then I have failed." There was a roaring in her ears. "If you ever see your horse again, tell her what happened to me." She swayed and fell, on the edge of consciousness.

He caught her before she fell. In his cold grip, she remembered a road from which there was no turning back, a road in a forest full of stars. She could have sworn he cursed, under his breath. Then she could feel his arm beneath her knees, beneath her shoulders, and he picked her up.

Carrying her, he strode out of the great feasting-hall.

17

Memory

S HE WASN'T UNCONSCIOUS, EXACTLY, BUT THE WORLD HAD GONE
gray and still. She smelled smoke-tinged night and pine. When she
tipped her head back she saw stars—a whole world of stars—as though
she flew between heaven and earth, like that wandering devil. The
frost-demon's feet did not groan in the snow, his breath made no plume
in the cold night. She heard the creak of cold-stiffened hinges. New
smells—fresh birch and fire and rot. She was deposited unceremoni-
ously onto something hard, and hissed when the shock of it jarred both
her bones and her bruises. She lifted her arm, and saw her hand sticky
with blood, the wrist cut deep.

Then she remembered. "Midnight," she gasped. "Is it still midnight?"

"It is still midnight." Candles flared suddenly: waxen lumps in
niches in the wall. Her gaze flew up and found the frost-demon watching her.

The air was hot and close. To her surprise, she saw they were in a
bathhouse. She tried to sit up, but she was bleeding too fast; it was a
struggle to stay conscious. Gritting her teeth, she reached to tear a strip
of her skirt, found that she could not with one hand useless.

Raising her head, she snapped at him, "Did you bring me here to
watch me bleed to death? You are going to be disappointed. I am getting used to spiting people by surviving."

"I can imagine," he returned mildly. He was standing over her. His gaze, sardonic, still curious, took in her damaged face, dropped to her bloody wrist. She was holding it in an iron grip, trying to halt the flow of blood. Her blood was on his cheek, on his robe, his white hands. He wore his power like another skin.

"Why a bathhouse?" she asked him, trying to control her breathing. "Only witches or wicked sorcerers go to a bathhouse at midnight."

"Appropriate then," he said, his voice dry. "And you are still not afraid? With your blood pouring out of you? Where have you come from, wanderer?"

"My secrets are my own," said Vasya, between gritted teeth.

"Yet you asked me for my help."

"I did," she said. "And you cut my wrist open."

"You knew that was going to happen the instant you challenged me."

"Very well," she said. "Wondering who I am? Then help me. Otherwise you will never know."

He did not answer, and when he moved she did not hear him, only felt a breath of cold air, strange in the heat of the room. He knelt before her. Their eyes met. She saw a flicker of unease run through him, as though some crack—some small crack—had opened in the wall of ice in his mind. Without a word, he cupped his hand; water pooled in the palm. He let the water fall into the wound on her wrist.

Where the water touched her raw flesh, pain blazed up. She bit the inside of her cheek to keep from screaming. The pain died as fast as it had risen, leaving her shaken, a little sick. The cut on her wrist was gone, and only a line of white remained, catching the light, as though ice were embedded in the scar.

"You are healed," he said. "Now tell me—" He fell silent. Vasya followed his gaze. There was another scar on her palm, where he had wounded her—and healed her—once before.

"I did not lie," said Vasya. "You know me."

He did not speak.

"You once tore my hand with yours," she went on. "Smeared your fingers in my blood. Later, you healed the mark you'd made. Can't you remember? Remember the dark, the dead thing, the night I went into the forest for snowdrops?"

He got to his feet. "Tell me who you are."

Vasya forced herself to stand as well, though she was still light-headed. He took a step back. "I am called Vasilisa Petrovna. Do you believe now that I know you? I think you do. You are afraid."

"Of a wounded maiden?" He was scornful.

Sweat rolled down the hollow of her spine. A fire in the inner room snapped fingers of flame, and even there in the outer room, it was hot. "If you do *not* mean to kill me," said Vasya, "and you do not remember me, then why are we here? What can the lord of winter have to say to a servant-girl?"

"You are no more a servant-girl than I am."

"At least I am not a prisoner in this village," said Vasya. She was near enough to catch his gaze and hold it.

"I am a king," he said. "They make a feast in my honor; they give me sacrifices."

"Prisons are not always made of walls and chains. Do you mean to spend eternity feasting, lord?"

His expression was cold. "A single night only."

"Eternity," she said. "You have forgotten that too."

"If I cannot remember, then it is not eternity to me." He was getting angry. "What matter? They are my people. You are only a madwoman, come to plague good people on Midwinter night."

"At least I wasn't planning to kill any of them!"

He did not reply, but cold air rushed through the bathhouse, setting the candle-flames to swaying. There was little space in that outer room; they were almost shouting in each other's faces. The crack in his defenses widened. She could not reason away whatever magic kept him forgetful. But emotion dragged his memory a little nearer the surface. So did her touch. So did her blood. The feeling between them was still there. He did not need to remember; he felt it, just as she did.

And he had brought her here. Despite all he'd said, he had brought her here.

Her skin felt thin, as though a breath would bruise it. Vasya had always been reckless in battle; that same recklessness had her in its grip now. *Deeper than memory,* she thought. *Mother of God, forgive me.*

She reached out. Her hand with its white scars paused a breath from his cheek; his hand shot up, his fingers closed on her wrist. For a second they stood motionless. Then his grip slackened, and she touched his face, the fine, ageless bones. He didn't move.

Low, Vasya said, "If I may defer my death an hour, winter-king, I am going to bathe. Since you have brought me to a bathhouse."

He did not react, but his stillness was answer enough.

THE INNER ROOM WAS utterly dark, save for the glow of the hot stones in its oven. Vasya left him standing behind her. She was shaken by her own temerity. In a life littered with questionable decisions, she wondered if she was doing the most foolish thing she'd ever done.

Determinedly, she stripped off her clothes, laid them in a corner. She ladled water on the rocks and sat, arms wrapped about her knees. But the blissful languor of the heat could not overtake her. She did not know if she was more afraid that he would go away or that he wouldn't.

He slipped through the door. She could barely see him in the dark; only knew his presence by the shift of the steam as he moved through it.

She lifted her chin, to hide sudden fright, and said, "Won't you melt?"

He looked affronted. But then, unexpectedly, he laughed. "I will try not." He sank with undiminished grace onto the bench opposite her, leaned on his knees, his hands laced together. Her glance lingered on his long fingers.

His skin was paler than hers; he made nothing of nakedness. His stare was cool and frank. "You had a long road," he said. She could not see his eyes in the shadows, but felt his gaze like a hand. Whatever he had not seen of her skin before, he was seeing it now.

"And it is not over," she said. With unsteady fingers, she touched the scab on her cheek, raised her eyes to his, wondered if she was hideous, wondered if it mattered. Still he didn't move. The faint light lit him in pieces: a shoulder, a hollow beneath the ribs. She realized that she was considering him, throat to feet, and that he was watching her do so. She blushed.

"Will you not tell me your secret?" he asked.

"What secret?" retorted Vasya, laboring to keep her voice steady. His hands were motionless, but his glance still traced the lines of her body. "I already told you. My people have need of you."

He shook his head, raised his eyes to hers. "No, there is something more. Something there in your face every time you look at me."

As I could, I loved you.

"My secrets are mine, Gosudar," said Vasya sharply. "We sacrifices may take things to the grave as well as anyone else."

He lifted a brow. "I have never met a maiden who looked less like she meant to die."

"I don't," said Vasya. Still short of breath, she added, "I did want a bath, though, and I am getting one; that is something."

He laughed again, and their eyes caught.

Him too, Vasya thought. *He is afraid too. For he knows no more than I where this will end.*

Yet he brought me here, he stayed. He wounded me and healed me. He remembers, and he doesn't.

Before she could lose her nerve, Vasya slipped off the bench and knelt between his knees. His skin had not warmed with the steam. Even in the smoke-smelling bathhouse, the scent of pine, of cold water hung about him. His face did not change, but his breathing quickened. Vasya realized she was trembling. Once again, she reached up, touched her palm to his face.

A second time, he caught her wrist. But this time, his mouth grazed the scar in the hollow of her hand.

They looked at each other.

Her stepmother had liked to frighten her and Irina with tales of wedding-night horrors; Dunya had assured her that it was not quite so.

It felt like the wildness would burn her up from the inside out.

He traced her lower lip with his thumb. She could not read his expression. "Please," she said, or thought she said, just as he closed the distance between them and kissed her.

The fire was barely embers in the stove, but they didn't need the light. His skin was cool under her hands; her sweat streaked them both. She was shivering all over; she didn't know what to do with her hands. It was too much: skin and spirit, hunger and her desperate loneliness, and the rising tide of feeling between them.

Perhaps he felt the uncertainty beneath the desire, for he broke off, looking at her. The only sound was their breathing, his as harsh as hers.

"Afraid *now?*" he whispered. He had pulled her with him onto the wooden bench; she was sitting crosswise in his lap, one of his arms about her waist. His free hand drew lines of cool fire on her skin, from ear to shoulder, followed her collarbone, dipped between her breasts. She could not control her breathing.

"I'm supposed to be frightened," Vasya snapped, sharper than was warranted because she was, in fact, frightened, and angry too because she could barely think, let alone speak, while his hand came up again, and this time slid down her spine, curved lightly around her ribs, found her breast and lingered there. "I am a maiden. And you—" She trailed off.

The light hand stilled. "Afraid I will hurt you?"

"Do you mean to?" she asked. They both heard the tremor in her voice. Naked in his arms, she was more vulnerable than she'd ever been.

But he was afraid too. She felt it in the restrained tension of his touch, could see it now in his black-shadowed eyes.

Again, they looked at each other.

Then he half-smiled, and Vasya realized suddenly what the other feeling was, beneath the fear and desire rising between them.

It was mad joy.

His hand shaped the curve of her waist. He drew her mouth down to his again. His answer was more breath than word, breathed into her ear.

"No, I will not hurt you," he said.

"Vasya," he said into the darkness.

They had made it into the outer room, in the end. When he'd drawn her down to the floor, it was onto a mound of heaped blankets that smelled like the winter forest. They were beyond speech by then, but it didn't matter. She didn't need words to call him back to her. Only the slide of her fingers, the heat of her bruised skin. His hands remembered her, when his mind did not. It was in his touch, easing over her half-healed wounds; it was in his grip, and the look in his eyes, before the candles burned low.

Afterward, lying half-drowsing in the dark, she could still feel the pulse of his body in hers, and taste the pine on her lips.

Then she jerked upright. "Is it still——?"

"Midnight," he said. He sounded weary. "Yes, it is midnight. I will not let you lose it."

His voice had changed. He'd said her name.

She rose on one elbow, felt herself blushing. "You remembered."

He said nothing.

"You set the Bear loose to save my life. Why?"

Still he said nothing.

"I came to find you," she said. "I learned to do magic. I got the help of the firebird, you didn't kill me—*stop looking at me like that.*"

"I did not mean——" he began, and just like that she was angry, to mask a gathering hurt.

He sat up, drew away from her, the line of his spine stiff in the near-dark.

"I wanted it," she said to his back, trying not to think of every notion of decency she had ever been taught. Chastity, patience, lie with men only for the bearing of children, and above all do not enjoy it. "I thought—I thought you did too. And you——" She couldn't say it; instead she said, "You remembered. A small enough price, for that." It didn't feel small.

He turned so she could see his face; he didn't look as though he believed her. Vasya wished now she were not sitting naked, a hands-breadth away from him.

He said, "I thank you."

Thank you? The words struck coldly, after the last hours' heat. *Maybe you wish you did not remember,* she thought. *Part of you was happy here, feared and beloved, in this prison.* She didn't say it.

"The Bear is free in Rus'," said Vasya instead. "He has set the dead to walking. We must help my cousin, help my brother. I came to get your help."

Still Morozko said nothing. He had not drawn further away from her, but his glance had turned inward, remote, unreadable.

She added with sudden anger, "You owe us your help; you are the reason that the Bear is free in the first place. You didn't need to bargain with him. I walked out of the pyre myself."

A little light came into his face. "I wondered if you would. But it was still worth it. When you drew me back to Moscow, I knew then."

"Knew what?"

"That you could be a bridge between men and chyerti. Keep us from fading, keep men from forgetting. That we weren't doomed after all, if you lived, if you came into your power. And I had no other way to save you. I—deemed it worth the risk, whatever came after."

"You might have trusted me to save myself."

"You meant to die. I saw it in you."

She flinched. "Yes," she said softly. "I suppose I did mean to die. Solovey had fallen; he died under my hands, and—" She broke off. "But my horse would have called me foolish to give up. So, I changed my mind."

The wild simplicity of the night was fading into endless complications. She had never imagined that he'd set his realm and his freedom at hazard purely for love of her. Part of her had wondered anyway, but of course he was king of a hidden kingdom, and he could not make his decision so. It was the power in her blood he'd wanted.

She was tired and cold and she ached.

She felt more alone than before.

Then she was angry at her own self-pity. For cold there was a remedy, and damn this new awkwardness between them. She slid again beneath the heavy, heaped-up blankets, turned her back to him. He did not move. She balled her body up on itself, trying to get warm alone.

A hand, light as a snowflake, brushed her shoulder. Tears had gathered in her eyes; she tried to blink them away. It was too much: his presence, cold and quiet, the reasonable and practical explanations, to contrast with the overwhelming memory of passion.

"No," he said. "Do not grieve tonight, Vasya."

"You would never have done it," she said, not looking at him. "This——" A vague gesture took in the bathhouse, them. "If you had been able to remember who I was. You would never have saved my life if I hadn't been—if I hadn't been——"

His hand left her shoulder. "I tried to let you go," he said. "Again and again I tried. Because every time I touched you—even looked at you—it drew me nearer to mortality. I was afraid. And yet, I could not." He broke off, continued. "Perhaps if you hadn't been what you are, I would have found it in myself to let you die. But—I heard you scream. Through all the mists of my weakness, after the fire in Moscow, I heard you. I told myself I was being practical, I told myself you were our last hope. I told myself that. But I thought of you in the fire."

Vasya turned to face him. He shut his lips tight, as though he'd said more than he wished.

"And now?" she asked.

"We are here," he said simply.

"I am sorry," she said. "I didn't know how else to bring you back."

"There was no other way. Why do you think my brother had such faith in his prison? He knew of no tie strong enough to draw me back to myself. Nor did I."

Morozko didn't sound happy about it. It occurred to Vasya that he might feel just as she did: raw. She put out a hand. He did not look at her, but his fingers closed about hers.

"I am still afraid," he said. It was a truth, baldly offered. "I am glad you are alive. I am glad to see you again, against all hope. But I do not know what to do."

"I am afraid too," she said.

His fingertips found her wrist, where the blood surged against her skin. "Are you cold?"

She was. But . . .

"I think," he said wryly, "all things considered, we should be able to share the same blankets a few hours more."

"We must go," said Vasya. "There is too much to do; there is not time."

"An hour or three won't make a great difference, in this country of Midnight," said Morozko. "You are all worn to shadows, Vasya."

"It will make a difference," she said. "I can't fall asleep, here."

"You can now," he said. "I will keep you in Midnight."

To sleep—to really sleep . . . Mother of God, she was weary. She was already beneath the blankets; after a moment, he slid beneath them too. Her breath came short; she clenched her fists on an impulse to touch him.

They watched each other, warily. He moved first. His hand stole up to her face, traced the sharp line of her jaw, brushed the thick line of the scab from the stone. She shut her eyes.

"I can heal this for you," he said.

She nodded once, vain enough to be glad that at least there would be only a white scar instead of a scarlet one. He cupped his hand, trickled water onto her cheek, while she set her teeth against the flare of agony.

"Tell me," he said, after.

"It is a long story."

"I assure you," he said. "I will not grow old in the telling of it."

She told him. She started with the moment he'd left her in the snowstorm in Moscow and finished with Pozhar, Vladimir, her journey into Midnight. She was wrung out at the end, but calmer too. As though she'd laid the skeins of her life out neatly, and there was less of a tangle in her soul.

When she fell silent, he sighed. "I am sorry," he said. "For Solovey. I could only watch."

"And send me your mad brother," she pointed out. "And a token. I could have done without your brother, but the carving—comforted me."

"Did you keep it?"

"Yes," she said. "It brings him back when I—" She trailed off; it was too fresh, still.

He tucked a short curl behind her ear, but said nothing.

"Why are you afraid?" she asked him.

His hand dropped. She did not think he would answer. When he did, it was so low she barely caught the words. "Love is for those who know the griefs of time, for it goes hand in hand with loss. An eternity, so burdened, would be a torment. And yet—" He broke off, drew breath. "Yet what else to call it, this terror and this joy?"

It was harder this time, to move close to him. Before, it was— uncomplicated, reckless, joyful. But now emotion freighted the air between them.

His skin had warmed with hers, beneath the blankets; he might have been a man except for his eyes, ancient and troubled. It was her turn to push his hair back where it fell over his brow; it curled coarse and cold beneath her fingers. She touched the warm place behind his jaw, and the hollow of his throat, laid her spread fingers on his chest.

He covered her hand with his, traced her fingers, her arm, then her shoulder, slid his hand from spine to waist, as though he meant to learn her body by touch.

She made a sound in her throat. The coolness of his breathing touched her lips. She did not know if he had moved, or if she had, to bring them close together. And still his hand moved, gently, coaxing suppleness from her. She couldn't breathe. Now that they were no longer talking, she could feel the tension gathering in him—shoulder to hand—where his fingers dug into her skin.

One thing to take the wild stranger to herself. Another to look into the face of an adversary-ally-friend and . . .

She wound her fingers in his hair. "Come here," she said. "No— closer."

He smiled then: the slow, unknowable smile of the winter-king. But there was a hint of laughter in it she'd never seen. "Be patient," he murmured into her mouth.

But she could not, not an instant more; rather than answer, she caught him by the shoulders and rolled him over. She felt the strength in her body then, saw the shift and play of muscle in the faint candle-light: hers and his. She bent forward to breathe into his ear: "Never give me orders."

"Command me, then," he whispered back. The words went through her like wine.

Her body knew what to do then, even if her mind did not quite, and she took him into herself, snow and cold and power and years and that elusive fragility. He said her name once, and she barely heard, lost as she was. But after, when she lay pliant, curved into his body, she whispered, "You are not alone, anymore."

"I know," he whispered. "Neither are you."

And then, finally, she slept.

18

On the Backs of
Magic Horses

H E ROSE FROM THE TANGLED HEAP OF SNOW-COLORED FURS SOME unmarked hours later. She did not hear him go, but felt his absence. It was still midnight. She opened her eyes, shivering, and sat up. For an instant, she did not know where she was. Then she remembered and lurched to her feet, afraid. He was gone, he had vanished into the night, she had dreamed it all . . .

She seized hold of herself; would he really vanish without a word?

She didn't know. The madness had gone from her; she was only cold now, teeth set against a rush of shame. The voices of her upbringing sounded loud in her ears, all of them accusing.

Teeth sunk into her lower lip, she went to retrieve her clothes. Damn this shame, and damn the darkness. She turned her head, and light flared all at once from the candle in the wall-niche. Lighting it shook her not at all, as though her mind had accepted at last a world where she could make things burn.

Groping, she found her shift, drew it over her head. She was standing in the doorway between rooms, undecided and chilly, when the outer door opened.

The candlelight highlighted the bones of him, and filled his face with shadows. He had the bundle of her boy's clothes in his hands. She caught the sound of voices and crunching footsteps outside the bath-house.

Fear filled her, unbidden. "What is happening outside?"

He looked rueful. "I think that between us we have sealed the murky reputation of bathhouses."

Vasya said nothing. In her mind, she was hearing again the sound of the mob in Moscow.

She saw him understand. "You were alone then, Vasya," he said. "Now you are not." She had both hands on the inner doorframe, as if men were coming in to drag her out. "Even then, you still walked out of the fire."

"It cost me," she said, but the gnarled hand of fear loosened its grip on her throat.

"The village isn't angry," Morozko said. "They are delighted. There is power in this night." She felt a blush creeping along her cheekbones. "Do you wish to stay? It is hard for me to linger, now."

She paused. It must be like coming to a place that had been home, but wasn't anymore. Like trying to fit back into a skin already shed.

"Do your lands border my great-grandmother's?" Vasya asked him suddenly.

"They do," said Morozko. "How do you think my table once had strawberries for you, and pears and snowdrops?"

"So you knew the story?" she pressed. "Of the witch and her twin girls? You knew Tamara was my grandmother?"

"I did," he said. He looked wary now. "And before you ask, no, I never meant to tell you. Not until the night of the snowstorm in Moscow, and by then it was too late. The witch herself was either dead or lost in Midnight. No one knew what had become of the twins, and I could remember nothing of the sorcerer, who had made magic to set himself apart from death. All these things I learned later."

"And you thought me only a child, a tool to your purposes."

"Yes," he said. Whatever he thought or felt or hoped was buried deep, and locked tight. *I am not a child anymore*, she might have said, but the truth of *that* was written in his eyes on her. "Never lie to me again," she said instead.

"I will not."

"Will the Bear know you are free?"

"No," he said. "Unless Midnight tells him."

"I don't think she will meddle so," said Vasya. "She watches."

In his silence this time she could hear a thought unspoken.

"Tell me," she said.

"You needn't go back to Moscow," he said. "You've seen enough horror, and caused enough pain. The Bear will do his best to see you slain now: the worst death he can devise, especially if he finds out I remembered. He knows I would grieve."

"It doesn't matter," she said. "It is our fault he is free. He must be bound again."

"With what?" Morozko demanded. The candle leaped up with a violet flame. His eyes were the color of the fire; his outlines seemed to fade, until he was wind and night made flesh. Then he shook off the mantle of power and said, "I am winter; do you think I will have any power in summertime Moscow?"

"You needn't make it cold in here to score a point," said Vasya, resentfully. "We have to do *something*." She took her own clothes from his hands. "Thank you for these," she added, and went to the inner room to dress. At the threshold, she called back, "Can you even go out into the summertime world, winter-king?"

His voice behind her was reluctant. "I don't know. Perhaps. For a little time. If we are together. The necklace is destroyed but—"

"But we don't need it anymore," she finished, realizing. The tie between them now—layers of passion and anger, fear and fragile hope—was stronger than any magical jewel.

Dressed, she returned to the doorway. Morozko was standing where she'd left him. "We could perhaps get to Moscow, but to what end?" he said. "If the Bear finds out we are coming, he will delight in setting a trap, so that I must watch, helpless, while you are slain. Or perhaps one where *you* must watch while your family suffers."

"We will just have to be clever," said Vasya. "We got Muscovy into this; we are going to get her out."

"We ought to return to my own lands, come to him in winter when I am stronger. Then we'd have a chance of victory."

"He surely knows that," Vasya returned. "Which means that whatever he is planning, he must do it this summer."

"It might be your undoing."

She shook her head. "It might. But I am not going to abandon my family. Will you come with me?"

"I have said you are not alone, Vasya, and I meant it," he said. But he sounded unhappy.

She managed the ghost of a smile. "You are not alone either. By all means, let us continue repeating it until one of us believes it." Briskly, she managed to say without tremor, "If I go out there, will the village try to kill me?"

"No," said Morozko, and then he smiled. "But a legend might be born."

She flushed. But when he extended a hand, she took it.

The village had indeed gathered outside the bathhouse. They drew back when the door opened. Their eyes roved from Vasya to Morozko, hand-fast, disheveled.

Yelena stood at the front of the crowd, shoulder to shoulder with the man who had tried to save her. She flinched when Morozko turned to her. It was to Yelena that the frost-demon spoke, although the whole village heard. "Forgive me," he said.

She looked shocked. Then she gathered her dignity and bowed. "It was your right. But—" She looked more closely at his face. "You are not the same," she whispered.

Just as Vasya had seen the years gone from his eyes, this woman could sense the weight of their return. "No," said Morozko. "I have been saved from forgetfulness." He glanced at Vasya and spoke so that the whole village heard. "I loved her, and a curse made me forget. But she came for me and broke the curse and now I must go. My blessing on you all, this winter."

Whispers of wonder, even joy. Yelena smiled. "We are doubly blessed," she said to Vasya. "Sister." She had a gift in her hands: a magnificent long cloak, wolf without, rabbit within. She gave it to Vasya, embraced her. "Thank you," she whispered. "May I have your blessing on my firstborn?"

"Health and long life," said Vasya, a little awkwardly. "For your child, joy in love, and a brave death, a long time from now."

Zimnyaya Koroleva, they said. The winter-queen. It frightened her. She tried to compose her features.

Morozko stood beside her, deceptively calm, but she could sense the feeling rushing between him and his people: a pull like a current. His eyes were a deep and astonishing blue. Perhaps he wished even now to go back, to take his place in the feasting, to feed forever on this worship.

But if he doubted his course, he did not let it show on his face.

Vasya was relieved when all the people turned at the sound of hoofbeats. Delight bloomed on a dozen faces. Two horses came flowing over the palisade, one white and one gold. They cut through the crowd, and trotted up to the two of them. Morozko, without a word, leaned his forehead against the neck of the white mare. The horse put her head around and lipped at his sleeve. Pain shot through Vasya, seeing it. "I forgot you too," he said to the mare, low. "Forgive me."

The white mare shoved him with her head, ears back. *I don't know why any of us waited for you. It was very dark.*

Pozhar scraped a hoof in the snow in obvious agreement.

"You waited as well," Vasya said to her, surprised.

Pozhar bit Vasya on the arm and stamped. *I am not waiting again.*

Vasya said, rubbing the new bruise, "I am glad to see you, lady."

Morozko said, in some wonder, "She has never taken a rider willingly in all the years of her life."

"She has not taken one now," said Vasya hastily. "But she helped to guide me here. I am grateful." She scratched Pozhar's withers. Pozhar, despite herself, leaned into the scratches. *You took too long,* said the mare again, just to show she didn't in any way enjoy being coddled, and stamped again.

Vasya's new cloak lay heavy on her shoulders. "Farewell," she said to the people. They were round-eyed with wonder. "They think they see a miracle," Vasya said, low, to Morozko. "It doesn't feel like one."

"And yet," he replied, "a girl alone rescued the winter-king from forgetfulness and stole him away with magic horses. That is miracle enough for one Midwinter." Vasya found herself smiling as he vaulted to the white mare's back.

Before he could offer—or not offer—to take her up before him, she said firmly, "I am going to walk. I came here on my own feet, after all."

Walking had been a slogging nightmare of deep snow without snow-shoes, but she didn't say that.

The pale eyes considered her. Vasya wished he wouldn't. He so obviously saw past her pride—not wanting to be carried away across his saddlebow—to the deeper emotion. The shock of Solovey breaking, falling, was still too raw in memory. It felt wrong now to ride away in triumph.

"Very well," he said, and surprised her by dismounting.

"You needn't," she said. The two horses' bodies shielded them from the crowd. "You can't mean to march out of the village like a cowherd? It is beneath your dignity."

"I have seen uncounted dead," he returned coolly. "Touched them, sent them on. But I have never done anything to remember them. I can walk now with you, because you cannot ride Solovey beside me. Because he was brave, and he is gone."

She hadn't wept for Solovey. Not properly. She had dreamed of him, waked screaming for him to run, felt his absence as a dull, poisonous ache. But she hadn't wept, except for a few quelled tears after she nearly slew the mushroom-spirit. Now she felt the tears starting, stinging. Lightly, Morozko touched his finger to the first, as it ran down to her jaw. It froze at his touch, fell away.

Somehow the act of walking out of that midnight village, while the horses paced beside them, drove home Solovey's loss in a way that none of the last days' shocks had. When they had passed the palisade and gone back into the winter forest, Vasya buried her face in the white mare's mane and she cried all the dammed-up tears that one night in Moscow had left inside her.

The mare stood patiently, blowing warm air onto her hands, and Morozko waited, silent, except that once, he laid cool fingers on the back of her neck.

When at last her tears quieted, she shook her head, wiped her running nose, and tried to think clearly. "We have to go back to Moscow." Her voice was hoarse.

"As you say," he said. He still didn't look happy about it. But he didn't object again.

If we are going all the way back to Moscow, the white mare put in un-expectedly, *then Vasya must get on my back. I can carry both of you. It will be quicker.*

Vasya had her lips open in a refusal, but then she noticed Morozko's expression. "She will not let you say no," he said mildly. "And she is right. You will only exhaust yourself, walking. It is you who must hold Moscow in your mind; if I guide us, it will be winter when we arrive."

At least they were out of sight of the village now. Vasya vaulted to the mare's back and Morozko got on behind her. The white mare was more finely built than Solovey, but the way she moved reminded her— Trying not to think of the bay stallion, Vasya looked down at Moroz-ko's hand, lying relaxed on his knee, remembered instead his hands on her skin, his hair coarse and cold, tumbled dark across her breasts.

She shivered at the memory and pushed it away too. They had sto-len those hours in Midnight; now they must think only of outmaneu-vering a clever and implacable enemy.

But— For distraction, she forced herself to ask a question whose answer she feared. "To bind the Bear—must I sacrifice myself as my father did?"

Morozko did not immediately say no. Vasya began to feel a little sick to her stomach. The mare set off lightly through the snow; more snow drifted down from the sky. Vasya wondered if he called it down in his distress, if it were involuntary, like the beat of a heart. "You promised you'd not lie to me again," said Vasya.

"I will not," said Morozko. "It is not so simple as exchanging your life for his binding, the two things interchangeable. Your life is not tied to the Bear's liberty; you are not just a—token in our war."

She waited.

"But I gave him power over me," said Morozko, "when I yielded up my freedom. My twin and I will not be equals in a fight, now." The words came out gratingly. "Summer is his season. I do not know how to bind him, except with the power of a life freely given, or a trick—"

Pozhar said suddenly, *What about the golden thing?* The mare had drifted close enough to catch their conversation.

Vasya blinked. "What golden thing?"

The mare threw her head up and down. *The golden thing the sorcerer made! When I wore it, I couldn't fly. I had to do what he said. It is powerful, that thing.*

Vasya and Morozko looked at each other. "Kaschei's golden bridle," said Vasya, slowly. "If it bound her—might it bind your brother?"

"Perhaps," said the winter-king, brows drawn together.

"It was in Moscow," said Vasya, speaking faster and faster in her excitement. "In the stable, Dmitrii Ivanovich's stable. I pulled it off her head and threw it down, the night Moscow burned. Is it still in the palace? Perhaps it melted in the fire."

"It would not have melted," Morozko said. "There is a chance." She could not see his face, but his hand on his knee closed slowly into a fist.

Vasya, without thinking, leaned over and scratched Pozhar's neck with delight. "Thank you," she said. The mare tolerated it a moment before she sidled away.

Part Four

19

Allies

Summer came with unnatural suddenness, fell on Moscow like a conquering army. Fires broke out in the forest, so that the city was palled with smoke and no one could see the sun. Folk went mad from the heat; drowned themselves in the river seeking coolness, or simply dropped where they stood, scarlet-faced, bodies dewed with clammy sweat.

The rats came with the warmth, creeping out of the merchant-boats while men unloaded silver and cloth and forged iron for the sticky, sweltering markets of Moscow. They thrived in the smother, drawn to the reek of Moscow's middens.

The first folk to fall sick lived in the posad: the airless, crowded huts by the river. They began to cough, to sweat, and then to shiver. Then the smooth swellings showed, at throat and groin, and then black spots.

Plague. The word rippled through the city. Moscow had seen plague before. Dmitrii's uncle Semyon had died of it, with his wife and his sons in one terrible summer.

"Close up the houses of the sick," said Dmitrii to the captain of his guard. "They are not to go out—no, not even to go to church. If a priest can be found to bless them, let the priest go in, but that is all. Tell the guards at the city-gate; anyone who seems ill is not allowed within the walls." Folk still whispered in hushed tones of the death of Dmitrii's uncle: dying swollen like a tick, black-spotted, his own attendants afraid to come near him.

The man nodded, but he was frowning. "What?" Dmitrii demanded. The night of the Tatar attack had decimated Dmitrii's city guard. In the aftermath of the riot and Vasya's burning, he'd built it up again, larger than before, but they were still inexperienced.

"This sickness is the curse of God, Gosudar," said the captain. "Surely it is only right that men be allowed to go and pray? All the people's prayers together may yet reach the ears of the Almighty."

"It is a curse that flies from man to man," said Dmitrii. "What are the walls of Moscow for if not to keep out evil?"

One of his boyars there in his anteroom said, "Forgive me, Gosudar, but—"

Dmitrii turned, scowling. "Can I not give orders without debate from half the city?" Ordinarily he humored his boyars. They were mostly older than he, and had ensured that he had a throne to inherit when he came of age. But the shocking heat sapped his strength and brought on a sick, weary anger. He'd had no word from either of his cousins. The Prince of Serpukhov had taken all the silver Muscovy could muster, and had gone south to plead their case before the temnik Mamai. Sasha was supposed to be bringing back Father Sergei. But Sasha had not returned, and reports came out of the south that Mamai was still gathering up his ulus, as though he'd never heard Vladimir's message at all.

"The people are afraid," said the boyar carefully. "Thrice have the dead come walking since the season turned. Now this? If you shut the gates of Moscow and deny church to the sick, I do not know what they will do. Already there is much talk that the city is cursed."

Dmitrii understood war, and the managing of men, but curses were outside his experience. "I will take thought for the comfort of the city," he said. "But we are not cursed." In his own heart, though, Dmitrii wasn't sure. He wanted Father Sergei's advice, but the old monk was not there. So instead, grudgingly, the Grand Prince turned to his steward. "Send for Father Konstantin."

"THE FAIR-HAIRED PRINCE IS no fool," said the Bear. "But he is young. He has sent a messenger for you. When you go to him, you must convince him to let you give service in the cathedral. Call the people together and pray for rain or salvation or whatever it is men ask of their gods in this age. But call them together."

Konstantin was alone in the scriptorium of the Archangel, wearing only the lightest of cassocks; sweat dewed his forehead, his upper lip. "I am painting," he said. He turned a pot of color in the light. His colors lay before him like a string of jewels—some were actually made from precious stones. At Lesnaya Zemlya, he had made his colors from bark and berries and leaves. Now anxious boyars showered him with lapis for his blues and jasper for his reds. They paid the finest silversmiths in Moscow to make icon-covers for him, of hammered silver, studded with pearls.

The third time dead things came whispering through the streets, it had taken the whole night to drive them off: first one, then another, and finally a third. "It cannot seem to be too easy," the Bear had told him afterward, when Konstantin had wakened screaming from a dream of dead faces. "Do you think the defeat of a single child-upyr would have been enough to win over all Moscow, peasant and boyar? Drink wine, man of God, and do not fear the darkness. Have I not done all I promised?"

"Every last thing," Konstantin had said miserably, shivering in his cooling sweat. He was to be made bishop. He had been granted property commensurate with his dignity. The people of Moscow worshipped him with wild-eyed fervor. But that did not help him in the night, when he dreamed dead hands, reaching.

Now, in the scriptorium, Konstantin turned away from his wooden panel, found the devil standing just behind him. His breath left him silently. He could never get used to the demon's presence. The beast knew his thoughts, waked him from nightmares, whispered advice in his ear. Konstantin would never be free of him.

Perhaps I don't wish to be, Konstantin thought in his more clear-headed moments. Always, when he met the devil's single eye, the creature stared steadily back.

The beast saw him.

Konstantin had waited to hear the voice of God for so long, but God was silent.

This devil never stopped talking.

Nothing would quiet Konstantin's nightmares, though. He'd tried drinking mead, to thicken his sleep, but the honey-wine only made his head ache. Finally, in desperation, Konstantin asked the monks for brushes and wooden panels, for oil and water and pigment, and set himself to writing icons. When he painted, his soul seemed to exist only in his eye and hand; his mind went quiet.

"I can see you are painting," said the Bear, with an edge. "In a monastery, alone. Why? I thought you wanted earthly glories, man of God."

Konstantin swept his arm at the image on the panel. "I have my earthly glories. And this? Is it not glorious too?" His voice was thick with bitter irony: the icon painted by a man without faith.

The Bear peered over Konstantin's shoulder. "That is a strange picture," he said. His thick finger went out to trace the image.

The image was of Saint Peter. He was dark-haired and wild-eyed, hands and feet streaming blood, his eyes turned blindly to heaven, where angels waited. But the angels had eyes as flat and inimical as the swords in their hands. The host welcoming the apostle to heaven looked more like an army holding the gates. Peter had not the serene look of a saint. His eyes saw, his hands gestured, expressive. He was as alive as Konstantin's gift, and the raw, wretched hunger the priest could not uproot from his soul, could make him.

"It is very beautiful," said the Bear. His finger traced over the lines without quite touching; he looked almost perplexed. "How do you make it live—so? You have not magic."

"I don't know," said Konstantin. "My hands move without me. What do you know of beauty, monster?"

"More than you," said the Bear. "I have lived longer and seen more. I can make dead things live, but only in mockery of the living. This—is something else."

Was that wonder, in that sardonic, single eye? Konstantin couldn't be sure.

The Bear reached out and turned the icon's wooden panel to the wall. "You still must go and give service in the cathedral. Have you forgotten our bargain?"

Konstantin threw his brush aside. "What if I don't? Will you damn me? Steal my soul? Put me to torture?"

"No," said the Bear, and touched his cheek, lightly. "I will disappear, be gone, fling myself back into the fiery pit and leave you all alone."

Konstantin stood still. Alone? Alone with his thoughts? Sometimes this devil seemed like the only thing real in this hot, nightmarish world.

"Don't leave me," said Konstantin. It came out a grinding whisper.

The thick fingers stroked his face with surprising delicacy. Eyes wide and densely blue rose to meet a single gray eye, a face seamed with scars. The Bear breathed his answer into Konstantin's ear. "I was alone for a hundred lives of men, bound in a clearing beneath an unchanging sky. You can make life with your hands, of a kind I've never seen. Why would I ever leave you?"

Konstantin did not know whether to be relieved or terrified.

"But," murmured the Bear, "the cathedral."

DMITRII DIDN'T AGREE. "Divine service for all Moscow?" he asked. "Father, be reasonable. Folk will faint from the heat, or perhaps be trampled. Feelings are running high enough already without calling everyone together to sweat and pray and kiss icons, pleasing as it may be to God." This last was tacked on as an afterthought.

The Bear, watching invisibly, said with satisfaction, "I do love sensible men. They always try to make sense of the impossible and they can't. Then they blunder. Come now, little father. Blind him with eloquence."

Konstantin gave no sign he heard, beyond a tightening of his mouth. But aloud he said, reproof in his tone, "It is God's will, Dmitrii Ivanovich. If there is any chance to lift this curse from Moscow we must take it. The dead are infecting Moscow with fear, and what if I am called too late? What if worse comes than upyry, and my prayers do not stop it? No, I think it better that the whole city pray together, and perhaps make an end of this curse."

Dmitrii was frowning still, but he agreed.

To Konstantin, the world seemed less real when he donned his new robes of white and scarlet, his collar high and stiffened in the back. Sweat ran like rivers down his spine as he put a hand to the door of the sanctuary.

The Bear said, "I wish to go in."

"Then go in," said Konstantin, his mind elsewhere.

The devil made a sound of impatience and took Konstantin's hand. "You must bring me with you."

Konstantin's hand curled in the demon's. "Why can't you go in yourself?"

"I am a devil," said the Bear. "But I am also your ally, man of God."

Konstantin drew the Bear into the sanctuary with him, and gave the icons a spiteful look. *See what I do, when you will not speak to me?* The Bear looked about him curiously: at the gilding, and jeweled icon-covers, at the scarlet and blue of the ceiling.

At the people.

For the cathedral was packed with people, a shoving, swaying throng, smelling of sour sweat. Crammed together before the icon-screen, they wept and they prayed, watched over by the saints and also by a silent devil with one eye.

For the Bear walked out with the clergy, when the doors of the ico-nostasis were thrown open. Surveying the crowd, he said, "This bodes well. Come now, man of God. Show me your quality."

When he began the service, Konstantin did not know whom he chanted for: the watching throng or the listening demon. But he flung all the torment of his tattered soul into it, until the whole cathedral wept.

Afterward, Konstantin went back to his cell in the monastery, kept against the furnishing of his own house, and lay down, wordless, in his sweat-soaked linen. His eyes were shut, and the Bear did not speak, but he was there. Konstantin could feel the dazzling, sulfurous presence.

Finally the priest burst out, without opening his eyes, "Why are you silent? I did what you asked."

The Bear said, almost growling, "You have been painting the things you will not say. Shame and sorrow and all the tedious rest. It is all there, in your Saint Peter's face, and today you sang what you cannot bring yourself to utter. I could feel it. What if someone realizes? Are you trying to break your promise?"

Konstantin shook his head, his eyes still shut. "They will hear what they want to hear and see what they want to see," he said. "Make what I feel their own, without understanding."

"Well, then," said the Bear, "men are great fools." He let it go. "In any case, that scene in the cathedral should make enough." Now he sounded pleased.

"Enough what?" said Konstantin. The sun had gone down by then; the green dusk brought some respite from the savage heat. He lay still, breathing, seeking in vain a breath of cool air.

"Enough dead," said the Bear, unsparing. "They all kissed the same icon. I have use for the dead. Tomorrow you have to go to the Grand Prince. Secure your place with him. That monk of witch's getting— Brother Aleksandr—he is going to come back. You must see to it that his place by the Grand Prince's side is not waiting for him."

Konstantin lifted his head. "The monk and the Grand Prince have been friends from boyhood."

"Yes," said the Bear. "And the monk saw fit to lie to Dmitrii, more than once. Whatever stiff-necked oaths he has sworn since, I assure you, it will not be enough to get back the prince's trust. Or is it harder than setting a mob to kill a girl?"

"She deserved it," Konstantin muttered, throwing an arm over his eyes. The blackness behind his eyelids gave him back a bruised, deep-green gaze, and he opened his eyes again.

"Forget her," said the Bear. "Forget the witch. You are going to drive yourself mad with lust and pride and regret."

That was too close to the bone; Konstantin sat up and said, "You cannot read my mind."

"No," the Bear retorted. "But I can read your face, which is much the same thing."

Konstantin subsided into the rough blankets. Softly, he said, "I thought I'd be satisfied."

"It is not your nature to be satisfied," said the Bear.

"The Princess of Serpukhov wasn't at the cathedral today," said Konstantin. "Nor her household."

"That would be because of the child," said the Bear.

"Marya? What about her?"

"Warned," said the Bear. "The chyerti warned her. Did you think you killed all the witches in Moscow when you burned the one? But never fear. There will be no more witches in Moscow before the first snow."

"No?" Konstantin breathed. "How?"

"Because you brought all Moscow to the cathedral today," said the Bear, with satisfaction. "I needed an army."

"THEY MUSTN'T GO!" MARYA had cried to her mother. "No one!"

Daughter and mother each wore the thinnest of shifts, sweat dewing their faces, identical dark eyes glassy with weariness. In the terem that summer, all the women lived in twilight. There were no fires lit indoors, no lamps or candles. The heat would have been unbearable. They opened the windows at night, but fastened them all tightly by day, to keep in what coolness they could. So the women lived in gray darkness and it told on all of them. Marya was pallid under her sweat, thin and drooping.

Gently Olga said to her daughter, "If folk wish to go pray at the cathedral, I can hardly prevent them."

"You have to," said Marya urgently. "You have to. The man in the oven said. He said that people will come away sick."

Olga considered her daughter, frowning. Marya hadn't been herself since the heat gripped them. Ordinarily, Olga would have taken her family out of the city, to the rough-built town of Serpukhov proper, where they could at least hope for some quiet and cooler air. But this year there were reports of fires to the south, and if anyone so much as put a nose out of doors, they saw a hellish white haze and breathed the smoke. Now there was plague in the posad outside the walls, and that settled it. She would keep her family where it was. But—

"Please," said Marya. "Everyone has to stay here. With our gates shut."

Olga was still frowning. "I cannot keep our gates shut forever."

"You won't have to," said Marya, and Olga noticed uneasily the directness of her daughter's gaze. She was growing up too quickly. Something about the fire and its aftermath had changed her. She saw things her mother did not. "Just until Vasya gets back."

"Masha—" Olga began gently.

"She is coming back," said her daughter. She did not shout it defiantly, did not weep or plead with her mother to understand. She just said it. "I know it."

"Vasya wouldn't dare," said Varvara, coming in with damp cloths, a jar of wine that had been packed in straw in the cool cellar. "Even assuming she lives still, she knows what a risk it would be to all of us." She handed the cloth to Olga, who dabbed her temples.

"Has that ever stopped Vasya?" Olga asked, taking the cup that Varvara gave her. The two women exchanged worried glances. "I will keep the servants from the cathedral, Masha," Olga said. "Though they will not thank me for it. And—if you—hear—that Vasya has come, will you tell me?"

"Of course," said Marya at once. "We must have supper ready for her."

Varvara said to Olga, "I do not think she will come back. She has gone too far."

20

The Golden Bridle

VASYA'S HEAD WAS FULL OF WINTER MIDNIGHTS, AND SHE WAS shaking with the want of light. She wasn't sure they would ever come out at all. They rode without pause, over ridges and valleys glazed with ice, filled up with darkness as if they'd never seen day. Morozko's presence at her back was no comfort here; he was a part of the long, lonely night, untroubled by the frost.

She tried to think of Sasha, to think of Moscow and daylight and her own life waiting for her on the other side of the darkness. But the touchstones of her life had all been thrown into disarray, and it grew harder and harder to focus her mind, as they rode through the icy night.

"Stay awake," Morozko said in her ear. Her head was lolling on his shoulder; she jerked upright, half in a panic, so that the white mare slanted a reproving ear. "If I guide us, we will end somewhere on my own lands, in the deep of winter," he continued. "If you still want to make it to Moscow, in summer, you must stay awake." They were crossing a glade full of snowdrops, stars overhead and the faint sweetness of the flowers at her feet.

Hastily Vasya straightened her back, tried to refocus her mind. The darkness seemed to mock her. How could you separate the winter-king from winter? Impossible even to try. Her head swam.

"Vasya," he said, more gently. "Come with me to my own lands. Winter will come soon enough to Moscow. Otherwise—"

"I am not asleep yet," she said, suddenly fierce. "You set the Bear free; you must help me bind him."

"With pleasure. In winter," he said. "It is only a breath of time, Vasya; what are two seasons?"

"Little to you, perhaps, but a great deal for me and mine," she said.

He did not argue again.

She was thinking of that forgetfulness, the strange slip of reality that made fire from nothing, or kept the eyes of all Moscow from seeing her. Impossible that the winter-king should walk abroad in summer. Impossible, impossible.

She clenched her fists. *No,* she thought. *It isn't.*

"A little farther," she said, and wordless, the white mare cantered on.

At last, when Vasya's concentration was wavering like a flame in a high wind, when exhaustion ate at her, and his arm about her waist was the only thing keeping her upright, the cold grew a little less fierce. Then mud showed under the snow. Then they were in a world of rustling leaves. The white mare's hooves rimed the leaves with frost where they fell, and still Vasya hung on.

Finally, she and Morozko and the two horses stepped between one night and the next, and she saw a campfire nestled in the bend of a river.

In the same instant, the full weight of summer's heat fell on her body like a hand, and the last trace of winter fell away behind them.

Morozko sagged weightless against her back. She was alarmed to see his hand growing fainter and fainter, as frost dissolves at the touch of warm water.

Vasya half-turned and caught hold of his hands. "Look at me," she snapped. *"Look at me."*

He raised absolutely colorless eyes to hers, set in a face equally colorless, without depth, the way light flattens in a snowstorm. "You promised not to leave me," Vasya said. "*You are not alone,* you said. Are you so easily forsworn, winter-king?" Her hands crushed his.

He straightened up. He was still there, though faint. "I am here," he said, and the ice of his breathing stirred, impossibly, the leaves of a summertime wood. A note of wry humor entered his voice. "More or less." But he was shaking.

You are back in your own midnight now, Pozhar informed them, indifferent to impossibilities. *I am going. My debt is paid.*

Vasya cautiously let go of Morozko's hands. He did not immediately vanish, and so she slid down the white mare's shoulder. "Thank you," Vasya said to the golden mare. "More than I can say."

Pozhar flicked an ear, spun, and trotted off without another word.

Vasya watched the mare go, a little forlorn, trying, yet again, not to think of Solovey. The campfire by the river glimmered bright in the darkness. "Traveling by midnight is all very well," Vasya muttered. "But it involves far too much creeping up on folk in the dark. Who do you suppose that is?"

"I have no notion," said Morozko shortly. "I can't see." He said it matter-of-factly, but he looked shaken. In winter, his senses stretched far.

They crept nearer, and halted outside the firelight. A gray mare stood without hobbles on the other side of the flames. She raised her head uneasily, listening to the night.

Vasya knew her. "Tuman," she breathed, and then she saw three men camped beyond the mare, sleeping rough. Three fine horses and a pack-horse. One of the men was just a dark bundle wrapped in a cloak. But the others were sitting upright beside the fire, talking, despite the late hour. One was her brother, his face thinned with days of travel, raw with sunburn. There were threads of white in his hair. The other was the holiest man in Rus', Sergei Radonezhsky.

Sasha's head came up, seeing the horses restless. "Something in the wood," he said.

Vasya didn't know how a monk—even her brother—would react to her just then, drenched as she was in magic and darkness, hand-fast with a frost-demon. But she nerved herself and stepped forward. Sasha wrenched round, and Sergei rose to his feet, spry despite his years. The third man jerked upright, blinking. Vasya recognized him: Rodion Oslyabya, a brother of the Trinity Lavra.

Three monks, dirty from days on the road, camping in a clearing in the summer night. Painfully ordinary; they made the winter midnights at her back feel like a dream.

But it wasn't. She had brought the two worlds together.

She didn't know what would happen.

THE FIRST BROTHER ALEKSANDR saw of his sister was a slim figure with a bruised face. He blasphemed in his mind; he sheathed his sword, offered up prayers, and ran to her.

She was so thin. Every plane of her face was blade-sharp: a skull picked out with firelight. But she returned his embrace with strength, and when he looked at her he saw her lashes wet.

Perhaps he was weeping, too. "Marya said you were alive. I— Vasya—I am sorry. Forgive me. I wanted to go find you. I—Varvara said you had gone beyond our reckoning, that you—"

She cut into this flow of words. "There is nothing to forgive."

"The fire."

Her face hardened. "It is over, brother. Both fires."

"Where have you been? What happened to your face?"

She touched the scar across her cheekbone. "This is from the night the mob came for me in Moscow."

Sasha bit his lip. Father Sergei broke in, his voice sharp. "There is a white horse there in the wood. And a—shadow."

Sasha spun, his hand again going to the hilt of his sword. In the darkness, just touched by the edges of the firelight, stood a mare, white as the moon on a winter night.

"Yours?" Sasha said to his sister, and then he looked again. Beside the mare, the shadow was watching them.

Again, he put a hand to his sword-hilt.

"No," said his sister. "You don't need it, Sasha."

The shadow, Sasha realized, was a man. A man whose eyes were two points of light, colorless as water. Not a man. A monster.

He drew his sword. "Who are you?"

MOROZKO MADE NO ANSWER, but Vasya could feel the anger in him. He and the monks were natural enemies.

Catching her brother's eye, she saw with an unpleasant feeling that Sasha's fury wasn't just the impersonal disdain of a monk for a devil. "Vasya, do you know this—creature?"

Vasya opened her mouth, but Morozko stepped into the light and spoke first. "I marked her from her childhood," he said coolly. "Took her into my own house, bound her to me with ancient magic, and put her on the road to Moscow."

Vasya glared wordlessly at Morozko. Her brother's disdain was obviously not one-sided. *Of all the things he might have said to Sasha first.*

"Vasya," Sasha said. "Whatever he has done to you—"

Vasya cut him off. "It doesn't matter. I have ridden across Rus' dressed as a boy; I have walked alone into darkness and come out alive. It is too late for your scruples. Now—"

"I am your brother," said Sasha. "It concerns me; it concerns every man in our family that this—"

"You left us when I was a child!" she interrupted. "You have given yourself first to your religion and second to your Grand Prince. My life and my fate lie beyond your judgment."

Rodion broke in, bristling. "We are men of God," he said. "That is a devil. Surely nothing more needs to be said?"

"I think," said Sergei, "that a little more must be said." He did not speak loudly, but everyone turned to him.

"My daughter," said Sergei calmly, "we will hear your tale from the beginning."

THEY SAT DOWN AROUND the fire. Rodion and Sasha did not sheathe their swords. Morozko did not sit at all; he paced, restless, as though he did not know which he disliked more: the monks and their hostile firelight or the hot summer darkness.

Vasya told the entire story, or the parts of it she could. She was hoarse by the end. Morozko did not speak; she got the impression that it was taking all his concentration not to disappear. Her touch might have helped, or her blood, but her brother kept a brooding eye on the frost-demon, and she thought it better not to provoke him. She kept her arms around her knees.

When her voice wound raggedly to a halt, Sergei said, "You have not told us everything."

"No," said Vasya. "There are things that have no words. But I have spoken the truth."

Sergei was silent. Sasha's hand still toyed with the hilt of his sword. The fire was dying; Morozko seemed paradoxically more real in the faint red glow than he had in the full light of flames. Sasha and Rodion looked at him with open hostility. To Vasya it seemed suddenly that her hope was a foolish one; that it was impossible that these two powers would make common cause. Trying to put all her conviction into her voice, she said, "There is evil walking free in Moscow. We must face it together, or we will fall."

The monks were silent.

Then, slowly, Sergei said, "If there is an evil creature in Moscow, then what is to be done, my daughter?"

Vasya felt a stir of hope. Rodion made a sound of protest, but Sergei raised a hand, silencing him.

"The Bear cannot be slain," said Vasya. "But he can be bound." She told them all she knew of the golden bridle.

"We found it," said Sasha, breaking in unexpectedly. "In the ruin of the burned stable the night—the night of—"

"Yes," said Vasya swiftly. "That night. Where is it now?"

"In Dmitrii's treasure-room, if he hasn't melted it for the gold," said Sasha.

"If you and Sergei tell him together what it is for, will he give it to you?"

Sasha's mouth was open on what obviously was a *yes*. Then he frowned. "I don't know. I haven't— Dmitrii doesn't trust me as he once did. But he has great faith in Father Sergei."

Vasya knew the admission hurt. And she also knew why Dmitrii didn't trust her brother.

"I am sorry," she said.

He shook his head once, but said nothing.

"You cannot trust the Grand Prince's faith in anyone," Morozko broke in for the first time. "Medved's great gift is disorder, and his tools are fear and mistrust. He will know that both of you are coming, and will have planned for it. Until he is bound, you cannot trust anyone; you cannot even trust yourselves, for he makes men mad."

The monks exchanged glances.

"Can the bridle be stolen?" Vasya asked.

All the monks looked pious at that and did not answer. She wanted to pull her hair in exasperation.

IT TOOK THEM A long time to lay their plans. By the time they had finished, Vasya was desperate to sleep. Not just for rest, but because to sleep here in her own midnight meant that there would be light when she awakened. All that time they talked, she was still in Midnight. They all were: caught fast in the darkness with her. She wondered if Sasha asked himself what had delayed the dawn.

When she'd had enough, Vasya said, "We can speak again in the morning," got up and left the fire. She found a place thick with old pine-needles, and wrapped herself in her cloak.

Morozko bowed to the monks. A faint mockery in the gesture brought angry color to Sasha's face.

"Until morning," said the winter-king.

"Where are you going?" Sasha demanded.

Morozko said simply, "I am going down to the river. I have never seen dawn on moving water."

And he vanished into the night.

SASHA WANTED TO FLING himself down in frustration and fear. He wanted to strike down that shadow-creature, he wanted to rid his mind of the thought of it whispering in the dark to his maiden sister. He stared at the place where the demon had vanished, while Rodion watched him with concern and Sergei with understanding.

"Sit down, my son," said Sergei. "It is not a time for anger."

"Are we then to make a deal with a demon? It is sin, God will be angry—"

Sergei said reprovingly, "It is not for men and women to presume what the Lord wishes. That way lies evil, when men put themselves too high, saying, I know what God wants, for it is also what I want. *You* may hate the one she calls the winter-king, for the way he looks at your sister. But he has not harmed her; she says he has saved her life. You could not do as much for her."

That was severe, and Sasha flinched. "No," he said, low. "I could not. But perhaps he has damned her."

"I do not know," said Sergei. "We cannot know. But our business is with men and women: the helpless, and the afraid. That is why we are going to Moscow."

Sasha was silent a long time. Finally, wearily, he threw a log on the fire and said, "I do not like him."

"I fear," said Sergei, "that he does not care in the slightest."

Vasya woke in brilliant daylight. She leaped to her feet and lifted her face to the sun. Out of the country of Midnight, at last; and she hoped never to take that dark way again.

For a moment, she enjoyed the warmth. Then the heat began to gather, inexorable. Sweat slid between her breasts and down her spine. She was still wearing the wool shirt from the house at the edge of the lake, though now she wished for linen.

Her bare feet drank coolness from the dew-damp earth. Morozko was only a few paces off, grooming the white mare. She wondered if he'd kept near them that night, or if he'd gone wandering, touching the summer earth with strange frost. The monks still slept, in the easy way men sleep in daylight in summer.

Morozko's fur and embroidered silk was gone, as though he could not maintain the trappings of power in the harsh light of day. He might have been any peasant, feet bare in the grass, except his steps starred the earth with frost, and the cuffs of his shirt dripped cold water. A little coolness hung about him, even in the humid morning. She breathed it in, comforted, and said, "Mother of God, the heat."

Morozko looked grim. "That is the Bear's work."

"In winter, I have often wished for mornings like this," Vasya said, to be fair. "To be warm all the way through." She went over to stroke the white mare's neck. "And in summer, I remember how suffocating such mornings are. Do you get hot?"

"No," he said shortly. "But the heat tries to unmake me."

Remorseful, she put a hand on his, where it moved on the mare's withers. The connection between them flared to life, and his outline looked a little less vague. His hand curled around hers. She shivered, and he smiled. But his eyes were far away; he could not enjoy the reminder of his own weakness.

She dropped her hand. "Do you think the Bear knows you're here?"

"No," said Morozko. "I will try to keep it that way. Best we take two days on the road, and go into Moscow in bright morning."

"Because of the dead things?" said Vasya. "The upyry? His servants?"

"They only walk at night," he said. His colorless eye was savage. Vasya bit her lip.

An old war, Ded Grib had called it. Had she made herself a third power in it as the chyert suggested? Or merely taken the winter-king's side? The wall of years between them suddenly seemed as insurmountable as it had been before the night in the bathhouse.

But she forced herself to say crisply, "I imagine that by the end of the day even my brother would sell his soul for cold water. Please do not bait him."

"I was angry," he said.

"We won't be traveling with them for long," she said.

"No," he returned. "I will endure the summer as long as I can, but, Vasya, I cannot endure it forever."

They ate nothing; it was too hot. All of them were flushed and sweating even before they started off. They took the narrow track that wound alongside the Moskva, approaching the city from the east. Vasya's stomach knotted with nerves. Now that they'd come to it, she did not want to go back to Moscow. She was deathly afraid. She trudged through the dust, trying to remember that she could do magic, that she had allies. But it was hard to believe, in the harsh light of day.

Morozko had let the white mare go, to graze beside the river and keep out of the sight of men. He was staying out of sight himself: little more than a cool breeze ruffling the leaves.

The sun rose higher and higher over the swooning world. Gray shadows lay like bars of iron along the trail. To their left ran the river. To their right was a vast wheat-field, red-gold as Pozhar's coat, hissing as a hot wind flattened the stalks. The sun was like a mallet between the eyes. The path coated their feet with dust.

On and on they walked, still passing the wheat. It seemed endless. It seemed . . . Suddenly Vasya halted, shading her eyes with a hand, and said, "How large is this field?"

The men stopped when she did; now they looked at each other. No one could tell. The hot day seemed interminable. Morozko was nowhere to be seen. Vasya peered out over the wheat-field. A whirlwind of dust spun through the red-gold grass; the sky was dull with yellow haze, the sun overhead—still overhead . . . How long had it been overhead?

Now that they'd stopped, Vasya saw that the monks were all flushed and breathing fast. Faster than before? Too fast? It was so hot. "What is it?" asked Sasha, wiping the sweat from his face.

Vasya pointed to the whirlwind. "I think—"

Suddenly, with a muffled gasp, Sergei slumped over his horse's mane and toppled sideways. Sasha caught him; Sergei's placid horse didn't move, only tilted a puzzled ear. Sergei's skin was scarlet; he'd stopped sweating.

Behind the monks, Vasya glimpsed a woman with fair skin and hair bleached white, raising a pair of cutting shears in one bone-colored hand.

Not a woman. Without thinking, Vasya leaped, caught the chyert's wrist, forced it backward.

"I have met Lady Midnight," said Vasya to her, not letting go. "But not her sister Poludnitsa, whose touch, they say, strikes men with heat-sickness."

Sasha was kneeling in the dust now, holding Sergei and looking stricken. Rodion had run for water. Vasya wasn't sure he'd find any. The wheat-field at noon was the realm of Midday, and they had stumbled into it.

"Let me *go*!" hissed Poludnitsa.

Vasya did not slack her grip. "Let *us* go," she said. "We have no quarrel with you."

"No quarrel?" The chyert's white hair snapped like straw in the sultry wind. "Their bells will be the end of us. That is quarrel enough, don't you think?"

"The bell-makers wish only to live," said Vasya. "As we all do."

"If they can only live by killing," snapped Lady Midday. "Better they all die." Rodion came back without water; Sasha had risen to his feet, a hand on the searing hilt of his sword, but he couldn't see who Vasya was talking to.

Vasya said to Midday, "Their deaths are yours; men and chyerti are bound together for good or ill. But it can be for good. We can share this world." To show her good intentions, Vasya reached out and bloodied her thumb on the shears. Behind her, she heard the monks gasp, and realized that the touch of her blood had allowed them to see the demon.

Midday laughed, shrill. "Are *you* going to save us, little mortal child? When the Bear has promised us war, and victory?"

"The Bear is a liar," said Vasya.

Just then Sergei's thready voice whispered behind her, "Fear and flee, unclean and accursed spirit, visible through deceit, hidden by pretense. Whether you be of the morning, noonday, midnight, or night, I expel you."

Midday cried out, this time in real pain; she dropped her shears, fell back, vanishing, vanishing . . .

"No!" Vasya cried to the monks. "It's not what you think. It's not what *they* think." She lunged and seized Midday's wrist, keeping her from disappearing utterly.

"I see you," she said to her, low. "Live on."

Midday stood an instant, wounded, afraid, wondering. Then she was swept up in a whirlwind and vanished.

Morozko stepped out of the noonday glare. "Didn't your nurse warn you about wheat-fields in summer?" he asked.

"Father!" Sasha cried, just as Vasya turned back to the monks. Sergei was breathing too fast; his pulse vibrated in his throat. Morozko might have hesitated, but, muttering something, he knelt in the dust, laid long fingers against the frantic pulse in the monk's neck. As he did, he breathed out, his other fist clenched hard.

"What are you doing?" Sasha demanded.

"Wait," said Vasya.

The wind rose. Sluggishly at first, then faster, flattening the wheat. It was a cold wind: a wind of winter, pine-smelling, impossible in all the heat and the dust.

Morozko's jaw was set; his outline grew fainter even as the wind grew stronger. In a moment he would disappear, his presence as unimaginable as a snowflake at high summer. Vasya caught him by the shoulders. "Not yet," she said into his ear.

He shot her a brief look and hung on.

As the air cooled, Sergei's breathing and rabbit-fast pulse began to slow. Sasha and Rodion looked better too. Vasya was drinking in the cold air with great gulps. But Morozko's outline was wavering badly now, despite her grip.

Unexpectedly, Sasha asked, "What can I do?" Hope had won out over the censure on his face.

She glanced at him in surprise, and said, "See him. And remember." Morozko's lips thinned, but he said nothing.

Sergei drew a deep breath. The air about them was cool enough to dry the sweat beneath Vasya's stifling shirt. The wind faded to a breeze. The sun had moved; the heat was still intense, but not deadly. Morozko dropped his hand, bowed forward, gray as spring snow. Vasya kept her hands on his shoulders. Cold water ran down her fingers, over his shoulders.

All were silent.

"I don't think we're going any farther for a while," Vasya said, looking from the frost-demon to the sweat-stained monks. "No point in doing the Bear's work for him, and perishing before we get there."

No one said anything to that.

THEY FOUND A LITTLE HOLLOW of the river, cool with grass and moving water. The river rolled brown at their feet, running fast toward Moscow, where the Moskva and the Neglinnaya joined. In the distance, thick with haze, they could see the sullen city itself. A little way beyond them, the river was full of boats.

It was too hot to eat, but Vasya took a little bread from her brother and sprinkled crumbs in the water. She thought she caught a flash of bulging fish-eyes, a ripple that was not part of the current, but that was all.

Sasha, watching her, said abruptly, "Mother—Mother put bread in the water too, sometimes. For the river-king, she said." Then he shut his lips tight. But to Vasya it sounded like understanding, it sounded like apology. She smiled tentatively at him.

"The demon meant to kill us," said Sergei, his voice still hoarse.

"She was afraid," said Vasya. "They are all afraid. They do not want to disappear. I think the Bear is making them more afraid, and so they lash out. It wasn't her fault. Father, exorcisms will only drive more of them to the Bear's side."

"Perhaps," said Sergei. "But I did not wish to die in a wheat-field."

"You didn't," said Vasya. "Because the winter-king saved your life."

No one said anything.

She left them in the shade, rose and went downstream, out of earshot. She sank down in the tall grasses, dabbled her feet in the water and said aloud, "Are you all right?"

Silence. Then his voice spoke in the summertime stillness. "I have been better."

He stepped soundlessly through the grass and sank to the earth beside her. It was somehow harder to look at him now, as the eye slides, without comprehension, over any impossible thing. She narrowed her eyes and kept looking until the feeling passed. He sat with his knees drawn up, staring out at the glaring-bright water. Sourly he said, "Why should my brother fear my freedom? I am less than a ghost."

"Does he know now?"

"Yes," said Morozko. "How could he not? Calling the winter wind, so . . . I could not have made clearer sign of my presence short of shouting it to his face. If we still mean to go to Moscow, we will have to go today, despite the risk of sunset. I had hoped to avoid night and the upyry both, but if he is going to send his servants to try to kill you anyway, better we have the bridle first."

Vasya shivered in the midday sun. Then she told him, "There is a reason chyerti like Lady Midday are on the Bear's side."

"Many perhaps. Not most," Morozko returned. "Chyerti don't want to disappear, but most of us know what folly it is, to go to war with men. Our fates are bound together."

She said nothing.

"Vasya, how close did my brother come to persuading *you* to join him?"

"He didn't come *close*," she said. Morozko raised a brow. Lower, she added, "I thought about it. He asked me what loyalty I could have to Rus'. The mob of Moscow killed my horse."

"You freed Pozhar, who set fire to Moscow," Morozko said. He was looking out at the water again. "You caused the death of your sister's infant, though she was ready to die to give the babe life. Perhaps you only paid for your foolishness."

His tone was wounding, the words sword-sharp in their suddenness. Startled, she said, "I did not mean—"

"You came into the city like a bird in a cage of reeds, battering yourself against the bars and breaking them—do you wonder that it ended as it did?"

"Where should I have gone?" she snapped. "Home, to be burned as a witch? Should I have heeded you, worn your charm, married, had children, and sat sometimes by the window, fondly remembering my days with the winter-king? Should I have let—"

"You should think before you do things." He bit off the words, as though her last question had stung.

"This from the frost-demon who set this whole realm at hazard to save my life?"

He said nothing. She swallowed more hot words. She did not understand what lay between them. She was neither wise nor beautiful. None of the tales spoke of both wanting and resentment, of grand gestures and terrible mistakes.

"The chyerti would be worshipped," said Vasya, moderating her tone. "If the Bear had his way."

"*He* would be worshipped if he had his way," said Morozko. "I do not think he cares what happens to chyerti, so long as they serve his ends." He paused. "Or what happens to men and women themselves, dead in his scheming."

"If I wished to throw my lot in with the Bear, I would not have come to find you in the first place," Vasya said. "But yes, sometimes I think it is a bitter thing, to go back and try to save that city."

"If you spend all your days bearing the burden of unforgotten wrongs you will only wound yourself."

She glared at him, and he looked back, narrow-eyed. Why was he angry? Why was she? Vasya knew about marriages, carefully arranged; she knew about swains courting yellow-haired peasant girls in the midsummer twilight. She had listened to fairy tales since before she could speak. None of those prepared her for this. She had to clench her hands into fists to keep from touching him.

He drew away, jerkily, just as she took a deep, shaken breath and turned her gaze again to the water. "I am going to go to sleep in the sunshine," she said. "Until Father Sergei is ready to go on. Will you disappear if I do?"

"No," he said, and he sounded as if he resented it. But she was hot and sleepy and could not bring herself to care. She curled up in the grass near him. The last thing she felt was his light, cold fingers in her hair, like an apology, as she fell suddenly and completely asleep.

SASHA FOUND THEM A little while later. The frost-demon sat upright, watchful. The slanting summer light seemed to shine through him. He raised his head as Sasha approached, and Sasha was startled at the look on his face at that moment, unguarded, there and gone. Vasya stirred.

"Let her sleep, winter-king," said Sasha.

Morozko said nothing, but one hand moved to smooth Vasya's tousled black hair.

Watching them, Sasha said, "Why did you save Father Sergei's life?"

Morozko said, "I am not noble, if that is what you are thinking. The Bear must be bound anew, and we cannot do it alone."

Sasha was silent, turning that over. Then he said abruptly, "You are not a creature of God."

"I am not." His free hand, lying loose, had an unnatural stillness.

"Yet you saved my sister's life. Why?"

The devil's gaze was direct. "First for my own scheming. But later because I could not stand to see her slain."

"Why do you ride with her now? It cannot be easy, a frost-demon at high summer."

"She asked it of me. Why all these questions, Aleksandr Peresvet?"

The epithet was given half in earnest, half in mockery. Sasha had to swallow a surge of rage. "Because after Moscow," he said, trying to keep his voice even, "she went to a—dark country. I was told I could not follow her there."

"You could not."

"And you could?"

"Yes."

Sasha took this in. "If she goes into the darkness again—will you swear not to abandon her?"

If the demon was surprised, he gave no sign. His face remote, he said, "I will not abandon her. But one day she will go where even I cannot follow. I am immortal."

"Then—if she asks—if there is a man who can warm her, and pray for her, and give her children—then let her go. Do not keep her in the dark."

"You ought to make up your mind," said Morozko. "Swear not to abandon her or give her up to a living man? Which shall it be?"

His tone was cutting. Sasha's hand strayed to his sword. But he did not grasp it. "I don't know," he said. "I never protected her before; I do not know why I should be able to now."

The demon said nothing.

Sasha said, "A convent would have broken her." Reluctantly he added, "Even a marriage, no matter how kindly the man, how fair the house."

Still Morozko did not speak.

"But I am afraid for her soul," said Sasha, voice rising despite himself. "I am afraid for her alone in dark places, and I am afraid for her with you at her side. It is sin. And you are a fairy tale, a nightmare; you have no soul at all."

"Perhaps not," agreed the winter-king, but still the slender fingers tangled with Vasya's hair.

Sasha ground his teeth. He wanted to demand promises, pledges, confessions, if only to delay the realization that there were some things he couldn't change. But he bit back the words. He knew they wouldn't do any good. She had survived the frost and the flame, had found a harbor, however brief. Perhaps that was all anyone could ask, in the world's savage turning.

He stepped back. "I will pray for you both," he said, voice clipped. "We are going soon."

21

Enemy at the Gate

IT WAS EARLY EVENING, BRIGHT AND STILL, THE GRAY SHADOWS long and softening to violet, by the time they made their way down the parched bank of the Moskva and found a ferry to take them across.

The ferryman only had eyes for the monks. Vasya kept her head down. With her cropped hair, her rough clothes, her gawkiness, she passed for a horse-boy. At first it was easy to forget where she was, as she busied herself getting the horses to stand quiet in the rocking boat. But she found her heart beating faster and faster and faster as they approached the far side of the river.

In her mind's eye, the Moskva was sheeted with ice, red with fire-light. Men and women seethed around a hastily built pyre. Perhaps even now they were floating over the very spot where the last ashes of her would have sunk into the indifferent water.

She barely made it to the side of the boat, and then she was heaving into the river. The ferryman laughed. "Poor country boy, never been on a boat before?" Father Sergei, with kindly hands, held her head as she retched. "Look at the shore," he said, "see how still it is? Here is some clean water, drink. That's better."

It was the icy touch on the back of her neck, cold, invisible fingers, that drew her back to herself. *You are not alone,* he said, in a voice no one but she could hear. *Remember.*

She sat up, grim-faced, and wiped her mouth. "I'm all right, Father," she said to Sergei.

The boat ground against a dock. Vasya took hold of the packhorse's halter, led him ashore. The rope slid against her sweating hands. People were pushing to get into the city before the gates were shut for the night. It was not difficult to fall a little behind the three monks. Morozko's cold presence paced invisibly beside her. Waiting.

Would anyone recognize her—the witch they thought they'd burned? There were people in front and behind; people all around. She was afraid. The air smelled of dust and rotten fish, and sickness. Sweat trickled between her breasts.

She kept her head down, trying to look insignificant, trying to control her racing heart. The stink of the city was calling up memories faster than she could push them back: of fire, of terror, of hands tearing at her clothes. She prayed no one would wonder why she wore a thick shirt and jacket in the heat. She had never in her life felt so hideously vulnerable.

The three monks were stopped at the gate. The gate-guards held sachets of dried herbs to mouth and nose as they prodded carts and asked questions of travelers. The river darted points of light into their eyes.

"Say your name and your business, strangers," said the captain of the guard.

"I am no stranger. I am Brother Aleksandr," said Sasha. "I have returned to Dmitrii Ivanovich, accompanying the holy father Sergei Radonezhsky."

The captain scowled. "The Grand Prince ordered you brought to him when you arrived."

Vasya bit her lip. Smoothly, Sasha said, "I will go to the Grand Prince, in due course. But the holy father must go first to the monastery, to rest and say prayers of thanks for his safe arrival." Vasya's hands were slippery on the lead-rope of the horse.

"The holy father may go where he chooses," said the captain flatly. "But to the Grand Prince *you* will go, according to orders. I will have men escort you. The Grand Prince has taken advice, and he does not trust you."

"Who has advised him?" Sasha demanded.

"The wonder-worker," said the gate-guard, and a little emotion entered his flat voice. "Father Konstantin Nikonovich."

The Bear knows we are coming now, Morozko had said to Sergei and Sasha, as they made their way along the Moskva toward the city in the sweltering afternoon. *It is possible you will be delayed at the gate. If so—*

Vasya could scarcely breathe around the panic in her throat. But she managed to mutter to the pack-horse at her side: "Rear!"

The creature broke into a frenzy of heavy-limbed bucking. Next moment, Sasha's battle-trained Tuman reared up as well, lashing out with her fore-hooves. Rodion's horse too began capering heavily, right at the gate, and then Sergei raised his voice, rich and full despite his age, to say, "Come, Brother, let us all pray—" just as Tuman kicked one of the guards. When the confusion was at its height, Vasya slipped through the gate, Morozko in her wake.

Forget. Just like that other night on this same river. Forget that they could see her. Of course, the guards might not have seen her even without magic, so effectively had the three monks drawn all eyes.

She waited in the shadow of the gate. Waited for Sasha to come through with Sergei, so that she could follow them, invisibly, to the Grand Prince's palace, be let in with them, unseen, then go and steal the bridle.

"Am I an utter fool, brother?" asked a familiar voice. Somewhere in its light tones was the clashing of armies, the screaming of men. The Bear stood in the shadow of the gate and seemed to have grown since the last time she saw him, as though nourished by the miasma of fear and sickness swirling about Moscow. "The city is mine," he said. "What do you expect to do, coming here like a ghost in the company of a pack of monks? Betray me to the new religion? See me exorcised? No, I am stronger. You won't have a pleasant prison of forgetfulness this time; it will be chains and long darkness. After I kill her and make her my servant in front of you."

Morozko didn't speak. He had a knife of ice, though the blade dripped water when it moved. His eyes met hers once, wordless.

She ran.

"Witch!" shouted the Bear, in the voice that men could hear. "Witch, there is a witch there!" Heads began to turn; then his voice was cut off abruptly. Morozko had flung his knife at his brother's throat; the Bear had slammed it aside and then the two were grappling like wolves, invisible in the dust.

Vasya fled, heart hammering in her throat, effacing herself in the shadow of buildings.

SHE TRIED NOT TO THINK of what was happening behind her; Sasha and Sergei set to distract Dmitrii, Morozko holding off the Bear.

The rest was up to her.

If it comes to it, I cannot keep him distracted forever, Morozko had said. *Until sunset, not longer. And by sunset it won't matter. He will have the dead, he will have the power of men's fears, that rise in the dark. He must be bound by sunset, Vasya.*

So she ran now, the sweat smarting in her eyes. The gazes of chyerti fell on her like a hail of stones, but she did not turn to see. People went heavily about their business, gasping and sweat-soaked, holding sachets of dried flowers to ward off sickness, paying little heed to a single gawky boy. A dead man lay huddled in a corner between two buildings, flies in his open eyes. Vasya swallowed nausea and ran on. With every step she had to fight down panic at being in Moscow again, and alone. Every sound, every smell, every turn of the streets brought back paralyzing memories; she felt like a girl in a nightmare, trying to run through clinging mud.

The gates of the palace of Serpukhov had been reinforced and reinforced again; spikes of wood lined the top, and there were guards on the gate. She paused, still fighting that stomach-clenching dread, wondering how she was going to—

A voice spoke from the wall-top. She had to look three times before she saw the speaker. It was Olga's dvorovoi. He reached his two hands down to her. "Come," he whispered. "Hurry, hurry."

When she caught the outstretched hands of the dvorovoi, she found them strangely solid. Olga's house-spirits had been little more than mist, before. But now the chyert's hands pulled strongly. Vasya scrabbled for purchase, got a hand up to the top of the wall and pulled herself over.

She dropped to the ground on the other side and found a brassy, silent dooryard, with only a few servants moving slowly. She breathed, groped for the forgetfulness that kept them from seeing her. She could barely manage it. Just there, Solovey had . . .

"I must speak to Varvara," Vasya said to the dvorovoi, between clenched teeth.

But the dvorovoi had her by the hand, and was hustling her in the direction of the bathhouse. "You must see our lady," he said.

SHE WAS LYING CURLED like a puppy in the bathhouse. It was not too hot inside. The bannik must be doing what he could for her, Vasya thought. All the house chyerti must be doing what they could for her. Because she . . .

Marya sat up and Vasya was shocked when she saw the child's face; her eyes set about with rings like bruising.

"Aunt!" Marya cried. "Aunt Vasya!" And she hurled herself sobbing into Vasya's arms.

Vasya caught the child and held her. "Masha, love, tell me what has happened."

Muffled explanations sounded from somewhere around Vasya's breastbone. "You were gone. And Solovey was gone and the man in the oven said the Eater would send dead people into our houses if he could. So I talked to the chyerti and I gave them bread and I cut my hand and gave them blood like you said, and Mother kept us all home from church—"

"Yes," Vasya said with pride, cutting into the flow of words. "You did so well, my brave girl."

Marya straightened abruptly. "I am going to get Mother and Varvara."

"That is a good idea," said Vasya, mindful of the waning day. She didn't like the idea of skulking in the bathhouse while Marya played messenger. But she dared not allow the servants to see her, and she was not enough in control of herself to rely on half-understood magic. Terror was still waiting to snatch her by the throat.

"The chyerti said you'd come back," Marya said happily. "They said you'd come and we'd go to a place by the lake where it's not hot and there are *horses*."

"I hope so," said Vasya fervently. "Now hurry, Masha."

Marya ran off. When she had gone, Vasya took a few deep breaths, fighting to compose herself. She turned her head to the bannik. "I have wept for a nightingale," she said. "But Marya—"

"Is your heir and your mirror," returned the bannik. "She will have a horse and they will love each other as the left hand loves the right. She will ride far and fast when she is grown." He paused. "If you and she survive."

"It is a good future," said Vasya, and then bit her lip, remembering.

"The Bear scorns the house-chyerti, as tools of men," said the bannik. "We will help you as we can. His votary is afraid of us."

"His votary?"

"The priest with golden hair," said the bannik. "The Bear took the priest as his own, and gave him the second sight that frightens him so, now. They are bound together."

"Oh," said Vasya. Much was suddenly obvious to her. "I am going to kill that priest." It wasn't even a vow. It was a statement of fact. "Will it weaken the Bear?"

"Yes," said the bannik. "But it might not be so easy. The Bear will protect him."

Just then, Marya came running back into the dim bathhouse. "They're coming," she said, and frowned. "I *think* they will be glad to see you."

Olga and Varvara appeared in her wake. Olga looked not so much glad as shaken. "It seems you are destined to astonish me with sudden meetings, Vasya," she said. Her voice was crisp, but she took Vasya's hands and held them tightly.

"Sasha said you knew I survived."

"Marya knew," said Olga. "And Varvara. They told us. I had doubts but—" She broke off, searching her sister's face. "How did you escape?"

"It doesn't matter," broke in Varvara. "You put us all in danger once, girl. Now you are doing it again. Did anyone see you?"

"No," said Vasya. "They didn't see me jumping off my own pyre either, and they will not see me now."

Olga paled. "Vasya," she began, "I am sorry—"

"It doesn't matter. The Bear means to dethrone Dmitrii Ivanovich," said Vasya. "To send this whole land into chaos. We must stop him." She swallowed hard, but managed to say steadily, "I must get into Dmitrii Ivanovich's palace."

22

The Princess and the Warrior

S ASHA'S DIVERSION WORKED BETTER THAN HE COULD HAVE HOPED. Tuman, riled by the shouting and trained for war, reared, lashed out, reared again. More guards came, and more, until the three monks were at the center of a noisy throng.

"He is back."

"The witch's brother."

"Aleksandr Peresvet."

"Who is that with him?"

There was no chance of anyone seeing Vasya, Sasha thought grimly. They were all looking at him. More and more people were gathering. The guards looked now as though they didn't know whether to turn inward to him, or outward, so as not to put their backs to the angry crowd. A lettuce came hurtling, rotten, from somewhere out of the crowd, burst at the feet of Sergei's horse. The horses jolted into motion, beginning to climb the hill of the kremlin. More vegetables flew; then a stone. Sergei still sat unruffled on his horse, raised a hand and blessed the crowd. Sasha moved his horse up by his master, protecting Sergei with his body and Tuman's. "This is madness," he muttered. "Rodion—both of you—go to the Archangel. This might get worse. Father—please. I will send word."

"Very well," said Sergei. "But be careful." Sasha was glad when

Rodion and his big horse plowed a way through the crowd, and were gone. The guards were hustling him up toward Dmitrii's palace now; it was becoming a race to see if he would get there before the crowd grew too thick.

But they did get there, and Sasha was glad to hear the gate shut behind him, to dismount in the dust of the dooryard. The Grand Prince was outside, watching a man put a three-year-old colt through his paces. He did not look well, that was Sasha's first thought. He looked heavy and haggard, soft in the jaw, and in his face was a strange dull anger.

The golden-haired priest was standing right behind Dmitrii and *he* looked lovelier than he ever had. His lips and hands were as delicate as a woman's, his eyes impossibly blue. He was dressed as a bishop, his head raised listening to the clamor of the uneasy city. There was no triumph in his face, only a sureness of power that Sasha found infinitely worse.

Dmitrii caught sight of Sasha and stiffened. There was no welcome in his face, only a new, strange tension.

Sasha crossed the dooryard, keeping a wary eye on the priest. "Gosudar," he said to Dmitrii, formal. He did not want to speak of Father Sergei, not with that cold-eyed man listening.

"Come back *now*, Sasha?" Dmitrii burst out. "Now, when the city is full of sickness and unrest, and all the people need is an excuse?" He stopped to listen to the rising noise outside; they were thronging the gates.

"Dmitrii Ivanovich—" Sasha began.

"No," said Dmitrii. "I will not hear you. You will be put under lock, and pray it is enough to quiet the crowd. Father—if you would tell them?"

Konstantin said, with the perfect tone of courageous sorrow, "I will tell them."

Sasha, hating the man, said, "Cousin, I must speak with you."

Dmitrii's eyes met his and Sasha could have sworn that there was something in them, a warning. Then Dmitrii's expression iced over. "You will be put under key," he said. "Until I consult with holy men and decide what to do with you."

"Eudokhia is pregnant again and afraid," Olga said to Vasya. "She will be glad of any diversion. I can get you past the gate."

"It is a risk," Vasya replied. "I had thought Varvara and I could go. Two servants with a message. Who will notice? Or I alone, even. Or you could give me a man you trust, to boost me over the wall." She told them briefly about the capricious invisibility she had discovered in herself, the night of the burning.

Olga crossed herself, and then, frowning, shook her head. "Whatever strange powers you have discovered, Dmitrii still has a large guard on the gate. And what will happen to the manservant if someone sees *him*? Moscow is half-wild. All are afraid of plague, and they are afraid of the dead, and of curses. Indeed, Moscow has been much afraid this summer. I am the Princess of Serpukhov; I can get through the gate most easily. Dressed as my servant, you will be little remarked if someone *does* see you."

"But you—"

"Tell me it is not needful," Olga retorted. "Tell me that to leave things as they are won't put my children in danger, and my husband, and my city. Say that, and I will gladly stay home."

Vasya could not, in conscience, say anything of the kind.

Olga and Varvara were efficient. With scarcely a word spoken, they found Vasya the dress of a servant. Olga bid her horses be harnessed in haste. Marya begged to be allowed to go, but Olga said, "Dear heart, the streets are full of sickness."

"But *you're* going," said Marya, rebellious.

"Yes," said Olga. "But you cannot be spared, my brave love."

"Take care of her," said Vasya to Olga's dvorovoi, and she hugged Marya tightly.

The sisters left the palace of Serpukhov as twilight was thickening to dusk. The closed carriage was stuffy; the sun hovered red. From outside came the murmurs of unrest, the smell of putrefaction from the overcrowded city. Vasya, dressed as a serving-girl, felt more naked than she ever had in her boy's clothes. "We must get back behind your walls before sunset," she said to Olga, laboring to keep her voice even. The fear had begun to rise in her again, when they went back out into Moscow. "Olya, if I am delayed, you will go home without me."

"Of course I will," said Olga. Not for her a grand and foolish sacrifice; Vasya knew she was already taking more of a risk than she wanted. They rode a few moments in silence. Then— "I do not know what to do for Marya," Olga admitted abruptly. "I am doing my best to protect her, but she is too like you. She speaks to things I cannot see; she is growing more elusive every week."

"You cannot protect her from her own nature," said Vasya. "She does not belong here."

"Perhaps she doesn't," Olga said. "But in Moscow I can at least protect from those that mean her ill. What will happen if folk find out her secret?"

Vasya said slowly, "There is a house by a lake, in a wild country. That is where I went, after the fires in Moscow. It is where our grandmother came from, and our great-grandmother. It is in our blood. I am going to go back, when this is over. I am going to build a place that is safe for men and chyerti. If Marya came with me, she would grow up free. She could ride horses, and if she wishes to marry, she may. Or not. Olya, she will wither here. All her life she would mourn something she did not know she'd lost."

The lines of worry deepened about Olga's mouth and eyes. But she didn't answer.

A new silence fell between them. Then Olga spoke again, startling her. "Who was he, Vasya?"

Vasya's eyes flew up.

"Credit me with a little perception at least," said Olga, answering her look. "I have seen enough girls wed."

"He," said Vasya, finding herself suddenly nervous again, in a different way. "He is—" She stumbled to a halt. "He is not a man," she admitted. "He—is one of the unseen folk."

She expected Olga to be shocked. But Olga only frowned. Her eyes searched her sister's face. "Were you willing?"

Vasya did not know if Olga would be more horrified if Vasya had been willing or if she had not. But there was only truth. "I was," she said. "He has saved my life. More than once."

"Are *you* wed?"

Vasya said, "No. I do not—I do not know if we can be. What sacrament would bind him?"

Olga looked sad. "Then you are living beyond the sight of God. I fear for your soul."

"I don't," said Vasya. "He "—she stumbled, finished—"he has been a joy to me." And, drily, "Also a great source of frustration."

Olga smiled a little. Vasya remembered that years before, her sister had been a girl who had dreamed of love and raven-princes. Olga had laid aside the dream, as women must. Perhaps she did not regret it. For the raven-prince was strange and secret; he would draw you out into a dangerous world.

"Would you like to meet him?" Vasya asked suddenly.

"I?" Olga asked, sounding shocked. Then her lips firmed. "Yes. Even a girl in love with a devil needs someone to negotiate for her."

Vasya bit her lips, not sure whether to be glad or worried.

They were getting to Dmitrii's gate now. The general noise of the city had heightened. A crowd clamored outside the gate. Her skin crawled.

Then a single, musical voice rose above the shouting. It silenced the mob. Controlled it.

A voice she knew. Vasya felt the greatest shock of fear she'd ever known. Her breath came short; her skin broke out in a clammy dew of sweat. Only Olga's merciless hand on her arm recalled her.

"Don't you dare faint," said Olga. "You say you can make yourself unseen. Will *he* be able to see you? He is a holy man. And he wished you dead, once."

Vasya tried to think around the fear beating like wings in her skull. Konstantin wasn't a holy man, but—he could see chyerti now. The Bear had given him that power. Could he see her? "I don't know," she admitted.

They were rolling to a stop. Vasya thought she would choke if she could not get a breath of fresh air.

Konstantin's voice spoke again, cool and measured, just outside. She had to clench her teeth and her fists to keep from making a sound. Her whole body shook.

Now there came the sounds of a crowd that was parting, grudgingly, to let them through. Olga sat still on her woolen cushion, seemingly unruffled. But her eye fell with some concern on Vasya, gray-faced and sweating.

Vasya managed to speak between her clenched teeth. "I'm all right, Olya. Just—remembering."

"I know," said Olga, and drew a deep breath. "All right," she said firmly. "Follow my lead." There was no time for more. The gate creaked, and then they were in the dooryard of the Grand Prince of Moscow.

THE EVENING SUN WAS SLANTING, and Olga was blinding in a jeweled headdress, her long hair plaited up with silk, hung with silver ornaments. She got out first. Vasya, holding on to her courage as hard as she could, stepped out in her wake. Olga at once seized her sister's arm, ostensibly for support. But it was the Princess of Serpukhov in control; she was dragging Vasya toward the steps of the terem, holding her up when she faltered.

"Don't look back," Olga muttered. "He will come back through the gate in a moment. But the terem is safe. Wait a little, then I will send you out on an errand; keep out of sight and you'll be all right."

That sounded like sense. But a glance at the sun showed it slanting ever farther. They had an hour at most, and Vasya found her mind so crowded with fear and fearful memory that she could hardly think.

There was the new stable, built over the ruin of the old. Now they were on the terem-steps, which Vasya had last climbed in darkness to rescue Marya. Somewhere at her back was Konstantin Nikonovich, who had nearly killed her in the cruelest way possible. And now he had the king of chaos for his ally.

Where was Morozko now? Where were Sasha and Sergei? How—?

Olga hurried them on, regal. They climbed the steps, were admitted. Vasya, fighting for self-control, felt relief for once when the terem-door was shut behind them. But now they were in the workroom that Kaschei had filled with illusions, where he had almost killed Marya and her—

Vasya's gulp of air was almost a sob, and Olga shot her a stern look—*don't you dare break now, sister*—just as Eudokhia Dmitreeva, Grand Princess of Moscow, seized upon Olga with delight. Kept in their airless rooms, Eudokhia and her women were desperate for any diversion.

Vasya crept off to stand against the wall with the other servants. She could barely draw a full breath around the grip of fear on her lungs. In a moment, Olga would judge it safe and . . .

The door of the terem opened. Vasya froze.

Konstantin's golden hair gleamed in the dimness. His face was serene as ever, but his gaze was puzzled, wary.

Vasya pressed herself into the shadows near the wall, just as Olga glanced up, caught sight of Konstantin, and at once swooned with perfect accuracy and startling skill. She fell directly onto a table of sweetmeats and wine, sending everything flying up in a great sticky wash.

If Sasha's theatrics at the gate had been a little stilted, everyone was taken in by Olga's diversion. Immediately the women flocked; even Konstantin, at the doorway, took a few steps into the room. There was just enough room for Vasya to get around him.

He can't see you. Believe it, believe it . . .

She ran for the door.

But he could see her. She heard his indrawn breath, and turned her head.

Their eyes met.

A mingling of shock and horror and rage and fear crossed his face. Her legs shook, her stomach was full of acid. In an instant like a lightning-strike, they both stood frozen, staring at each other.

Then she turned and ran. It wasn't anything so noble as running to find the bridle, to put an end to all this. No, she was fleeing for her life.

Behind her, she heard the terem-door slam open, heard his rich voice raised, shouting. But she'd already ducked into the nearest door, passed a room full of weavers like a wraith, gone back outside again, descending. All the quivering panic of the last hours had broken open; all she wanted to do was run.

She slipped through another doorway, found the room empty, and with a wrench of desperate effort, paused and forced herself to think.

The bridle. She must get the bridle. Before dusk. If she could only keep everyone safe until midnight, perhaps the Midnight-road could save them. Perhaps.

Or perhaps she'd die, screaming.

Voices sounded just outside the outer door. There was a second door, leading farther into Dmitrii's palace; she fled through. The place was a warren. Low-ceilinged, dim rooms, many of them full of goods: skins and barrels of flour and silk-figured carpets. Other rooms housed workshops for weaving and carpentry, the souter, the bootmaker.

Vasya, still running, came to a room full of bales of wool and hid herself behind the biggest. Kneeling, she drew her little belt-knife and, with shaking fingers, cut her hand, and turned her palm so that the drops pattered onto the floor.

"Master," she said to the air, in a voice that cracked, "will you help me? I mean this house no harm."

Below her, in the dooryard, Vasya heard curses, the shouts of men, the screams of women. A servant came running through the room of bales. "They are saying there is someone in the palace."

"A witch!"

"A ghost!"

Dmitrii's faded domovoi stepped out from behind one of the bales of wool. He whispered, "You are in danger here. The priest will kill you for hatred, and the Bear to spite his brother."

"I don't care what happens to me," said Vasya, her bravado belied by her shallow-breathed voice, "so long as my sister and brother live. Where is the treasure-room?"

"Follow me," said the domovoi, and Vasya drew a deep breath and followed. She was grateful suddenly for every scrap of bread she'd ever given a household-spirit, for now all those homely tributes, bread and blood, quickened the domovoi's feet, as he led her deep into the mad jumble of Dmitrii's palace.

Down, and down again, to an earth-smelling passage and a great, iron-bound door. Vasya thought of caves and traps. She was still breathing faster than the exertion called for.

"Here," said the domovoi. "Hurry." Next moment, Vasya heard the sound of heavy feet, tramping. Shadows moved on the walls; she had only a moment.

Seized again by terror, she forgot she could be invisible; she forgot to ask the domovoi to open the door. Instead she lurched forward, driven by the sound of feet above, and put a hand on the treasure-room door. Reality twisted; the door gave. With a gasp, she tumbled inside and scrambled into a corner behind some bronze-chased shields.

Voices sounded in the corridor.

"I heard something."

"You imagined it."

A pause.

"The door is ajar."

A creak as the door swung open. A heavy step. "There is no one here."

"What fool left the door unlocked?"

"A thief?"

"Search the room."

After all this? Were they to find her so, drag her up into Moscow, where Konstantin would be waiting?

No. No they would not.

A crack of thunder sounded suddenly outside, as though to give voice to her panic and her courage both. The palace shook. There came a sudden roar of rain.

The men's torches went out. She heard them swearing.

Her hands trembled. The sounds of storm, the darkness all around, the great door opening at her touch, were like three pieces of a nightmare. Reality was shifting too fast to understand.

The men's shock at the noise and unexpected darkness had won her a reprieve, but that was all. They would relight their torches. They would search, and find her. *Could* she make herself invisible this time? When they were searching for her in this small room?

She wasn't sure. So instead Vasya clenched her fists and thought of

Morozko. She thought of the sleep like death that the winter-king held in his hands. Sleep. The men would go to sleep. If she could only forget they were awake.

She did. And they did. They crumpled to the packed-dirt floor of the treasure-room. Their cries died away.

Morozko was there, between one blink and the next. She hadn't put the men to sleep. *He* had. He was there, himself, real, in the treasure-room with her.

Now the winter-king was turning pale eyes on her. She stared. It was really him. Pulled to her, somehow, as she remembered his power. As though drawing him to her was easier than calling down sleep herself.

Summoned. She'd summoned the winter-king like a stray spirit.

They both realized it at the same time. The shock in his face mirrored the feeling in hers.

For an instant, they were silent.

Then he spoke. "A thunderstorm, Vasya?" he said, with effort.

Speaking between dry lips, she whispered, "It wasn't me. It just happened."

Morozko shook his head. "No it didn't just happen. And now, with the rain, it is dark enough outside. He need no longer delay. Fool, I cannot keep him distracted from a cellar!" Morozko wasn't wounded, but he looked—battered—in a way she could not define, and his eyes were wild. He looked as though he'd been fighting. He probably had been, until she pulled him away, unknowing.

"I didn't mean to," she said, her voice small. "I was so frightened." Reality was rippling around her like cloth in a high wind. She wasn't sure if he was really there or if she'd just imagined him. "I *am* so frightened . . ."

Without thinking she cupped her palms and found them suddenly full of blue flames, and she could see his face properly. Fire in her hands . . . It didn't burn her. She was on the edge of mad laughter, as blind terror mingled with newfound power. "Konstantin saw me," she said. "I ran. I was so afraid; I couldn't stop remembering. So I called a thunderstorm. And now you're here. Two devils and two people—"

She knew she wasn't making sense. "Where is the bridle?" She cast around, gripping the fire in her two hands as though it were an ordinary lamp.

"Vasya," said Morozko. "Enough magic. Let it go. Enough for one day. You will bend your mind until it breaks."

"It is not my mind bending," she said, lifting up the fire between them. "You are here, aren't you? It is everything else. It is the whole world *bending*." She was shaking; the flames jerked back and forth.

"There is no difference between the world without and the world within," said the winter-king. "Close your hands. Let go." He shoved the locked door farther open to give them a little light from the passageway. Then he turned back to her, put his hands around hers, folded her fingers around the flames. They vanished, swift as they had come. "Vasya, my brother's very presence stirs up fear, and in its wake, he brings madness. You must—"

She hardly heard him. Shaking, she looked all around her for the golden bridle. Where was Olga? What had Konstantin done? What was he doing now? She broke away from Morozko, knelt beside a great iron-bound chest. When she pushed the lid, it gave. Of course it did. There were no locks in a nightmare. This was a dream; she could do what she liked. Was she truly in a cellar, a fugitive, back in Moscow, had she summoned a death-god?

"*Enough,*" said Morozko from behind her. "You will drive yourself mad with impossibilities." His cool, insubstantial hands fell on her shoulders. "Vasya listen, listen, *listen to me.*"

Still she didn't hear him; she was staring at the contents of the chest, hardly noticing the shaking of her hands.

This time, he lifted her up bodily, turned her, saw her face.

He whispered something harsh under his breath and said, "Tell me things that are true. *Tell me.*"

She stared at him blindly and said, beginning to laugh hysterically, "Nothing is real. Midnight is a place and there is a storm outside from a clear evening and you were not here and now you are and I am *so frightened*—"

Grimly, he said, "Your name is Vasilisa Petrovna. Your father was a country lord named Pyotr Vladimirovich. As a child you stole honey-cakes—no, look at me." He lifted her face forcibly to his, kept on with his strange litany. Telling her true things. Not part of the nightmare.

Mercilessly he went on, "And then your horse was killed by the mob."

She jerked in his grip, denying the truth of it. Perhaps, she thought suddenly, she could make it so that Solovey had never died, here in this nightmare where anything was possible. But he shook her, lifted her chin so that she had to meet his eyes again, spoke into her ear, the voice of winter in this airless cellar, reminding her of her joys and her mistakes, her loves and her flaws, until she found herself back in her own skin, shaken but able to think.

She realized how close she had come, in that dark treasure-room, with reality collapsing like a rotten tree, to going mad. Realized, too, what had happened to Kaschei, how he had become a monster.

"Mother of God," she breathed. "Ded Grib—he said that magic makes men mad. But I didn't really understand . . ."

Morozko's eyes searched hers, and then some indefinable tension seemed to go out of him. "Why do you think so few people do magic?" he asked, getting hold of himself, stepping back. She could still feel the impress of his fingers, realized how hard he had been gripping her. As hard as she'd held him.

"Chyerti do," she said.

"Chyerti do tricks," he said. "Men and women are far stronger." He paused. "Or they go mad." He knelt beside the chest she had opened. "And it is easier to fall prey to fear and madness, when the Bear is abroad."

She drew a deep breath, and knelt beside him before the open chest. In it lay the golden bridle.

Twice before she had seen it, once in daylight on Pozhar's head and once again in a dark stable, where the gold paled to nothing beside the mare's brilliance. But this time it lay on a fine cushion, glimmering with an unpleasant sheen.

Morozko took the thing in his hands, so that the pieces of it spilled like water across his fingers. "No chyert could have made this," he said, turning it over. "I do not know how Kaschei did it." He sounded torn between admiration and horror. "But it would, I think, bind anything it was put on, flesh or spirit."

She reached down flinching hands. The gold was heavy, supple, the bit a horrible, spiked thing. Vasya shuddered in sympathy, thinking of the scars on Pozhar's face. Hastily she undid the straps and buckles, reins and headstall, so that she was left with two golden ropes. The bit she flung to the floor. The other pieces lay in her hands like quiescent snakes. "Can you use these?" she asked, offering them to Morozko.

He put a hand to the gold, hesitated. "No," he said. "It is a magic made by mortals, and for them."

"All right," said Vasya. She wound the golden ropes one about each wrist, making sure she could snap them loose quickly, at need. "Then let's go find him."

Outside there came another crack of thunder.

23

Faith and Fear

KONSTANTIN FINISHED QUIETING THE CROWD AT THE GRAND PRINCE of Moscow's gates. The Princess of Serpukhov's carriage was being unharnessed; the woman herself had already disappeared, with her attendant, up the terem-steps.

One day, Konstantin thought grimly, he wasn't going to soothe the people of Moscow anymore but rouse them to savagery once again. He remembered the power of that night: all those thousands receptive to his softest word.

He craved that power.

Soon the devil had promised. *Soon.* But now he must go back to the Grand Prince, and make sure that Dmitrii gave no hearing to Aleksandr Peresvet.

He turned to cross the dooryard, and saw a little, wispy creature blocking his way.

"Poor dupe," said Olga's dvorovoi.

Konstantin ignored him, lips set thin, and strode across the dooryard.

"He lied to you, you know. She's not dead."

Despite himself, Konstantin's steps slowed; he turned his head. "She?"

"She," said the dvorovoi. "Go into the terem now, and see for yourself. The Bear betrays all who follow him."

"He wouldn't betray me," said Konstantin, eyeing the dvorovoi with disgust. "He needs me."

"See for yourself," whispered the dvorovoi again. "And remember— you are stronger than he."

"I am only a man; he is a demon."

"And subject to your blood," whispered the dvorovoi. "When the time comes, remember that." With a slow smile, he pointed up the terem-steps.

Konstantin hesitated. But then he turned toward the terem.

He hardly knew what he said to the attendant. But it must have worked, for he stepped through the door, and stood a moment, blinking in the dimness. The Princess of Serpukhov, without once glancing his way, swooned. Konstantin felt an instant's disgust. Only a woman, come to visit her fellows.

Then a servant ran for the door, and he recognized her.

Vasilisa Petrovna.

She was alive.

For a long, electric moment he stared. A scar on her face, her black hair cropped short, but it was her.

Then she bolted and he shouted, hardly knowing what he said. He followed her, blindly, casting around to see where she'd gone—only to see the Bear in the dooryard.

Medved was dragging a man in his wake. Or—not a man. Another devil. The second devil had colorless, watchful eyes, and was strangely familiar. The edges of him seemed to bleed into the shadows of the failing day.

"She is here," said Konstantin raggedly to the Bear. "Vasilisa Petrovna."

For an instant it seemed the second devil smiled. The Bear spun and struck him across the face. "What are you planning, brother?" he said. "I see it in your eyes. There is something. Why have you let her come back here? What is she doing?"

The devil said nothing. The Bear turned back to Konstantin. "Summon men; go and get her, man of God."

Konstantin didn't move. "You knew," he said. "You knew she was alive. You lied."

"I knew," said the devil, impatient. "But what difference does it make? She's going to die now. We'll both make sure of it."

Konstantin had no words. Vasya had lived. She'd beaten him after all. Even his own monster had been on her side. Had kept her secret. Could it be that everyone was against him? Not only God, but the devil too? What had it all been for: the suffering and the dead, the glory and the ashes, the heat and the shame of that summer?

The Bear had filled the gaping hole of his faith with his sheer electrifying presence, and Konstantin had come, as though despite himself, to believe in something new. Not in faith, but in the reality of power. In his alliance with *his* monster.

Now the belief shattered at his feet.

"You lied to me," he said again.

"I do lie," said the Bear, but he was frowning now.

The second devil raised his head and looked between them. "I could have warned you, brother," he said, his voice dry and exhausted. "Against lying."

In that moment two things happened.

The second devil suddenly disappeared, as though he'd never been there at all. The Bear was left gaping at his empty hand.

And Konstantin, rather than go out and join the palace guard in searching for Vasya, plunged back into the terem without a sound, his soul aflame with desperate purpose.

THE WILD-EYED DOMOVOI MET Vasya and Morozko just outside the treasure-room. Vasya said, "What is happening?"

"It is dark now; the Bear is going to let them in!" cried the domovoi, every hair standing on end. "The dvorovoi can't hold the gates, and I don't think I can keep the house."

Another crack of thunder sounded. "My brother is done with subtleties," said Morozko.

"Come on," said Vasya.

They burst out of the palace, onto a landing, and looked down at a landscape transformed. It was raining, hard and steadily, lit by intermittent flashes of lightning. The dooryard was swimming in mud already, but in the center was a knot of men, strangely still.

Guards, Vasya saw, squinting through the rain. Olga's guards, and Dmitrii's, standing bewildered.

The knot of them broke apart. Vasya glimpsed Konstantin Nikonovich, his golden head rain-wet in the middle of the dooryard.

He was holding her sister Olga by the arm.

He had a knife to the princess's throat.

His beautiful voice was shouting Vasya's name.

The guards, Vasya could see, were torn between fear for the princess and bewildered submission to the holy madman. They stood still; if any remonstrated with Konstantin it was lost in the noise of falling water. If a guard moved nearer, Konstantin backed up, holding the knife right against Olga's throat.

"Come out!" he roared. "Witch! Come out or I'll kill her."

Vasya's first, overwhelming instinct was to sprint down to her sister, but she forced herself to pause and think. Would revealing herself win Olga any respite? Perhaps, if Olga disavowed her. Yet Vasya hesitated. The Bear was standing behind the priest. But Medved wasn't really watching Konstantin. His gaze was turned out into the rain-soaked darkness. "Calling the dead," said Morozko, his eyes on his brother. "You must get your sister out of the dooryard."

That settled it. "Come with me," she said, gathered her courage and stepped bareheaded out into the rain. The guards might not have recognized her in the stormy dusk: a girl who was supposed to be dead. But Konstantin's eyes locked on her the instant she stepped into the dooryard and he fell utterly silent, watching her come toward him.

First one guard's head turned, then another. She heard their voices: "Is that—?"

"No, it can't be."

"It is. The holy father knew."

"A ghost?"

"A woman."

"A witch."

Now their drawn weapons were turning toward her. But she ignored them. The Bear, the priest, her sister—those were the only things she could see.

Such a current of rage and bitter memory ran between her and Konstantin that even the guards must have felt it, for they made a path for her. But they closed ranks again at her back, swords in their hands.

Stark in Vasya's mind was the last time she'd faced Konstantin Nikonovich. Her horse's blood lay between them, and her own life.

Now it was Olga who was caught up in their hatred; Vasya thought of a cage of fire, and she was deathly afraid.

But her voice didn't shake.

"I am here," said Vasya. "Let my sister go."

KONSTANTIN DIDN'T SPEAK IMMEDIATELY. The Bear did. Was it her imagination or did his face show an instant of unease? "Still in your right mind?" the Bear said to Vasya. "A pity. Well met again, brother," he added to Morozko. "What magic pulled you from my grip before—?" He broke off, looking between Vasya and the winter-king.

"Ah," he said, softly. "Stronger than I would have guessed: her power and your bond both. Well it is no matter. Hoping to be beaten again?"

Morozko made no answer at all. His eyes were on the gate as though he could see beyond the bronze-studded wood. "Hurry, Vasya," he said.

"You can't stop it," said Medved.

Konstantin flinched at the sound of the Bear's voice. His knife was fraying the cloth of the veil about Olga's face. As though she were speaking to a frightened horse, Vasya said to Konstantin, "What do you want, Batyushka?"

Konstantin didn't answer; she could see he didn't really know. All his prayers had earned him only silence from God. Yielding up his soul to the Bear had won him neither that creature's honesty nor his loyalty. In the stinging grip of his own self-hatred, he wanted to hurt her by any means, and had not thought beyond.

His hands shook. Only Olga's headdress and veil were keeping her from being cut by accident. The Bear cast a benign eye over the scene, drinking up the raw emotion of it, but most of his attention was still on the world outside Dmitrii's walls.

Olga was white to the lips but dignified still. Her eyes met Vasya's without a tremor. With trust.

Vasya said to Konstantin, showing him her open palms, "I will yield myself up to you, Batyushka. But you must let my sister go up into the terem, let her go back to the women."

"Trick me, witch?" Konstantin's voice had lost none of its beauty, but the control was gone; it boomed and cracked. "You yielded to the fire too; but it was all a trick. Am I to be taken in again? You and your devils. Bind her hands," he added to the guard. "Bind her hands and feet. I will keep her in a chapel where devils cannot get in uninvited, and she cannot trick me again."

The guards stirred uneasily, but none of them made a decisive movement forward.

"Now!" screamed Konstantin, stamping his foot. "Lest her devils come for us all!" His glance went with horror from Morozko at Vasya's shoulder, to the Bear at his own side, to the house-chyerti gathered in the yard, watching—

Not watching the drama in the dooryard. Watching the gate. Despite the rain, Vasya caught a whiff of rot. A little curl of triumph was playing about the Bear's lips. There was no time. She must get Olya away . . .

A new voice fell into the tense silence. "Holy Father, what is this?"

Dmitrii Ivanovich strode into the dooryard. Attendants scurried, disregarded, at his back; his long yellow hair was dark with water, curling up under his cap. The guards parted to let the Grand Prince through. He halted in the center of the ring, looked directly at Vasya. In his face was wonder. But not, Vasya noted, surprise. She met Dmitrii's eyes with sudden hope.

"See?" snapped Konstantin, not slacking his grip on Olga. He had regained some control of his voice; the word snapped out like a fist.

"There is the witch that set fire to Moscow. She was, we thought, justly punished. But through black magic, here she stands." This time the guards growled agreement. A dozen blades were pointed at Vasya's breast.

"Hold them a few moments longer," said the Bear to Konstantin. "And we will have victory."

A spasm of rage crossed Konstantin's face.

"Vasya, tell Dmitrii you must pull back," said Morozko. "There is no time."

"Dmitrii Ivanovich, we must get into the palace," said Vasya. "Now."

"A witch indeed," said Dmitrii coldly to Vasya. "Back to the fire you will go, I will stake my reign on it. We do not suffer witches to live. Holy Father," he said to Konstantin. "Please. Both these women will face the harshest justice. But it must be justice before all the people, not in the mud of the dooryard."

Konstantin hesitated.

The Bear snarled suddenly. "Lies; he is lying. He knows. The monk told him."

The gate shook. Screams sounded from the city. Thunder flashed in the streaming heavens. "Back!" snapped Morozko suddenly. This time the men heard him. Heads turned uneasily, wondering who had spoken. There was horror in his face. "Back now behind walls or you'll all be dead by moonrise."

There was a smell riding the wind that lifted every hair on her body. More screams came from the city. In a flash of lightning, the dvorovoi could be seen now with both hands against the shaking gate. "Batyushka, *I beg you*," she said to Konstantin, and threw herself in supplication in the mud at his feet.

The priest's eyes followed her down, just for a moment, but it was enough. Dmitrii leaped for Olga, dragged her away from the priest just as the gate flew open. Konstantin's knife caught in Olga's veil, tore it away from her chin on one side, but Olga was unwounded, and Vasya was on her feet once more and scrambling back.

The dead came into the dooryard of the Grand Prince of Moscow.

THE PLAGUE HAD NOT been as bad as it could have been, that summer. Not as bad as ten years before; it only sputtered among the poor of Moscow like tinder that refused to catch completely.

But the dead had died in fear and those were the ones the Bear could use. Now the result of the summer's work came through the gate. Some wore their grave-clothes, some were naked, their bodies marked with the blackened swellings that had killed them. Worst of all, in their eyes was still that fear. They were still afraid, seeking in the darkness for anything familiar.

One of Dmitrii's guards cried out, staring, "Holy Father, save us!"

Konstantin made not a sound; he was standing frozen, the knife still in his hand. Vasya wanted to kill him, as she'd never wanted to kill anyone in her life. She wanted to bury that knife in his heart.

But there was no time. Her family meant more than her own sorrow.

Faced with Konstantin's silence, the guards were backing up, their nerve wavering. Dmitrii was still supporting Olga; unexpectedly he spoke to Vasya, his voice clear and calm. "Can those things be slain like men, Vasya?"

Vasya spoke Morozko's answer, as he said it into her ear. "No. Fire will slow them, and injury, but that is all."

Dmitrii shot the sky an irritated glance. It was still pouring rain. "Not fire. Injury then," he said and raised his voice to call concise orders.

Dmitrii had not Konstantin's control, the liquid beauty of tone, but his voice was loud and brisk, even cheerful, encouraging his men. Suddenly they were no longer a knot of frightened men, backing away from something horrible. Suddenly they were warriors, massed to face a foe.

Just in time. Their blades steadied just as the dead things ran for them, openmouthed. More and more dead things were coming through the gate. A dozen—more.

"Morozko!" Vasya snapped. "Can you—?"

"I can put them down if I touch them," he said. "But I cannot command them all."

"We have to get into the palace," Vasya said. She was supporting Olga now; her sister, used to the smooth floors of her own terem, was clumsy in the sloppy dooryard. Dmitrii had gone forward with his men and Olga's; they had formed a hollow square, bristling with weapons, about the women, all of them backing up together toward the door of the palace.

Konstantin stood still in the rain, as though frozen. The Bear stood beside him, eyes alight, shouting his army on, joyful.

The first upyry collided with Dmitrii's guards. A man screamed. Konstantin flinched. Little more than a boy, the man was already on the ground, his throat torn away.

Morozko's touch was gentle, but his face was savage as he sent that upyr back down into death, whipped round to do the same to two others.

Vasya knew that she and Olga weren't going to reach the door. More and more upyry were flowing into the lightning-lit dooryard. The guards' hollow square was surrounded, and only their frail bodies stood between Olga and . . .

They had to bind the Bear. They had to.

Vasya squeezed her sister's hand. "I have to help them, Olya," she said.

"I'll be all right," said Olga firmly. "God go with you." Her hands clasped in prayer.

Vasya let go her sister's hand and came up beside Dmitrii Ivanovich, in line with his men.

The men were holding the dead things off with spears, looks of sick terror on their faces, but Dmitrii had to step forward to behead one, and another ran up, taking advantage of the break in the line.

Vasya shut her fists and forgot that the dead thing was not burning.

The creature caught like a torch, then another, a third. They didn't burn long; the rain put out the fire and the dead things were still coming, blackened and moaning.

But Dmitrii saw. As the nearest dead thing caught fire, his sword sheared through water and flame, glittering, and cut off the thing's head.

He shot Vasya a grin of unfeigned delight. There was blood on his cheek. "I knew you had unclean powers," he said.

"Be grateful, cousin," Vasya retorted.

"Oh, I am," said the Grand Prince of Moscow, and his smile put heart in her, despite the drenching rain, the dooryard packed with nightmarish things. He surveyed the dooryard. "But I hope you have better than little fires—cousin."

She found herself smiling at the acknowledged kinship, even as Dmitrii buried his sword in another upyr, leaping back to the protection of his men's spears at the last moment. She set three more alight, horribly, only for the rain to douse them again. The dead things were wary now of the men's blades, and deathly afraid of Morozko's hands. But the death-god was only a wraith in the rain, a black shape remote and terrible, and already six living men were down, not moving.

The Bear had grown gigantic, fatted with summer's heat, with sickness and suffering, and to Vasya his voice seemed louder than the thunder, urging his army on. Medved did not look like a man anymore; he wore the shape of a bear, shoulders broad enough to blot out the stars.

Dmitrii put his sword through another one, but it stuck. He refused to relinquish it, and Vasya dragged him back to the safety of the square of guards just in time. The square had shrunk.

"You are both bleeding," said Olga, only a slight tremor in her voice, and Vasya, glancing down, saw that she was; her arm was grazed, and Dmitrii's cheek.

"Never fear, Olga Vladimirova," said Dmitrii to her. He was smiling still, bright and calm, and Vasya understood anew why her brother gave this man such loyalty.

From the ring of guards, a man screamed, and Morozko leaped, too late to save him. The Bear laughed even as Morozko flung the dead thing down. Still more were coming into the dooryard.

"Where is Sasha now?" Vasya demanded of Dmitrii.

"Gone to the monastery for Sergei, of course," said the Grand Prince. "I sent him as soon as the priest went mad. A good thing too. Yon's the work of holy men, not warriors; we're going to die if we don't get help." He said this quite matter-of-factly: a general weighing his force's chances. But then his narrow-eyed gaze found Konstantin, who was standing motionless beside the Bear's hulking shadow. There was death in it. The dead took no notice of the priest.

"I knew the priest was up to something, the way he harped on my cousin's wickedness," said Dmitrii. He took off another dead thing's head, speaking in grunts. "I had Sasha thrown in prison just to draw Konstantin out. When I went down to see him, Sasha told me everything. In the nick of time too. I thought the priest a bit of a charlatan. But I never would have thought—"

To Dmitrii, it looked as though Konstantin were doing it all himself, controlling the dead. He couldn't see the Bear. Vasya knew better. She could see Konstantin's face tormented in the flashes of lightning; she could see the Bear's too, ferocious, joyful, indomitable.

Vasya said, "I must get to Konstantin. He is standing beside the devil that is causing all this. But I cannot cross the dooryard alive."

Dmitrii pursed his lips. But he did not speak. After a brief pause, he nodded once, turned and began giving his men crisp orders.

"You have no power over the dead," whispered the voice of the dvorovoi in Konstantin's ear. Konstantin barely flinched at the sound, so lost was he in horror. "But you have power over him."

Slowly, Konstantin turned. "Do I?"

"Your blood," said the dvorovoi, "will bind the devil. You are not powerless."

Vasya's nose was full of the smell of earth and rot and dried blood. The air was full of hissing rain and shuffling footsteps. The whole scene was illuminated luridly by a flash of lightning. She could hear Olga, still protected by the ring of men, praying softly and continuously.

There was a terrible blaze of blue-white light in Morozko's face, his hair plastered to his skull with the rain; he did not look human. She could see the stars of the forest beyond life reflected in his eyes. She seized his arm, as he passed near the ring of men. He rounded on her. For a moment, the full weight of his strange power, his endless years, looked out at her from his gaze. Then a little humanity bled back into his face.

"We have to get to the Bear," said Vasya.

He nodded; she wasn't sure he could speak.

Dmitrii was still giving orders. To Vasya he said, "I am splitting the men in two. Half will stay with the princess. The other half will form a wedge, and cut across the dooryard. Do what you can to help us."

Dmitrii finished giving orders, and the men immediately split. Olga was surrounded by a shrunken ring, pushing back toward the door of the palace.

The rest made a wedge and drove forward, shouting, toward the Bear and Konstantin, through the packed mass of dead.

Vasya ran with them, and a dozen upyry bloomed into flame on either side. Morozko's swift hand caught the dead by wrist and throat, banishing them.

There were so many. Their progress slowed, but still they came nearer the Bear. Nearer. Now the men were faltering. In their faces was sick fright. Even Dmitrii looked suddenly afraid.

The Bear was doing it; he grinned. As the men wavered, the upyry drove forward with renewed strength. One of Dmitrii's men fell, his throat torn away, and then another. A third shrieked with horror as sharp teeth sank into his wrist.

Vasya set her jaw. The fear buffeted her, too, but it wasn't real. She knew that. It was the Bear's trick. She loosed the fire from her soul again, and this time it flared from the Bear's streaming coat.

Medved turned his head, snapping, and the fire instantly died. But she had used his moment of inattention. While Morozko kept the dead things off her, she threw herself across the last few steps, unwound the golden rope from her wrist and flung it over his head.

The Bear dodged, somehow. He dodged the links as they flew. Laughing, he lunged, jaws open, to snatch at Morozko. Though the frost-demon ducked, Vasya didn't have time for another try, for the movement had pulled Morozko from the side and the dead things had closed round her. "Vasya!" Morozko shouted. A slimy hand caught at her hair; she didn't bother to look before she set the creature afire. It fell back, howling. But there were so many. Dmitrii's wedge had splintered; men were fighting individual battles all over the dooryard. The Bear was keeping Morozko from her, and the dead were closing in once more . . .

A new voice sounded from the direction of the gate. Not a chyert or a dead thing.

It was her brother standing there, sword in hand. Beside him stood his master, Sergei Radonezhsky. They both looked disheveled, as though they'd had a hard ride through dangerous streets. The rain ran down Sasha's drawn sword.

Sergei lifted his hand and made the sign of the cross. "In the name of the Father," he said.

Astonishingly, the dead things froze. Even the Bear stilled at the sound of that voice. Somewhere in the dark, a bell began to ring.

A touch of fear showed even in the winter-king's eyes.

The lightning flashed again, illuminating Konstantin's face, which had gone slack with horrified wonder. Vasya thought, *He believed there was nothing more in this world than devils and his own will.*

Sergei's praying was quiet, measured. But his voice cut through the hammering rain, and every word echoed clearly around the dooryard.

The dead still didn't move.

"Be at peace," finished Sergei. "Do not trouble the living world again."

And, impossibly, all the dead crumpled to earth.

Morozko breathed out a single, shattered breath.

Vasya saw the Bear's face contorted with rage. He had underestimated men's faith, and just like that, his army was gone. But Medved himself was still unbound, still free. Now he would flee, into the night, into the storm.

"Morozko," she said. "Quickly—"

But the lightning flashed again, showed them Konstantin, his golden hair rain-dark, standing before the hulking shadow of the Bear. A gust brought the priest's carrying voice clearly to her ears. "You lied about that too, then," said Konstantin, his voice small but clear. "You said there was no God. But the holy father prayed and—"

"There isn't a God," Vasya heard the Bear say. "There is only faith."

"What is the difference?"

"I don't know. Come, we must go."

"Devil, you lied. You *lied again*." A break in that flawless voice, a croak like an old man coughing. "God was there—there all the time."

"Perhaps," said the Bear. "And perhaps not. The truth is that no one knows, man or devil. Come with me now. They will kill you if you stay."

Konstantin's eyes were steady on the Bear's. "No," he said. "They won't." He raised a blade. "Go back to wherever you crept from," he said. "I have one power. The devils told me this too, and once I was also a man of God."

The Bear's clawed hand shot out. But the priest was faster. Konstantin drew the knife swiftly across his own throat.

The Bear caught the knife, wrenched it away. Too late. Neither one made a sound. The lightning flashed again. Vasya saw the Bear's face, saw him catch Konstantin as he fell, put hands—human hands now—to the blood pouring through the split skin of the priest's throat.

Vasya stepped forward and whipped the rope round the Bear's neck, drew it tight.

He didn't dodge this time. He couldn't, caught already by the priest's sacrifice. Instead he just shuddered, head bowed beneath the rope's power.

Vasya wrapped the other golden thing about his wrists. He didn't move.

She should have felt triumph then.

It was over, and they had won.

But when the Bear lifted his eyes to hers, there was no longer any rage in his face. Instead his eyes looked beyond her, found his twin. "Please," he said.

Please? Please have mercy? Set me free once more? Somehow, Vasya didn't think so. She didn't understand.

The Bear's eyes went again to the priest dying in the mud; he barely seemed to notice the golden rope.

Triumph in Morozko's voice, and a strange note, like unwilling understanding. "You know I won't."

The Bear's mouth twisted. It wasn't a smile. "I know you won't," he said. "I had to try."

The gold and blue head was dark with rain, pale with death. Konstantin's hand rose, streaming blood in the darkness. The Bear said, *"Let me touch him, damn you,"* to Vasya, and she stepped back bewildered, allowing the Bear to kneel and catch the priest's wavering hand. He closed his own thick fingers tight around it, ignoring the bound wrists. "You are a fool, man of God," he said. "You never understood."

Konstantin said, in a blood-filled whisper, "I never understood what?"

"That I do keep faith, in my own fashion," said the Bear. A twist of his lips. "I did love your hands."

The artist's hand, with its expressive fingers and cruel, tapering nails, was limp as a dead bird in the chyert's grip. In Konstantin's eyes, already milky, fixed on the Bear, was an expression of puzzlement. "You are a devil," he said again, gasping for air as the blood left his body. "I don't—aren't you vanquished?"

"I am vanquished, man of God."

Konstantin stared, but Vasya could not tell what he was looking at. Perhaps he was seeing the face above him: a creature he loved and reviled as he loved and reviled himself.

Perhaps he was only seeing a starlit wood, and a road that had no turning.

Perhaps there was peace for him, there at the end.

Perhaps there was only silence.

The Bear lowered Konstantin's head to the mud, the hair golden no more, but dark with blood and water. Vasya realized she had her hand pressed to her mouth. The wicked were not supposed to mourn, or to regret, or to have seen their silent God at last, in the steadfastness of another's faith.

Slowly, the Bear unclenched his hand from the priest's, slowly he stood. The golden rope seemed to weigh him down, shining its sickly gleam. Still wrapped in golden cord, the Bear's hands closed tightly about the winter-king's. "Brother, lead the priest gently," he said. "He is yours now, and not mine." His eyes went back to the crumpled form in the mud.

"Neither of ours, in the end," said Morozko. Vasya found her hands moving to cross herself, almost without being aware of it.

Konstantin's open eyes were full of rainwater, spilling over, sliding down his temples like tears. "Your victory," the Bear said to Vasya and bowed, sweeping a gesture over the field of the dead. His voice was colder than she'd ever heard Morozko's. "I wish you joy of it."

She said nothing.

"You have seen our end in that man's prayers," said the Bear. His chin jerked toward Sergei. "Brother, you and I will stay locked in our endless war, even as we fade into ash and frost, and the world is changed. There is no hope now for the chyerti."

"We are going to share this world," Vasya said. "There will be room for all of us: men and devils and bells too."

The Bear only laughed softly at her. "Shall we go, my twin?"

Morozko, without a word, swept out a hand, caught the gold binding the other's wrists. An icy wind leaped up and the two faded into the darkness.

THE WATER WAS SLUICING down Dmitrii's hair, his bloody sword-arm. He crossed the dooryard with a heavy step, pushing his rain-drenched hair out of his eyes. "I am glad you are not dead," he said to Vasya. "Cousin."

She said wryly, "I, too."

Dmitrii spoke to Vasya and her brother both. "Take the Princess of Serpukhov home," he said. "And then—come back, both of you. Secretly, for God's sake. This is not over. What comes next will be worse than a few dead men."

Without another word, he left them, made his splashing way across the dvor, already calling orders.

"What is coming?" Vasya asked Sasha.

"The Tatars," said Sasha. "Let's get Olya home; I want some dry clothes."

Part Five

24

Turnings

ONCE OLGA WAS SAFE IN THE TEREM OF HER OWN PALACE, VASYA and Sasha changed their filthy dripping clothes and hurried back to the Grand Prince. Vasya threw the fur cloak they'd given her in Midnight about her shoulders; the rain had broken the heat and it was chilly in the wet darkness.

They were let quietly in through the postern and brought up at once, in silence, to Dmitrii's small antechamber. The wind was roaring through windows flung wide. There were no attendants, only a table ready-laid, with a jar and four cups, and bread and smoked fish and pickled mushrooms. Simple fare, for Sergei's sake; the old monk was with Dmitrii, waiting for them. He drank honey-wine slowly and he looked very tired.

Dmitrii stood out, vivid and restless, unwearied among the vines and flowers and saints painted on his walls. "Sit, both of you," he said, when Sasha and Vasya appeared. "I will have to consult with my boyars tomorrow, but first I wish to be decided in my own mind."

Wine was poured out, and Vasya, who had taken only a few tasteless mouthfuls when they stopped to rest by the river, now made her way steadily through bread and the good oily fish, listening all the while.

"I should have known," began Dmitrii. "That yellow-haired charlatan, sweeping into Moscow to exorcise the dead things. We thought it was divine power. And all the time he was in league with the devil."

Vasya wished Dmitrii wouldn't speak of it. She kept seeing Konstantin's face as it had looked in the rain.

"We are well rid of him," Dmitrii continued.

Sergei said, "You have not summoned us all, weary as we are, to gloat."

"No," said Dmitrii, his triumphant mood fading. "I have been getting reports—the Tatars are on the lower Volga, marching north. Mamai is still coming. No word of Vladimir Andreevich. The silver—"

"The silver was lost," said Vasya, remembering.

Every head in the room swiveled.

"Lost in a flood," she continued. She set aside her cup and straightened her back. "If the silver was your ransom for Muscovy, Dmitrii Ivanovich, then Muscovy has not been ransomed."

They were still staring. Vasya looked steadily back. "I swear it is true. Do you wish to know how I know?"

"I do not," said Dmitrii, crossing himself. "I'd rather know more. Is Vladimir dead? Alive? Captured?"

"That I do not know," said Vasya. She paused. "But I could find out."

Dmitrii only frowned at that, thoughtfully, and paced the room: grim, restless, leonine. "If my spies confirm what you say about the silver, then I will send word to the princes of Rus'. We have no choice. We have to muster at Kolomna before the dark of the moon, then march south to fight. Or are we to allow all Rus' to be overrun?" Dmitrii spoke to them all, but his eyes were on Sasha, who had once pleaded with him not to engage the Tatar in the field.

Now Sasha only said, with a grimness to match Dmitrii's, "Which of the princes will come to the muster?"

"Rostov, Starodub," said Dmitrii, ticking off the principalities on his fingers. He was still pacing. "The ones in my vassalage. Nizhny Novgorod, for its prince is my father-in-law. Tver, to honor the treaty. But would I had the Prince of Serpukhov. He is clever in council, and loyal, and I will need his men." He halted in his pacing, his eyes on Vasya.

"What of Oleg of Ryazan?" Sasha asked.

"Oleg won't come," said Dmitrii. "Ryazan is too close to Sarai, and Oleg is cautious by nature; he won't risk it, regardless of what his boyars want. He'll march with Mamai, if anything. But we'll fight anyway, without Ryazan and without Serpukhov, if we must. Do we have a choice? We tried ransoming Muscovy, but we could not. Shall we submit, or *shall we fight?*" This time the question was addressed to all three of them.

No one said anything.

"I will send to the princes tomorrow," said Dmitrii. "Father"—here he turned to Sergei—"will you come with us, and bless the army?"

"I will, my son," said Sergei. He sounded weary. "But you know even a victory will cost you."

"I'd avoid war if I could," said the Grand Prince. "But I can't and so—" His face shone. "We will fight at last, after a summer of fear and cringing. God willing, it will be our time to throw off the yoke."

And God help them all, Vasya thought. When Dmitrii spoke so, they believed him. She knew, without asking, that the princes would come to his mustering. *God help us all.*

The Grand Prince turned abruptly to Vasya. "I have your brother's sword," he said. "And I have the holy father's blessing. But what will I have from you, Vasilisa Petrovna? I was sorry to think you dead. But then I heard you set fire to my city."

She got to her feet to face him. "I am guilty before you, Gosudar," said Vasya. "Yet twice I helped defeat this city's enemies. The fire was my fault, but the snowstorm that followed—I summoned that, too. As for punishment? I was punished." She turned her head so the mark on her cheek showed stark in the firelight. Subtly, her hand closed on the carved nightingale in her sleeve, but that was not a sorrow she meant to parade before these men. "What do you want of me?"

"Twice you were nearly burned alive," said Dmitrii. "Yet you came back, to save this city from evil. Perhaps you should be rewarded. What do *you* want, Vasilisa Petrovna?"

She knew her answer, and didn't mince words. "There is a way to know if Vladimir Andreevich is alive or dead. If he is alive, then I am going to find him. You muster in two weeks?"

"Yes," said Dmitrii warily. "But—"

She cut him off. "I will be there," she said. "And if Vladimir Andreevich is alive, he will be there too, with his men."

"Impossible," said Dmitrii.

Vasya said, "If I succeed, then I will consider my debt paid, to you and to this city. And now? I would ask you for your trust. Not for a boy named Vasilii Petrovich, who never existed, but for myself."

"Why should I trust you, Vasilisa Petrovna?" asked Dmitrii, but his gaze was intent. "You are a witch."

"She defended the Church from evil," said Sergei, and made the sign of the cross. "Strange are the works of God."

Vasya crossed herself in turn. "Witch I may be, Dmitrii Ivanovich, but the powers of Rus' must be allies now—prince and Church must join with the unseen world. Otherwise there is no hope of victory."

First I needed men to help me defeat a devil, she thought. *Now I will need devils to help me defeat men.*

But who could do it other than she? *You can be a bridge between men and chyerti,* Morozko had said. She thought she understood that, now.

For a moment, there was no sound but the triumphant wind, pouring in through the windows. Then Dmitrii simply said, "I will trust you." He laid a light hand on her head, a prince's blessing on a warrior. She went very still under the touch. "What do you need?"

Vasya thought. She was still glowing with the words, *I will trust you.* "Clothes such as a tradesman's son might wear," she said.

"Cousin," Sasha broke in. "If she goes, then I must go with her. She's made enough journeys without her kin."

Dmitrii looked surprised. "I need you here. You speak Tatar; you know the country between here and Sarai."

Sasha said nothing.

Understanding came suddenly into Dmitrii's face. Perhaps he had remembered the night of the fire, Sasha's sister forced out into the dark alone. "I will not stop you, Sasha," he said reluctantly. "But you must be at the mustering, whether she succeeds or no."

"Sasha—" Vasya began, just as he went to her and said, low, "I wept for you. Even when Varvara told me you were alive, I wept. I despised myself, that I had let my sister face such horror alone, and I despised myself more when you appeared again at my campfire so changed. I am not letting you go alone."

Vasya put a hand on her brother's arm. "Then, if you come with me tonight—" Her grip tightened; their eyes met. "I warn you, the road leads through darkness."

Sasha said, "Then we will go through darkness, sister."

WHEN THEY GOT BACK to Olga's palace, Varvara was waiting for them at the bathhouse. Sasha bathed hastily and sought his bed. Midnight would come soon: the hour of their departure. But Vasya lingered. "I never said thank you," she told Varvara. "For that night on the river. You saved my life."

"I would not have," said Varvara. "I didn't know what I could do for you but mourn. But Polunochnitsa spoke to me. I had not heard her voice for so long. She told me what was wanted, and so I went down to the burning."

"Varvara," said Vasya. "In the country of Midnight—I met your mother."

Varvara's lips tightened. "I suppose she thought you were Tamara over again. Only a daughter she could control, one who was not in love with a sorcerer."

Vasya had no answer to that. Instead she said, "Why did you come to Moscow at all? Why be a *servant*?"

Old anger showed in Varvara's face. "I have not the gift of seeing," she said. "I cannot see chyerti; I can hear the stronger ones and speak a little of the speech of horses, that is all. There was no wonder for me in my mother's kingdom, only cold and danger and isolation, and later my mother's wrath. She had dealt too harshly with Tamara. So, I left her, went in search of my sister. In time I came to Moscow, this city of men. I found Tamara there, but already beyond my aid, dim and wandering, bowed down by grief beyond her strength. She had borne a child, that I protected as I could." Vasya nodded. "But when the child went north to marry, I did not follow. She had her nurse, and her husband was a good man. I didn't want to live in another land with only forest and no people. I liked the sound of the bells, the color and hurry of Moscow. So I stayed, and waited. In time, another girl of my blood came, and I grew whole again, caring for your sister and her children."

"Why be a servant, though?"

"Do you ask?" Varvara demanded. "Servants have more freedom than noblewomen. I could walk about as I wished, go into the sun with my head uncovered. I was happy. Witches die alone. My mother and my sister showed me that. Has your gift brought *you* any happiness, fire-maiden?"

"It has," said Vasya, without elaborating. "But grief as well." A little anger threaded her voice. "Since you knew them both—Tamara and Kasyan—why did you do nothing for her, after she died? Why did you not warn us, when Kasyan came to Moscow?"

Varvara did not move, but suddenly her face showed sharp lines and hollows; the echoes of old grief. "I knew my sister haunted the palace; I could not get her to go, and I did not know why she lingered. Kasyan I did not know when he came. He wore a different face in Moscow than the one he wore when he seduced Tamara by the lake at Midsummer."

She must have seen the doubt in Vasya's eyes, for she burst out, "I am not like you, with your immortal eyes, your mad courage. I am only a woman, unworthy of my bloodlines, who has done what I could to care for my own."

Vasya said nothing to that but put out a hand, and took Varvara's in hers, and neither of them spoke a moment. Then Vasya said, with effort, "Will you tell my sister?"

Varvara had her mouth open on what was obviously a sharp reply—and then she hesitated. "I never dared before," said Varvara grudgingly. There was a thread of doubt now in her voice. "Why would she believe me? I do not appear old enough to be anyone's great-aunt."

"I think Olga has seen enough wonders lately to believe you," said Vasya. "I think you should tell her; it would give her joy. Although I see your point." Vasya looked at Varvara with new eyes. Her body was strong, her hair yellow, barely touched with white. "How old are you?"

Varvara shrugged. "I don't know. Older than I look. Our mother never told me who sired us. But I always assumed my long life was some gift of his. Whoever he was. I am happy here, truly, Vasilisa Petrovna. I never wanted power, only folk to care for. Save Moscow for them, and take my wild Marya somewhere she can breathe, and I will be content."

Vasya smiled. "I will do that—Aunt."

VARVARA LEFT, AND VASYA finished her bath and dressed. Clean, she stepped out into the covered walkway that connected the bathhouse to the terem. The rain was still falling, but more gently. The lightning was sparser now as the storm moved on.

It took Vasya a moment to pick out the shadow. She stilled, the bathhouse door rough at her back.

Thin-voiced, she spoke. "Is it done?"

"It is done," Morozko returned. "He is bound by my power, by his own votary's sacrifice, and by Kaschei's golden bridle: all three together. He will never win free again." The rain fell cold now, beating down summer's dust.

Vasya let go the door. The rain whispered on the roof. She crossed the walkway, until she could see his face, until she could ask a question that troubled her. "What did the Bear mean," she asked, "when he said *please?*"

Morozko frowned, but rather than answer in words, he lifted his cupped hand. Water collected in his palm. "I wondered if you would ask," he said. "Give me your hand."

Vasya did. He let the water run lightly over the cuts on her arm and fingers. They healed with that startling spear of agony, there and gone. She jerked her hand back.

"Water of death," said Morozko, letting the remaining droplets scatter. "That is my power. I can restore flesh, living or dead."

She'd known he could heal since the first night she met him and he healed her frostbite. But she hadn't connected it to the fairy tale, hadn't considered—

"You said you could only heal wounds that you'd inflicted."

"I did."

"Another lie?"

His mouth set hard. "A part of the truth."

"The Bear wanted you to save Konstantin's life?"

"Not save it," he said. "I can mend flesh, but he was already too far gone. Medved wanted me to mend the priest's flesh, so *he* could bring him back. Together, my brother and I can restore the dead, for Medved's gift is the water of life. That is why he said *please*."

Frowning, Vasya considered her healed fingers, the scars on palm and wrist.

"But," Morozko added, "we never act together. Why would we? He is monstrous, he and his power both."

"The Bear mourned," said Vasya. "He mourned when Father Konstantin—"

Morozko made a sound of impatience. "The wicked can still mourn, Vasya."

She didn't reply. She stood still, while the rain fell all around them, overwhelmed again by all the things she didn't know. The winter-king was part of the lingering storm; his humanity only a shadow of his true self, his power rising as summer waned. His eyes glittered in the darkness. Yet he had cared for her, schemed for her. Why should she give the Bear or Konstantin a passing thought? They were murderers both, and they were both gone.

Shaking off her unease, she said, "Will you come meet my sister? I promised."

Morozko looked surprised. "Come to her as your suitor and ask her permission?" he asked. "Will it change anything? It might make it worse."

"Still," said Vasya. "Otherwise I—"

"I am not a man, Vasya," he said. "No sacrament will bind me; I cannot marry you under the laws of your god or your people. If you are looking for honor in your sister's eyes, you will not find it."

She had known that was true. But— "I'd like you to meet her anyway," said Vasya. "At least—perhaps she will not fear for me."

There was a silence and then she realized that he was shaking with silent laughter. She crossed her arms, offended.

He looked at her, crystalline-eyed. "I am not likely to reassure any-one's sister," he said, when he stopped laughing. "But I will, if you like."

OLGA WAS IN MARYA'S CHAMBER, watching over the child's sleep. The marks of long strain shadowed the girl's pale, pinched face. She had taken on too great a labor too young, and Olga looked scarcely less weary.

Vasya halted in the doorway, suddenly unsure of her welcome.

The bed was covered in feather-stuffed ticking, with furs and woven wool. For a moment, Vasya wanted to be a child again, to fall into bed beside Marya and go to sleep while her sister stroked her hair. But Olga turned at Vasya's soft-footed approach, and the wish vanished. One could not go backward.

Vasya crossed the room, touched Marya's cheek. "Will she be all right?" Vasya asked.

"She is only tired, I think," said Olga.

"She was very brave," said Vasya.

Olga smoothed her daughter's hair and said nothing.

"Olya," Vasya said awkwardly. All the composure she'd found in Dmitrii's hall seemed to have deserted her. "I—I told you that you would meet him. If you wish."

Olga frowned. "*Him*, Vasya?"

"You asked. He is here. Will you see him?"

Morozko did not wait for an answer, nor did he walk through the door like a person. He simply stepped out of the shadows. The domo-voi had been sitting beside the stove; now he shot to his feet, bristling; Marya stirred in her sleep.

"I mean them no harm, little one," said Morozko, speaking first to the domovoi.

Olga had lurched to her feet too; she was standing in front of Marya's bed as though to defend her child from evil. Vasya, stiff with apprehension, suddenly saw the frost-demon as her sister did: a cold-eyed shadow. She began to doubt her own course. Morozko turned away from the domovoi, bowed to Olga.

"I know you," Olga whispered. "Why have you come here?"

"Not for a life," Morozko said. His voice was even, but Vasya felt him wary.

Olga said to Vasya, "I remember him. I remember. *He took my daughter away.*"

"No—he—" began Vasya, clumsily, and Morozko shot her a hard look. She subsided.

His face was unchanged, but his whole body was taut with strain. Vasya understood why. He'd wanted to go near enough to humanity to be remembered, so he could go on existing. But Vasya had pulled him nearer and nearer still, like a moth to a candle-flame. Now he must look at Olga, understand the torment in her eyes, and carry it with him down the long roads of his life.

He didn't want to. But he didn't move.

"It is little comfort," Morozko said carefully. "But your elder daughter has a long life before her. And the younger—I will remember her."

"You are a devil," said Olga. "My little girl didn't even have a name."

"I will remember her regardless," said the winter-king.

Olga stared at him a moment and then suddenly broke; her whole body bowed with grief. She put her face in her hands.

Vasya, feeling helpless, went to her sister, wrapped tentative arms about her. "Olya?" she said. "Olya, I'm sorry. I'm so sorry."

Olga made no answer and Morozko stood where he was. He did not speak again.

There was a long silence. Olga took a deep breath. Her eyes were wet. "I never wept," she said. "Not since the night I lost her."

Vasya held her sister tightly.

Olga gently put Vasya's arms aside. "Why my sister?" she asked Morozko. "Why, of all the women in the world?"

"For her blood," said Morozko. "But later for her courage."

"Have you anything to offer her?" Olga asked him. And, with an edge, "Besides whispers in the dark?"

Vasya bit back her sound of protest. If the question took Morozko aback, it didn't show. "All the lands of winter," he said. "The black trees and the silver frost. Gold and riches made by men; she may fill her hands with wealth, if she desires it."

"Will you deny her the spring and the summer?"

"I will deny her nothing. But there are places she can go where I cannot easily follow."

"He is not a man," Olga said to Vasya, not taking her eyes off the winter-king. "He will not be a husband to you."

Vasya bowed her head. "I have never wanted a husband. He came with me out of winter, for Moscow's sake. It is enough."

"And you think he won't hurt you, in the end? Remember the dead girl in the fairy tale!"

"I am not she," said Vasya.

"What if this—liaison means your damnation?"

"I am damned already," Vasya said. "By every law of God and man. But I do not wish to be alone."

Olga sighed and said sadly, "As you say, sister." Abruptly, she said, "Very well. My blessing on you both—now send him away."

VASYA FOLLOWED MOROZKO OUT. He even went through the door this time, in ordinary fashion. But when he was outside, he halted, head bowed, like a man after hard labor.

He managed to say to her through gritted teeth, "The bathhouse." She took his hand and pulled him there with her, shut the door on darkness, forgot a candle wasn't burning. Four flared up at once. He sank to one of the benches of the outer room and drew a shuddering breath. A bathhouse was a place of birth and of death, of transformation and of magic, and perhaps of memory. He could breathe easier there. But—

"Are you all right?" she asked.

He didn't answer. "I cannot stay," he said instead. His eyes were pale as water, his hands locked together, the bones of them stark in the candlelight. "I cannot. It is not my time yet, here. I must go back to my own lands. I—" He broke off, then said, "I *am* winter, and have been too long separate from myself."

"Is that the only reason?" she asked.

He wasn't looking at her now. Forcibly, he relaxed his clenched hands, laid them on his knees. Almost inaudibly, he said, "I cannot learn any more names. It draws me too near—"

"Too near what? Mortality? Can you become mortal?" she asked.

He was taken aback. "How? I am not made of flesh. But it—tears at me."

"Then it will always tear at you, I think," said Vasya. "So long as we—unless—you forget me."

He rose to his feet. "I have made that choice already," he said. "But I must return to my own lands. You are not the only one who can be driven mad with impossibilities; I cannot endure this one anymore. I do not belong in the summertime world. Vasya, you have done all you must. Come with me."

At his words, a bolt of longing tore through her, for blue skies and deep snow, for wild places and for silence, for his fire-lit house in the fir-grove, for his hands in the darkness. She could go with him, and leave all the doings of men behind her, leave this city that had cost Solovey his life.

But even as she thought it, she said, "I can't. It isn't over."

"Your part in this is over. If Dmitrii fights the Tatars, then that is a war of men, and not of chyerti."

"A war the Bear brought about!"

"A war that might have happened anyway," retorted Morozko. "A war that's been threatening for years."

She put a hand to her cheek, where lay the scar from a stone flung as she was led to her death. "I know," she said. "But I am Russian, and they are my people."

"They put you in the fire," said Morozko. "You owe them nothing. Come with me."

"But—who will I be, if I go with you?" she demanded. "Just a snow-maiden, the winter-king's bride, forgotten by the whole world, just like you!"

She saw him flinch at the words. Biting her lips, she asked, in a calmer voice, "Who am I, if I cannot help my people?"

"Your people are more than a single, ill-conceived battle."

"You freed your brother because you thought I could keep the chy-

erti from fading out of the world. Perhaps I can. But the other Rus'—
the Rus' of men and women—paid the price, and I am going to make it
right again. The Bear's mischief did not end with Moscow; my task is
not over."

"And if it gets you killed? Do you think I want to bear you away
into the dark and then never see you again?"

"I know you don't." She dragged in a deep breath. "But I still have
to try."

For her sake, Morozko had made common cause with her brother,
asked her sister's forgiveness, gone into Moscow in summer, bound the
Bear. But she had reached the limits of both his strength and his will.
He would not fight Dmitrii's war.

She would, though. Because she wanted to be more than a snow-
maiden. She wanted Dmitrii's faith, and his hand on her head. She
wanted a victory, brought about by her courage.

But she also wanted the winter-king. In the smoke and dust and
stink of Moscow, he was a breath of pine and cold water and stillness.
She could not think for wanting him.

He saw her waver. Their eyes met in the darkness, and he closed the
distance between them.

He wasn't gentle. He was angry, and so was she, baffled and wanting, and their hands were rough on each other's skin. When she kissed
him, he felt like flesh under her hands, drawn sharply into reality by the
place and the hour, and by her own passion. The silence stretched out,
as their hands said the things they could not, and Vasya almost told him
yes then. She almost let him carry her to his white horse, bear her away
into the night. She didn't want to think anymore.

But she must think. Tamara had let her own demon lull her with
dreams of love until she'd lost everything that mattered.

She wasn't Tamara. Vasya yanked away, gasping for breath, and he
let her go.

"Go back to winter then," she heard herself saying, her voice
hoarse. "I am taking the road through Midnight to find my brother-in-
law, if he is alive. I am going to help Dmitrii Ivanovich win his war."

Morozko stood still. Slowly the anger and confusion and desire
faded from his expression. "Vladimir Andreevich is alive," he said

only. "But I do not know where he is. Vasya—I cannot walk this road beside you."

"I will find him," said Vasya.

"You will find him," Morozko said, with weary certainty. He bowed, remote, any feeling locked deep in his eyes. "Look for me at the first frost."

He slipped out of the bathhouse like a wraith. She hurried to follow, angry still, but not wanting him to go like that, with a wound unhealed between them. She'd pitched him against his own nature, a foe that was too great.

He went out into the dooryard, and raised his face to the night. For an instant, the wind was the true deep wind of winter that freezes the breath in your nostrils.

Suddenly he turned back to her, and the feeling was there again in his face, as though he could not help it.

"Be well, and do not forget, Snegurochka," he said.

"I will not. Morozko—"

He was only half there; the wind seemed to blow through him.

"As I could, I loved you too," she whispered.

Their eyes met. Then he was gone, gone on the rising wind, blown through the wild air.

25

The Road Through Darkness

S ASHA AND VASYA LEFT JUST BEFORE MIDNIGHT.

"I am sorry," Sasha said to Olga before they left. "For what I said, at our last parting."

Olga almost smiled, but the corners of her mouth turned down. "I was angry too. You'd think I'd be used to farewells, brother."

"If it goes ill for us in the south," said Sasha, "you mustn't stay in Moscow. Take the children to Lesnaya Zemlya."

"I know," said the Princess of Serpukhov, and brother and sister exchanged grim glances. Olga had lived through three sieges; Sasha had been fighting Dmitrii's battles since the two were scarcely out of boyhood.

Watching them, Vasya was reminded, uncomfortably, that though she had seen much, she had never seen war.

"Go with God, both of you," said Olga.

Vasya and Sasha slipped out of Moscow. Below the gate, the posad slept. The swift, cold wind had driven out the reek of sickness. At least the dead would lie quiet.

Vasya led her brother into the woods, to the same place where Varvara had first sent her through Midnight—how long ago had it been? Two seasons had passed in Rus' since that night, but Vasya had lost count of the days she'd lived herself.

Somewhere in Moscow, a bell rang. The city walls loomed white beyond the trees. Vasya took her brother's hand. It was midnight. The darkness took on a wilder texture: a new menace and a deeper beauty. She stepped forward, pulling her brother with her. "Think of our cousin," she said. One step, two, and then Sasha let out a soft, shocked breath.

Moscow was gone. They stood in a sparse elm-copse, dry and warm. There was dust instead of mud between Vasya's bare toes, and the big late-summer stars hung low overhead. A different midnight.

"Mother of God," Sasha whispered. "These are the woods near Serpukhov."

"I told you," said Vasya. "It is a swift road, but—" She broke off.

The black stallion Voron emerged from between two trees. His rider's morning-star eyes glowed in the darkness.

Sasha's hand went to the hilt of his sword. Perhaps the country of Midnight had wakened something in his blood, for he could see horse and rider. "That is Lady Midnight," said Vasya, not taking her eyes off the chyert. "This is her realm." She inclined her head.

Sasha crossed himself. Polunochnitsa smiled at him, mocking, and slid down from her horse's back.

"God be with you," Sasha said, cautiously.

"I certainly hope not," returned Polunochnitsa. Voron tossed his black head, his ears set unhappily. Turning to Vasya, Midnight said, "In my realm again? And proud of your victory?"

"We did win," Vasya said, wary.

"No," said Midnight. "You didn't. What do you think the real battle is, you arrogant fool? You never understood, did you?"

Vasya said nothing.

Between her teeth, Midnight said, "We hoped—*I* hoped—that you were different. That you would break their endless round of revenge and imprisonment. But you *encouraged* their war, those idiot twins."

"What are you talking about?" Vasya demanded. "We saved Moscow from the dead. I do not know why you are angry. He is wicked, the Bear. Wicked. Now he is bound. Rus' is safe."

"Is it?" Midnight asked. "You still don't understand." Fury and disgust and—disappointment—snapped in her eyes. "You cannot rule the chyerti, or keep the house by the lake, or save us from fading out of life. You failed. The way to the lake is shut to you; I am shutting it, and risking the old woman's wrath. She will have no heir. Farewell, Vasilisa Petrovna."

Then she was gone fast as she'd appeared, a whirl of pale hair, vaulting to Voron's back. The last Vasya heard of her was the sound of fading hoofbeats. Shaken, Vasya stared at the place where she'd been. Sasha looked merely puzzled. "What did that mean?"

"I do not understand why she is angry," said Vasya. But she was uneasy. "We have to go on. Follow me close. We must not be separated."

They walked cautiously, for Vasya feared Midnight's anger, in this place of her power. Sasha followed her, starting at shadows, bewildered by the changing nights. But still he followed her. He trusted her.

Vasya blamed herself, later.

26

The Golden Horde

THEY HAD NO WARNING. THEY SAW NO GLEAM FROM FAR OFF, heard no noise. They merely stepped suddenly from darkness, into firelight filled with laughter.

For an instant, they both froze.

The revelers froze too. Vasya had a brief impression of weapons: curved swords and short bows unstrung. She could smell horses, see the shine of their eyes, watching from beyond the firelight.

All around them, men sprang to their feet. They weren't speaking Russian. It sounded like the words she'd heard once on a dark winter night when she'd rescued girls from—from—

"Get back!" Vasya said to Sasha. Out of the corner of her eye, she glimpsed pale hair, Midnight's set, triumphant face. She thought she heard a whisper: "Learn or die, Vasilisa Petrovna."

Swords in a dozen men's hands. Her brother's sword reflected the firelight when he drew it. "Tatars!" Sasha snapped. "Vasya, go."

"No!" She was still trying to pull him back. "No, we must only walk back into Midnight—" But the men were closing in around them; she could not see the Midnight-road. "Vasya," said Sasha in a voice more terrible for its calm, "I am a monk; they will not kill me. But you . . . Run. *Run!*" He drove himself at the men, knocking them aside. She backed away from the melee, willed the campfire into a sudden storm of light. The renewed fire drove the Tatars back just as her brother's sword met another, sparking.

There was the Midnight-road, just beyond the light. The fire flared again, frightening the men, and she called, "Sasha, this way—"

Or started to say. For the hilt of a sword caught her on the temple, and the world went dark.

SASHA, SEEING HIS SISTER FALL, dropped his sword and said, in Tatar, to the man who had struck her down, "I am a man of God, and that is my servant. Do not hurt him."

"Indeed, you *are* a man of God," returned the Tatar. He spoke Russian, lightly accented. "You are Aleksandr Peresvet. But this is not your servant."

The voice was vaguely familiar, but Sasha could not see the Tatar's face. The man stood over Vasya, on the other side of the fire, and pulled the girl upright. Her eyelids fluttered; a gash across her forehead poured a maze of blood across her face.

"*This* is your witch of a sister," said the Tatar. He sounded both pleased and mystified. "How came you both here? Spying for Dmitrii? Why would he spend his cousins, so?"

Shocked silent, Sasha said nothing. He'd recognized the other man. "Come on," added the Tatar in his own tongue. He heaved Vasya over his shoulder. "Tie the monk's hands, and follow me. The general will want to know of this."

SOMEONE WAS CARRYING HER. Every footfall jarred her head. She vomited. Pain like shards of ice shot through her skull. The man carrying her exclaimed in disgust. "Do that again," said a half-familiar voice, "and I'll beat you myself, when the general's done."

She tried to look about her, seeking for the Midnight-road. But she couldn't see it. She must have lost it when she fell unconscious. Now the night was drawing on and she and Sasha were trapped until the next day's midnight.

Her senses swam. She couldn't make herself and her brother disappear under the eyes of the entire camp. Maybe she could—but even as she tried to plan, her thoughts fractured.

Something loomed before her, dimly seen, just as she drifted back to awareness. It was a round building, made of felt. A flap was thrust aside and she was borne through the gap. Terror locked her throat and stomach. Where was her brother?

Men inside—she couldn't tell how many. Two stood in the center, finely dressed, illuminated by a small stove and a hanging lamp. The person carrying her let her fall. Floundering, she managed to drag herself to her knees. She had an impression of wealth: the lamp was of worked silver; there was a smell of fat meat and carpet under her knees. All around was the disorienting buzz of a tongue she didn't understand. Sasha was thrown down beside her.

One of the finely dressed men was a Tatar. The other was a Russian; it was he who spoke first. "What is this?" he asked.

"This—" echoed that almost-familiar voice from behind her. Vasya tried to twist around and had to freeze, gasping, at the pain in her head. But then the man stepped forward, and she could see his face. She knew him. He had nearly killed her once, in a forest outside Moscow. With the help of a wicked sorcerer, he had nearly deposed Dmitrii Ivanovich.

"It seems," said Chelubey in Russian, smiling at her, "that Dmitrii Ivanovich has devised a novel means to rid himself of his cousins."

THE TALL ONE, the one they were calling temnik—*general*—had to be Mamai, though Sasha knew him by reputation only. He didn't recognize the Russian.

"Cousins?" asked the temnik, in his own tongue. Mamai was a man in his middle years, weary, dignified, gray. He'd been loyal to Berdi Beg, one of the innumerable khans, but Berdi held the throne for only two years. Mamai had been plotting to regain his lost position ever since, hampered by the fact that he himself was not descended from the Great Khan. Sasha knew—probably the Tatar's whole army knew—that Mamai had to defeat Dmitrii decisively, or a rival faction in the warring Horde would rise up and make an end of him.

Men with everything at stake were dangerous.

"This man is the holy Aleksandr Peresvet—surely you have heard of him," said Chelubey, but his eyes were on Vasya. "And this other one—when I first met him in Moscow, they told me he was highborn: Aleksandr Peresvet's brother. That was a lie." Softly, Chelubey continued, "*This* is not a boy at all but a girl—a little witch-girl. Disguised as a boy, she deceived all Moscow. I wonder very much why Dmitrii has sent them here—a witch and a monk. Spies? Will you tell me, devushka?" The last question was put to Vasya, almost gently. But Sasha heard the menace behind it.

His sister met Chelubey's eyes, wordless. Her eyes were wide and terrified; her face bloody. "You hurt me," she whispered, in a trembling, abject tone Sasha had never heard from her in his life.

"I'll hurt you worse," said Chelubey placidly. It wasn't a threat so much as a statement of fact. "Why are you here?"

"We were set upon," she whispered, voice still quivering. "Our men were killed. We came toward the fire for help." Her eyes were vast and dark, confused and terrified, her cheek crusted with blood. She bowed her head, and then looked up at Chelubey again. This time two tears cut tracks in the blood on her face.

Sasha thought she was overdoing it, playing the helpless girl, but then she saw Chelubey's face slide from wariness to contempt. In his mind, he breathed a prayer of gratitude. Drawing Chelubey's attention back to himself, he said, "Don't frighten her. We came upon you by accident. We are not spies."

"*Indeed*," said Chelubey silkily, turning. "And is your sister also traveling with you, alone, dressed so immodestly, by *accident*?"

"I was taking her to a convent," lied Sasha. "The Grand Prince desired it of me. Our train was set upon by robbers; we were left alone, without succor. They tore her dress; they left us with nothing, save what you see. We wandered hungry for some days, saw your fires and came. We thought to receive help, not indignities."

"It puzzles me, though," said Chelubey with acid irony. "Why is the nearest adviser of the Grand Prince of Moscow taking his sister to a house of religion at such a time?"

"I advised Dmitrii Ivanovich against going to war," said Sasha. "In anger, he ordered me from his side."

"Well," broke in Mamai briskly, "if that is so, then you will have no difficulty informing us of your cousin's intentions and dispositions, so you can get back to praying."

"I know nothing of Dmitrii's dispositions," said Sasha. "I told you—"

Chelubey backhanded him across the face, hard enough to send him to the floor. Vasya cried out and threw herself at Chelubey's feet, getting in his way before he could kick Sasha in the stomach. "Please," she cried. "Please, don't hurt him."

Chelubey shook her off, but stared frowning down as she knelt before him, hands clasped. Vasya would never be taken for a beautiful woman, but her bold bones and vast eyes caught the gaze somehow, and held it. Sasha, his lips bleeding, was disturbed to see the men's attention once more on her, in a way it hadn't been before. And she was encouraging them, damn her, to keep them from him.

"Forgive me," said Chelubey calmly, "if I don't believe your brother."

"He has only spoken the truth," she whispered, her voice small.

Mamai turned abruptly to the Russian. "What say you, Oleg Ivanovich? Are they lying?"

The Russian's bearded face was quite inscrutable, but Sasha recognized the name. The Grand Prince of Ryazan, who had sided with the Tatar.

Oleg pressed his lips together. "I cannot say if they're lying. But the monk's tale seems more likely than not. Why would Dmitrii Ivanovich send two of his own cousins to spy, and one a girl dressed as a man?" His glance at Vasya was wholly disapproving.

"She is a witch; she has strange powers," insisted Chelubey. "She made our campfire burn unnaturally; she bewitched my horse in Moscow."

All eyes went to Vasya. Her gaze was unfocused; her lips trembled.

Blood still welled from the cut in her head, and a lump was forming. She was crying softly.

"Indeed," said Oleg after a telling silence. "She is a fearful sight. What is the girl's name?" The last was in Russian.

Vasya looked blank and didn't answer. Chelubey raised his hand once more, but Oleg's voice caught him before the blow fell. "Do you strike bound girls now?"

"I told you," said Chelubey, angry. "She is a witch!"

"I see no evidence of it," said Oleg. "I will add that it is late, and perhaps we can determine their fate in the morning."

"I will occupy myself with them," said Chelubey. In his eyes was an eager light, the memory of Moscow's humiliations fresh. Perhaps he was curious about the green-eyed girl who dressed as a boy. Perhaps he'd even been there, on the river that day, when Kasyan exposed her secret before all Moscow, in the cruelest way possible. "Dmitrii Ivanovich will ransom her," said Sasha. "If she is unharmed."

They ignored him.

"Very well," said Mamai. "Occupy yourself with them and tell me what you learn. Oleg Ivanovich—"

"The Metropolitan will have something to say if he dies under torture," said Oleg. Sasha took a steadying breath.

"See that he lives," Mamai added to Chelubey.

"General," Oleg said to Mamai, his eyes on Vasya once more, "I will keep the girl with me this night. Perhaps, separated from her brother, alone and afraid, she will say more to me."

Chelubey looked put out. He had his mouth open to speak, but Mamai forestalled him, looking amused. "As you like. Skinny though, isn't she?"

Oleg bowed and hauled Vasya to her feet. Vasya hadn't understood most of the conversation as it had been largely in Tatar. Her eyes locked on Sasha. "Don't be afraid," he said.

Cold comfort. She wasn't afraid for herself; she was afraid for him.

27

Oleg of Ryazan

Outside Mamai's tent, Oleg hissed between his teeth. Two armed men appeared and followed them. They looked Vasya over curiously, before schooling their faces to blankness. She was terrified for her brother. It had all happened too fast. Midnight might mock and threaten, but Vasya had never dreamed that her great-grandmother's servant would betray her to the Tatars. *Why*, in God's name?

You failed, Midnight had said.

Oleg pulled her onward. She tried to think. If she could get herself away, could she come back for her brother at the next day's midnight? In this great camp, face sticky with blood, magic seemed as distant as the uncaring stars.

Another round tent, smaller than Mamai's, loomed out of the dark. Oleg thrust her through the flap, followed her in, dismissed his dubious-looking attendants.

No stove this time, and only a single clay lamp. She had a brief impression of an austere space, a neat heap of furs, and then Oleg spoke. "Traveling to a convent, are you? Dressed so? Set upon by bandits? Then you and your brother were foolish enough to stumble on Chelubey's fire? Am I a fool? Tell me the truth, girl."

She tried to collect her wits. "My brother told you the truth," she said.

"You're no coward, I'll give you that." His voice quieted. "Devushka, I can help you. But I must have the truth."

Vasya let her eyes fill. It wasn't difficult. Her head ached abominably. "We told you," she whispered again.

"Fine," said Oleg. "Just as you like. I will give you back to Chelubey tomorrow and he will get the truth out of you." He sat down to take off his boots.

Vasya watched him a moment. "You are a man of Rus', fighting on the enemy's side," she said. "Do you expect me to trust you?"

Oleg looked up. "I am fighting beside the Horde," he said very precisely, laying a boot aside. "Because I am not eager, as Dmitrii Ivanovich seems to be, to have my city razed, my people carried off as slaves. That doesn't mean I cannot help you. Nor does it mean that I won't see you suffer greatly if you cross me."

The second boot joined the first, and then he pulled his cap off, tossed it on the heap of furs. He looked her over, his glance appraising. *Forget,* she thought. *Forget he can see you—* But she couldn't focus her mind; there was a white-hot bar of pain in her head. His feet bare, Oleg stalked over to her. Wordless, he took her bound wrists in one hand and felt her over for other weapons with the other. She was unarmed. Someone had taken her knife, after she was struck down beside Chelubey's fire. "Well," he said, as he ran his hands down her body, "I suppose you are a girl after all."

She stamped on his foot. He struck her across the face.

When she came to, she found herself sprawled on the ground. He'd cut her bonds. She raised her head. He was sitting on his heap of furs, running a whetstone over the unsheathed sword across his knees.

"Awake?" he said. "Let's start again. Tell me the truth, devushka."

She hauled herself laboriously to her feet. "Or what? Are you going to torture me?"

A flicker of distaste crossed his face. "It might not occur to you, determined as you are to suffer nobly, but you are better off with me than with Chelubey. He was shamed in Moscow; the whole army knows the tale. *He* will torture you. And if he is feeling inspired, perhaps he will force you in front of your brother, to pass along a little share of the humiliation."

"Is that my choice then? Be raped publicly there or privately here?"

He snorted. "Fortunately for you, I prefer women who look and behave like women. Tell me what I want to know, and I will protect you from Chelubey."

Their eyes locked. Vasya took a deep breath, and gambled. "I have a message from the Grand Prince of Moscow."

His features sharpened. "Do you? Strange choice of messenger."

She shrugged. "I'm here, aren't I?"

Oleg laid sword and whetstone aside. "That is true. But perhaps you are lying. Have you a token? If so, did you eat it? I'll swear it's not on you now."

She didn't know if she could do it. But she made her voice steady when she said, "I have a sign."

"Very well. Show me."

"I will," she said. "If you tell me why Chelubey said that Dmitrii Ivanovich had devised a novel way to get rid of his cousins."

Oleg shrugged. "The Prince of Serpukhov is a prisoner here as well. Wasn't Dmitrii wondering where he had got to?" Oleg paused. "Ah. Messenger, are you? Or a rescue party? Either way it seems unlikely."

Vasya didn't reply.

"In any case it was bad planning on Dmitrii's part," finished Oleg. "Now Mamai has *three* of his first cousins." He crossed his arms. "Now. What is this sign of yours?"

Ignoring her splitting headache, Vasya cupped her hands and filled them with the memory of fire.

Swearing, Oleg scrambled up and back from the fire in her fingers.

She was still kneeling on the floor; she looked up at him through the flames. "Oleg Ivanovich, Mamai is going to lose this war."

"A ragtag army of Rus' is going to lose to the Golden Horde?" But Oleg's voice was thin and breathless; his eyes were on the flames. He reached out to touch, then jerked back at the heat. The fire didn't hurt her, though she could see the hairs on her arms crisping. "A fine trick," he said. "Has Dmitrii made alliance with devils? It won't defeat an army. Do you know how many horses Mamai has? How many arrows, how many men? If every man in Rus' fought on Dmitrii's side, he'd still be outnumbered two to one."

But Oleg did not take his eyes off Vasya's hands.

Vasya was straining every nerve, through pain, through headache, to keep her face unruffled, to keep steady the memory of fire. Oleg had sided with the enemy to protect his people. A practical man. One she could perhaps reason with. "Tricks with fire?" she said. "Is that what you think? No. Fire and water and darkness all together; the old powers of this land are going to battle alongside the new." She hoped it was true. "Your general *is going to lose*. I am the sign of it, and the proof."

"That Dmitrii Ivanovich has sold his soul for black sorcery?" Oleg made the sign of the cross.

"Is it black sorcery to defend the soil that bore us?" She shut her hands abruptly, extinguishing the flames. "Why did you take me from Chelubey, Oleg Ivanovich?"

"Misplaced kindness," said Oleg. "Also, I do not like Chelubey." He reached out a flinching hand to touch her palms, which were quite cool.

"Dmitrii's side has powers you cannot see," she said. "*We* have powers you cannot see. Better to fight for your own, Oleg Ivanovich, than defend a conqueror. Will you help me?"

She could have sworn he hesitated. Then a bitter smile spread over his face. "You are very persuasive. Now I could almost believe that Dmitrii sent you. He is cleverer than I gave him credit for. But it has been a long time since I believed in fairy tales, devushka. I will do this much. I will tell Mamai that you are only a foolish convent-bound girl, that you should be given into my household instead of sold as a slave. You may do your fire-tricks for me, in Ryazan, after the war is over. Don't let anyone see you doing them. The Tatars have a horror of witches."

The agony in her head was rising again. Darkness came up at the edges of her vision. She caught his wrist. Tricks, gambles, deceptions deserted her. "Please," she said.

Through the mists of gathering unconsciousness she heard his whispered reply. "I will make you this bargain: if you, alone, can find and save your brother and the Prince of Serpukhov—and do it in such a way as to make my men and my boyars question *their* allegiance— then perhaps that will be *sign* enough and I will heed you. Until then, I am for the Tatar."

SHE WASN'T SURE IF she slept that night, or if the pain in her head had merely sent her back into unconsciousness. Her dreams were shot through with faces, all watching her, waiting. Morozko troubled, the Bear intent, Midnight angry. Her great-grandmother, the madwoman lost in Midnight. *You passed three fires, but you did not understand the final riddle.*

And then she dreamed of her brother, tortured, until Chelubey, laughing, killed him.

She came gasping awake, in the darkness before dawn, to find herself lying in warmth and softness. Someone had even wiped the crusted blood from her face. She lay still. Her headache had subsided to a dull murmur. She turned her head and saw Oleg, lying awake beside her, on his stomach, watching her. "How does one learn to cup fire in one's hands?" he asked, as though continuing a conversation from the night before.

The pale light of early dawn was seeping in around them. They were sharing a pile of furs. She shot upright.

He failed to move. "Outraged virtue? After you appear in a Tatar camp at midnight dressed as a boy?"

She was out from under the furs like a cat, and perhaps the look on her face convinced him for he added mildly, looking amused, "Do you think I'd touch you, witch? But it's a long time since I slept warm with a girl, even a bony one. I thank you for that. Or would you have preferred the ground?"

"I would have," she said coldly.

"Very well," said Oleg placidly, getting up himself. "Since you are determined to suffer, you may walk tied to my stirrup, so that Mamai doesn't think I've gone soft. You are going to have a long day."

OLEG LEFT THE TENT, which he called a ger. Vasya's mind was racing. Escape? Forget they could see her and walk through the camp until she found her brother? But could she forget they could see *him*? And what if he was wounded? No, she decided reluctantly. It was better, wiser, to wait until midnight. She wasn't getting two chances.

Oleg sent a man in to her, carrying a cup full of something foul-smelling. Mare's milk, fermented. It was thick, clotted, sour. Her stomach roiled. When Oleg himself reappeared, he said, "Doesn't smell like much, I know, but Tatars march for days on that alone—and the blood of their horses. Drink it, witch-girl."

She drank, trying not to choke. When Oleg moved to tie her hands afresh, she said, "Oleg Ivanovich, is my brother all right?"

He drew the ropes tight around her wrists, looking at first as though he did not mean to answer. Then he said shortly, "He's alive, although he might be wishing he weren't. And he has not changed his story. I told Mamai that you knew nothing, that you were only an idiot girl. He believed me, although Chelubey did not. Be wary of him."

At midnight, Vasya told herself, trying not to shake. *We must only survive until midnight.*

Oleg pulled her outside the tent, into the rising sun, and she quailed. In broad daylight, the encampment was bigger than a town, bigger than a city. Tents and horse-lines stretched as far as she could see, half-blocked by scrubby woods. There were hundreds of men. Thousands. Tens of thousands. Her mind would go no higher. There were more horses than men, carts on every side. How would Dmitrii muster an army to match this one? How could he possibly hope to defeat them?

Oleg's horse was a stocky, big-headed bay mare. Her eye was kind and intelligent. Oleg slapped the mare's neck with affection.

Hello, Vasya said to the bay, with her body, in the speech of horses.

The bay flicked a dubious ear. *Hello,* she said. *You are not a horse.*

No, she said, as Oleg fastened the rope about her wrists to his saddle and vaulted to the mare's back. *But I understand you. Can you help me?*

The mare looked puzzled, but not unwilling. *How?* she asked, and jolted into a trot at the touch of Oleg's calf. Vasya, trying to think of a way to explain, was hauled stumbling along with them, praying that her strength would hold.

SHE SOON REALIZED THAT Oleg was keeping her close in part to humiliate her, but also to keep her from the nastier elements of an army on the march. Perhaps he'd believed her more than he appeared, about having been sent from Dmitrii Ivanovich. Perhaps he was even not so loyal to the Tatar as he appeared. The first time someone threw horse-dung at her, Oleg turned with a deceptively soft word, and she was not troubled again.

But the day was hard, and the hours passed slowly. Dust got in her eyes, her mouth. It rained halfway through the morning, and the dust turned to mud, and she was relieved for a space until she began to shiver, her wet clothes chafing. Then the sun came out, and she was back to sweating.

The bay mare was persuaded to make Vasya's way as easy as she could, by keeping straight so she didn't pull Vasya off her feet. But the mare was required to keep up a steady trot, hour after hour. She tugged Vasya in her wake. The girl was panting, her limbs afire, the cut on her head throbbing. Oleg did not look back.

They did not stop until the sun was high, and then only briefly. As soon as they halted, Vasya crumpled against the bay's comfortable shoulder, shuddering. She heard Oleg dismount. "More witchcraft?" he asked her mildly.

She hauled up her aching head and blinked at him resentfully.

"I raised this one from a foal," he explained, slapping the mare's neck. "She hasn't bitten you yet, and now you're leaning on her like she's a plow-horse."

"Maybe she just doesn't like men," Vasya said, wiping the sweat from her brow.

He snorted. "Perhaps. Here." He handed her a skin of mead, and she gulped, wiping her mouth with the back of her hand. "We go until dark," he said, putting a foot in the stirrup. "You are stronger than you look," he added. "Fortunately for you."

Vasya only prayed she'd make it to midnight.

Before Oleg could remount, his mare slanted an ear and Chelubey cantered up. Oleg turned, looking wary. "Not so proud now, are you, girl?" Chelubey said in Russian.

Vasya said, "I want to see my brother."

"No, you don't. He's having a worse day than you," said Chelubey. "He could make it easier for himself, but he just repeats the same lies, no matter what the flies do to his back."

She swallowed a wave of nausea. "He is a man of the Church," she snapped. "You have no right to hurt him!"

"If he had stayed in his monastery," said Chelubey, "I wouldn't. Men of the Church should confine themselves to praying." He bent nearer. Heads were turning among Oleg's men. "One of you is going to tell me what I want to know, or I will kill him," he said. "Tonight."

Chelubey had brought his horse right up alongside Oleg's. Vasya did not move, but suddenly the bay mare lashed out with both hind feet, catching Chelubey's horse in the flank. The horse squealed, shied, threw his rider and backed, eyes wild, two hoof-shaped gashes in his coat.

Oleg's bay wheeled, rearing, and yanked Vasya to the ground. Vasya was glad of that, even as she tumbled painfully into the dust. No one would realize she'd done it on purpose. Oleg sprang forward, caught his horse's bridle.

All his men were laughing.

"Witch!" snapped Chelubey, hauling himself out of the dust. To Vasya's surprise he looked a little afraid, as well as enraged. "You—"

"You cannot blame a girl for my horse's bad temper," said Oleg mildly, from behind her. "You brought your mare too close."

"I am going to take her with me now," said Chelubey. "She is dangerous."

"The mare or the girl?" Oleg asked innocently. The men laughed again. Vasya kept her eyes on Chelubey. The Russians were edging up on either side of her, closing ranks against the Tatar. Someone had caught Chelubey's horse. He was staring at her with a kind of enraged fascination. But then, abruptly, he turned away, saying, "Bring the girl to me at nightfall." With that he remounted and spurred off along the dusty column.

Vasya watched him go. Oleg was shaking his head. "I thought Dmitrii Ivanovich a man of sense, at least," he said. "But to spend his cousins like water, and for what?" Seeing her face still white and afraid, he added, with rough comfort, "Here," and gave her a hunk of flatbread. But she couldn't have eaten to save her life; she thrust the food in her sleeve for later.

~~~~~

THE AFTERNOON DRAGGED ON, and the men of Ryazan began to experience something strange. Their horses were slowing down. It wasn't lameness, and it wasn't sickness. But though the men kicked and spurred, their horses would only break into a lumbering gallop, then halt a few paces later, ears flattened.

Oleg and his men found themselves falling behind the fast-moving Tatar column. By nightfall, they were out of sight of the main body. Only the dust, faint against the green-yellow sky, showed the location of the rest of the army.

Vasya felt battered in every limb. Her head was throbbing with the effort of negotiating silently with a whole column's worth of horses. Fortunately, Oleg's mare was a sensible creature, held in awe by the others. She was a great help in creating the delay Vasya needed. If Vasya was to be dragged back to Chelubey, she wanted it to be at or near midnight.

They came to a ford, stopped to let the horses drink. Vasya, with a gasp, knelt at the riverbank herself. Gulping water, she was quite unprepared when Oleg took her by the upper arms, pulled her upright, turned her around, hands still wet. "All right," he said grimly. "Is it you?"

"Is what me?" Vasya asked.

He shook her once, slamming her teeth together on her tongue. She tasted blood. She was reminded that, whatever small kindnesses this prince chose to show her, he would betray Dmitrii Ivanovich to keep his own people safe; he would kill her without a qualm. "I've protected you; do I deserve deceit?" Oleg demanded. "Chelubey said you'd ensorcelled a horse in Moscow. I had my doubts, but——" A half-ironic sweep of his hand took in the vanished column. "Here we stand. Are you doing something to the horses?"

"I haven't been out of your sight," she said, and did not trouble to keep the exhaustion and defeat out of her voice. "How could I have done something to the horses?"

He considered her a few moments more, narrow-eyed, and then he said, "You are planning something. What is it?"

"Of course, I am planning," she said tiredly. "I am trying to think of a way to save my brother's life. I haven't thought of anything clever yet." She let her eyes rise to his. "Do you know a way, Oleg Ivanovich? I will do anything to save him."

He drew in a half-breath, looking uneasily into her eyes. "Anything?"

She made no reply, but she met his eyes.

He pressed his lips together; his glance went from her eyes to her mouth. Suddenly he let her go, turned away. "I will see what can be done," he said, voice clipped.

He was an honorable man, she thought, and not a fool; he might threaten but he'd not lie with Dmitrii's cousin. But that he was angry meant he was tempted. And he *was* angry; she could see the cords in his neck. But he didn't shake her again, and he had stopped thinking about the horses, which was what she wanted.

As for the rest—well, she meant to be gone, and her brother with her, before the question was raised again.

Oleg remounted, spurred his mare, yanked her on. There was no more stopping.

It was full night, well after moonrise, by the time Oleg's Russians found their place in the host. Their horses were fresh, having enjoyed Vasya's game greatly, but the men were sweating, sullen, sore.

Comments that sounded like good-natured abuse were hurled from all sides as the Russians straggled into camp in the moonlight. The exhausted men snapped at their restless horses. Oleg had not taken his eyes off her, Vasya was sure, for the last hour of marching. When they finally halted, he swung from the saddle and contemplated her grimly. "I must take you to Chelubey."

A little cold tendril of fear wormed its way through her belly. But she managed to say, "Where? Where is my brother?"

"In Mamai's ger." He must have seen the involuntary fear in her eyes, for he added roughly, "I won't leave you there, girl. Work on the most ignorant face you can manage. I must see the men settled first."

She was left sitting on a log, with a guard nearby. Vasya looked up at the moon, tried to feel the hour in her bones. It was late, certainly. Her clothes, sweat-soaked in the day's heats, chilled her now. She drew in a deep breath. Close enough to midnight? It would have to be.

Her head was clear now, though she was very tired. The nausea was gone, the pain in her head. She tried to push aside her fear for her brother, and concentrate. Small things. Little magic that was not beyond her strength and would not send her mad. Sitting on the day-warm earth, she forgot that her bonds were tight.

And she felt the rope give. Just a little. She forced herself to relax. The rope gave a little more, subtly. Now she could move her chafed wrists, turn them.

She looked round, caught the amiable eye of Oleg's bay. The mare, obligingly, reared, squealing. All the Russian horses did. Simultaneously, they went into a very ecstasy of fear, bucking, heaving wild-eyed on their pickets, thrashing against their hobbles. All around, Vasya heard men cursing. They streamed over to the horse-lines, even Vasya's guard. No one was looking at her. A twist, and she had yanked her wrists free. The chaos in the camp was spreading, as though the horses' panic was infecting their fellows.

She didn't know where Mamai's tent lay. She ducked into the confusion of milling men and horses, put a hand on the good bay's neck. The mare was still saddled; there was even a long knife attached to the saddlebag. "Will you carry me?" she whispered.

The bay tossed her head good-naturedly, and Vasya vaulted to her back. Suddenly she could see over the confusion. She nudged the mare forward, glancing back over her shoulder.

She could have sworn she saw Oleg of Ryazan, watching her go and saying not a word.

28

Pozhar

VASYA WHISPERED TO THEIR HORSES OF FIRE AND WOLVES AND terrible things. Wherever she went, she left the encampment in chaos. Campfires flared, throwing out sparks. Dozens of horses—more— were panicking all at once. Some bolted outright, trampling men with their passage; others merely reared and bucked and thrashed against their ropes. Vasya rode the bay mare through a wave of maddened creatures. More than once she was glad of the horse's steady feet and good sense. Danger was a fizz in her throat and stomach.

Darkness and chaos, she thought, were better allies even than magic.

Drawing nearer Mamai's tent, Vasya slid from the mare's back. "Wait for me," she said to the horse. The mare put her nose down obligingly. The horses here were bucking too; there were men everywhere, cursing. She gathered her courage and slipped inside Mamai's tent, praying under her breath.

Her brother was there, alone. His arms were wrenched up and bound to the pole that held the tent. He was bare to the waist, his back raw with whip-marks; he had bruises on his face. She ran to him.

Sasha raised exhausted eyes to her face. He was missing two fingernails on his right hand. "Vasya," he said. "Get out."

"I will. With you," she said. She had the knife from Oleg's saddle; now with a single slash, she cut his bonds. "Come on."

But Sasha was shaking his head dazedly. "They know," he said. "That you stirred up the horses. Chelubey—said something about a bay stallion, and a mare in Moscow. He knew it was you, as soon as the noise started. They—they planned for it." Sweat had run down into his beard; it gleamed at his temples, on his bare tonsured head. She whipped round.

They were standing in the opening of the tent: Mamai and Chelubey, watching, with men crowding behind them. Chelubey said something in his own tongue and Mamai answered. There was something avid in their stares.

Vasya, not taking her eyes off the two men, reached down to help her brother to his feet. He rose when she pulled, but it was obvious that every movement was agony.

"Step away from him. Slowly," said Chelubey to her in Russian. She could see her slow death in his eyes.

Vasya had had enough. She wasn't dazed with a blow to the head now. She set the tent on fire.

Flames leaped from the tent flaps in a dozen places; both men sprang backward, with cries of alarm. Vasya seized her brother and pulled him, limping, to the other side of the tent, used the knife to slice through the felt.

Rather than go out, she waited, holding her breath against the smoke, and whistled once between her teeth. The good bay mare came, and even knelt when Vasya asked, despite smoke and gathering flame, so that Sasha could get onto her back.

He couldn't stay on the horse by himself. Vasya had to get up in front of him, pull his arms about her waist. "Hold on," she said. The mare bolted, just as a shout went up from behind. She risked a glance back. Chelubey had seized a horse, just as she broke out of the smoke. Half a dozen men had joined him; they were riding her down. It was a race, to see if midnight would come or her pursuers catch her first.

At first, she thought it was one she could win. Her bones told her that midnight was not far off, and the mare had a good turn of speed.

But the camp was crowded and churning; unable to bull their way straight through, they had to dodge and turn. Sasha was holding on to her for all he was worth, his breath leaving him in a silent wheeze of pain with each fall of the horse's hooves. The plucky little mare was already beginning to labor under the weight of two.

Vasya breathed, and allowed the whole memory of the night of the burning in Moscow to come back to her. The terror and the power. Reality twisted, just as every campfire in the Tatar army sprang up into a triumphant column of flames.

Dizzy, struggling to keep a grip on herself, Vasya risked another look back, trying to see around her brother. Most of the men pursuing them had sheared off, their horses panicking. But a few had kept control of their horses, and Chelubey had not faltered. Her mare's sprint was beginning to fade. No sign of Midnight.

Chelubey shouted at his horse. Now he was level with their bay mare's flank. He had a sword in one hand. Vasya touched the mare and she sheared off, ears laid back, but it cost them more speed; Chelubey was herding them toward the camp once more, boxing them in. Sasha was heavy at her back. Now Chelubey was level with them again, his horse the faster. He lifted his sword a second time.

Before it could fall, Sasha heaved himself sideways, tackled the Tatar, threw him to the ground.

"Sasha!" she screamed. The mare's pace freshened at once, the weight off her back, but Vasya was already wheeling the horse round. Her brother and Chelubey were fighting on the ground, but the Tatar had the upper hand. His fist snapped Sasha's head back; she saw a glitter of blood in the fire. Then he was rising to his feet, leaving her brother where he lay. Chelubey called his horse, shouting at the other riders.

Sasha dragged himself to his knees. There was blood on his mouth. His lips formed a single word—*Run*.

She hesitated. The mare felt it and slowed.

Just then, a streak of flame shot across the heavens.

It was like a star falling: scarlet and blue and gold. The streak of flame dropped lower, lower, surged like a wave, and suddenly there was a tall golden mare, glowing in the grass, galloping alongside them.

Cries of rage and wonder from the Tatars.

"Pozhar," Vasya whispered. The mare slanted an ear at the other horse, turned her other ear back to the men riding them down. *Get on my back.*

Vasya didn't question it. She stood up, balancing on the bay mare's back as she galloped. Pozhar had shortened her stride to pace the other horse and Vasya stepped sideways, lightly, and dropped to the mare's golden withers. The mare's skin was burning-hot between her knees.

A few of the oncoming men had bows; an arrow whistled past her ear. They were just inside bowshot, angling back toward the place where her brother lay. What to do? Miraculously, she had Pozhar's speed now, but her brother was on the ground. Another arrow whistled past her cheek just as she glimpsed the Midnight-road.

An idea came to her then, so reckless her breath caught. With the rage and terror in her heart, the limits of her knowledge and her skill so miserably evident, she could think of nothing else.

"We have to get back to this same midnight. We have to come back for him," Vasya told the mare grimly. "But we need to get help first."

You didn't understand, Midnight had said.

The mare set foot on the Midnight-road and they were swallowed up by the night.

THEY WOULD GET BACK to the Tatar camp on the same midnight—she would not have left otherwise. But it felt hideously like she'd abandoned her brother to die, as she galloped through the wild darkness, trees lashing at her face. She sobbed into the mare's neck for a stride or two, in horror, in fear for Sasha, in sheer disgust at her own blundering, at the limits of her skill.

The golden mare did not move like Solovey. Solovey was round through the barrel and easy to ride. Pozhar was faster, leaner, her withers a hard ridge, her stride a great heave and surge, like riding the crest of a flood.

After a few moments, Vasya raised her head and got control of herself. Could she do it? She couldn't even have contemplated it, were her mind not full of the sight of her brother, bloody, surrounded by enemies. She tried to think of something else.

Anything.

She couldn't.

So she concentrated on where she wished to go. That part was easy, and quick. Her blood knew the way; she scarcely needed to think of it.

After only few minutes of galloping, they burst out of the black woods into a familiar field, hissing with wheat half-harvested. The sky was a river of stars. Vasya sat up. Pozhar slowed, dancing, wild.

A small village stood on a little rise, beyond the cleared fields. It was indistinct against the stars, but Vasya knew its every fold and curve. Longing closed her throat. It was midnight, in the village where she'd been born. Somewhere near, in his own house, was her brother Alyosha, her sister Irina.

But she wasn't there for them. One day, she might go back—bring Marya back to meet her people, to eat good bread sitting in warm summer grass. But now she could not look for comfort here. She was on another errand.

"Pozhar," said Vasya. "Why did you come back?"

Ded Grib, said the mare. *He's been getting news from all the mushrooms in Rus', as self-important as you could wish, telling everyone he is your greatest ally. Today he came to me saying you were in danger again and that I was a great lump for not helping. I went to find you only to silence him, but then I saw the fires you made. They were good fires.* The mare sounded almost approving. *Besides, you don't weigh very much. You aren't even uncomfortable.*

"Thank you," said Vasya. "Will you carry me farther?"

That depends, said the horse. *Are we going to do anything interesting?*

Vasya thought of Morozko, far away in the white silence of his winter world. There was a welcome for her there, she knew. But not help. She might pull him, a shadow, out once more from winter, but to what end? He could not fight off an army of Tatars as he was, and save her brother.

She could only think of one who might be able to.

She said grimly, "More interesting than you might wish." Once more, she wondered if she was being fatally rash.

But then she thought of Midnight. What had she meant when she said, *We hoped that you were different.*

Vasya thought she knew.

At her touch, Pozhar wheeled and galloped back through the trees.

29

Between Winter and Spring

THERE IS A CLEARING ON THE BORDER BETWEEN WINTER AND SPRING. Once Vasya would have said that the cusp of spring was a moment. But now she knew that it was also a place, at the edge of the lands of winter.

At the center of the clearing stood an oak-tree. Its trunk was vast as a peasant's hut, its branches spread like the roof-beams of a house, like the bars of a prison.

At the foot of the tree, leaning on the trunk, knees drawn up to his chest, sat Medved. It was still midnight. The clearing was dark; the moon had sunk below the horizon. There was only Pozhar's light, echoed by the gleam of gold that bound the Bear's wrists and throat. Utter silence in the forest all around, but Vasya had the distinct impression of unseen eyes, watching.

Medved didn't move when he saw them, except his mouth quirked in an expression very far from a smile. "Come to gloat?" he asked.

Vasya slid off the mare's back. The demon's nostrils flared, taking in her disheveled appearance, the cut on her temple, feet caked with mud. Pozhar backed uneasily, ears locked on the Bear, remembering perhaps the teeth of his upyry in her flank.

Vasya stepped forward.

His unscarred brow lifted. "Or are you come to seduce me?" he asked. "My brother not enough for you?"

She said nothing. He couldn't draw back, pressed against the tree, but the single eye opened wider. He was tense, bound tight by the gold. "No?" he said, still mocking. "Then why?"

"Did you mourn the priest?" she asked.

The Bear tilted his head and surprised her by saying simply, "Yes."

"Why?"

"He was mine. He was beautiful. He could create and destroy with a word. He put his soul in his singing, in his writing of icons. He is gone. Of course, I mourn."

"You shattered him," she said.

"Perhaps. Though I did not make the cracks."

Perhaps it was a fitting epitaph for Father Konstantin, to be regretted by a chaos-spirit. The Bear was leaning his head against the bole of the tree, as though untroubled, but the single eye was fixed on her. "Devushka, *you* are not here to lament Konstantin Nikonovich. Then why?"

"My brother is a prisoner of the Tatar general Mamai. And my brother-in-law with him," she said.

The Bear snorted. "Kind of you to tell me. I hope they both die screaming."

She said, "I cannot free them alone. I tried, and I failed."

The eye took in her disheveled appearance again. "Did you?" His smile was almost whimsical. "What does that have to do with me?"

Vasya's hands were shaking. "I mean to save them," she said. "And after must save Rus' from invasion. I cannot do it alone. I joined the war between you and your twin, when I helped Morozko bind you. But now I want you to join *my* war. Medved, will you help me?"

She had shocked him. The gray eye widened. But his voice was still light. "Help you?"

"I will make you a bargain."

"What makes you think I'll keep it?"

"Because," she said, "I don't think you want to spend eternity under this tree."

"Very well." He leaned forward, as far as the gold would allow. The words were scarcely more than a breath against her ear. "What bargain, devushka?"

"I will undo this golden thing," she said. She traced the line of the binding, throat to wrist to hand. The golden bridle wanted to hold on; it was a tool made to bend one creature to another's will. It resisted her, but when she slipped a finger beneath and pulled it just a little away from his skin, it gave.

Medved shuddered.

She did not want to see hope in his eyes. She wanted him to be a monster.

But monsters were for children. He was powerful, in his own fashion, and for her brother's sake, she needed him.

Thinking of that, she opened the skin of her thumb on her dagger. His hand reached out involuntarily, drawn to the virtue in her blood. She drew away before he could touch her.

"If I release you, then you will serve me as Midnight serves my great-grandmother," said Vasya grimly. "You will fight my battles and connive at my victories; if I summon, you will answer. You will swear never to lie to me, but give true counsel. You will not betray me, but always keep faith. You will also swear never again to turn your plagues onto Rus': no terror or fire or dead alive. Under those conditions, and those alone, will I free you."

He laughed. "The effrontery," he said. "Just because my brother abased himself for your ugly face? Tell me why *I* should be your dog?"

Vasya smiled. "Because the world is wide and very beautiful, and you are tired of this clearing. I saw how you looked at the stars the night by the lake. Because, as you have noticed, I am like a chaos-spirit myself, and where I go disorder goes too. You enjoy that sort of thing. Because the fight between you and your brother is over, for you are both joining *my* war. And—perhaps you will like serving me. It would be a battle of wits at least."

He snorted, "*Your* wits, witch-girl?"

"They are improving," said Vasya, and touched his face with the hand she'd cut on her knife-blade.

He jerked back, even as his flesh grew more solid beneath her fingers. His hands flexed under the golden binding.

He stared at her, breathing shallowly. "Oh, now I know why my brother wanted you," he whispered. "Sea-maiden, witch's daughter.

But one day you will go mad with magic. Just like every witch, every sorcerer that ever lived. And then you will be mine. Perhaps I'll just . . . wait."

"One day," said Vasya mildly, dropping her hand, "I will die. I will go into the darkness, into the wood between worlds where your brother guides the dead. But I will still be myself. If I am mad, I will not be yours. And dead I will not be his."

He breathed out half a laugh, but the gray eye was sharp. "Perhaps," he said. "Still, exchange prison for slavery? Wear the golden rope here, trapped by the priest's blood? Or wear it elsewhere, a slave to your will? You haven't offered me nearly enough to get me to help you."

Pozhar squealed suddenly. Vasya did not look round, but somehow the sound gave her courage. She knew she'd never keep the mare's loyalty if she took a slave—any slave—with the help of that golden thing.

She took a deep breath. "No, you will not wear the rope. I am not Kaschei the Deathless. I am going to take your oath. Will it bind you, Medved?"

He stared.

She went on, "I imagine it might, since your own twin took your word. Swear to me, and I will free you. Or would you prefer sitting here to fighting a war?"

Avid hunger in his face, there and gone. "A war," he breathed.

She fought nerves, made herself speak calmly. "Between Mamai and Dmitrii," she said. "You should know. You were the one that ensured the silver would be lost."

He shrugged. "I only cast bread on the water, devushka. And see what comes up to eat it."

"Well, war is kindled; Dmitrii had no choice. And you, lover of battles, can help us. Will you swear to me, and come into the night?" She rose and stepped back. "Or perhaps you prefer to stay; perhaps it is beneath your dignity to be a girl's servant."

He laughed and laughed, and then he said, "In a thousand lives of men, I have never been anyone's servant." He gave her another long look. "And it will enrage my brother." She bit her lip. "You have my oath—Vasilisa Petrovna." He put his bound wrist to his mouth and bit his hand suddenly, just where finger met thumb. Blood, clear and sulfur-smelling, welled out. He put out a thick-fingered hand.

"What does your blood do to someone who is not dead?" she asked.

"Karachun told you, did he?" he said. "It gives you life, wild girl. Haven't I sworn not to harm you?"

She hesitated, and then clasped his hand, her blood sluggish on his skin, his blood stinging where it touched. She felt a jolt of unpleasant energy, burning away her weariness.

Pulling her hand away, she said, "If you are forsworn, then back to this tree you will go, tied hand and foot and throat with this golden thing. And I will put out your other eye and you may live in darkness."

"You were such a sweet child, when I first met you by this very tree," remarked the Bear. "What happened?" His voice was mocking, but she could feel the tension in him, when she began to undo the golden clasps.

"What happened? Love, betrayal, and time," said Vasya. "What happens to anyone who grows to understand you, Medved? Living happens." Her hands slid along the oily gold, working at the buckles. She wondered briefly how Kaschei had made it. Somewhere, perhaps, there was an answer, somewhere there were secrets of magic beyond the setting of fires, the seeing of chyerti.

One day, perhaps, she would learn them, in far countries, beneath wilder skies.

Then the gold slithered away, all in a rush. The Bear was very still, flexing his unbound hands with a disbelief he couldn't quite conceal. She got to her feet. The gold was in two pieces: what had been the reins and the headstall of the bridle. She wrapped them around her wrists: a terrible prince's ransom, shining.

The Bear rose, and stood beside her. His back was straight; his eye glittered. "Come then, mistress," he said, half-mocking. "Where shall we go?"

"To my brother," said Vasya grimly. "While it is still midnight, and he is still alive. But first—"

She turned, seeking, in the darkness. "Polunochnitsa," she said.

She had no doubts of her guess, and indeed, the midnight-demon stepped at once into the clearing. Voron's great hooves crunched the bracken at her back.

"You betrayed me," said Vasya.

"But you understood at last," said Polunochnitsa. "It was never your task to pick out the good from the wicked. Your task was to unite us. We are one people." The rage was gone from her face.

Vasya stalked forward. "You could have told me. They tormented my brother."

"It is not something you can be told," said Polunochnitsa. "It is something you must come to understand."

Her great-grandmother had said the same. Vasya could feel the Bear watching. He breathed out a laugh as she, wordless, unspooled the golden rope, snapped it out, caught Polunochnitsa around the throat. The midnight-demon tried to wrench back, but couldn't, caught by the power in the gold. She made a single, shocked sound and stood still, wide-eyed.

Vasya said, "I do not like being betrayed, Polunochnitsa. You took no pity on me after the fire; you had no pity on my brother. Perhaps I should leave *you* tied to a tree."

The black stallion reared, squealing. Vasya didn't move, though the great hooves were a handsbreadth from her face. "I will take her with me, Voron, if you kill me."

The horse subsided, and Vasya had to harden her heart. Midnight was looking at her with genuine fear. "Medved owes me allegiance now, and so do you, Polunochnitsa. You will not betray me again."

The midnight-demon was staring at her with horror and unwilling fascination. "You are Baba Yaga's heir in truth now," she said. "When you have finished with the dealings of men, go back to the lake. At midnight, the witch will be waiting."

"I am not finished yet," Vasya said grimly. "I am going to save my brother. You are going to swear an oath to me as well, Lady Midnight, and you are going to help me."

"I am sworn to your great-grandmother."

"And, as you said, I am her heir."

Their eyes locked, a silent battle of wills. Midnight was the first to lower hers. "I swear then," she said.

"What do you swear?"

"To serve you and to heed you, and never to betray you again."

Vasya, with a snap, freed Polunochnitsa of the golden rope. "I swear to sustain you as I can," she said. "With blood and with memory. We can no longer afford to fight amongst ourselves."

The Bear said lightly, from behind, "I think I am going to enjoy this."

30

The Enemy of
My Enemy

SASHA WAS ONLY VAGUELY AWARE OF WHAT HAPPENED, AFTER HE threw Chelubey from the saddle. He hadn't been thinking clearly when he did it. Merely that there was a sword, and his sister's vulnerable throat, and he hated the Tatar as he'd never hated anyone in his life. Hated his impersonal cruelties, his clever mind, his soft questions.

So, when the Tatar drew up alongside them, Sasha saw an opening and didn't hesitate. But he was wounded, and Chelubey strong. A blow to his jaw shot sparks across his sight, and then Chelubey shouted over Sasha's head, urging other men on. Sasha dragged himself to his knees, saw his sister, still mounted, wheeling her horse to come back for him.

Vasya, he tried to shout. *Run.*

Then the world went dark. When he came to, he was still lying on the ground. Chelubey stood over him. "She's gone," Sasha heard a voice say. "Disappeared." He let out a breath of relief, just as Chelubey drew back and kicked him in the ribs. The bone cracked; Sasha doubled up, lacking the breath to scream.

"I think," said Chelubey, "that after the night's excitement, the general will have no further objections to you dying while I torture you. Get him on his feet."

But the men weren't looking down at Sasha anymore. They were backing up, with expressions of horror.

THE ROAD BACK THROUGH Midnight was short. Vasya's blood cried out for her brother; and Pozhar had no objection to galloping through the forest at reckless speed. Voron raced alongside them. The black stallion was far swifter than any mortal horse, but still he labored to match the golden mare's pace.

Vasya mourned in silence even as she savored the strength of the mare beneath her. The firebird was not, and never would be, her other self, and Pozhar's grace reminded Vasya of her loss all over again.

The Bear paced the horses in silence. He had let go the shape of a man; he ran as a great shadow-beast, nourished by her blood. As they went, he sniffed at the sky, barely containing a bared-teeth eagerness.

"Hoping for killing?" said Vasya.

"No," said the Bear. "I care naught for the dead. Mine are the suffering living."

"Our task is to save my brother," Vasya said sharply. "Not to make people suffer. Are you so quickly forsworn, Medved?"

The two pieces of golden rope shimmered eerily on her wrists. He shot them a dark look and said, a growl just entering his voice, "I have promised."

"Ahead," said Midnight. Vasya squinted into the darkness. Fires broke up the night in front of them; the wind brought them the smell of men and horses.

Vasya sat back and Pozhar slowed, grudgingly. Her nostrils flared, disliking the smell of men. "I left my brother on the north side of the camp, not far from a stream," said Vasya to Polunochnitsa. "Is he still there?"

In answer, Midnight slid down from her horse, put a light hand on the stallion's neck, whispered. Voron reared up against the sky, mane flying lightly as feathers, and then a raven flew into the night.

"Solovey never did that," Vasya said, watching the black horse change and fly.

"Take his other form? He was too young," said Midnight. "A colt still. The young ones only change with difficulty. He'd have learned to control his own nature if—"

"He'd had time," Vasya finished flatly. The Bear glanced at her, half-smiling, as though he could taste the hurt.

"We must follow Voron," said Midnight.

"Get up behind me then," said Vasya. "Unless—Pozhar, do you mind?"

The mare looked as though she were considering saying no, just to remind them that she could. *Very well*, she said irritably, switching her tail.

Vasya put an arm down; the chyert seemed to weigh nothing at all. Riding double on the mare, they surged forward, the Bear at Pozhar's flank. Ahead, the trees thinned, and a single raven croaked from the darkness.

THE TATARS WERE STILL where she'd left them. Some were still mounted; others stood in a ragged circle. Two reached down, heaving, and Vasya glimpsed the dim shape of her brother being dragged to his feet. He was limp, his head hung down.

"Can you frighten them off?" said Vasya to the Bear, hearing her voice shake, quite beyond her control.

"Perhaps, mistress," said Medved, and grinned his vast dog-grin at her. "Do keep panicking. It helps me."

She just stared at him, stone-faced, and he relented. "Do something else useful then. See that tree there? Set it afire."

A flicker of remembered fire, and the tree burst into flames. It was disturbing, how easy it had become. Being near the Bear fanned the chaos in her own heart. His eye found hers. "It would do you good to go mad," he murmured. "It would make it easier. You could do any magic you pleased—if you were mad. Storms and lightning and noonday darkness."

"Be silent!" she said. The fire on the tree grew bigger, sending out a sweep of golden light. Reality wavered; she dug her nails into her palms, and whispered her own name, to make it stop. She forced her voice to calm. "Are you going to frighten them off or not?"

Still smiling, the Bear turned wordless toward the huddle of men and began to creep closer. Their horses backed up, nostrils flared. Wide-eyed, the men faced the night, swords in their hands.

Within the firelight, a shadow grew. A strange, crawling, mutable shadow, slinking toward men and horses. The shadow of an unseen beast.

The Bear's soft voice seemed to come from the shadow itself. "Interfere with my servant?" he whispered. "Lay hands on what is mine? You'll die for it. You'll die screaming."

His voice got into the men's ears, got into their minds. His shadow crawled nearer, sending twisted shapes dancing across the fire-beaten ground. The men were trembling. A soft, unearthly snarl filled the night. The shadows seemed to spring. At the same moment, a flicker of memory from Vasya made the flames leap in the burning tree.

The men's nerve broke. They fled, mounted or afoot, until there was only one alone, standing over her brother's prone form, shouting at the running men. They had let Sasha fall as they escaped.

The single man was Chelubey. Vasya nudged Pozhar then and rode into the light.

Chelubey blanched. His sword-blade dipped. "I warned them," he said. "Oleg and Mamai—those fools. I warned them."

Vasya gave him a dazzling smile, without warmth. "You shouldn't have told them I was a girl. Then they might have believed that I was dangerous."

Pozhar's eyes were embers, her mane, smoke and sparks. A touch to her flank drove the mare into a rear. She lashed out with her forefeet, and even Chelubey's nerve broke then. He fled, leaped to his own horse's back, shot away. Pozhar, half-maddened, sprang in pursuit. Vasya curbed her after a few bolting strides. Her blood was up; she had to fight her own urge, as well as the mare's, to ride Chelubey down. It was as though the Bear's presence goaded them both to rashness.

Well, he could goad all he liked; Vasya would make decisions for herself. "My brother," she said, seizing control of herself, and Pozhar was persuaded, with difficulty, to turn.

The Bear looked mildly disappointed. Ignoring him, Vasya dropped to the ground at her brother's side. Sasha was curled up, arms wrapped around his body. Blood showed on his mouth, on his back, black in the firelight. But he was alive. "Sasha," she said, cradling his head. "Bratishka."

Slowly, he looked up. "I told you to run," he croaked.

"I came back."

"That was disappointingly easy," said the Bear from behind her. "What now?"

Sasha tried to sit up, made a small sound of pain. "No," Vasya said. "No, don't be afraid. He helped me." She was feeling her brother over gently. The blood on his hand and back had gone cold and sticky, and his breath was short with pain, but she could find no fresh wounds. "Sasha," she said. "I must go into the camp, and find Vladimir Andreevich. Can you stand? You can't stay here."

"I think I can stand," he said. He tried, struggling. Once he put his weight on his injured hand and made a sound not far from a scream. But he got himself upright, leaning heavily on her. She staggered under his weight; her brother was barely conscious.

Perhaps that was a blessing, considering how he'd feel about her allies.

"Will you take him up on Voron?" Vasya asked Polunochnitsa. "And hide him from the Tatars?"

"You want me to nursemaid a monk?" Polunochnitsa asked, disbelieving. Then her expression turned curious. It occurred to Vasya that a chyert might be persuaded to try any unusual thing just to relieve the boredom of eternity.

"Swear you won't hurt him, or allow him to be hurt, or frighten him," Vasya said. "Meet us here. We are going to get my cousin."

At that Sasha croaked, "Am I a nursing babe, Vasya, that she must swear all those oaths? Who is this?"

"Travel by midnight would awaken the sight in even a monk," put in the Bear. "That is interesting."

Reluctantly Vasya answered Sasha, "Lady Midnight."

"The one who hates you?"

"We came to an arrangement."

Midnight gave Sasha an appraising look. "I swear it, Vasilisa Petrovna. Come, monk, and get on my horse."

Vasya wasn't sure of the wisdom of trusting Midnight with her brother, but she had little choice.

"Come on," she said to the Bear. "We have to free the Prince of Serpukhov, and then we must persuade Oleg of Ryazan that he is fighting for the wrong side."

Following her, the Bear said reflectively, "I might even enjoy that. Although it rather depends on your method of persuasion."

VASYA'S FIRES HAD BURNED down to scarlet embers, but they glowed on every hand, illuminating the Tatar encampment with a hellish light. Weary men were catching the foam-streaked horses and whispering among themselves; the air of unease was palpable. The Bear surveyed the remains of turmoil with a critical eye. "Admirable," he said. "I'll make a creature of chaos of you yet."

She feared she was already halfway there, but she was not saying that to him.

The Bear said, "What do you mean to do?"

Vasya told him her plan.

He laughed. "A few shambling corpses would be better. Nothing better for getting people to do what you want."

"We are not disturbing any more dead souls!" snapped Vasya.

"You may find it tempting, before the end."

"Not tonight," said Vasya. "Can you set fires, yourself?"

"Yes, and put them out too. Fear and fire are my tools, sweet maiden."

"Can you smell my cousin?"

"Russian blood?" he asked. "Do you think me a witch in a fairy tale?"

"Yes or no."

He lifted his head and snuffed the night. "Yes," he said, growling a little. "Yes, I suppose I can."

Vasya turned to have a quick word with Pozhar. Then she followed the Bear into the Tatar camp on foot. As she did, she took a deep breath and forgot that she was anything but a shadow, walking beside another shadow. One with teeth.

Invisibly, they slipped into the chaos of the camp, and the Bear, in his element, seemed to grow. He moved unerringly through the noise, the little knots of still-frightened horses, and where he passed, the horses shied and fires flared. Men turned clammy faces toward the darkness. He grinned at them, blew sparks into their clothes.

"Enough," said Vasya. "Find my cousin. Or I will bind you with more than just promises."

"There is more than one Russian here," said the Bear irritably. "I can't—" He caught her eye and finished almost meekly, except for a hint of sudden laughter in his eyes. "But that one smells like the far north."

She followed him, quicker now. Finally, he halted near the center of the camp. Instinctively she wanted to flatten herself, hiding in the shadow of a round tent, but that would mean she believed the soldiers could see her.

They couldn't. She held that thought and stayed where she was.

A bound man was kneeling, silhouetted, beside a well-tended fire. All around, soldiers were soothing their restive horses.

Three men stood near the fire, arguing. With the light behind them, it took her a moment to recognize Mamai and Chelubey and Oleg. She wished she could understand what they were saying.

"They are deciding whether or not to kill him," said the beast beside her. "It seems your escape has made them wary."

"You understand Tatar?"

"I understand the speech of men," said the Bear, just as a dazzle of fresh light poured over the camp, panicking the horses all over again. Vasya didn't look up. She knew what she would see: Pozhar soaring overhead, streaming smoke, her fiery wings making arcs of scarlet and blue, gold and white.

I can't make the earth catch fire like I did in the city, Pozhar had said, when Vasya asked. *That was—I was so angry, I was maddened with anger. I can't do it again.*

"You don't have to," Vasya returned. "Just dazzle them. It will send a message to my countrymen." She patted the horse comfortingly, and Pozhar bit her on the shoulder.

Now all around the camp, men looked to the sky. A babble of renewed talk broke out. She heard the snap of bowstrings, saw a few arrows arc up into the night, but Pozhar was keeping out of range. A wondering cry, quickly silenced, rose from one of the Russians: "Zhar Ptitsa!"

"Can you make it so they can see you?" Vasya asked the Bear, not taking her eyes off the general.

"With your blood," he said.

She gave him her grazed hand; he clung greedily, then she yanked her fingers back again.

"At the right moment then," she said.

Holding fast to the knowledge that they could not see her, she crept into the light. The three men were still arguing, shouting at each other now, while the bird, shining, impossible, soared overhead.

Vasya walked up behind them, unspooled her golden rope, and wrapped it around Mamai's throat.

He managed a choked gasp, and then he froze, caught by Kaschei's magic and her own will.

Everyone in sight froze too. They could see her now. "Good evening," said Vasya. It was hard to get the breath to speak steadily. The eyes of two dozen expert bowmen were on her; many of them already had arrows up.

"You can't kill me before I kill him," she said to them. "Even if you fill me with arrows." In one hand, she had the golden rope, but in the other was her knife, pressed to Mamai's throat. She thought she heard Oleg's voice, interpreting, but she didn't look around to see.

Chelubey had drawn his sword; he took one furious step toward her, then stopped at Mamai's wordless, pained sound.

"I am here for the Prince of Serpukhov," said Vasya.

Mamai made another inarticulate croak, and then said something that sounded like an order. "Silence!" she snapped, and he stood rigid when she pressed the dagger a little more into his neck.

Oleg was gaping at her like a landed fish. Above them the firebird cried again, wheeling, bright against the clouds. The Tatars' horses plunged. Out of the corner of her eye, Vasya glimpsed men, as though despite themselves, lifting their faces to the light.

Chelubey was the first to recover his wits. "You won't leave here alive, girl."

"If I don't," said Vasya, "and Vladimir Andreevich doesn't, then your leader doesn't either. Will you risk it?"

"Loose your arrows!" snapped Chelubey as Vasya gashed the general's throat just hard enough to make him cry out. Copper-smelling blood ran over her hands. The bowmen hesitated.

Medved took advantage of the moment to come strolling out of the night: a vast shadow-bear. A hell-light of amusement shone in his good eye.

A single bowstring twanged, the shot wild. Then a terrified stillness fell.

Vasya spoke into the silence. "Free the Prince of Serpukhov, or I will set the whole camp afire and lame every horse. And *he* will eat what's left." She jerked her chin at the Bear. The beast obligingly bared his teeth.

Mamai croaked something. His men hurried. Next moment, the man from the river, her sister's husband, was coming warily toward her.

He seemed unhurt. His eyes widened when he recognized the boy by the water. Vasya said, "Vladimir Andreevich." He looked as though he thought the rescue might be worse than the captivity. She tried to reassure him. "Dmitrii Ivanovich sent me," she said. "Are you all right? Can you ride?"

He dipped his chin in a wary nod, crossed himself. No one moved.

"Come with me," said Vasya to her cousin. He did, still looking uncertain. She began to back up, still holding on to Mamai by the golden rope.

Oleg had not spoken, but he was watching her very intently. She took a deep breath.

"Now," she said to the Bear.

Every fire in the encampment went out at once, every lamp and torch. The firebird was the only light, soaring overhead. Then Pozhar swooped low and the horses all plunged at their pickets again, neighing shrilly.

Over the din, in the darkness, Vasya whispered in the general's ear, "Continue on this course, and you will die. Rus' will have no conquerors." She thrust him into the arms of his men, caught her cousin's hand and pulled him into the shadows, just as three bows twanged. But she had already vanished into the night, and with her the Bear and Vladimir Andreevich.

The Bear was laughing as they ran. "They were so frightened, of a little skinny witch-girl. It was delicious. Oh, we will teach this whole land to fear, before the end." He turned his good eye on her and added censoriously, "You should have cut the leader's throat properly. He will live, none the worse."

"They gave me my cousin. In honor, I could not—"

The Bear whooped unpleasantly. "Hear the girl! The Grand Prince of Moscow gives her a task and she decides on the spot that *she's* a boyar, stuffed to the brim with the courtesies of war. How long will it take you to learn better, I wonder?"

Vasya said nothing. Instead she turned aside at a horse-line just at the edge of camp, cut a picket, said, "Here, Vladimir Andreevich. Mount up."

Vladimir didn't move. His eyes were on the Bear. "What black devilry is this?"

Happily, the Bear said, "The worst kind."

Vladimir made the sign of the cross with a hand that shook. Someone shouted in Tatar. Vasya whipped round and saw that Medved, enjoying their terror, had made himself visible against the sky. Vladimir Andreevich was on the edge of fleeing back to his enemies.

Furious, Vasya uncoiled a golden rope, and said, "Are we allies or no, Medved? I am getting tired of you."

"Oh, I do not like that thing," said the Bear. But his mouth closed; he seemed to shrink. Men were coming nearer.

"Get on the horse," Vasya said to Vladimir.

There was no saddle or bridle, but the Prince of Serpukhov heaved himself to the gelding's back, just as Vasya vaulted onto a piebald mare.

"Who are you?" whispered Vladimir, his voice cold with fright.

"I am Olga's younger sister," said Vasya. "Go!" She slapped the haunch of Vladimir's mount, and then they were away, over the grass, dodging between sparse trees, seeking the dark, and leaving the Tatars at last behind them.

The Bear laughed at her as they galloped away. "Now, don't tell me you didn't enjoy that," he said.

Answering laughter rose in her: the giddy joy of striking fear in her enemies' hearts. She tamped it down, but not before her eyes met the gaze of the king of chaos, and she saw her own reckless delight reflected there.

SASHA AND MIDNIGHT WERE just where Vasya had left them, double-mounted on Voron. Pozhar met them there too, in the form of a horse. Her every footfall made sparks; her eye was molten.

Vasya felt a surge of relief at the sight of them.

"Brother Aleksandr," said Vladimir, still sputtering. "Can it be—"

"Vladimir Andreevich," said Sasha. "Vasya." And to her surprise, Sasha slid down Voron's back just as she got off her Tatar mare. They embraced.

"Sasha," she said. "How—" His back had been bound, and his hand. He moved stiffly, but not in a haze of pain.

He glanced back at Polunochnitsa. "We rode into the dark," he said, frowning as though it were hard to remember. "I was barely conscious. There was the sound of water on rock. A house that smelled of honey and garlic. And an old woman there who bound my back. She said— she said she preferred daughters, but that I would do. Would I like to stay? I don't know what I answered. I slept. I don't know how long. But every time I woke, it was still midnight. Then Polunochnitsa came and said I had slept long enough, and she brought me back. I almost—it seems like the old woman called after us, sadly, but I might have dreamed it."

Vasya raised an eyebrow at Polunochnitsa. "You took him to the *lake*? How long was he there?"

"Long enough," said Midnight, unrepentant.

"You didn't think it would send *him* mad?" Vasya asked, with an edge.

"No," said Polunochnitsa. "He was asleep, mostly. And also, he is very like you." She gave Sasha a proprietary look. "Besides he couldn't sit upright and reeked of blood, and that irritated me. It was easier to let the witch fix him. She regrets Tamara, you know, as much as she is angry."

Vasya said, "It was kind then, my friend," to the midnight-demon. Polunochnitsa looked simultaneously suspicious and pleased.

"You have met our great-grandmother," Vasya added to her brother. "She is a madwoman who lives in Midnight. She is cruel and lonely, and sometimes kind."

"The old woman?" said Sasha. "I—no. Surely not. Our great-grandmother must be dead."

"She is," said Vasya. "But that doesn't matter, in Midnight."

Sasha looked thoughtful. "I would go back. When this is over. Cruel or no, she seemed to know a great many things."

"Perhaps we can go together," said Vasya.

"Perhaps," said Sasha. They grinned at each other, like children contemplating adventures, instead of a witch and a monk on the cusp of battle.

Vladimir Andreevich was shooting them both black looks. "Brother Aleksandr," he broke in stiffly, making the sign of the cross. "This is a strange meeting."

"God be with you," said Sasha.

"And what in God's *name*—" began the Prince of Serpukhov, before Vasya interjected hastily.

"Sasha will explain," she said, "while I perform one last errand. If we are fortunate, we will have company on the way north."

"Better hurry," said the Bear. He was looking critically over the Tatar camp where they had begun relighting their fires. Pozhar's ears twitched at the faint noise of their furious shouting. "They're like a stirred-up beehive."

"You're coming with me," she told him. "I don't trust you out of my sight."

"Quite right," said the Bear and looked up at the sky with a sigh of pleasure.

WHEN OLEG OF RYAZAN came back to his tent at last, he looked like a man who'd lived eternities in one night. He pushed the flap aside, walked in and stood silent a moment. Vasya let out a soft breath, and his clay lamp flared to life.

Oleg looked utterly unsurprised. "If the general finds you, he will kill you slowly."

She stepped into the lamplight. "He is not going to find me. I came back for you."

"Did you?"

"You have seen the firebird in the sky," she said. "You have seen flames in the night and horses running mad. You have seen the Bear in the shadows. You have seen our strength. Your men are already whispering of the strange power of the Grand Prince of Moscow, that has reached even into the camp of the Tatar."

"Strange power? Perhaps Dmitrii Ivanovich has no care for *his* immortal soul, but am *I* to damn my soul, allying myself with devils?"

"You are a practical man," Vasya said gently. She stepped closer. He knotted his hands together. "You did not choose to side with the Tatar for loyalty, but for survival's sake. Now you see that the opposite may be true. That we can win. Under the Khan you will never be more than a vassal, Oleg Ivanovich. If we win, then you will be a prince in your own right."

It was an effort to keep her voice even. She had begun to shake with spending too long in Midnight. The Bear's presence made that worse too. The chyert was a knot of deeper darkness, listening from the shadows.

"Witch, you have your brother and your cousin," said Oleg. "Are you not content?"

"No," said Vasya. "Summon your boyars and come with us."

Oleg's eyes were darting around the tent as though he could—not see, but sense—the Bear's presence. The clay lamp guttered; the darkness around it deepened.

Vasya aimed a glare at Medved, and the dark retreated a little.

"Come with us and have victory," Vasya said.

"Maybe a victory," murmured the Bear from behind her. "Who knows?"

Oleg was shrinking nearer the lamplight, without quite knowing what frightened him.

"Tomorrow," said Vasya. "Have your men fall behind the main body again. We'll be waiting."

After a long silence, Oleg said firmly, "My men will stay with Mamai."

She heard the echo of her failure in the words, just as the Bear let out a sigh of pleased understanding.

Then Oleg finished, and Vasya understood. "If I am to betray the general, better to wait until the right moment."

Their eyes met.

"I love a clever traitor," said the Bear.

Oleg said, "My boyars want to fight on the Russian side. I thought it my task to constrain their foolishness. But—"

Vasya nodded. Had she convinced him to risk his place and his life with naught but tricks and chyerti—and her own dogged faith? She looked him in the face, and felt the burden of his belief. "Dmitrii Ivanovich will be at Kolomna in a fortnight," she said. "Will you come to him then, and lay your plans?"

Oleg said, "I will send a man. But I cannot go myself. Mamai would suspect."

Vasya said, "You can go yourself. I will take you there and back in the course of a single night."

Oleg stared. Then grim humor touched his face. "On your mortar? Very well, witch. But know that even combining our strength, Dmitrii and I might as well be two beetles plotting to break a boulder."

"Where is your faith?" said Vasya, and smiled suddenly. "Look for me at midnight, in two weeks."

31

All the Russias

THE MEN OF RUS' MUSTERED AT KOLOMNA OVER THE COURSE OF FOUR gray, chilly days. One by one the princes came: Rostov and Starodub, Polotsk, Murom, Tver, Moscow, and the rest, as a cold rain whispered over the muddy fields.

Dmitrii Ivanovich set his tent in the middle of the gathering host, and the first night they were all assembled, he summoned his princes to him to take counsel.

They were grim, heavy with fatigue from mustering and marching in haste. It was well after moonset when the last of them crowded into Dmitrii's round felt tent, shooting each other wary looks. Midnight was not far off. Outside lay the Russian horse-lines, their wagons and their fires, stretching in every direction.

All that day, the Grand Prince had been getting reports. "The Tatars are assembling here," he said. He had a map; he pointed to a marshy place, on the curve of the Don river, at the mouth of a smaller tributary. Snipes' Field it was called, for the birds in the long grass. "They are waiting for reinforcements; units from Litva, mercenaries from Caffa. We must strike before their reinforcements can come up. Three days' march and battle at dawn on the fourth day, if all goes well."

"By how much do they outnumber us now?" demanded Mikhail of Tver.

Dmitrii did not answer. "We will form two lines," he continued.

"Here." He touched the map again. "Spears, shields, to hem in the horses, and use the forest to guard our flanks. They do not like attacking in the woods—it turns their arrows."

"By how many, Dmitrii Ivanovich?" demanded Mikhail again. Tver had been a greater principality than Moscow for most of its history, and rivals for the rest; alliance did not sit easily on them.

Dmitrii could not avoid answering. "Twice our force," he said. "Perhaps a little more. But—"

Muttering went around the men. Mikhail of Tver spoke up again. He said, "Have you had word of Oleg of Ryazan?"

"Marching with Mamai."

The muttering redoubled.

"It matters not," Dmitrii went on. "We have men enough. We have the blessing of holy Sergius."

"Enough?" snapped Mikhail of Tver. "A blessing is *enough* perhaps to save our souls when we are slaughtered on the field, but not to win this fight!"

Dmitrii was on his feet. His voice temporarily silenced the men's murmurs. "Doubt the power of God, Mikhail Andreevich?"

"How will we know God is on our side? For all we know, God wants us to be humble, Christlike, and submissive to the Tatar!"

"Perhaps," said a calm voice from the flap of the tent. "But if that were the case, would He have sent you the princes of Serpukhov and of Ryazan too?"

Heads swiveled; a few put hands on the hilts of their swords. A light kindled in the Grand Prince's eyes.

Vladimir Andreevich walked into the tent. Behind him came Oleg of Ryazan. And behind them both Brother Aleksandr, who added, "God is with us, princes of Rus', but there is no time to waste."

THE GRAND PRINCE OF MOSCOW did not hear the whole tale until late that night, when all the planning was done. He and Sasha rode quietly out of camp, beyond the light and smoke and noise, until they came to a hidden hollow, with a low fire burning.

As he rode, Sasha noted uneasily that the moon had not yet set.

Vasya had made solitary camp and was waiting for them. Her feet were still bare, her face smudged, but she rose with dignity and bowed to the Grand Prince. "God be with you," she said. Behind her, in deeper darkness, stood Pozhar, glowing.

"Mother of God," said Dmitrii and crossed himself. "Is that a horse?"

Sasha had to swallow a laugh as his sister put out a hand to the mare, who promptly laid back her ears and snapped.

"A beast out of legend," Vasya returned. The mare snorted disdainfully and moved off to graze. Vasya smiled.

"A fortnight ago," said Dmitrii, searching her face in the moonlight, "you left at midnight to save one cousin. You came back with an army."

"Are you thanking me for it?" she asked. "It was achieved partially by sheer accident, the rest through blundering."

Vasya might make light of it, Sasha thought, but it had been a bitter fortnight. Through the Midnight darkness, they had ridden fast to Serpukhov, reducing Vladimir to prayers and muttering. Then had come the frantic mustering of Vladimir's men, the long marches in the rain, to reach Kolomna in time, for Vasya could not, she said, take so many men through Midnight.

"You would be surprised at how many victories come so," said Dmitrii.

Vasya was calm under his scrutiny. She and Dmitrii seemed to understand each other.

"You carry yourself differently," said the Grand Prince. Half-joking, he asked, "Have you come into a realm of your own, in your travels?"

"I suppose," she said. "A stewardship at least. Of a people as old as this land and of a strange country, far away. But how did you know?"

"A wise prince recognizes power."

She said nothing.

"You brought armies to my mustering," Dmitrii said. "If indeed have command of a realm, then will you bring your own people to this fight—Knyazhna?"

The word—*princess*—stirred Sasha strangely.

"Greedy for more men, Dmitrii Ivanovich?" Vasya asked. A little color had come into her face.

"Yes," he said. "I need every beast, every man, every creature, if we are to win."

Sasha had never seen the likeness between Dmitrii Ivanovich and his sister. But he saw it now. Passion, cleverness, restless ambition. She said, "I have paid my debt to Moscow. Are you asking me to gather my own people now, and bring them to your battle? Your priests might call them devils."

"Yes, I am asking," said Dmitrii after the faintest pause. "What do you want of me in exchange?"

She was silent. Dmitrii waited. Sasha watched the light on the grass where the golden mare grazed and wondered at the look on his sister's face.

Slowly, Vasya said, "I want a promise. But not just from you. From Father Sergei as well."

Puzzled but not unwilling, Dmitrii said, "Then we will go to him in the morning."

Vasya shook her head. "I am sorry—I would spare his years—but it must be here. And quickly."

"Why here?" Dmitrii asked sharply. "And why now?"

"Because," said Vasya, "it is midnight, there is no time to waste, and I am not the only one who must hear what he says."

SASHA WENT, GALLOPING ON his gray Tuman, and not long after he led Father Sergei into the clearing. The moon hung strange and still in the sky. Vasya, waiting for her brother, wondered if Sasha knew that she had caught the four of them in Midnight until she chose to ride on—or go to sleep. But there was no sleep for her yet, that night. While they waited for Sasha, she and Dmitrii sat around her sinking fire, passing a skin back and forth, talking low-voiced.

"Where do you get your fine horses?" Dmitrii asked her. "First the bay and now this one." He was eyeing Pozhar covetously. The golden mare laid back her ears and sidled away.

Vasya said drily, "She understands you, Gosudar. I didn't *get* her from anywhere; she chose to bear me. If you want to win the allegiance of a horse like her, you would have to go questing through darkness, across three times nine realms; I suggest you concern yourself with your own beleaguered country first."

Dmitrii looked undeterred. He had his mouth open on more questions. Vasya rose hastily when the monks appeared, and crossed herself. "Father bless," she said.

"May the Lord bless you," said the old monk.

Vasya took a deep breath and told them what she wanted.

Sergei was silent for a long time afterward, and Sasha and the prince watched him, frowning.

"They are wicked," said Sergei at last. "They are the unclean forces of the earth."

"Men are also wicked," Vasya returned passionately. "And good, and everything in between. Chyerti *are*, just as men are, just as the earth herself is. Chyerti are sometimes wise and sometimes foolish, sometimes good and sometimes cruel. God rules the next world, but what of this one? Men may seek salvation in heaven and also make offerings to their hearth-spirits, to keep their house safe from evil. Did not God make chyerti, as He made everything else in heaven and earth?"

She spread her hands. "This is the price of my aid: Swear to me you will not condemn witches to burn. Swear to me you will not condemn those who leave offerings in their oven-mouths. Let our people have both their faiths."

She faced Dmitrii. "So long as you or your descendants sit on the throne of Muscovy. And"—to Sergei—"your monks are establishing monasteries, building churches and hanging bells. Tell them also to let the people have their two faiths. For your promises, I will go into the night now, and I will bring the rest of Rus' to your aid."

No one spoke for a long time.

Vasya stood silent, straight and severe, and she waited. Sergei had his head bowed, his lips moving in silent prayer.

Dmitrii said, "If we do not agree?"

"Then," said Vasya, "I will leave tonight. I will spend my days trying to protect what I can for as long as I can. You both will do the same, and we will both be the weaker."

"If we agree, and we win this fight, what happens then?" asked Dmitrii. "If I have need of you again, will you come?"

"If you will do as I ask now," said Vasya, "then as long as your reign lasts, when you call, I will come."

Again, they measured each other.

"I agree," said Dmitrii. "If Father Sergei does. A strong country cannot afford to have its strength divided. Even if its powers are not all of men."

Sergei raised his head. "I will agree also," he said. "The ways of God are strange."

"Heard and witnessed," Vasya said, and then she opened her hand. There was a thin line of blood on the meat of her thumb, black in the dim moonlight. She let her blood fall to the earth and two figures appeared. One was a man with one eye. The other was a woman with night-colored skin.

Dmitrii jerked backward; Sasha, who had seen them all along, stood still. Sergei's eyes narrowed, and he muttered another prayer. "We have all witnessed your promise," said Vasya. "And we will hold you to your word."

DMITRII AND SERGEI, looking shaken, took their leave and rode back to their beds in Kolomna. Polunochnitsa said, "I have witnessed these men's promises. Must I linger? I am not Medved; I do not love, endlessly, the strange doings of men."

"No," said Vasya. "Go if you wish. But if I call again, will you come?"

"I will come," said Midnight. "If only to see the end. For you might have their promise, but you must keep your own now, and fight."

She bowed and vanished into the night.

Sasha lingered with his sister. "Where are you going?"

She didn't look up; she was throwing wet leaves over the fire. It went out with a hiss, plunging the clearing into gray starlight. "I am going to go find Oleg and take him back to his men," said Vasya, straightening up. "See that word doesn't get out that he was here; I am sure there are at least a few spies in Dmitrii's camp. Although——" She smiled suddenly. "Who would believe it? He was with Mamai today and will be with him tomorrow." She went to the golden mare.

Patiently, Sasha followed and said, "After that—then what do you mean to do?"

She had a hand on the mare's neck. Looking over her shoulder, she countered with another question. "Where does Dmitrii mean to engage the Tatars?"

"They are bringing up their forces at a place called Snipes' Field," said Sasha. "Kulikovo. A few days' march; Dmitrii must engage them before they finish gathering up their reinforcements. Three days, he says."

"If you stay with the army," Vasya said, "I will have no trouble finding it. I'll come back to you in three days."

"But where are you going?" her brother asked again.

"To harry the enemy." She wasn't looking at him when she said it. She was staring beyond him already, frowning into the dark. Pozhar, ears going back and forth, did not for once try to bite her.

Sasha caught her arm and spun her around. The mare shied irritably, blowing. His sister was scraped hollow with weariness, a fey glow in her expression. "Vasya." He made his tone cold, an antidote to the reckless laughter lurking in her eyes. "What do you think will become of you, living in darkness with devils, and doing black magic?"

"I?" she shot back. "I am becoming myself, brother. I am a witch, and I am going to save us. Didn't you hear Dmitrii?"

Sasha shot a glance beyond the golden mare, to where the one-eyed man watched, only faintly visible in the starlight and midnight darkness. His grip tightened on her arm. "You are my sister," said Sasha. "You are Marya's aunt. Your father was Pyotr Vladimirovich, of Lesnaya Zemlya. If you spend too long alone in the dark, you will forget that you are more than the witch of the wood, you will forget to come back into the light. Vasya, you are more than this night-creature, this——"

"This what, brother?"

"This *thing*," Sasha went on ruthlessly, with a jerk of his chin toward the watching devil. "He wants you to forget yourself. He would be glad if you went mad, went wild, were lost forever in dark woods, like our great-grandmother. Do you know the risk you are running, traveling alone with that creature?"

"She doesn't," put in the Bear, listening.

Vasya ignored him. "I am learning," she said. "But even if I were not—is there a choice?"

"Yes," Sasha said. "Come back to Kolomna with me and I will look after you."

"Brother, I can't; did you not hear my promise to Dmitrii?"

"Damn Dmitrii; he thinks only of his crown."

"Sasha, do not be afraid for me."

"I am though," he said. "For your life and for your soul."

"They are both in my keeping, and not yours," she said gently. But a little of the wildness had gone from her expression. She took a deep breath. "I will not forget what you said. I am your sister, and I love you. Even wandering in darkness."

"Vasya," he said, his voice heavy with reluctance. "Better even the winter-king than that beast."

"You both have an exaggerated idea of my brother's good qualities," said the Bear, just as Vasya snapped, "The winter-king is not here!" In a calmer voice, she went on, "For it is not winter. I must use the tools I have."

The mare shook her mane and stamped, obviously eager to be gone.

"We are going," said Vasya to her, as though the mare had actually spoken. Her voice was a little ragged. She pulled away. "Farewell, Sasha." She swung to the mare's back and looked down at her brother's troubled face. "I won't forget what you told me."

Sasha merely nodded.

"In three days," said Vasya.

Then the mare bounded forward, bucking, and his sister was at once lost in the night. The devil looked back, winked at Sasha, and followed.

Vasya left Oleg where she'd met him, at the edge of the scrubby steppe where his men were encamped, a day's march from Kulikovo. Pozhar cow-kicked the Grand Prince of Ryazan as he slid down her golden flank and said very definitely, *That is the last time I carry one of his kind ever again. He is heavy.*

Oleg said, at the same moment, "I will leave riding the horses of legend to you, witch-girl. It is like trying to ride a thunderstorm."

Vasya could only laugh. She said, "If I were you, I'd delay your march to join Mamai. They are going to have a bad few days. I will see you at the battle."

"God willing," said Oleg Ivanovich, and bowed.

Vasya inclined her head, turned Pozhar, and then they were back on the Midnight-road.

MOTHER OF GOD, I am tired of darkness, Vasya thought. Pozhar's sure feet made nothing of the night, the changing landscape, but there was no comfort in the surge of the mare's running, her jutting withers and swift strides. Vasya rubbed her face, and tried to focus her mind. Her brother's warning had shaken her. He was right. All the anchor-stones of her life had gone: home and family and sometimes it seemed her very self, lost in the fire. Even Morozko had gone, not to return until the snow fell. Now her companion in the darkness was a creature whose nature was madness given flesh. But sometimes he sounded ordinary, even sensible, and every time that happened she had to remind herself to keep up her defenses.

Now the Bear was pacing the golden mare, beast-shaped. "Men will not keep their word," he said.

"I do not recall asking for your opinion," she snapped.

"Better for chyerti to fight them, before they destroy us," the Bear went on. She could hear the echo of men screaming in his low voice. "Or better yet, let the Russians and the Tatars destroy each other."

"Dmitrii and Sergei will keep their word," she said.

"Have you ever thought what meddling in their war will cost you?" he said. "What price Dmitrii's promise and his admiration? I saw the look in your eyes when Dmitrii called you *princess*."

"Is the prize not worth the risk?"

"That depends," said the Bear, as they ran through Midnight. "I am not sure you know what you're risking."

She didn't answer. She didn't trust his seeming-sense any more than she trusted his wickedness.

THE LAKE WAS DARK in the moonlight, rippling black, white dazzles on the crests of the waves. No long, terrifying journey on foot for her this time; Vasya found the lake swiftly, as though her blood remembered it.

She and Pozhar and the Bear burst out of the trees and found themselves beside the great stretch of moonlit water. Vasya's breath caught in her throat and she slid down the mare's shoulder.

The horses were grazing where she'd last seen them, near the shore. This time they didn't run from her but stood, ghostly in the cold mist of early autumn night, raised their flawless heads and looked. Pozhar pricked her ears and called softly to her kin.

The witch's empty house stood black and still on its tall posts, on the other side of the field. Still a grim ruin, the domovaya asleep once more, perhaps, waiting in her oven. Vasya let herself briefly imagine the house warm with firelight, with laughter, her family close, the horses—a great herd—grazing in the starlight outside.

One day.

But that night, she was there neither for the house, nor for the horses.

"Ded Grib!" she called.

The little chyert, glowing green in the dark, was waiting for her in the shadow of the great oak. He gave a small cry, ran toward her, then halted halfway. Either he was trying to look dignified, or the Bear made him nervous, Vasya could not tell.

"Thank you, my friend," Vasya said to him, and bowed. "For asking Pozhar to come to me. You both saved my life."

Ded Grib looked proud. "I think she likes me," he confided. "That is why she went. She likes me because we both glow at night."

Pozhar snorted and shook her mane. Ded Grib added, "Why did you come back? Are you going to stay now? Why is the Eater with you?" The mushroom-spirit looked suddenly fierce. "He is not to kick over any of my mushrooms."

"That depends," said the Bear pointedly. "If my brave mistress does not give me something better to do than run to and fro in the dark, I will happily kick over all your mushrooms."

Ded Grib bristled. "He is not going to touch anything of yours," said Vasya to Ded Grib, glaring at the Bear. "He is traveling with me now. We came back for you because I need your help."

"I knew you couldn't do without me!" cried Ded Grib, triumphantly. "Even if now you have allies that are *bigger*." He gave the Bear a very hard look.

"This is going to be a terrible war," the Bear interjected. "What damage do you expect to do with a mushroom?"

"You'll see," said Vasya, and offered her hand to the little mushroom-spirit.

MAMAI'S ARMY WAS STRUNG out along the Don. The vanguard was already settled at Kulikovo, the reserves encamped in stages for a great distance to the south, ready to march up at first light. Moving softly through Midnight, Vasya and the mare and the two chyerti capped a small rise, and peered through the trees at the host below.

Ded Grib's eyes grew huge, seeing the scale of the sleeping enemy. His green-glowing limbs quivered. There were fires along the bank as far as the eye could see. "There are so many," he whispered.

Vasya, surveying the immense stretch of men and horses, said, "We'd best get to work then. But first—"

Pozhar would not take saddle or saddlebag; Vasya had to carry a pouch slung around her instead, annoying when riding fast. From it she withdrew bread and strips of hard smoked meat: Dmitrii's parting gift. She gnawed a bit herself, and without thinking, tossed some to her two allies.

Utter silence; she looked up to find Ded Grib holding his bit of bread, looking pleased. But the Bear was staring at her, holding the meat in his hand, not eating.

"An offering?" he said, almost growling. "You have my service; do you want still more of me?"

"Not at present," said Vasya coldly. "It's just food." She gave him a scowl and resumed chewing.

"Why?" he asked.

She had no answer. She hated his wantonness, his cruelty, his laughter, and hated it even more because something of her own nature called out in answer. Perhaps that was why. She could not hate him, for to do so would be to risk hating herself. "You have not betrayed me yet," said Vasya at last.

"As you say," said the Bear. But he still sounded puzzled. Holding her gaze, he ate. Then he shook himself and smiled down chillingly at the sleeping encampment, licking his fingers. Vasya, reluctantly, rose and went to join him. "I don't know about mold, little mushroom," said the Bear to Ded Grib. "But fear leaps between men like sickness. Their numbers won't help with that. Come, let us begin."

Ded Grib gave the Bear a frightened look. He had put his bread away; now he said tremulously to Vasya, "What do you want me to do?"

She brushed the crumbs from her shirt. A little food had restored her, but now a fearful night's work loomed.

"If you can—blight their bread," said Vasya, and turned away from the Bear's grin. "I want them hungry."

Down they went into the sleeping encampment, foot by foot. Vasya had wrapped rags around the faint shimmer of gold on her arms. Her knife or the Bear's claws tore the boxes and bags of the army's food, and where Ded Grib plunged his hands, the flour and meat began to soften and stink.

When Ded Grib seemed to have the idea, she left him and the Bear to creep unseen among the tents of Mamai, spreading terror and rot in their wake. For her part, she slipped down to the river to call the vodianoy of the Don.

"The chyerti have made an alliance with the Grand Prince of Moscow," she told him, low. When she had related all her tale, she then persuaded him to raise the river so that the Tatars would not sleep dry.

THREE NIGHTS LATER THE TATAR army was in disarray along its length, and Vasya hated herself anyway.

"You can't kill any of them asleep," she told the Bear, when he sniffed, grinning, at a man who thrashed in the grip of a nightmare. "Even if they can't see us, it's not . . ." She trailed off, with no words for her revulsion. Medved surprised her by shrugging and stepping back.

"Of course not," he said. "That is not the way. An assassin in the dark can be fought, can be found, and killed. Fear is more potent still, and people fear what they can't see, and don't understand. I will show you."

God help her, he had. Like some foul apprenticeship, she walked with the Bear through the Tatar camp and together they spread terror in their wake. She set fires in wagons and tents, made men scream at half-glimpsed shadows. She terrified their horses, though it hurt her to see them wild-eyed and running.

The girl and the two chyerti traveled from one end of the spread-out force to the other. They gave Mamai and his army no rest. Horses broke their pickets and fled. When the Tatars lit fires, the flames flared up without warning, and sent sparks into unsuspecting faces. The soldiers whispered that they were haunted by a beast, by monsters that glowed, by a ghost-girl with eyes too large in the sharp planes of her face.

"Men make themselves afraid," the Bear told her, smiling. "Imagining is worse than anything they actually see. All it takes is whispers in the dark. Come with me now, Vasilisa Petrovna."

By the third night he was swollen with pleasure like a tick. Vasya was worn to a thread, sick for the dawn. "Enough," she told them both, after yet another stretch roaming the camp, every sense on alert, half-frightened, half-sharing the Bear's mad glee at the mischief.

"Enough. I am going to find a place to sleep, and then we'll go back to my brother in the light." She could bear no more darkness.

Ded Grib looked relieved; the Bear, merely satiated.

The air was chilly and blank with cold mist. She found a sheltered hollow in the thickest part of the wood, well away from the main body of troops. Even wrapped in her cloak, on a bed of pine-boughs, she shivered. She dared not light a fire.

The Bear was untroubled by the weather. As a beast, he'd terrorized the Tatar camp, but now, at rest, he looked like a man. He lay contentedly in the bracken, looking up into the night with his arms behind his head.

Ded Grib was hiding under a rock, his green glow faint. Spoiling the Tatars' food had wearied and discouraged him. "They drink the milk of their horses," he'd said. "I can't spoil that. They won't be *too* hungry."

Vasya had no answer for Ded Grib; she was feeling sick herself. The panic of men and beasts seemed to echo in her bones, but still she didn't know if all their efforts would be enough to turn the tide of the coming battle. "You are quite disgusting," she told the Bear, seeing the flash of his teeth when he smiled.

He didn't even lift his head. "Why? Because I've been enjoying myself?"

The glimmering gold on Vasya's wrists reminded her, uneasily, of the covenant between them. She didn't speak.

He rolled onto his elbow to look at her, a smile playing about his twisted mouth. "Or because *you* have?"

Deny it? Why? It would only give him power. "Yes," she said. "I liked frightening them. They invaded my country, and Chelubey tortured my brother. But I am sick at myself too, and ashamed, and very tired."

The Bear looked faintly disappointed. "You ought to flog yourself a bit more over it," he said, and rolled onto his back once more.

That way lay madness: hiding from the worst parts of her own nature until, out of sight, they became monstrous growths to devour the rest of her. She knew that, and the Bear knew it too. "That was what Father Konstantin did. Look where it got him," she said.

The Bear said nothing.

The Tatar army was out of sight, but still close enough to smell. Even bone-tired, irritable with damp, she was oppressed by the sheer weight of their numbers. She had promised Oleg magic, but she didn't know if there was enough magic in the world to give Dmitrii his victory.

"Do you know what you are going to say to my brother, when the snow falls?" asked the Bear, still looking at the sky.

"What?" she said, jolted by the question.

"His power will be waxing now, as mine is waning. You can bind me with threats and promises, but soon"—the Bear sniffed the air—*"very* soon, you're going to have to face the winter-king. Do you mean to threaten *him?"* The Bear smiled slowly. "I'd like to see you try. Oh, he will be so angry. I enjoy this world: the ugliness and the beauty, and meddling in the doings of men. Karachun does not." The Bear winked at her. "For your sake he spent his strength, went into Moscow, fought me in summer, against his nature. But then you turned around and freed me. He will be very angry."

"What I say to him is not your concern," said Vasya coldly.

"It most certainly is," said Medved. "But I can wait. I like surprises."

She'd had no murmur of the winter-king since he left her in Moscow. Did Morozko know she'd set his brother free? Would he understand why? Did *she?* "I am going to sleep," she said to the Bear. "You are not to betray me or draw attention to us or use someone else to draw attention to us, or awaken me, or touch me, or—"

The Bear laughed and lifted a hand. "Enough, girl, you've already exhausted my imagination. Go to sleep."

She gave him one more narrow-eyed look, and then she turned over. The Bear reasonable, laughing, was much more dangerous than the beast in the clearing.

SHE WAS AWAKENED, a little before daybreak, by a scream. Heart hammering, she lurched to her feet. The Bear was peering through the trees, looking quite untroubled. "I was wondering when they were going to notice," he said without looking round.

"Notice what?"

"That village there. I imagine most of the villagers took what they could and fled, with the army camped so close. But—someone didn't. And your Tatars are tired of mare's milk."

Vasya, feeling sick, crossed to his vantage point.

It was only a tiny village, hidden in a fold of the land, sheltered by great trees. It probably would have gone unnoticed, had the Tatars not been roaming for food to fill their bellies. Even she hadn't seen it.

She wondered if the Bear had.

But now it was afire in a dozen places.

Another scream, smaller and thinner now. "Pozhar," said Vasya. The mare sidled up to her, huffing unhappily; for once she made no objection when Vasya vaulted to her back.

"Far be it from me," said the Bear, "to curb your so-charming impulses, but I doubt very much you'll like what you see." He added, "And you could be killed."

Vasya said, "If I can put folk to such risk, the least I can do is—"

"The *Tatars* put them at risk—"

But Vasya was already gone.

By the time she got to the tiny hamlet, the houses had burned almost to the ground. If there had been animals, there weren't any now. Silence, emptiness. Unwilling hope rose in her. Perhaps *all* the villagers had run at the first sign of the Tatars; perhaps it was only a pig, dying, that had made a sound like a scream.

That was when she heard the small, choking moan, not quite a cry.

Pozhar's ears swiveled; at the same time, Vasya saw a slender dark shape, huddled near a burning house.

Vasya slid down Pozhar's shoulder, caught the woman and dragged her back from the flames. Her hand came away sticky with blood. The woman made a fainter sound of pain, but did not speak. The light of the burning houses illuminated her, pitilessly. She'd had her throat cut, but not well enough to kill her at once.

She'd also been pregnant. Laboring perhaps. That was why she'd not fled when her people did. If anyone had stayed with her, Vasya couldn't see. There was only the woman, scrapes on her hands, where she had pushed off men, and blood—so much blood—on her skirts. Vasya laid a hand on her belly, but it didn't stir, and there was a great, seeping wound there too . . .

The woman was gasping for air, her lips turning blue. Her dim eyes sought Vasya's face. Vasya took her bloody hand in hers.

"My child?" the woman whispered.

"You'll see her soon," said Vasya, steadily.

"Where is she?" said the woman. "I can't hear her cry. There were men—oh!" A choking gasp. "Did they hurt her?"

"No," said Vasya. "She is safe, and you will see her. Come, we will pray to God."

Otche Nash—the Lord's Prayer was soft and familiar, comforting; the woman joined in as she could even as her stare grew fixed and empty. Vasya didn't know she'd begun to cry until a tear fell onto their joined hands. She lifted her head to see the death-god standing there, his white horse at his side.

Their eyes met, but his face was without expression. Vasya shut the woman's eyes, laid her on the earth and stepped back. He did not speak. Her body lay still on the earth, but nonetheless the death-god seemed to gather the woman in his arms, gently, and put her on his horse. Vasya made the sign of the cross.

We can share this world.

He turned his eyes again to Vasya's face. Was there a flicker of feeling there? Anger? A question? No—only the death-god's ancient indifference. He swung to the white mare's back and rode away, silent as he'd come.

Vasya was soaked with the woman's blood and burning with shame, that she'd been sleeping in the woods thinking herself clever, while others bore the burden of the Tatars' anger.

"Well," said the Bear, coming up beside her, "you've put an end to my brother's indifference, that's certain. Poor fool, is he doomed to regret every dead girl he carries away over his saddlebow?" The Bear looked pleased at the prospect. "I congratulate you. I've been trying to make him feel things for years, rage mostly, but he's as cold as his season."

Vasya barely heard him.

"It will be delightful to see what happens when the snow comes," the Bear added.

She only turned her head slowly. "There is no priest," she said, low. "I could do nothing for her."

"Why would you?" asked the Bear, impatient. "Her own people will come out of hiding soon enough, and they will pray and weep and do all that's needful. Besides, she's dead, she won't care."

"If I—if I hadn't—"

The Bear gave her a look of outright scorn. "Hadn't what? You are playing for all of Rus' seen and unseen, not one peasant girl's life."

She pressed her lips together. "You might have woken me," she said. "I could have saved her."

"Could you?" the Bear asked calmly. "Perhaps. But I enjoyed the screaming. And you told me not to wake you."

She turned away from him and vomited. When she had done, she rose and got water from the stream. She washed the blood from the dead woman's body and composed her limbs. Then Vasya went back to the stream and scrubbed herself, by the light of the dying fires, heedless of the chill. She scraped at her skin with handfuls of sand until she was shuddering with cold. Then she cleaned the blood from her clothes, and put them wet on her body.

When she had done, she turned around to find the Bear and Ded Grib both watching her. Neither said a word. Ded Grib looked solemn. The Bear's face was free for once of mockery; he looked puzzled instead.

Vasya shook the water from her hair and addressed Ded Grib first. "Do you mean to come to the battle, my friend?"

Ded Grib shook his head slowly. "I am only a mushroom," he whispered. "I do not like the fear and the fire, and I am tired of these fighting-men; they have no care for growing things."

"I have liked it," said Vasya, determined not to spare herself. "The fear and the fire of these last nights. It made me feel free, and strong, to make others afraid. Others paid the price for my pleasure. Ded Grib, I will see you at the lake, God willing."

Ded Grib nodded, and vanished between the trees. The sun was just rising. Vasya took a deep breath. "Let us go to Dmitrii Ivanovich, and make an end."

"The first sensible thing you've said since you woke up," said the Bear.

32

Kulikovo

THE RUSSIANS RODE DOWN TO KULIKOVO AT THE CLOSE OF THE third day, and made camp. Even Dmitrii was silent, except to give the necessary orders, settling the men for the night, deploying his forces for the dawn. He'd had reports, of course, of the numbers. But reports were different than seeing something with his own eyes.

Mamai had finished bringing up his main host. They spread out in a single line across the field, as far as the eye could reach.

"The men are afraid," said Sasha to Dmitrii and Vladimir, as they rode down to the mouth of the Nepryadva, a tributary of the Don, to reconnoiter the ground. "Praying will not make them less so. We may tell them all the day that God is on our side but the men can see the numbers across the field. Dmitrii Ivanovich, they have more than twice our force, and more are coming up."

"*I* can see the numbers across the field," put in Vladimir. "I am not happy myself."

Dmitrii's and Vladimir's attendants were riding out of earshot, but even they looked at the opposing host and whispered, sallow-faced.

"There is nothing to do now," said Dmitrii. "Besides praying, feeding the men well this night, and getting them into battle tomorrow before they have time to think too much."

"There is one other thing we could do," said Sasha.

Both his cousins turned to look at him.

"What?" said Vladimir. He'd been suspicious of Sasha ever since their reunion, wary of his unholy allies and of the existence of Vasya, his sister-in-law with her strange powers.

"Challenge them to single combat," said Sasha.

A silence fell among the three of them. Single combat was a kind of augury. It wouldn't halt the battle, but the winner would have God's favor, and everyone in both armies would know it.

"It would put heart in the men," said Sasha. "It would make all the difference."

"If our champion won," said Vladimir.

"If our champion won," acknowledged Sasha, but his eyes were on Dmitrii.

Dmitrii did not speak. *His* eyes were on the mud and water of the open field, and beyond, to where the Tatars waited, their horses numberless as autumn leaves in the westering light. Beyond them, the Don river lay like a bar of silver. For three days, it had rained, heavy and cold. Now the sky had darkened and seemed to promise early snow.

Slowly Dmitrii said, "Do you think they'd agree to such a thing?"

"Yes," said Sasha. "I do. Are they to seem afraid to send a champion out?"

"If I ask and they agree, then whom should I name to fight for us?" said Dmitrii. But he spoke in the tone of a man who knows the answer.

"Me," said Sasha.

Dmitrii said, "I have a hundred men who could do it. Why you?"

"I am the best fighter," said Sasha. He wasn't boasting, but stating a fact. "I am a monk, a servant of God. I am your best chance."

Dmitrii said, "I need you at my side, Sasha, not—"

"Cousin," said Sasha fiercely. "I broke my father's heart, leaving home as a boy. I have not been true to my vows, for I could never stay quiet at the monastery. But *never* have I betrayed the soil that bore me; I have kept faith with it and defended it. I will defend it now, before both our hosts."

Vladimir said, "He is right. It might make all the difference. Frightened men are beaten men, you know it as well as I." Grudgingly he added, "And he fights well."

Dmitrii still looked unwilling. But he looked again at the host opposing them, half-obscured now by the dying light. "I will not deny you," said Dmitrii. "You are the best of us. The men know it." He paused again. "Tomorrow morning then," he said heavily. "If the Tatars are willing. I will send a messenger. But you are not to get yourself killed, Sasha."

"Never," said Sasha, and smiled. "My sisters would be angry."

IT WAS ALMOST FULL DARK when Sasha left the princes for the night. Dmitrii's messenger had not yet returned, but he needed to sleep, against whatever the day brought.

He had no ger, just a fire of his own, a patch of dry earth, and his horse hobbled near. When he got closer, he saw the golden mare standing next to his own Tuman.

Vasya had built up his fire and seated herself beside it. She looked weary and sad. The fey, mad creature of the night at Kolomna was gone.

"Vasya," he said. "Where have you been?"

"Harrying an army, in the company of the most ill-natured of devils," said Vasya. "Learning yet again the limits of what I can do." Her voice cracked.

"I think," said Sasha gently, "that you've done too much."

She rubbed her face, still slumped on the log between the horses' feet. "I don't know if it was enough. I even tried to creep in and kill the general, but he is well guarded now—learned his lesson after I got Vladimir away. I—I didn't want to die trying. I set fire to his tent though."

Sasha said firmly, "It was enough. You gave us a chance when there was none before. It was enough."

"I tried setting men afire," she said, with choked confession, the words spilling out. "I tried—while the Bear laughed. But I couldn't. He said that it is hardest to do magic on creatures that have a mind of their own and I didn't know enough."

"Vasya—"

"But I set other things afire. Bowstrings and wagons. *I* laughed, to see them burn. And—they killed a woman. A woman in labor. Because their supply was spoiled, and they were angry and hungry."

Sasha said, "God rest her spirit then. But Vasya—stop. We have a chance. Your courage gave it to us, and your blood. It is enough. Do not lament what you cannot change."

Vasya said nothing, but when her distracted eyes fell on his fire, the flames leaped high, even though there was precious little wood in it to burn, and her fists clenched so that her nails bit into her palms. "Vasya," said Sasha sharply. "Enough of that. When did you last eat?"

She thought. "I—yesterday morning," she said. "I could not bear to wait and go back into Midnight, so Pozhar and I came here as the crow flies, staying out of sight of Mamai's army."

"Very well," said Sasha firmly. "I am going to make soup. Yes, here. I have my own supply and I am capable—we do not have serving-women in the Lavra. You are going to eat and then sleep. Everything else can wait."

It was a measure of her weariness that she didn't argue.

They didn't speak much, while the water boiled, and when he dished out her food, she said, almost inaudibly, "Thank you," and swallowed it down. Three bowls, with flatbread of flour paste on a hot rock, and a little color had come back into her face.

He handed her his cloak. "Go to sleep," he said.

"What about you?"

"Tonight, I mean to pray." He thought of telling her then, about what the next day might hold. But he didn't. She looked so worn, so tired. The last thing she needed was a night of broken sleep, afraid for him. And it was possible the Tatars would refuse the challenge.

"Stay near at least?" she said.

"Of course I'll stay."

She nodded once, eyelids already heavy. Sasha, studying her, surprised himself by saying, "You look just like our mother."

Her eyes opened at that; sudden pleasure drove away the shadows in her face. He said, smiling, "Our mother always put bread in the oven at night. For the domovoi."

"I did the same," said Vasya. "When I lived at Lesnaya Zemlya."

"Father teased her for it. He was always content, in those days. They—they loved each other very much."

Vasya was sitting up now. "Dunya did not speak much of her. Not when I was old enough to remember. I think—I think Anna Ivanovna forbade it. For our father did not love her, and he had loved our mother."

"They were a joy to each other," said Sasha. "Even as a boy, I could see it."

It was hard to speak of that time. He had ridden away the year after his mother died. Would he have stayed, if she had lived? He didn't know. Ever since he came to the Lavra, he had tried to forget the boy he had been: Aleksandr Petrovich, with his faith and his strength, his enthusiasms and foolish pride. The boy who had worshipped his mother.

But now he found himself remembering. He found himself talking. To his sister, he spoke of Midwinter feasts, and childhood mishaps, of his first sword, his first horse, his mother's voice raised laughing in the forest ahead of him. He spoke of her hands, her songs, her offerings.

Then he spoke of the Lavra in winter, the deep calm of the monastery, the bell ringing out over the dreaming forest, the slow round of prayers that marked the cold days, the steady faith of his master, whom men came to see from many days' travel in all directions. He spoke of the days on horseback, and the nights around his fire; he spoke of Sarai and Moscow and places in between.

He spoke of Russia. Not of Muscovy, or Tver, or Vladimir, the principalities of the sons of Kiev, but of Russia itself, of its skies and its soil, its people and its pride.

She listened in rapt stillness, eyes vast and filled like cups with shadow. "That is what we are fighting for," said Sasha. "Not for Moscow, or even Dmitrii; not for the sake of any of her squabbling princes. But for the land that bore us; man and devil alike."

33

On the Cusp of Winter

VASYA AWAKENED TO THE TOUCH OF EARLY SNOW ON HER FACE.

Sasha had fallen asleep at last, the murmur of his prayers stilled, in the deep hush of night. The air had a crisp bite; the earth was just rimed with frost. The men's voices all around had sunk to silence. All who could sleep were sleeping, to gather strength against the dawn.

A chill wind raced through the Russian camp, fluttering their banners, and sending snow in eddies over the earth.

Vasya took a deep breath and got to her feet, pausing to lay the cloak over her sleeping brother. She saw the Bear. He was in the form of a man, standing perfectly still, beyond the red coals of their fire. He was watching the scanty flakes drift down from the sky.

"It is early for snow," said Vasya.

For the first time, there was a hint of fear beneath the exalted malice in the Bear's face. "It is my brother's power waxing," he said. "One more test, sea-maiden. And it might be the hardest."

Vasya straightened her back.

The winter-king rode out of the dark, as though the cold wind had blown him to her, his mare's hooves soundless against the muddy, white-glazed earth.

The two armies, even her sleeping brother, might not have existed. There was only herself, the king of chaos, and the king of winter, wrapped in a whirl of new snow. Morozko was not the thin, almost formless creature of high summer, nor was he the magnificent velvet-clad lord of midwinter. He was dressed all in white; the first bitter breath of the new season.

He halted and slid from the back of his horse.

Her throat was dry. "Winter-king," she said.

He surveyed her, up and down. He did not look at the Bear, but his not-looking had a force all its own. "I knew you meant to fight, Vasilisa Petrovna," he said, after a moment. "I didn't know the manner you would choose."

Only then did his glance find his brother. A spark of old hatred leaped between them. "You were always insufferable, Karachun," said the Bear. "What did you think would happen, when you left her to fight a war she had no notion how to win?"

"I thought you had learned some wisdom," said Morozko, turning back to Vasya. "You have seen what he is capable of."

"You knew what he was capable of, better than I," said Vasya. "Yet you also freed the Bear because you were desperate. I was desperate too. Just as he swore you an oath then, he has sworn one to me now."

She raised her hands. The two ropes glowed at her wrists, power quiescent in the oily gold. "Has he?" said Morozko, with a cold glance at them. "And after he swore? What then? Have you been roving about, terrorizing men in his company? Have you gotten a taste for cruelty?"

"Do you not know me?" she said. "I have loved danger since I was a child. But I have never loved cruelty."

Morozko's eyes searched her face, searched and searched until she looked away, getting angry. He snapped, "Look at me!"

She snapped back, "What are you looking for?"

"Madness," he said. "Malice. Do you think all dangers posed by the Bear are obvious? He will work on your mind, until one day you laugh at bloodshed and suffering."

"I am not laughing yet," she said, but his eyes went again to the gold on her wrists. Was she supposed to feel ashamed? "I have taken power where I could find it. But I have *not* turned to evil."

"Have you not? He is clever. You will fall unknowing."

"I haven't had *time* to fall, knowing or unknowing." She was really angry now. "I have been running through the dark, trying to save all who have need of me. I have done good and I have done evil, but I *am* neither. I am only myself. You will not make me ashamed, Morozko."

"Truly," said the Bear to her, "I hate to agree with him, but you should probably feel guiltier over it. Berate yourself a bit."

She ignored him. Nearer she stepped to the winter-king, until she could read his face, even in the dark. And there was feeling there for her to read: anger, hunger, fear, even grief, his indifference torn to shreds.

Her anger left her. She took his hand. He let her have it, his fingers cool and light in hers. She said softly, "I called every power of this land to war, winter-king. It had to be done. We cannot fight amongst ourselves."

"He killed your father," said Morozko.

She swallowed. "I know. And now he is bound to help save my people." She lifted her free hand, touched his cheek. She was close enough now to see him breathe. She framed his face with her fingers, drew his eyes back to her. The snow was falling faster from the sky. "Will you fight with us tomorrow?" she asked.

"I will be there for the dead," he said. His glance strayed away from her, to the camp at large. She wondered how many would see the next day's dusk. "You need not be there at all. It is not too late. You've done what you can; you've kept your word. You and your brother can—"

"It is too late," she said. "Sasha would never leave Dmitrii now. And I—I too am pledged."

"Pledged to your pride," retorted Morozko. "You want the obedience of chyerti and the admiration of princes, so you are taking this mad risk alongside Dmitrii. But you have never seen a battle."

"No, I haven't," she said, her voice gone as cold as his. She had dropped her hands, but she did not step back. "Though yes, I want Dmitrii's admiration. I want a victory. I even want power, over princes and chyerti. *I am allowed to want things, winter-king.*"

They were near enough to breathe the other's breath. "Vasya," he said, low. "Think beyond this one battle. The world is safer if the Bear is in his clearing, and you must live; you cannot—"

She cut him off. "I already have. And I swore your brother wouldn't have to go back. We understand each other, he and I. Sometimes it frightens me."

"I am not surprised," he said. "Spirit of sea and fire that you are; he is the worst parts of your own nature writ large." His hands were on her shoulders now. "Vasya, he is a danger to you."

"Then keep me safe." She raised her eyes to his. "Pull me back, when he drags me too far down. There is a balance to be struck here too, Morozko, between him and you, between men and chyerti. I was born to be in between—do you think I don't know it?"

His eyes were sad. "Yes," he said. "I know." He looked up at the Bear again, and this time the two brothers were silent, measuring each other. "It is your choice and not mine, Vasilisa Petrovna."

Vasya heard the Bear exhale and realized that he really had been afraid.

She let her head fall forward an instant to the wool and fur of Morozko's shoulder, felt his hands slide around her back and hold her there briefly, suspended between day and night, between order and chaos. *Take me somewhere quiet,* she wanted to say. *I cannot bear the noise and the stink of men anymore.*

But the time for that was past; she had chosen her course. She lifted her head and stepped back.

Morozko reached into his sleeve and drew out something small and shining.

"I brought this for you," he said.

It was a green jewel on a cord, rougher than the formal perfection of the sapphire necklace she'd once worn. She did not touch it, but stared, wary. "Why?"

"I went far away," said Morozko. "That is why I did not come to you, even dreaming, even when you plucked the Bear from his prison. I went south, through the snows of my own kingdom; I took the road to the sea. There, I called Chernomor, the sea-king, out of the water, who has not been seen for many lives of men."

"Why did you go?"

Morozko hesitated. "I told him what he never knew, that the witch of the wood had borne him children."

She stared. "Children? To the king of the sea?"

He nodded once. "Twins. And I told him that among his grandchildren's children was one I loved. And so, the sea-king gave this to me. For you." He almost smiled. "There is no magic in it now, and no binding. It is a gift."

She still didn't reach for the jewel. "How long have you known?"

"Not as long as you think, although I wondered whence your strength. I wondered if it could be only the witch, a mortal woman with magic who'd passed her talent to her daughters. But then I saw Varvara, and I knew it was more than that. Chernomor has fathered sons, now and again, and often they have their father's magic, and lives that are longer than the lives of men. So I asked Midnight for the truth, and she told me. You are the sea-king's great-grandchild."

"Will I live a long time then?"

"I do not know—who could know? For you are witch and chyert and woman too; a descendant of Russian princes and Pyotr Vladimirovich's daughter. Chernomor might know; he said he would answer questions, but only if you came to see him."

It was too much to take in. But she took the jewel. It was warm in her hand; she caught a faint whiff of salt. It felt as though he'd handed her a key to herself, but one she could not examine. There was too much else to do.

"Then I will go to the sea," she said. "If I survive the dawn."

He said heavily, "I will be at the battle. But my task is still the dead, Vasya."

"Mine is the living," said the Bear, and he smiled. "What a pair we are, my twin."

34

Lightbringer

GRIM DAY, AND ALL ABOUT THEM THE ARMY WAS STIRRING; BEYOND, far out on the great field of Kulikovo, the Tatars were awake. The Russians could hear the Tatars' horses snorting into the chill. But nothing could be seen; the world was obscured in thick mist.

"No battle until the fog burns off," said Sasha. He had no stomach for food, but he drank a little mead, passed the bottle to Vasya. When he woke, he'd found her already awake, sitting alone before his renewed fire, a line between her brows, pale but composed.

It was cold, the sky gray above the mist, promising more early snow. Then the sun heaved a cold rim over the edge of the earth, and the mist began to thin. He drew a deep breath. "I must go to Dmitrii. He is waiting for a messenger. Whatever happens, I will find you before the fighting begins. In the meantime, go with God, sister. You are to go unseen and run no risks."

"No," she said and smiled reassuringly. "My business is with chyerti this day. Not with the swords of men."

"I love you, Vasochka," he said, and left her.

THE MESSENGER HAD RETURNED, and the Tatars had accepted Dmitrii's challenge. They had also brought the name of Mamai's champion. Sasha and Dmitrii heard it with the same cold thrill of rage.

"I have dozens of men who would take your place," said Dmitrii. "But—"

"Not with this champion," said Sasha. "If he is not to be yours, then he is mine, brother."

Dmitrii did not disagree. They stood together in his tent, while attendants ran in and out. All about them was the neighing and the ringing of steel and the shouts of the waking army. The Grand Prince offered his cousin bread, and Sasha forced a little of it down.

"Besides," Sasha added, keeping the anger from his voice. "Another man would take the glory for his own city: for Tver or Vladimir or Suzdal. It must be for Rus' and for God, brother, for on this field we are one people."

"One people," said Dmitrii thoughtfully. "Did your sister return? With her—followers?"

"Yes," said Sasha, and gave his cousin a dark look. "She is tempered like steel now and so very young, and I blame you for pulling her into this."

Dmitrii did not look repentant. "She knows the stakes as well as I."

Sasha said, "She says let men beware of the river. And also to trust that the trees will conceal them, and to fear neither storm nor fire."

"I can't decide if that is welcome or ominous," said Dmitrii.

"Perhaps both," said Sasha. "Nothing about my sister is simple. Brother, if I—"

Dmitrii shook his head sharply. "Do not say it. But yes—she will be as a sister to me too; she need fear nothing from my hand."

Sasha bowed his head and said not a word.

"Come then," said Dmitrii. "I will arm you."

Mail shirt and cuirass, a shield, a leaf-shaped spear, red at the haft. Good boots, cuisses for his thighs. A pointed helm. It was soon done. Sasha's fingertips felt cold. "Where is your armor?" he asked Dmitrii. The Grand Prince was dressed as a minor boyar, one of hundreds.

Dmitrii looked cheerful, like a boy caught in mischief. His attendants, the ones Sasha could see, looked simultaneously anxious and exasperated. "I had one of my boyars change places with me," he said. "Do you think I want to sit on a hill clad in scarlet? No. I will fight properly, and I will not give the Tatar bowmen a better target than I can help."

"Your cause is defeated if you are slain," said Sasha.

"My cause is defeated if I am not the leader of this host," said Dmitrii. "For Rus' will fracture, if I am not lord. They will be as leaves in defeat, scattering in a strong wind, or they will be overproud in victory, each trying to claim a greater share than the others. No, I will play for the great prize. What else is there?"

"What indeed?" said Sasha. "I have served you as well as God, cousin," he said. "And been proud to do it. For all I've done—or not done—forgive me."

"Do we talk of forgiveness, brother?" said Dmitrii. "The left hand does not beg forgiveness of the right." He clapped Sasha on the back. "Go with God."

Armed, they went out to where the army waited, drawn up on the field of Kulikovo. It was a little before noon by then, and the mist was burning away.

"I must find my sister," said Sasha. "I did not bid her a proper farewell."

"There is not time," said Dmitrii. A man brought his horse, and he swung to the saddle. As the sun broke through the last of the fog, he raised a hand to shade his eyes. "Look, there is their champion now."

Dmitrii was right. The Tatar champion had appeared and a roar echoed from a hundred thousand throats. Sasha, his heart beating fast, mounted Tuman. The steady mare only pricked her ears at the noise. "Tell her farewell, since I cannot," he said.

As Sasha rode out onto the great sloshing field before the two hosts, he thought he saw a flash of gold: Pozhar galloping unseen among the host of Rus'. Sasha raised his hand to the glimmer. It was all he could do.

Go with God, little sister.

VASYA MOUNTED POZHAR as soon as her brother left to go to the Grand Prince. The Bear was snuffing the air, pleased, Vasya thought, at the tension. He turned a teeth-baring grin to her. "What now, mistress?"

Morozko had left her just as dawn touched the sky. There was still something of his presence in the cold mist, the few snowflakes just drifting down in the wind that riffled the pennants of the Russian host. She felt caught again between them: the Bear's joy in battle and Morozko's grief at destruction. The Bear's presence and the winter-king's absence.

Very well; Morozko's work was with the dead.

Hers was with the living.

But not, just now, with men.

The first one she saw was like a great black bird with the face of a woman. She soared across the battlefield, rippling banners with her wings, and though men could not see her they looked up, as though they felt her shadow upon themselves and upon the day.

The next was the leshy, stepping softly to the border of his forest; the scrubby forest that ringed the battlefield, the forest that currently concealed Vladimir Andreevich and his cavalry, waiting for the right moment to charge.

Vasya nudged Pozhar and the golden mare, streaming sparks, galloped between the ranks of men, the tents, so that Vasya could go have a word with the forest-lord.

"I will keep the men hidden," said the leshy, when Vasya had clasped his twiggy fingers with her bloody ones, "and bewilder their enemies. For your promises and the Grand Prince's, Vasilisa Petrovna."

So it was all across the battlefield. While Sasha armed, and men ate and drew up rank on rank, the chyerti gathered in the thick mist. The vodianoy gurgled in his river; his daughters the rusalki waited on the banks. Some Vasya knew by sight. Many she didn't. But still they came until the battlefield was teeming, haunted, and she felt the weight of their eyes, and their trust.

The thick mist had begun to burn away. She was already sweating, despite the chill, with nerves and with exertion, riding Pozhar here and there to rally and dispose and encourage her own people in and around Dmitrii's.

Finally there came a single long blast from a trumpet, and Vasya let her attention return to the world of men. She looked across the great swampy field. Mist still lay in patches between the Tatars and the Russians, but now the Tatars could be seen.

Vasya's heart sank.

There were so many. What could a little fear do to a mass of men that great? Their line stretched out as far as she could see; the snorting of their horses was like a rumble far away. Clouds massed in the north, heavy with snow, and the occasional flake tumbled down. Dmitrii had his best troops in the van, with Mikhail, the Grand Prince of Tver, on the left flank. Vladimir, the Prince of Serpukhov, was on the right, but concealed in the thick trees.

Somewhere behind Mamai's line, Oleg and his boyars were waiting, too, waiting for another signal, to fall upon the Tatars from behind.

All around the chyerti waited, flickering like candle-flames in the corner of her eyes.

The Bear, at her side, surveying them, said, "I have lived a long time, but I have never seen such a magic as this, to draw all our people into war as one." There was a hell-light of anticipation in his eyes.

Vasya made no answer; she only prayed she'd done the right thing. She tried to think what else she could do but couldn't think of anything.

Pozhar was restive now, barely ridable. Tension lay thick in the air. Here was no concealing darkness; the mist was gone. There was nothing to hide the fact that a hundred thousand men were about to start killing each other. The battle would start soon. Where was Sasha?

The Bear appeared at her side and gave the field a look of joy. "Mud and screaming," he said. "Chyerti and men fighting together. Oh, it will be glorious."

"Do you know where my brother is?" said Vasya.

The Bear smiled wolfishly. "There," he said, and pointed. "But you can't go to him now."

"Why not?"

"Because your brother is fighting that Tatar Chelubey in single combat. Didn't you know?"

She whipped around, horrified. But it was too late, already too late; the armies were drawn up and now two figures appeared from each side, riding toward each other, on a gray horse and a chestnut.

"You knew and waited to tell me," she said.

"I may serve you," said the Bear. "I may even enjoy it. But I will never be trustworthy. Besides, rather than talk to me *before*, you spent the night arguing with my brother who, no matter how blue-eyed, cannot know the army like I do. Your loss."

Pozhar threw her head up, sensing Vasya's sudden urgency; she said, "I must go to him," just as the Bear hurled himself snarling in her way.

"Are you a fool?" he demanded. "Do you think there is no man, out of all of them, with the wit to see you or that golden horse? Can you rely on it, when all eyes will be fixed on your brother? Can you be sure that no Tatar will raise no cry of treachery?" And seeing Vasya staring at him, stone-faced, frozen, he added, "The monk will not thank you. That Tatar tortured him; he is doing it for Dmitrii, for his country, for himself. It is his glory, not yours."

She turned round, indecisive, agonized.

They were all drawn up, the armies of Rus' and the armies of Mamai, and shivering in the dawn mist, their mail cold and heavy. Among them were the powers that no one could see. The vodianoy of the Don, waiting to drown the unwary. The leshy of the woods, concealing men in his branches. The grinning king of chaos. The lesser chyerti of wood and water.

And unseen, powerful, aloof, the king of winter. He was in the clouds in the north, the hard, chill wind, the occasional snowflake on her cheek. But *he* would not come down and stand among them. He would not fight Dmitrii's war. She had seen the terrible knowledge in his eyes: *My task is with the dead.*

I could be far from here, Vasya thought, seeing her hands tremble. *I could be far away, beside the lake, or at Lesnaya Zemlya, or in a clean forest with no name.*

Instead I am here. Oh Sasha, Sasha, what have you done?

ALONE, BROTHER ALEKSANDR RODE onto the swampy field of Kulikovo, rode between the spears of Dmitrii's vanguard and out into the open space between the two armies. There was no sound but Tuman's soft snorting breath, and the suck of her hooves in the sodden earth.

A man on a tall red horse rode out to meet him. More than a hundred thousand men on that field, and still it was quiet enough for Sasha to hear the wind rising, sighing as though in sorrow, blowing down the last of the leaves.

"A fair morning," said Chelubey, sitting easily on his stocky Tatar horse.

"I am going to kill you," said Sasha.

"I think not," said Chelubey. "In fact I am sure not. Poor holy man, with the scars on your back and your torn hand."

"You cheapen this," said Sasha.

Chelubey's face was grim now. "What is this to you? A game? A spiritual quest? It is only men against men, and whichever side prevails, there will be women wailing and blood on the earth."

Without another word, he wheeled his horse around and cantered a few paces away, turned and stood waiting.

Sasha did likewise. Still, all was silent. Strange, in all that gray morning, with men in the ten thousands waiting. Once more he thought he glimpsed a single horse glowing gold in the last of the mist, a slender rider on her back; at her side was a hulking black shadow. He breathed a silent prayer.

Then Sasha raised his spear and shouted, and at his back came a roar from sixty thousand throats. When had the Rus' last come together? Not since the days of the grand princes of Kiev. But Dmitrii Ivanovich had drawn them together, there on the cold bank of the river Don.

Chelubey shouted in turn, his face bright with joy; the sound of all his people shouting at his back. Tuman stood steady beneath her rider, and at Sasha's touch she shot forward. Chelubey kicked his powerful chestnut and then they were racing across the marshy ground, mud and water flying from beneath their horses' hooves.

VASYA WATCHED THEM GALLOP, her heartbeat strangling-fast in her throat. Their horses threw great arcs of mud with each stride. Chelubey's spear dipped at the last moment, to catch her brother in the breastbone. Sasha's shield deflected the full force of the blow; his own spear rattled along the scale on Chelubey's shoulder, and broke.

Vasya put a hand to her mouth. Sasha dropped his broken spear-haft and drew his sword just as Chelubey wheeled his chestnut, icy calm. The Tatar still had both his spear and his shield; he guided his mare with his knees. Sasha's sword had less than half his reach.

A second pass. This time, at the last instant, Sasha touched Tuman's side. The quick-footed mare feinted left, and Sasha's sword came down on Chelubey's spear-haft. Now they were both armed only with swords, and wheeling their horses once more.

Now it was close-work, striking, feinting, drawing back. Even from a distance, the ringing of their swords came clearly to her ears.

The Bear smiled with pure unfeigned joy, watching.

Chelubey's chestnut mare was a little quicker than Tuman. Sasha was a little stronger than Chelubey. By now, both men had mud on their faces, dirt and blood on the necks of their horses, and they grunted each time their heavy swords struck.

Vasya's heart was in her mouth, but she couldn't help him. Nor would she. This was his moment; his teeth were bared, and in his face was glory. Her palms were bloodied with the impress of her nails.

Fine snow stung her face. Vasya could hear the voices of chyerti rising too, and also the voices of Russians, calling encouragement to her brother.

Sasha parried another thrust and scored a strike along Chelubey's ribs, tearing away the chain mail. Chelubey blocked a second blow with his sword, and then the two men had their swords pressed hilt to hilt. Sasha did not falter; he heaved with all his strength and threw Chelubey out of the saddle.

The Bear roared when the Tatar fell, and all the men on both sides screamed out. Chelubey and Sasha were grappling in the dirt, swords gone, only their hands and fists now. Then Sasha's hand, groping, found his dagger.

He buried it to the hilt in Chelubey's throat.

All around the Russians shouted victory; all of Vasya's chyerti cried out likewise. Sasha had won.

Vasya let out a shaken breath.

The Bear sighed, as though in the most profound satisfaction.

Sasha stood straight, his bloody sword in his hand. He kissed it and lifted it to heaven, saluting God and Dmitrii Ivanovich.

Vasya thought she heard a single voice, Dmitrii's voice, calling to his men, "God is on our side! Victory is sure! Ride now! Ride!" And then the Russians were charging, all of them, massed, screaming the name of the Grand Prince of Moscow, and of Aleksandr Peresvet.

Sasha turned, straight-backed, as though to call to his horse and join the charge. But he didn't call.

The Bear turned to look at Vasya, his eyes eager and intent. And then Vasya saw it, the great rent in Sasha's leather armor, where a sword-thrust had found its mark, unseen in the melee.

"No!"

Her brother turned his head as though he could hear her. Tuman had come back to him, and he put a hand to the pommel of her saddle, as though to vault to her back.

Instead he fell to his knees.

The Bear laughed. Vasya screamed. She did not know such a sound was in her. She leaned forward; Pozhar shot forward, raced across the open field toward Sasha, outstripping the converging armies. The Bear followed her; faintly she could hear the voices of the chyerti of Rus', running with the Russians.

But Vasya had stopped thinking of victory. On either side the armies were rushing up, but in the middle of the field there was nothing but Tuman, wild with fright, and Chelubey dead, facedown in the mud and water. Vasya had no thought to spare for either, for her brother was still kneeling in the mud but shaking violently now, the blood spilling from his lips. He looked up. "Vasya," he said.

"Shh," she told him. "Don't talk."

"I am sorry. I meant to live. I did."

Pozhar silently knelt in the mud for them. "You're going to live anyway. Get on the horse," Vasya said.

She had no notion of how it must have hurt him to obey her. The ground shook from the thunder of two armies. He could not sit upright, but slumped, deadweight.

"He is going to die," said Medved at her side. "Better to take vengeance."

Without a word, Vasya gashed her hand on her brother's sword. Blood poured over her fingers. She smeared it across the Bear's face, putting all she had of will in it.

"Take vengeance for me," she said flatly.

The Bear shuddered with strength. His eye blazed up, brighter than Pozhar at midnight. Watching her, he snatched Sasha's helm off the muddy ground and bit deep into his own hand. Blood poured down, clear as water but acrid with the smell of sulfur, pooling in the cupped bronze.

"I give you my power in exchange," he said, and his glance was sly. "To make the dead rise."

Then he was gone, disappearing into the fray, terror his weapon. Vasya, balancing the helmet, got up onto Pozhar behind her brother. The mare, ears pinned, stood up despite her double burden, mud on her legs and belly. Fast as a star she galloped away, while all around them the battle was joined.

35

The Starlit Road

Vasya could feel every strike of Pozhar's hooves, as though she were the one mortally wounded. The mare twisted and turned, avoiding armies and chyerti both; once she jumped clean over a dead horse. All the while, Vasya gripped her brother, gripped the helmet with its strange burden. And she prayed.

At last they broke clear of the battle, and left the omnipresent roar behind them, concealing themselves in the trees that lined the river. They found a space of quiet in a little copse. They were not terribly far from the battle; the roaring seemed to shred the earth and sky. Vasya thought she could hear the Bear laughing.

The copse was a little higher than the marsh; Vasya slid from Pozhar's back just in time to catch her brother as he fell. He almost sent her sprawling into the water. It took all her strength to halt him, and lay him on the soft earth. His lips were blue, his hands cold.

She stared at the water in the helm. *Make the dead alive. But he isn't dead. Morozko—Morozko where are you?*

Sasha's eyes looked up, but they did not see her. Perhaps he saw a road beneath a starry sky: a road from which there is no turning back. "Vasya?" he asked. His voice was little more than a breath now.

She had nothing but her two hands: with her fur cloak she wiped the blood and earth from her brother's face, held his head in her lap.

"I am here," she said. Tears unbidden spilled from her eyes. "You have won. The army is sure of its victory."

His eyes brightened. "I am glad," he said. "I am—"

He turned his head a little; his stare became fixed. Vasya turned to follow his gaze, and there was the death-god, waiting. He was on foot; his horse a faint shape, pale as mist at his back. She looked at him long, and there were no words between them. Once she had begged, once she had railed at him, for coming to claim those she loved. Now she only looked, and saw her glance go through him like a sword.

"Could you have saved his life?" she whispered.

His answer was the merest shake of his head. But he came, still wordless, and knelt beside her. Frowning, he cupped his hands. Water, clear and clean, gathered in his palms, and he let it trickle out onto her brother's face. Where the water touched, the cuts, bruises, the grime vanished, as though washed away. Vasya, not speaking either, helped him. They worked slowly and steadily. Vasya pulled aside the stained and broken armor, and Morozko let the water run. In the end, her brother's face and torso were clean and unmarked; he looked asleep, peaceful, unwounded.

But he did not stir back to life.

She reached for the helmet.

Morozko's troubled glance followed the movement. Hope was beating in her throat, a fragile, burning thing. "Can this bring him to life in truth?"

Morozko looked reluctant. "Yes," he said.

Vasya lifted the helmet, tipped it toward her brother's lips.

Morozko put out a hand to stay her. "Come with me first."

She did not know what he meant. But when he offered her his hand, she took it; their fingers met, clasped, and she found herself in the place beyond life: the forest with its road, its net of stars.

Her brother was waiting for her there, upright, a little pale, starlight in his eyes. "Sasha," she said.

"Little sister," he said. "I didn't say goodbye, did I?"

She ran forward and embraced him, but he felt icy cold, distant in her arms. Morozko watched them.

"Sasha," Vasya said eagerly. "I have something that will bring you back. You can live on, come back to us, to Dmitrii."

Sasha was looking out into the distance, down the star-strewn road as though with longing. Hastily, she said, "This," holding out the dented helmet. "Drink it," she said. "And you will live again."

"But I am dead," he said.

She shook her head. "You need not be."

He was backing up. "I have seen the dead return. I will have no part in it."

"No!" she said. "It is different this way—it is—it is like Ivan, in the fairy tale."

But her brother was still shaking his head. "This is not a fairy tale, Vasya. I will not risk my immortal soul, returning to life when I have left it."

She stared at him. His face was quiet, sad, immovable. "Sasha," she whispered. "Sasha, please. You can live again. You can go back to Sergei, and Dmitrii and Olga. Please."

"No," he said. "I—I fought. I yielded my life and I was glad to give it. It is for others to make it matter. My death is Dmitrii's now—and—and yours. Guard this land. Make it whole."

She stared at him. She could not believe. Wild thoughts darted through her brain. Perhaps, in the living world, she could force the water between his lips. But then—but then . . .

It wasn't her choice. She thought of Olga's rage when Vasya had decided the same question for her. She remembered Morozko's words: *It is not your choice to make.*

Trying to control her voice, she said, "Is this what you want?"

"It is," said her brother.

"Then—then God be with you," said Vasya, her voice breaking. "If—if you see Father and—and Mother—tell them I love them. That I have wandered far, but not forgotten. I—I will pray for you."

"And I for you," said her brother, and smiled suddenly. "I will see you again, little sister."

She nodded but could not speak. She knew her face was crumbling. But she embraced her brother; she stepped back.

And then Morozko spoke softly, but his words were not for her. "Come with me," he said to Sasha. "Do not be afraid."

36

The Army of Three

SHE TUMBLED BACK TO HERSELF, BOWED OVER HER BROTHER'S UN-marked body, sobbing. She did not know how long she wept, while the battle raged nearby. It was a soft hoofbeat that drew her back, and a cold presence behind her.

She turned her head to see the winter-king. He slid from the back of his horse and looked at her.

She had no words for him. Gentle speech or a soft touch would have shattered her, but he offered neither. Vasya shut her brother's eyes, whispered a prayer over his head. Then she got to her feet, soul full of restless violence. She could not bring her brother back. But the thing he had wanted—the thing he had worked for—that she could do.

"Only for the dead, Morozko?" she said. She reached out a hand, still smeared with her brother's blood and her own, from where she'd cut it for the Bear.

He hesitated.

But in his face was an echoing savagery; he looked suddenly like he had on a Midwinter midnight: proud, young, dangerous. There were traces of Sasha's blood on his hands too.

"And for the living, beloved," he said, low. "They are my people too."

He caught her bloody hand in his and all around the wind shrieked; the cry of the first snowstorm. Her soul was all restless fire, and when she looked up at Pozhar, the golden mare was drawn equally taut; she pawed the ground once. They mounted their horses together, and wheeled and galloped back to the battle, on the breast of a newborn storm.

Flames in her hands; in his grip was the power of bitterest winter.

A shout came from the field, as the Bear, laughing, caught sight of them.

"We must find Dmitrii," called Vasya, shouting over the noise, as she sent Pozhar hurtling through a knot of Tatar warriors who were galloping down a group of Russian pikemen. The beasts scattered with sudden fright, spoiling their swearing riders' aim.

A swift wind leaped up and blew wide an arrow that would have struck her, and Morozko said, "There is his standard."

It was at the apex of a small rise, in the first line of battle; they turned thither, cutting a swath through fighting men as they did. The snow was falling thicker and thicker now. A hail of arrows was targeting Dmitrii's position. A wedge of horsemen was pushing through, trying to get to that vulnerable banner.

The white mare and Pozhar, light on their feet, cut through the battle faster, but the Tatars were closer and it was a race between them. Ears flat to her head, Pozhar dodged and sprang and galloped, while Vasya shouted at the Tatars' horses. A few heard her and faltered, but not enough. The ground under the enemy's feet grew slippery with ice, but the Tatars' horses were sturdy beasts, used to running on all surfaces, and even that didn't sway them. Snow blew in their faces, blinding the riders, but still the skillfully timed arrows flew.

"Medved!" Vasya shouted.

The Bear appeared on her other side, still with that edge of shrieking laughter in his voice. "Such joy," he crowed. He was a beast, bathed in men's blood and howling with delight, stark contrast to Morozko's gathered silence on her other side. Together the three of them made a wedge of their own, and bulled through the fighting. Vasya set fires at their feet, swiftly smothered by the wet field, the fast-falling snow. Morozko blinded them, turned their arrows with a pranking wind.

Medved simply terrified all in his path.

It was a race between them and the Tatars to see who could get to Dmitrii's position first.

The Tatars won. Arrows flying, they slammed into Dmitrii's standard like a wave, a few strides before Vasya and her allies. The standard fell, crumpled to mud; all around were shouts of triumph. Still those arrows fell, deadly accurate. The white mare was hanging close to Pozhar's flank; most of Morozko's efforts were spent to keep arrows from Vasya and the two horses.

Dmitrii's guard was smashed apart; his horse reared and went over. Then three Tatars were on him, hacking.

Vasya shouted, and Pozhar slammed into them with brute force. Who needed a sword, riding the golden mare? Her hooves shattered them, drove off their horses; sudden fires leaped up at their feet and they were flung back. Vasya slid down the mare's shoulder and knelt at the Grand Prince's head.

His armor was hacked; he was bleeding from a dozen wounds. She pulled off his helmet.

But it wasn't the Grand Prince of Moscow at all. It was a young man she didn't know, dying.

She stared. "Where is the Grand Prince?" she whispered.

The young man could hardly speak; blood bubbled between his lips. He looked up at her with unseeing eyes. She had to bend near to catch the words. "The van," he whispered. "The first line of battle. He gave me his armor, so the Tatars would not know him. I was honored. I was . . ."

The light faded from his eyes.

Vasya closed them, turned.

"The line of battle," she said. "Go!"

TATARS EVERYWHERE, FIGHTING. Arrows flying from all sides. Morozko was riding knee to knee with Vasya, keeping arrows from her with grim tenacity. With the Bear they cut through battles when they could, bringing snow, fire, terror.

"The line is wavering," put in the Bear conversationally. His eye still glittered, his fur spiked with blood. "Dmitrii is going to have to—"

Then she heard Dmitrii's voice. Undimmed, hale, roaring out over all the clash of armies. "Fall back!" he cried.

"That is not ideal," said the Bear.

"Where is he?" said Vasya. She could hardly see through the snow and the thrash of fighting men.

"There," said Morozko.

Vasya looked. "I can't see."

"Come on then," said the winter-king. Shoulder to shoulder they fought their way through the press. Now she could see Dmitrii, still mounted, dressed in the armor of an ordinary boyar, his sword in his hand. Whooping, he ran a man through, used his horse's weight to boost another man out of his saddle. There was blood on his cheek, his arm, his saddle, and the neck of his horse. "Fall back!"

The Tatars were advancing. All around, the arrows flew. One grazed her arm; she barely felt it. "Vasya!" snapped Morozko, and she realized her upper arm was bleeding.

"The Grand Prince has to live," said Vasya. "All this is for naught if he dies—"

And then Pozhar was level with Dmitrii's horse, rearing, forcing another attacker back.

Dmitrii turned and saw her. His face changed. He leaned over and seized her arm, heedless of her wounds or his.

"Sasha," he said. "Where is Sasha?"

Battle had numbed her, but at his words, the fog around her mind thinned a little—and beneath it was agony. Dmitrii saw it in her face. His own whitened. His lips firmed. Without another word to Vasya, he turned to his men again. "Fall back! Join the second line, bring them up."

It wasn't orderly. The Russians were breaking, fleeing, hiding themselves in the second line of battle, which was wavering badly. Now the Bear was nowhere to be seen, and—

Dmitrii said, turning back on her suddenly, "If Oleg was planning to take a hand, now is a good time."

"I'll go find him," said Vasya. To Morozko, she said, "Don't let him die."

Morozko looked as though he wanted to swear at her; there was mud on his face too, and blood. A long scratch marred the neck of his mare. He wasn't the aloof winter-king now. But he only nodded, turned his horse to keep up with Dmitrii.

Dmitrii said, "If Oleg hasn't betrayed us, tell him to fall in on Mamai's right flank," and then he whirled away calling more orders.

Vasya turned Pozhar, trying to sink once more into invisibility, cutting through the advancing Tatar line in search of Oleg.

SHE FOUND THE MEN of Ryazan fresh, waiting on a small rise, watching.

"This," said Vasya, riding up to him, "is not generally what is meant when you take an oath to a Grand Prince that you are going to fight."

Oleg just smiled at her. "When one is risking everything on a hammer-stroke, one waits until the stroke does the most good." He looked over the field. "That time is now. Ride down with me, witch-girl?"

"Hurry," said Vasya.

He called an order; Vasya wheeled Pozhar. The mare was glowing coal-hot, but Vasya couldn't feel it.

The men of Ryazan, shouting, raced down the rise at full stretch. Horns were blowing. Vasya fell in beside Oleg's stirrup, going to a little trouble to hold Pozhar to the pace of the racing horses. She saw the Tatars turning in shock, to meet an attack on an unexpected quarter, and then she saw another movement from the woods on Dmitrii's left flank—Vladimir's cavalry coming out of the forest at last, and the Bear among them, driving their horses on with the speed of terror. She could hear his whooping laughter.

And so they caught the Tatars between them—Oleg, Vladimir, and Dmitrii—and smashed the line to pieces.

BUT STILL IT HAD to be fought out, hour by bloody hour, and she did not know how long it had been—hours? days?—when at last a voice brought her back to herself. "Vasya," Morozko said. "It is over. They are fleeing."

It seemed a haze fell from her sight. She looked around and realized that they had met in the middle: Oleg, Vladimir, and Dmitrii, and also she, the Bear, and Morozko.

Dmitrii was half-fainting from his wounds; Vladimir supported him. Oleg looked triumphant. All around she saw only their own men. They had won.

The wind had dropped; the early snow fell steadily now. Lightly, silently, thickly, it covered dead enemies and dead friends alike.

Vasya just stared at Morozko, stupid with shock and weariness. A thin curtain of blood ran down from a scratch in the white mare's neck. He looked as weary as she, and as sad, dirt and blood on his hands. Only Pozhar was unwounded: still as sleekly powerful as she'd been that morning.

Vasya only wished she could say the same. Her arrow-grazed arm throbbed, and that wasn't even close to the pain in her soul.

Dmitrii had forced himself upright, deathly pale, and was walking over to her. She slid down Pozhar's shoulder and went to meet him.

"You have won," she said. There was no emotion in her voice.

"Where is Sasha?" said the Grand Prince of Moscow.

Water of Death, Water of Life

DMITRII'S MEN CHASED THEIR FOES ALL THE WAY BACK TO MECIA—
nearly fifty versts. Vladimir Andreevich, Oleg of Ryazan, and Mikhail
of Tver led the rout, the princes riding side by side like brothers, and
their men mingling like water, so that the eye could no longer tell who
was from Moscow or Ryazan or Tver, for they were all Russians. They
took the herds of Mamai's train and killed the puppet-khan he'd
brought; they sent the general himself fleeing to Caffa, not daring to go
back to Sarai, where his life would be forfeit.

But neither the Grand Prince of Moscow nor Vasya took part in the
rout. Instead, Dmitrii followed Vasya to a little sheltered copse not far
from the river.

Sasha lay where they'd left him, wrapped in Vasya's fur cloak, his
flesh clean, inviolate.

Dmitrii half-fell, stumbling from his horse, and caught his dearest
friend's body in his arms. He did not speak.

Vasya had no comfort for him; she was weeping too.

A long silence fell in that copse, as the long day ended, and the light
grew smoky and insubstantial. Snow still fell, softly, all around.

Finally, Dmitrii raised his head. "He should be taken back to the
Lavra," he said. His voice was hoarse. "To be buried with his fellows,
in consecrated ground."

"Sergei will say prayers for his soul," said Vasya. Her voice was as rough as his, with shouting and with weeping. She pressed the heels of her hands to her eyes. "He wandered the whole of this land," she said. "He knew it and he loved it. And now he will be bone, trapped in frozen earth."

"But there will be songs," said Dmitrii. "I swear it. He will not be forgotten."

Vasya said nothing at all. She had no words. What did songs matter? They would not bring her brother back.

It was night when the cart came to take her brother's body away. It came rumbling out of the dark, accompanied by a spill of noise and light, and Dmitrii's noisy attendants, all full of triumph, barely leavened by respect for the occasion. Vasya could not stand their noise, or their joy, and anyway, Sasha was gone.

She kissed her brother's forehead, and rose, and slipped away into the dark.

SHE DID NOT KNOW when Morozko and Medved appeared. She had the sense that she'd been walking alone a long time, with no notion of where she was or where she was going. She just wanted to get away from the noise and stink, the gore and the grief, the wild triumph.

But at some point, she raised her head and found them walking beside her.

The two brothers she had met in a clearing as a child, the two that had marked her life and changed it. They were both daubed with blood, the Bear's eyes alight with the remnants of battle-lust, Morozko grave, his face unreadable. The enmity between them was still there, but changed, somehow, transmuted.

It's because they aren't on opposite sides anymore, she thought, dim with exhausted grief. *God help me, they are both mine.*

Morozko spoke first, not to Vasya but to his brother.

"You still owe me a life," he said.

The Bear snorted. "I have tried to pay it. I offered her hers, I offered her brother his. Is it my fault that men and women are fools?"

"Perhaps not," said Morozko. "But you still owe me a life."

The Bear looked surly. "Very well," he said. "What life?"

Morozko turned to Vasya, looked a question. She only stared at him blankly. What life? Her brother was gone and the field was thick with dead. Whose life could she desire, now?

Morozko reached very carefully into his sleeve, drew out something wrapped in embroidered cloth. He unwrapped it, held it out with both hands to Vasya.

In was a dead nightingale, its body stiff and perfect, kept inviolate with the water of life. It looked like the carved one she had kept with her through all the long nights and hard days.

She stared from the bird to the winter-king, beyond speech. "Is it possible?" she whispered. Her throat was dust-dry.

"Perhaps," said Morozko, and turned back to his brother.

SHE COULD NOT BEAR to watch. She could not bear to listen. She walked away from them, almost afraid of her hope, coming so soon after grief. She could not bear to see them succeed and she could not bear to see them fail.

Even when hoofbeats came softly up behind her, she didn't turn. Not until a soft nose came down, lightly, on her cheek.

She turned her head.

And stared and stared and she could not believe. She couldn't move; she couldn't speak. It was as though speech or movement would break the illusion, shatter it and leave her desolate once more. She drank in the sight; his bay coat black in the darkness, the single star on his face, his warm dark eye. She knew him. She loved him. "Solovey," she whispered.

I was asleep, said the horse. *But those two, the Bear and the winter-king, they woke me up. I missed you.*

Her heart torn with exhaustion and shocked joy, Vasya threw her arms around the bay stallion's neck, and she wept. He was no ghost. He was warm, alive, smelling of himself, and the texture of his mane was agonizingly familiar against her cheek.

I will not leave you again, said the stallion, and put his head around to nuzzle her.

"I missed you so," she said to the horse, hot tears sliding into his black mane.

I am sure of it, said Solovey, nosing her. He shook his mane, looking superior. *But I am here now. You are the warden of the lake now? It has not had a mistress for a long time. I am glad it is you. But you should have had me. You would have done it all a great deal better if I'd been there.*

"I am sure of it," said Vasya, and she made a broken sound that was almost a laugh.

FINGERS TANGLED IN HER horse's mane, leaning on his broad, warm shoulder, she barely heard the Bear speak. "Well, this is all touching. But I am off. I have a world to see and her promise for my freedom, *brother.*" This last was added warily to Morozko. Vasya saw, when she opened her eyes, that the winter-king was eyeing his twin with un-dimmed suspicion.

"You are still bound to me," said Vasya to the Bear. "And to your promise. The dead will not rise."

"Men create enough chaos without me," said the Bear. "I am just going to enjoy it. Perhaps give a few men nightmares."

"If you do worse," said Vasya, "the chyerti will tell me." She raised her golden wrists, a threat and a promise.

"I will not do worse."

"I will call you again," she said. "If there is need."

"So you will," he said. "I may even answer." He bowed. And then he was gone, swiftly lost in the gloom.

THE BATTLEFIELD WAS EMPTY. The moon had risen, somewhere be-hind the clouds. The field was stiff with frost. The dead lay open-eyed, men and horses, and the living moved among them by torchlight, look-ing for dead friends, or stealing what they could.

Vasya looked away.

The chyerti had already slipped away, back to their forests and streams, holding Dmitrii's promise, and Sergei's, and Vasya's.

We can share this land. This land that we have kept.

Three chyerti remained. One was Morozko, standing silent. The second was a woman, whose dawn-pale hair slanted across the darkness of her skin. The third was a little mushroom-spirit, who glowed a sickly green in the darkness.

Vasya bowed to Ded Grib and Polunochnitsa, straight-shouldered and solemn, though she knew her face was swollen and blotched like a child's with grief and with painful joy. "My friends," she said. "You came back."

"You had your victory, lady," returned Midnight. "We are witnesses. You made your promises and you kept them. We are yours in truth, the chyerti. I came to tell you that the old woman—she is glad."

Vasya could only nod. What care had she for promises, either kept or broken? The price had been too high. But then she licked her lips and said, "Tell—tell my great-grandmother that I will come to her, in Midnight, if she will permit. For I have much to learn. And thank you. Both of you. For your faith. And your lessons."

"Not tonight," put in Ded Grib, in his high voice, practically. "You aren't learning anything tonight. Go and find somewhere clean." He fixed Morozko with a dark look. "Surely you know a good place, winter-king. Even if your realm is too cold for mushrooms."

"I know a place," said Morozko.

"I will see you beside the lake, in the moonlight," said Vasya to Ded Grib and Polunochnitsa.

"We will wait for you there," said Midnight, and then she and Ded Grib were gone as suddenly as they'd appeared.

Vasya leaned against Solovey's shoulder and the grief and the joy bewildered her equally. Morozko cupped his hands. "Let us go," he said. "At last."

Without a word, she put a foot in his hands and let him boost her onto Solovey's back. She did not know where they were going, save that it was the direction her soul told her was *away*. Away from the sound and the smell, the glory and the futility.

Solovey carried her gently, neck arched, and Pozhar, glowing in the darkness, shed heat upon them both.

Finally they crested a small rise. The whole blood-drenched battle-field lay clear at their feet. Vasya dismounted and went to Pozhar.

"Thank you, lady," she said. "Will you fly free now, as you have long wished to do?"

Pozhar lifted her head, aloof, and her nostrils flared, as if to test the winds of heaven. But then she bent her golden head, delicately, and lipped Vasya's hair. *I will be at the lake when you return*, she said. *You may prepare a warm place for me on stormy nights, and comb my mane.*

Vasya smiled. "It will be done," she said.

Pozhar slanted her ears back a fraction. *Do not neglect the lake. For it will always need a guardian.*

"I will guard it," said Vasya. "And I will watch over my family. And I will ride the world, in between times, through the farthest countries of dark and day. It is enough for one life." She paused. "Thank you," she added to the mare. "More than I can say."

Then she stepped back.

The mare threw her head up, small flames licking at the edge of her mane. One ear slanted toward Solovey, perhaps with a touch of co-quetry. He rumbled softly at her. Then the mare reared—up and up. Her wings flared, brighter than the pale morning sun, gilding all the snowflakes, making shadows of the whirling snow. Then the firebird soared aloft in a rush of glory. Men who watched from afar later told each other that they had seen a comet, a sign of God's blessing, flying between heaven and earth.

Vasya watched Pozhar go, eyes fixed on the brightness, and only looked down when Solovey nudged her in the small of her back. She buried her face in her horse's mane, breathed the reassuring smell of him. He had none of Pozhar's alarming tang of smoke. She could even, for an instant, forget the smell of blood and filth, fire and iron.

A coolness at her back, and she lifted her head and turned.

Morozko had dirt under his nails, a streak of soot on his cheek. The white mare behind him looked as weary as he, her proud head hanging low. She nuzzled Solovey, her colt, once, lightly.

Morozko looked weary, as men are weary, at the end of long labor. His eyes searched her face.

She took his hands in hers. "Will it be thus for you," she asked him, "so long as you live? To stand beside us, and to grieve for us?"

"I don't know," he said. "Perhaps. But—I think that I would rather feel pain than not feel anything at all. Perhaps I am grown mortal, after all."

His tone was wry, but then his arm closed around her tightly, and she put her arms around his neck and pressed her face to his shoulder. He smelled of earth and blood and fear, of that day's slaughter. But beneath, as always, were the scents of cold water and of pine.

She tilted her head up and pulled him down to her and kissed him fiercely, as though at last she could lose herself, forget duty and that day's horror in the touch of his hands.

"Vasya," he said, low, in her ear. "It is almost midnight. Where do you wish to go?" His hand was in the snarls of her hair.

"Somewhere with clean water," she said. "I am sick to death of blood. And then? North. To tell Olya how . . ." She trailed off, had to steady her voice before she continued. "Perhaps—after—we may ride to the sea together, and see the light on the water."

"Yes," he said.

She almost smiled. "And then? Well, you have a realm in the winter forest, and I have mine, on the bow-curve of a lake. Perhaps we might forge one country in secret, a country of shadows, behind and beneath Dmitrii's Russia. For there must always be a land for chyerti, for witches and for sorcerers, and for followers of the forest."

"Yes," he said again. "But for tonight, food and cool air, clean water and untainted earth. Come with me, Snegurochka. I know a house in a winter forest."

"I know," she said, and a thumb brushed away her tears.

She would have said she was too tired to vault to Solovey's back, but her body did it despite her.

"What did we gain?" Vasya asked Morozko as they rode away. The snow had stopped, the sky shone clear. The season of frost had barely begun.

"A future," returned the frost-demon. "For men will say in later years that this was the battle that made Rus' a nation of one people. And chyerti will live on, unfaded."

"Even for that, the price was very high," she said.

They were riding knee to knee; he made no answer. The wild darkness of Midnight was all about them now. But somewhere ahead, a light shone through the trees.

AUTHOR'S NOTE

ALMOST FROM THE EARLIEST DAYS OF DRAFTING *THE BEAR AND the Nightingale*, I knew I wanted to end my trilogy at the Battle of Kulikovo. This battle always seemed to me to create a natural point of reconciliation for many of the conflicts I wished to consider on the pages of these three books: the Rus' against the Tatars, Christian against pagan, Vasya trying to balance her own desires and ambitions with the needs of her family and her nation.

The path I charted to get to the battle has varied wildly since those early days. But the destination never changed.

The Battle of Kulikovo really happened. In 1380, on the Don river, Grand Prince Dmitrii Ivanovich acquired his historical moniker Donskoi, *of the Don,* by leading a combined force from several different Russian principalities against a host commanded by the Tatar temnik Mamai.

Dmitrii won. It was the first time the Russian people combined under the leadership of Moscow to defeat a foreign adversary. Some have argued that this event marks the spiritual birth of the nation of Russia. I have chosen to take it as such, although in reality, the historical significance of this battle is the subject of ongoing debate. Who, if not the novelist, has the right to cherry-pick historical interpretations that suit her best?

My fairy-tale version of this battle ignores the incredible amount of political and military maneuvering that led up to the event itself: the threats, the skirmishes, the deaths, the marriages, the delays.

But the great events of my version of Kulikovo are drawn from history:

A warrior-monk named Aleksandr Peresvet really fought in single combat with a Tatar warrior named Chelubey, and died victorious. Dmitrii really did trade places with one of his minor boyars, so that he could fight with his men, unmarked by the enemy. Oleg of Ryazan really did play an ambiguous role in the battle: perhaps he betrayed the Russians, perhaps he betrayed the Tatars, perhaps he merely strove to chart a path between the two.

All that is true.

And perhaps, beneath the battle recorded by history, there was fought another, between holy men and chyerti, over how they were to coexist in this land of theirs. Who knows? But the concept of *dvoeveriye*, dual faith, persisted in Russia up until the Revolution. Orthodoxy coexisted with paganism in peace. Who is to say that wasn't the work of a girl with strange gifts and green eyes?

Who is to say, in the end, that the three guardians of Russia are not a witch, a frost-demon, and a chaos-spirit?

I find it fitting.

Thank you for reading all the way to the end. I started this series in a tent on a beach in Hawaii when I was twenty-three years old, and now you are holding the final piece of that work in your hands.

I am still astonished by the journey, and more grateful than I can say that it happened.

A Note on
Russian Names

Russian conventions of naming and address—while not as complicated as the consonant clusters would suggest—are so different from English forms that they merit explanation. Modern Russian names can be divided into three parts: the first name, the patronymic, and the last, or family, name. In medieval Rus', people generally had only a first name, or (among the highborn) a first name and a patronymic.

First Names
and Nicknames

Russian is extremely rich in diminutives. Any Russian first name can give rise to a large number of nicknames. The name Yekaterina, for example, can be shortened into Katerina, Katya, Katyusha, or Katenka, among other forms. These variations are often used interchangeably to refer to a single individual, according to the speaker's degree of familiarity and the whims of the moment.

Aleksandr—Sasha
Dmitrii—Mitya
Vasilisa—Vasya, Vasochka
Rodion—Rodya
Yekaterina—Katya, Katyusha

PATRONYMIC

THE RUSSIAN PATRONYMIC IS always derived from the first name of an individual's father. It varies according to gender. For example, Vasilisa's father is named Pyotr. Her patronymic—derived from her father's name—is Petrovna. Her brother Aleksei uses the masculine form: Petrovich.

To indicate respect in Russian, you do not use Mr. or Mrs., as in English. Rather, you address someone by first name and patronymic together. A stranger meeting Vasilisa for the first time would call her Vasilisa Petrovna. When Vasilisa is masquerading as a boy, she calls herself Vasilii Petrovich.

When a highborn woman married, in medieval Rus', she would exchange her patronymic (if she had one) for a name derived from her husband's name. Thus Olga, who was Olga Petrovna as a girl, has become Olga Vladimirova (whereas Olga and Vladimir's daughter is called Marya Vladimirovna).

GLOSSARY

BABA YAGA~An old witch who appears in many Russian fairy tales. She rides around on a mortar, steering with a pestle and sweeping her tracks away with a broom of birch. She lives in a hut that spins round and round on chicken legs. In The Winternight Trilogy, she is Vasya's great-grandmother.

BANNIK~"Bathhouse dweller," the bathhouse guardian in Russian folklore.

BATYUSHKA~Literally, "little father," used as a respectful mode of address for Orthodox ecclesiastics.

BELIYE~Porcini, a kind of mushroom.

BOYAR~A member of the Kievan or, later, the Muscovite aristocracy, second in rank only to a knyaz, or prince.

BROTHER ALEKSANDR PERESVET~Historically a monk and member of the Trinity Lavra under Sergius of Radonezh; he fought a single combat with Chelubey to open the Battle of Kulikovo. Both men were killed, but according to Russian sources, Chelubey was unhorsed first.

BYZANTINE CROSS~Also called the patriarchal cross, this cross has a smaller crosspiece above the main crossbar, and sometimes a slanted crossbar near the foot.

CAFFA~A city in Crimea, now known as Feodosia. In the era of The Winternight Trilogy, the city was under the control of the Genoese.

CATHEDRAL OF THE ASSUMPTION~Uspenksy Sobor. Also known as the Cathedral of the Dormition. Commemorates the dormition (aka falling asleep, aka death of the Mother of God and her being taken to heaven). Located in the modern-day Moscow Kremlin, the original limestone structure was begun in 1326 and consecrated in 1327. The building presently on the site dates to the sixteenth century.

CHELUBEY~Called Chelubey by Russian chroniclers and Temir-Murza by his own countrymen, Chelubey was the champion for the Tatar side at the battle of Kulikovo. He was defeated by Aleksandr Peresvet.

CHERNOMOR~An old wizard and sea-king in Russian folklore whose name literally derives from "Black Sea." With his thirty-three sons he would come out of the sea to guard the island of the swan-maiden in the fairy tale of Tsar Saltan.

CHYERTI (SINGULAR: CHYERT)~Devils. In this case a collective noun meaning the various spirits of Russian folklore. Another, and possibly better, term is nyechistiye sili, literally "unclean forces," but that is an unwieldy mouthful for Anglophone readers.

DAN~Tribute; in this case, the tribute owed by the conquered Rus' to their Mongol overlords.

DED GRIB~Grandfather Mushroom. There is no historical source for this one; he was inspired by and is a shout-out to a character in the old Soviet children's movie *Morozko*.

DMITRII DONSKOI~Called Dmitrii Ivanovich in The Winternight Trilogy, he earned the moniker "of the Don" following his victory at the Battle of Kulikovo.

DOMOVOI~In Russian folklore, the guardian of the household, the household-spirit. Feminized in *The Winter of the Witch* as domovaya. In some sources, the domovoi had a wife, called the kikimora, but I felt that feminizing the name of the main household-guardian was more appropriate for a witch's house.

DVOR~Dooryard. The space between outbuildings in the property of a highborn medieval Russian.

DVOROVOI~The dooryard-guardian of Russian folklore.

ECUMENICAL PATRIARCH~The supreme head of the Eastern Orthodox Church, based in Constantinople (modern Istanbul).

GAMAYUN~A black bird in Russian folklore that speaks prophecy, generally depicted as a bird with a woman's head.

GER (YURT)—A portable round tent made of felt or skins and used by Mongol armies on the march. Generally they were taken down and put up each night, but the finest one, used by the Khan or the leader of the host, was often left intact and transported from place to place on a giant platform drawn by oxen.

GOLDEN HORDE—A Mongol khanate founded by Batu Khan in the twelfth century. It adopted Islam in the early fourteenth century, and at its peak ruled a large swath of what is now Eastern Europe, including Muscovy.

GOSPODIN—Form of respectful address to a male, more formal than the English "mister." Might be translated as "lord."

GOSUDAR—A form of address akin to "Your Majesty" or "Sovereign."

GRAND PRINCE (VELIKIY KNYAZ)—The title of a ruler of a major principality, for example Moscow, Tver, or Smolensk, in medieval Russia. The title *tsar* did not come into use until Ivan the Terrible was crowned in 1547. Velikiy Knyaz is also often translated as "Grand Duke."

GREAT KHAN—Genghis Khan. His descendants, in the form of the Golden Horde, ruled Russia for two hundred years.

HEGUMEN—The head of an Orthodox monastery, equivalent to an abbot in the Western tradition.

ICONOSTASIS (ICON-SCREEN)—A wall of icons with a specific layout that separates the nave from the sanctuary in an Eastern Orthodox church.

IVAN—This reference is to the fairy tale *Marya Morevna*, where Ivan, having been cut apart by the wicked sorcerer, is restored to life by his brothers-in-law, the bird-princes, who go and get him the water of death (which restores his flesh) and the water of life (which returns him to life).

IZBA—A peasant's house, small and made of wood, often with carved embellishments. The plural is *izby*.

KOKOSHNIK—A Russian headdress. There are many styles of *kokoshniki*, depending on the locale and the era. Generally the word refers to the closed headdress worn by married women, though maidens also wore headdresses, open in back, or sometimes just headbands, that revealed their hair. The wearing of kokoshniki was limited to the nobility. The more common form of head covering for a medieval Russian woman was a head scarf or kerchief.

KOLOMNA—A town that still exists today, part of the Moscow region. Its name likely derives from the Old Russian word for a bend in the river. Its official arms were granted by Catherine the Great. The historical location of Dmitrii's mustering of the Russian army before marching to Kulikovo.

KREMLIN—A fortified complex at the center of a Russian city. Although modern English usage has adopted the word *kremlin* to refer solely to the most famous example, the Moscow Kremlin, there are actually kremlins to be found in most historic Russian cities. Originally, all of Moscow lay within its kremlin proper; over time, the city spread beyond its walls.

KULIKOVO—Kulikovo Pole, literally "Snipes' Field." The location of the historic Battle of Kulikovo, which took place in 1380.

LESNAYA ZEMLYA—Literally, "Land of the Forest." Vasya, Sasha, and Olga's home village, the location for much of the action of *The Bear and the Nightingale*, referenced in *The Girl in the Tower* and *The Winter of the Witch*.

LETNIK—A calf-length, light woman's garment with long, wide sleeves, worn over a shift.

LISICHKI—Chanterelles, a kind of mushroom.

LITTLE BROTHER—English rendering of the Russian endearment bratishka. Can be applied to both older and younger siblings.

LITTLE SISTER—English rendering of the Russian endearment sestryonka. Can be applied to both older and younger siblings.

MATYUSHKA—Literally, "little mother," a term of endearment.

MEAD—Honey-wine, made by fermenting a solution of honey and water.

METROPOLITAN—A high official in the Orthodox church. In the Middle Ages, the Metropolitan of the church of the Rus' was the highest Orthodox authority in Russia and was appointed by the Byzantine Patriarch.

MONASTERY OF THE ARCHANGEL—The monastery's full name was Aleksei's Archangel Michael Monastery; it was more familiarly known as the Chudov Monastery, from the Russian word chudo, miracle. It was dedicated to the miracle of the Archangel Michael at Colossae, where the angel purportedly gave the power of speech to a mute girl. It was founded in 1358 by Metropolitan Aleksei.

MOSCOW (RUSSIAN: MOSKVA)—Currently the capital of the modern Russian Federation, Moscow was founded in the twelfth century by Prince Yury Dolgoruki. Long eclipsed by cities such as Vladimir, Tver, Suzdal, and Kiev, Moscow rose to prominence after the Mongol invasion, under the leadership of a series of competent and enterprising Rurikid princes.

MOSKVA RIVER—River along which Moscow was founded.

MUSCOVY—Derived from Latin *Moscovia,* from the original Russian appellation *Moscov,* the term refers to the Grand Duchy or Grand Principality of Moscow; for centuries, Muscovy was a common way to refer to Russia in the West. Originally Muscovy covered a relatively modest territory stretching north and east from Moscow, but from the late fourteenth to the early sixteenth century it grew enormously, until by 1505 it covered almost a million square miles.

NEGLINNAYA RIVER—Moscow was originally built on a hill between the Moskva and the Neglinnaya, and the two rivers formed a natural moat. The Neglinnaya is now an underground river in the city of Moscow.

OLEG OF RYAZAN—Also Oleg Ryazansky. The Grand Prince of Ryazan during the latter half of the fourteenth century. His role in the time leading up to the Battle of Kulikovo, and in the battle itself, is ambiguous. Some sources put him fully on the side of the Tatars. Others say he tried to play both sides, so as to come out ahead whoever won. He might have been the first one to bring word to Dmitrii that Mamai's forces were advancing on Kulikovo; he might have delayed his own arrival at the battle and turned aside Mamai's reinforcements to give Dmitrii a chance. He might have allowed his boyars to fight on the side of the Russians but hung back himself.

OTCHE NASH~Our Father, the opening phrase of the Lord's Prayer in Old Church Slavonic. Even today, the prayer is generally memorized and said in this older form rather than in modern Russian.

OVEN~The Russian oven, or pech', is an enormous construction that came into wide use in the fifteenth century for cooking, baking, and heating. A system of flues ensured even distribution of heat, and whole families would often sleep on top of the oven to keep warm during the winter.

PATENT~A term used in Russian historiography for official decrees of the Golden Horde. Every ruler of Rus' had to have a patent, or yarlyk, from the Khan giving him the authority to rule. Jockeying for the patents of various cities made up a good deal of the intrigue between Russian princes from the thirteenth century on.

POLUDNITSA~Lady Midday, sister to Lady Midnight, who wanders the hayfields and causes heatstroke with her cutting shears.

POLUNOCHNITSA~Literally, midnight woman; Lady Midnight, a demon that comes out only at midnight and causes children's nightmares. In folklore, she lives in a swamp, and there are many examples of charms sung by parents to send her back there. In *The Winter of the Witch*, this folkloric character is associated with Night, the servant of Baba Yaga in the fairy tale *Vasilisa the Beautiful*.

POSAD~An area adjoining, but not within, the fortified walls of a Russian town, often a center of trade. Over the centuries, the posad often evolved into an administrative center or a town in its own right.

POZHAR~Fire, bonfire; the name of the golden mare in *The Winter of the Witch*, who is also the firebird. You can see the root of her name in the Russian word for firebird, zhar-ptitsa.

RUBAKHA~A long-sleeved shift, the main undergarment for nearly all medieval Russian women, the only one consistently washed.

RUS'~The Rus' were originally a Scandinavian people. In the ninth century C.E., at the invitation of warring Slavic and Finnic tribes, they established a ruling dynasty, the Rurikids, that eventually comprised a large swath of what are now Ukraine, Belarus, and western Russia. The territory they ruled was eventually named after them, as were the people living under their dynasty, which lasted from the ninth century to the death of Ivan IV in 1584.

RUSSIA~From the thirteenth through fifteenth centuries, there was no unified polity called Russia. Instead, the Rus' lived under a disparate collection of rival princes (knyazey) who owed their ultimate allegiance to Mongol overlords. The word *Russia* did not come into common use until the seventeenth century. Thus, in the medieval context, the use of the word *Russia,* or the adjective *Russian,* refers to a swath of territory with a common culture and language, rather than a nation with a unified government. Hence the phrase "All the Russias" refers to these various states, rather than a unified whole.

SAPOGI~Short boots, generally made of multiple pieces of leather, with a rounded toe. In this era, they did not distinguish between left and right foot.

SARAFAN~A dress something like a jumper or pinafore, with shoulder straps, worn over a long-sleeved blouse. This garment actually came into common use only in the early fifteenth century; I included it in *The Bear and the Nightingale* slightly before its time because of how strongly this manner of dress evokes fairy-tale Russia to the Western reader.

SARAI~From the Persian word for "palace," the capital city of the Golden Horde, originally built on the Akhtuba River and later relocated slightly to the north. Various princes of Rus' would go to Sarai to do homage and receive patents from the Khan to rule their territories. At one point, Sarai was one of the largest cities in the medieval world, with a population of over half a million.

SERPUKHOV~Currently a town that sits about sixty miles south of Moscow. Originally founded during the reign of Dmitrii Ivanovich to protect Moscow's southern approaches, and given to Dmitrii's cousin Vladimir Andreevich (Olga's husband in *The Girl in the Tower*). Serpukhov did not get town status until the late fourteenth century. In *The Girl in the Tower* and *The Winter of the Witch,* Olga lives with her family in Moscow despite being the Princess of Serpukhov, because Serpukhov, at this time, consists of little more than trees, a garrison, and a few huts. The Prince of Serpukhov was the only lord in Muscovy who was not a vassal, i.e., was a prince in his own right and not subordinate to Moscow.

SNEGUROCHKA—Derived from the Russian sneg, snow, the Snow-Maiden, a character who appears in several Russian fairy tales. In *The Winter of the Witch*, it is also Morozko's nickname for Vasya.

SOLOVEY—Nightingale; the name of Vasya's bay stallion.

TEREM—The word refers both to the actual location where highborn women lived in Old Russia (the upper floors of a home, a separate wing, or even a separate building, connected to the men's part of the palace by a walkway) and more generally to the Muscovite practice of secluding aristocratic women. Thought to be derived from the Greek *teremnon* (dwelling) and unrelated to the Arabic word *harem*. This practice is of mysterious origin, owing to a lack of written records from medieval Muscovy. The practice of terem reached its height in the sixteenth and seventeenth centuries. Peter the Great finally ended the practice and brought women back into the public sphere. Functionally, terem meant that highborn Russian women lived lives completely separate from men, and girls were brought up in the terem and did not leave it until they married. The princess whose father keeps her behind three times nine locks, a common trope in Russian fairy tales, is probably derived from this actual practice.

TRINITY LAVRA (THE TRINITY LAVRA OF SAINT SERGEI)—Monastery founded by Saint Sergei Radonezhsky in 1337, about forty miles northeast of Moscow.

TUMAN—Mist; the name of Sasha's gray horse.

ULUS—Nation, tribe, followers.

UPYR—The Slavic version of a vampire. More monstrous and less elegant than the Western European variant.

VAZILA—In Russian folklore, the guardian of the stable and protector of livestock.

VEDMA—Vyed'ma, witch, wisewoman.

VERST—In Russian, versta (the English word *verst* derives from the Russian genitive plural, which is the form most frequently used in conjunction with a number). A unit of distance equal to roughly one kilometer, or two-thirds of a mile.

VLADIMIR~One of the chief cities of medieval Rus', situated about 120 miles east of Moscow. Its founding is said to date from 1108, and many of its ancient buildings are still intact today.

VLADIMIR ANDREEVICH~Called "the Bold" (khrabriy), he is the most well known of the princes of Serpukhov. He got his moniker for his courage in fighting in Dmitrii Donskoi's wars, and was also Dmitrii's first cousin and close adviser. In *The Winter of the Witch*, he is the husband of Vasya's sister Olga.

WRITING ICONS~A direct translation of the Russian phrase. In Russian, one uses the verb *to write* (pisat/napisat') for the making of icons.

ZAPONA~An ancient outer garment worn by maidens over a long-sleeved shift. It was just a rectangular length of fabric folded in half at the shoulders and with a round opening for the head. It was not sewn together on the sides, but belted at the waist.

THE LINEAGE OF

VASILISA PETROVNA

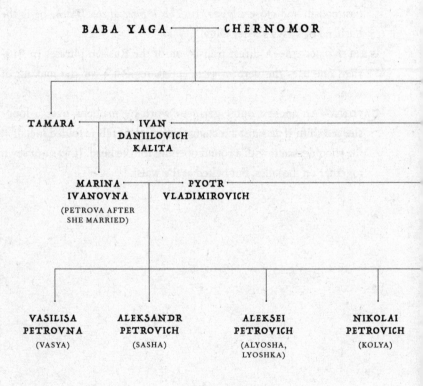

BABA YAGA ——————— CHERNOMOR

TAMARA ——————— IVAN
DANIILOVICH
KALITA

MARINA ——————— PYOTR
IVANOVNA   VLADIMIROVICH
(PETROVA AFTER
SHE MARRIED)

VASILISA   ALEKSANDR   ALEKSEI   NIKOLAI
PETROVNA   PETROVICH   PETROVICH   PETROVICH
(VASYA)   (SASHA)   (ALYOSHA,   (KOLYA)
                                    LYOSHKA)

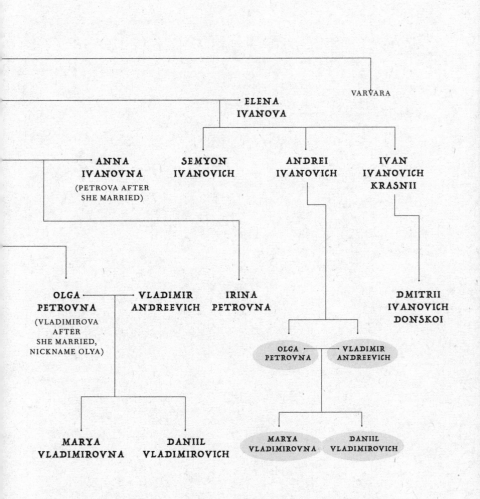

VARVARA

ELENA
IVANOVA

ANNA
IVANOVNA
(PETROVA AFTER
SHE MARRIED)

SEMYON
IVANOVICH

ANDREI
IVANOVICH

IVAN
IVANOVICH
KRASNII

OLGA
PETROVNA
(VLADIMIROVA
AFTER
SHE MARRIED,
NICKNAME OLYA)

VLADIMIR
ANDREEVICH

IRINA
PETROVNA

DMITRII
IVANOVICH
DONSKOI

OLGA
PETROVNA

VLADIMIR
ANDREEVICH

MARYA
VLADIMIROVNA

DANIIL
VLADIMIROVICH

MARYA
VLADIMIROVNA

DANIIL
VLADIMIROVICH

ACKNOWLEDGMENTS

SEVEN YEARS OF MY LIFE WENT INTO THE WINTERNIGHT TRILOGY, and more kindnesses from more people than I can possibly count. Writing a book is solitary, but finishing a book and publishing it is the work of many, in great and small ways. I am grateful to everyone who went into the forest with Vasya and me, back in 2011, and stuck it out to the bittersweet end.

To the Russian department at Middlebury College, current and former, I suppose this was a slightly unorthodox use of my education, but I am grateful for all those years of history, grammar, and conjugations, without which I would never have undertaken this series. Thanks, in particular, to Tatiana Smorodinskaya and Sergei Davydov, for being mentors and friends, and for checking my translation of Pushkin.

Huge thank-you to my agent, Paul Lucas, who was the very first person not my mom to read this book and believe in it, way back in 2014, and who has been a rock of good advice and common sense ever since. And to everyone at Janklow and Nesbit and Cullen Stanley International, especially Stephanie Koven, Brenna English-Loeb, and Suzannah Bentley.

To the people across the water at Ebury: Gillian Green, Stephanie Naulls, and Tess Henderson, thank you so much for bringing my work to readers in the UK, and thanks for your unfailing hospitality and cupcakes whenever I visited. Special shout-out to Vlad Sever and his team in Croatia who made the single most gorgeous edition of *The Bear and the Nightingale* I've ever seen.

To the folks at Del Rey and Ballantine who have made for my books and for me the very best publishing home a writer could have over the last few years: Thanks to Scott Shannon, Tricia Narwani, Keith Clayton, Jess Bonet, Melissa Sanford, David Moench, Anne Speyer, and Erin Kane.

To Jennifer Hershey, my brilliant editor. Thanks for keeping me going when I didn't think I could do it; thanks for four years' worth of good ideas, thanks for sticking with me through all those most questionable drafts. This series wouldn't exist without you.

To my housemates at Slimhouse: RJ and Pollaidh (girl, you're an honorary member), Garrett, Camila and Blue, you guys are the best family I could ask for. Having you in my life, rattling around the kitchen, telling bad jokes, making me try yet another terrible beer, and giving me a hard time about the boxes of books under my bed, has kept me sane and happy. Love you all.

To the Johnsons: Peter, Carol Anne, Harrison, and Gracie, thanks for your hospitality and your enthusiasm. To Abhay Morrissey, for taking me flying, literally, when I needed a break. To the Roxendals: Björn, Kim, Josh, David, Eliza, Dana, Mariel, Joel, Hugo, and all of you, thanks for letting me spend all those months on my couch, scribbling. To Allie Brudney, for being amazing, for coming out to every event you can, because college besties are forever. To Jenny Lyons and the rest of the staff of Vermont Book Shop, thanks for your unfailing support. To the folks at Stone Leaf Tea House, thanks for all those winter evenings I spent hanging out in your space, working on my book.

To my family: Mike Buls and Beth Fowler, John Burdine and Sterling Burdine, and Elizabeth Burdine. I love you all. Thanks for everything.

To Evan Johnson, who makes me eat and sleep when all I want to do is write, my running buddy and my adventure buddy, my partner and my best friend. I love you.

Finally, thanks to everyone—far more people than I can name, the booksellers and the book readers who read my book, told a friend, reviewed it somewhere. Thanks to everyone who has gone with Vasya on her journey.

I hope you'll come with me on the next one.

The
Winter
of the
Witch

*Katherine
Arden*

A
READER'S
GUIDE

Questions and Topics for Discussion

1. Sacrifice plays an important role in *The Winter of the Witch*. We see Morozko sacrifice himself for Vasya, Vasya sacrifice herself to protect her family, Solovey sacrifice himself for Vasya, Sasha sacrifice himself for Russia, Konstantin sacrifice himself for spite, and so on. What do you think the author is saying about the significance of sacrifice?

2. Discuss the ways in which Vasya and Morozko's relationship has changed over the course of the Winternight Trilogy. What are the various roles they have held in each other's lives, and where do they stand now?

3. Vasya meets a number of new chyerti that both help and hinder her along her journey. Do you have a favorite fairytale creature in this cast of characters?

4. Why do you think Konstantin is so obsessed with eliminating Vasya? Do you think his fixation on her is a result of hatred or passion? Is there a difference?

5. How does the loss of Solovey impact Vasya? Did she need to suffer this loss in order to fulfill her destiny? How do you feel about his return? Did it seem too convenient? Was it necessary?

6. Discuss Vasya's lineage. Were you surprised to learn that Vasya descends from Baba Yaga, the witch of the wood, and Chernomor, the sea-king? What do these familial ties imply about Vasya's abilities, the journey she has taken, and the path she will take from here?

7. Vasya wields her newfound magical powers throughout her mission to save both the magical and mortal worlds. What do you think

is the cleverest use of her powers? What is the most foolish thing she does with her magic abilities?

8.   How does Pozhar compare as a companion in Vasya's journeying to Solovey? Could Vasya have been successful without the help of the firebird?

9.   At one point it is said, "Medved's great gift is disorder, and his tools are fear and mistrust. . . . Until he is bound, you cannot trust anyone." How does Vasya earn the trust of the many chyerti and people she encounters? Is there a key to how she wins them over to her side in spite of the chaotic atmosphere Medved has created?

10.   Do you think Konstantin is warped by Medved, or was he already corrupt and therefore an easy target for the Bear's puppetry? By the end of the trilogy, do you think Konstantin is more of a villain or a victim?

11.   What do you think of Vasya's alliance with Medved? Did you think she would be able to trust him not to betray her?

12.   Vasya has long fought to find a balance between the magical world and the Christian church so that both may coexist. How does this struggle for coexistence relate to the world today?

13.   Throughout the series, Vasya has struggled to find her place in a society that dictates that a woman must either wed or become a nun. How has Vasya not only taken control of her own future but also influenced the fates of the many other women she has encountered along her journey?

14.   The concept of memory (and lack thereof) is an important theme: Vasya must use the power of "forgetting the world was ever other than as you willed it." To work her magic, Morozko is trapped by the loss of his memories, and the chyerti are desperate not to be forgotten in the minds of others. What does all this say about the power of memory?

15.   In this conclusion to the trilogy, do you think Vasya has finally found the acceptance that she always sought from her family? What about that of the larger community? And among the chyerti? Which group do you think she most reliably found support from throughout her journey—and which is most accepting of her in the end?

KATHERINE ARDEN is the *New York Times* bestselling author of the Winternight Trilogy: *The Bear and the Nightingale, The Girl in the Tower,* and *The Winter of the Witch.* She is also the author of the children's horror novels *Small Spaces* and *Dead Voices.* She lives in Vermont.

katherinearden.com

Facebook.com/katherineardenauthor

Twitter: @arden_katherine

Instagram: @arden_katherine

This book was set in Fournier, a typeface named for Pierre-Simon Fournier (1712–68), the youngest son of a French printing family. He started out engraving woodblocks and large capitals, then moved on to fonts of type. In 1736 he began his own foundry and made several important contributions in the field of type design; he is said to have cut 147 alphabets of his own creation. Fournier is probably best remembered as the designer of St. Augustine Ordinaire, a face that served as the model for the Monotype Corporation's Fournier, which was released in 1925.

EXPLORE THE WORLDS OF DEL REY BOOKS

READ EXCERPTS
from hot new titles.

STAY UP-TO-DATE
on your favorite authors.

FIND OUT about exclusive
giveaways and sweepstakes.

CONNECT WITH US ONLINE!
⊙ ◘ 🐦 @DelReyBooks